SHADOW
ON THE
VALLEY

ALSO BY KIRK MITCHELL:

Black Dragon
With Siberia Comes a Chill

SHADOW
ON THE
VALLEY

KIRK
MITCHELL

ST. MARTIN'S PRESS

NEW YORK

Production Editor: David Stanford Burr
Designer: Judith A. Stagnitto

Library of Congress Cataloging-in-Publication Data

Mitchell, Kirk.
        Shadow on the valley : a Civil War thriller / Kirk Mitchell.
                p.   cm.
        "A Thomas Dunne book."
        ISBN 0-312-10542-8
        1. Shenandoah River Valley (Va. and W. Va.)—History—Civil War, 1861–1865—Fiction.
        2. Serial murders—Shenandoah River Valley (Va. and W. Va.)—Fiction.   3. Shenandoah Valley Campaign, 1864 (August–November)—Fiction.
        4. Physicians—United States—Fiction.
        I. Title.
        PS3563.I7675S48   1994
        813'.54—dc20   93-43521
                                                                        CIP

First Edition: February 1994

10 9 8 7 6 5 4 3 2 1

SHADOW
ON THE
VALLEY

⊰ PROLOGUE ⊱

SEPTEMBER 17, 1862

ANTIETAM CREEK, MARYLAND

The sun came up through a mist left by the night's soft rain. All around him, ground and foliage began to steam as if hell were rising to take possession of the earth. Hands shaking, he removed the emerald sash from around his waist and tied it to the branch of an oak.

The silk dangled limp for an instant, then fluttered on the rising of the moist breeze.

"Here she comes!" a distant voice yelled, laughing, as if it were the most hilarious thing imaginable.

Then he flinched as solid shot, a big iron ball, crashed through the treetops. A limb fell groaning and crunched against the ground. The smell of sap filled the air.

"Steady," he told the stretchermen, musicians from the regimental band.

But they refused to meet his eyes. They started to melt away, heading back for the field hospital across the creek—without their litters. This wasn't their sort of music. The bastards.

He tried to shout for them to stop and stand firm for the sake of the wounded, but nothing came out of his mouth. Or maybe the words were covered by the sound of musket fire coming from the cornfield on the far side of the woods. Worse than anything he'd heard at Cedar Mountain or Second Bull Run. Something like a piece of burlap being slowly ripped in two.

A soldier hopped toward him, using the trunks of the trees for support. The man had to hop because his left foot was gone from the ankle.

He helped the soldier lie down, gave him a sip of whiskey. He thought about drawing the arteries out, tying them off with ligatures, but then realized that a tourniquet must do.

No time.

"Surgeon!" somebody else screamed as if his bowels were on fire.

He looked up.

He wasn't the surgeon, who was back at the field hospital, pointing with a sword for the steward and wound dressers to do this and that. He was the assistant surgeon, a second lieutenant whose uniform was just beginning to fade from the summer sun to a lighter blue, and he'd been ordered forward to set up a dressing station as close to the lines as he dared. He had nothing more at his disposal than a basin of water, a sponge, some bandages and a half-dozen tourniquets. A little whiskey and a Harvard education. Not even any stretchermen at this point.

But no matter.

More wounded were staggering out of the cornfield. Mostly shattered arms and legs, as expected. But more wounded than he'd ever seen at one time. The entire 12th Massachusetts Volunteer Infantry, it seemed, was sifting back through the woods toward his emerald sash. The pride of Beacon Hill. It was a regiment of blue bloods, with a sprinkling of fresh-off-the-boat Irish, until recently led by Colonel Fletcher Webster, the great Daniel Webster's son, who'd fallen at Second Bull Run.

And it was being used up in a few minutes.

Strangely, he found himself thinking of somber Bostonian parlors, those flimsy yellow telegrams from the Adjutant General that the butlers would bring into them on silver trays over the next several days.

Minié balls clipped the leaves. Still green with late summer. Not even a tinge of autumn yet. They floated down over the wounded, who were gathering around him, eyes big and empty with shock.

Twenty.

Then at least fifty. Among them casualties from the other regiments in the brigade, New Yorkers and Pennsylvanians.

And then a hundred, silently waiting in the shade for him to do something. A few moaned, but the rest were quiet, immobile except for those who were plucking at their clothes for a look at their wounds.

All the maimed in the world were being drawn to his sash.

He didn't know where to begin. His fingers wouldn't spring to work. Panic hit him that he'd forgotten how to do the simplest procedure.

Oh God of Israel, fortify me. And I promise that the next time there's a war, I won't volunteer.

"It's all right now, Surgeon," a soldier with white hair at the temples said compassionately, as if he were the unhurt one. "Take a minute to get a hold on yourself. You haven't seen the worst of it yet. How old are you, sir? You look awful young."

That shamed him and finally got him going.

Men without a scratch on them were coming back now in driblets. Some had left their muskets in the field.

"Where're your officers!" he finally managed to shout.

They ignored him.

"Got us a primary station here, boys!"

More and more of them were streaming out of the cornfield and toward the rear. The colors were coming back, the fabric in tatters, the last men breaking into a run. Behind them he saw nothing but enemy uniforms. White gaiters. Rebel yells trilled above the gunfire.

"Stop!" he cried. "Think of your wounded! It could be you lying here!"

But they shoved past him.

"Come on, boys!" And then he heard himself saying the damndest thing: "Think of your wives and sisters!"

His own dear sister lived in Richmond. Her husband, Israel, was Lee's best artillerist and might've been pounding away at the 12th Massachusetts even at that moment.

He grabbed the colors from a corporal who seemed glad enough to be rid of them.

Where was the color sergeant? And all the officers?

He started forward, waving the flag, but no one followed. He felt like a fool as the river of blue continued to press against him.

Then he used the flagstaff to bar the way for two privates. They halted. He expected mutiny, and one of them, an Irishman, a recruit he'd recently treated for syphilis, called him a son of a bitch.

"Least I've got a mother, soldier—and didn't just crawl out of a rotten potato like a maggot!"

The man slowly grinned, then said over his shoulder in a loud voice, "Hell, if a butternut Jew can make a stand, so can I!"

Others stopped. They actually turned and unsnapped their cartridge boxes, the poor crazy bastards.

He no longer felt the fool. Just scared out of his wits. And trapped into going on.

He led them out of the woods, and the field spread smokily before him. The ripened corn had been cropped to the ground by bullets and shot. The dead lay neatly in rows, murdered wholesale. It almost seemed as if they'd been ordered to lie down and die. He couldn't bear to look at them. Or at the Rebels rushing toward him, their white gaiters coming at him like the foamy skirt of a wave racing over the sand of the beach at home. South Carolina, oddly enough.

He fixed his gaze on a tidy, whitewashed building on the rise to the southwest. Cannon were firing from around it. A gray-clad figure, hunched in the saddle, loomed behind these batteries. His eyes seemed to shine even at a quarter mile, and he raised a gloved hand as if invoking death across the field.

"Put a twist on 'em, Surgeon darlin'," the Irishman said to his back.

He started to run, and the men gave out with a *hurrah*.

But suddenly he lost sight of the horseman with the dreadful eyes. The morning dimmed, and the colors tumbled out of his hands. He felt as if he'd just been caned. It'd been done to him in Charleston once. Caned on the upper arm.

He slowly raised his head and found himself sprawling on a bed of shredded cornstalks, his right shirtsleeve filling with blood. And then the earth began to swallow him. His right hand was useless, but he clawed at the dirt with his left.

To keep from being sucked under.

TWO YEARS LATER

⊰ CHAPTER 1 ⊱

Simon Wolfe rode into town on a milk-white mare.

Her first master, a hospital steward and a pompous little fellow, had called her Invicta. Invincible. But then the man had died of typhoid while Philip Sheridan's newly formed army was putting itself together in Harpers Ferry, and she'd come into Simon's possession. He promptly renamed her Naomi, which was more in keeping with her gentleness, and then bought her from the government when he grew more attached than he'd expected. Something about her calmed him. Like some men and women, she had a singularly fine temperament, maybe from birth, maybe from kind treatment when she was young.

"We're arrived, Sissy," he said, drawing rein in front of the courthouse. It was a handsome building for a town that had been half shabby even before the war. He lifted his cap off his head and used the crook of his left arm to smooth the tumble of damp black hair that played over his coat collar. His empty right sleeve was folded in two and pinned up.

"Why—greetin's, Col'nel!"

Behind the wrought-iron fence encircling the courthouse were several hundred Rebel prisoners, many of them wounded—although just the ambulatory, as the prostrated were still strewn over five miles of battlefield between Winchester and Opequon Creek to the north-east.

"Who sawed yourn off?"

These were rawboned men in threadbare uniforms, no two dressed alike. There was a greater variety of hats in one of their regiments than in a New York haberdashery, but they were shoeless, most of them.

Simon dismounted, picked his way through the blue provost guards and then the prisoners up to the front door. "Evenin', Col'nel," the same sunny voice piped up behind him, followed by some phlegmy chuckling all around. "I guess we back in the Union now. How 'bout we smoke on it?"

"Sure, boys," Simon said. "But I seem to be short on tobacco, for some damn reason. Cotton too."

They howled with laughter. Somehow, you never really got the morale on them. Sheridan had whipped them bloody today, sent their army reeling back up the Shenandoah Valley—but you couldn't tell that by their faces.

"Where you from, Col'nel?"

Simon ignored the question and went inside the courthouse.

A Confederate surgeon was operating in the judge's chambers. His apron was heavy with blood, and the spines of the law books to his back were flecked with red. He was using the desktop for a table.

Simon said, "Sir—"

A scream from the desk made both of them jump a little. The first shock of the injury was wearing off, and Simon doubted that the bottle of whiskey beside the amputation kit was doing much good.

"How're you set for chloroform?" Simon went on.

"Had a little ether earlier, Colonel," the Rebel surgeon said. "But it's gone. No opiates either." He offered his left hand, making it less awkward for Simon to shake. "Jonathan Jeffers, Terry's Brigade." The remnants of Stonewall's Division.

"Simon Wolfe, medical director."

"Which corps, sir?"

Simon paused. "Director for the Army of the Shenandoah."

"I see," Jeffers said, sounding surprised. Simon was but twenty-nine and suspected that he looked a bit younger than that.

"If you'll put off any operations you can, a wagon train's due any minute." Then Simon realized by the sudden brightening in the surgeon's eyes that he'd placed the accent.

"Pardon if I ask, Colonel . . ."

"Yes?"

"Are you related to Solomon Wolfe of Charleston?"

Simon paused again. "My father."

The surgeon glanced at the blue uniform. "A brilliant man."

"Yes," Simon said. The purplish tint behind the high windows reminded him of the hour. "I'm in need of a building that'll do for a transfer hospital. Also my administrative offices. I was hoping to use this one, but . . ." His voice trailed off to avoid any hint of accusation.

"May I suggest the old harness factory out along Amherst Street? It's empty. Two blocks west."

"I'm in your debt. I'll send chloroform and morphine as soon as our wagons arrive. Kindly tell my man what else you need—and it's yours."

"Thank you, Colonel Wolfe. We're using some of the churches. Christ Episcopal, New Lutheran and First Presbyterian."

"We'll look in on them."

"Bless you." Then Jeffers's smile of gratitude disappeared. "But you'll forgive me, won't you, if I lay your generosity to being Carolina-bred?"

"I was educated in Boston, sir. Good evening."

A breeze had risen and was flowing down between the tall fronts of the brick buildings. There'd been man-dropping heat all day. It was the third week of September, and no hint yet that summer was fading. Simon climbed heavily into the saddle, then just sat. He hadn't thought of his father in days. Naomi turned an eye, expecting him to cluck his tongue so they could be off. But he went on sitting with the rein slack in his hand, staring absently over the prisoners. This was the hour his father had summoned him to his study. To practice elocution in Greek, Latin and German. Then, after the bugler at the Citadel had sounded retreat, his mother's woman—that serene, handsome high-yellow face smiling over the tray—would bring in citron tarts and tea. Father and son would eat and drink in silence. And then Solomon Wolfe would intently watch the quadroon woman leave the room.

Simon stirred at last. "Let's go, girl."

Nearing the intersection with Amherst Street, he spotted his orderly, Otis Pamunkey, riding toward him alongside an infantry column. "At last!" Simon cried, and the orderly's broad Indian face lit up. "Where's our train?"

Pamunkey's fingers tugged at his nappy hair: his sign that something was a hairbreadth away.

"All right," Simon said. "Now, stay right here and turn our people up to that building." He pointed at the limestone structure that was no doubt the factory the Rebel surgeon had mentioned.

Then he galloped toward it himself.

The cavernous rooms were empty, as promised, but filthy from disuse. He quickly made up his mind where to put the wards and offices, then ran out onto the loading dock to meet a clatter of wheels. But instead of the supply wagons he'd hoped for, the vehicles were ambulances, trailing splatters of blood in the dust. The drivers were impatient to unload and be off again, but Simon made them commandeer brooms from nearby households and sweep out what would be the main ward. While they worked and grumbled, he went behind the building and tested the well water: it was good. He drank ravenously. His eyes fell on a nearby shed. It'd do for the dead house.

"Colonel Wolfe!" An indignant voice drew him out front again. "Where are you?"

"Obviously in the wrong place," Simon muttered to himself.

A wagon had finally arrived, but rather than the precious boxes marked "glass—with care" it carried one of the contract surgeons, Dr. Twiss, and his orderly. They looked like snake-oil peddlers in their civilian suits and black derbies.

"I'm here, as ordered." Twiss said. "But there was plenty to do at the hospital in Berryville Canyon."

"No doubt, but soon there'll be even more to do here."

"Where's Mother Haggerty and her nurses? I was told they'd be coming."

"The women'll be brought up in the morning," Simon said, "long as the Rebels don't counterattack tonight. Meanwhile, you'll have to make do with the male nurses."

"Convalescents are as useless as teats on a boar—"

"Doctor, please, we have wounded waiting."

"For surgery?" Twiss asked hopefully.

"For wound dressing." The surgeons of Simon's own staff, although administrative officers, would be pressed into cutting long before he'd ever let Twiss pick up a bone saw. Only one in a dozen surgeons actually performed operations. Thank God. Most had only six months of medical education from some rural college and a graveyard full of patients to prove it.

He turned an ear toward the south.

He heard skirmishing, but before he could decide what it meant he saw his supply train rounding the corner with Pamunkey in the lead. Good. But if Sheridan continued to chase the Rebels up the Valley tonight two, maybe three division hospitals would have to follow, or the ambulance ride back to Winchester would be too far.

A steward began to interrupt his calculations with a gripe that he and his wardmasters were hungry. But Simon cut him short and sent him running for the first wagon, where he grabbed two knapsacks of medicines and bandages. For Surgeon Major Jeffers at the courthouse.

Simon kept Pamunkey from dismounting by grasping his boot. "We'll need fresh straw for the floors. Wheat, if you can find it. Take a wagon—but don't get yourself captured. The area's stiff with Rebs."

Pamunkey had no sooner driven away than Callender Ames, the assistant medical director, rode up. The middle-aged lieutenant colonel got down off his lathered mount and winked at Simon without saluting. They'd worked together at Boston City Hospital before the war, and military courtesy was saved for when Sheridan was snooping around the hospital tents.

"What you have to say, Cal?" Simon asked.

"Pus," Ames said. "Stinking pus."

"That bad?"

"It's always that bad, and don't let the *beau sabres* tell you otherwise." But Ames was smiling a little. He gave his horse to a groom and limped up to Simon, the result of a shell fragment taken in the heel at Fredericksburg. "Hear that . . . ?" he asked, stroking his side-whiskers as he gazed off into the south. A bluish sheet of smoke hung there against the gathering nightfall.

Simon listened more keenly. Artillery fire now. If Jubal Early's army quit running and fought as ferociously as it had earlier today, Simon would have to concentrate the hospitals of three corps south of Winchester as soon as possible. Lately, it was like picking up and moving a city of five thousand every day.

"Go," Ames said as if reading Simon's mind. "I'll set up here and save a room for you."

"Rebel hospitals are in most of the churches, Cal. Surgeon-in-charge is at the courthouse."

"I'll make sure they get some help."

"And start taking over buildings for us. We can set up the tents later, if we know we're staying."

"Yes, yes—go, Simon."

"Get some rest if you can, Cal. Let the younger scalpels take the brunt of it."

"Oh pus."

Simon pulled himself up onto Naomi's back. She stamped a hoof. "Not much longer now, Sissy," he lied.

He himself wasn't much better off. He'd had all of an hour's sleep last night, and that had been spoiled by the nightmare. The East Woods at Antietam again, so lifelike he'd actually been relieved to be awakened at midnight by Pamunkey, who shook his shoulder. This was the general call. The entire army, thirty thousand strong, was being roused by nudges and whispers instead of bugles, so as to get the jump on Rebel Lieutenant General Jubal Early. Simon put on his boots with Pamunkey's help, feeling glassy, fragile, deeply sad. It'd been some months since the nightmare had affected him that power-fully.

He forced his mind back to the present.

A day of at least three thousand casualties, not counting the enemy wounded who'd been left behind. And what if Sheridan kept moving right on to Charlottesville, as Grant wanted?

Simon needed to talk to the general before starting south of town, but no one along the street knew where to find him until a headquarters courier hollered over the racket of limbered guns on the roll, "He's still in the field, Colonel—went forward about twenty minutes ago!"

Simon coaxed Naomi into the dusty space between two infantry battalions. A wave of lightheadedness came and went—should've gotten a bite to eat. At least a cup of coffee. Someday, he'd force himself to try what the troops did to ward off fatigue on the march—chew ground coffee. But just the thought turned his stomach.

Cannoneers were unlimbering their twelve-pounders out in the trampled wheat on both sides of the Valley Pike, but he could tell that they were in no mood for a fight. They weren't even bothering to dig trenches behind their guns. If the Rebels were as worn out, there'd be no counterattack. Maybe.

A wooden bridge arched over a small creek. Naomi stumbled on the first board, more from exhaustion than the sudden darkness. Simon halted. He stroked her ears, then got down and led her by the bridle.

Ahead, the soldiers broke ranks to loot some enemy who had been dropped in a circle by a shell, a neat rosette of corpses. The men gathered bunches of dry grass and set fire to them for light. Soon the ground was littered with envelopes and ambrotypes of wives and children. Simon stopped and looked down between his boots: a lock of red hair was unraveling on the breeze. Whoever she was, she didn't know about him yet. Queer to realize that. She was probably making supper right now, and didn't know.

"Back in formation, boys," their captain said. A boy himself.

But then a shoat squealed out of the weeds, and the entire company gave chase, whistling and hooting as they fanned out to catch the pig. Simon thought to help the captain get them back into order, but then he noticed a figure leaning weakly against a stone fence. An old woman. Her cap shone whitely against the nightfall. He let go of the bridle and stepped widely across a slough to her.

"*Bitte, nein!*" She squirmed against the fence like something small and cornered, clutching a hemorrhaging wound to her upper arm.

"*Ich bin ein doktor,*" he said before she might run away.

She stopped cowering, but stayed watchful of him.

He asked to see her injury. She hesitated, then spread the bloody rent in her sleeve. A saber cut. Some bastard had actually slashed her.

He closed his eyes for a moment, lips tightened, then asked in German, "Who did this, *Oma?*"

She didn't reply.

"Tell me so he can be punished . . . please."

She pointed south along the pike, her finger scratching the air like a twig. "A blue English."

"On a horse?"

"*Ja,* a black gelding."

Naomi was drinking noisily from the slough. Simon took a cotton compress from the saddle valise. "How long ago did this happen?"

"Minutes . . . he stole my milch cow."

Simon asked her to help him tie the compress on. "That's it, snugly now . . ." What could he say? The soldiers had been ordered to drive away the livestock, burn the crops—all part of Sheridan's mission to push up the Valley and leave so little that "crows flying over it for the balance of the season will have to carry their provender with them." With this campaign through the back door of the Blue Ridge, Grant hoped to break the stalemate at Petersburg, where the Army of the Potomac and the Army of Northern Virginia had gone into opposing trenches. But to get this done by sabering civilians?

"Why do you need my cow?"

"We don't," Simon said. "But the gray soldiers mustn't have it either."

"But we Brethren aren't with the gray English!"

"I know." Simon touched his palm to her wrinkled cheek, then, shamefaced, dropped his hand. He had come across Dunkers, or German Baptist Brethren, before. What he'd thought to be a schoolhouse across that cornfield at Antietam turned out to be a Dunker church. A tidy, devout people opposed to slavery. They'd been persecuted by Richmond for refusing to bear arms and now were being pauperized by Phil Sheridan.

Hoofbeats on the macadamized pike—a courier was on a dash south. Simon waved him to a halt.

"Sir?"

"What units lie ahead?"

"No idea, sir." His horse was dripping wet.

"Then who the hell are you with?"

"Wolverines." Michigan Brigade.

"And your commanding officer?"

"Brigadier Custer."

Oh yes. Custer. Simon had yet to be introduced. "Inform him that Colonel Simon Wolfe requests his presence at the hospital on Amherst Street in Winchester. The general's convenience, of course."

The courier saluted and was off again.

Simon turned back to the old Dunker woman, but she'd gone.

He listened for sounds of her over the tramp of brogans on the road, but heard only the *chuck-chuck* of a mockingbird from a nearby patch of woods. The whole of the sky had blackened, except for feathers of peach that fanned up from where the sun had set behind Little North Mountain. His gaze fell from these to a farmhouse on the hillock above. Reddish light showed from a second-story window. It guttered, then frenzied into sparks. Smoke began gushing out from under the eaves.

"Sergeant!" Simon cried toward the troops marching past, trusting that someone would answer.

A voice said after a moment, "Sir!"

"Detail some men to put out that fire!"

"Our orders are to keep marching. My lieutenant's somewhere behind—you can take it up with him."

Simon didn't wait for the officer. The night had suddenly blazed: the window curtains had erupted into flame. Alone, he rode through a gate in the stone fence and followed wagon ruts up to the dooryard.

He tethered Naomi to a sapling.

"Hello the house!" he cried, pounding on the front door. The latchstring had been taken in.

He hurried along the veranda to a window, but the darkened room was closed off from the rest of the lower story. He went around to the rear of the house.

The kitchen latch gave with a shove, but when he pushed the door all the way open, smoke billowed out and dropped him choking to his knees. The smoke was like molten lead, throat-searing. He scuttled backward into the fresh air, inhaled deeply, then crawled through the door. A roll of flame whooshed down the stairs on the far side of the kitchen, forcing him to flatten himself until it had dissipated into a black pall that hung a few feet above him.

Drops of liquid fire were seeping between the ceiling boards, plopping brightly on the floor around him. One landed on his coat. He patted it out and sniffed: coal oil.

He started to move across the kitchen, thinking to go upstairs and check the bedrooms, but an overturned churn blocked his way. He shoved it aside—and started. "God!"

A face was leering at him. Bulging eyes. A woman in a white cap. For a split second he thought she was the Dunker matron he'd just tended. But no, she was another, a much younger woman with a spray of raven-colored hair jutting out from under her cap. Simon steadied his fingers and reached across a jumble of butter tools to press one of her eyeballs. The tissue was flaccid.

Dead by some minutes.

He held his breath against the lowering smoke as he crouched over the corpse. Then he saw the bloodstain. He fumbled in his trouser pocket for his penknife and cut her skirt away from her midriff.

His eyes were tearing so badly it was some moments before he could make out the three piercing wounds. All to the lower abdomen. Low enough to make the womb seem the target of the thrusts. He shook his head, but then went on. The punctures weren't incised, as he'd expect from a saber. A bayonet then? The width of each wound was half that of the infantry weapon, although he reminded himself to take the elasticity of the skin into account. He glanced at her face again. Looks that still invited sexual desire, although she was on the verge of middle age. Was that what this was about then? He sliced away more homespun and examined the labia major for violence. Nothing unusual.

A ceiling board tumbled down and exploded into embers that skittered against the woman's legs, setting her skirt on fire. He grabbed her hand—it was still pliant—and began dragging her toward the door. But then, with a groan of failing rafters, the middle of the ceiling staved in. A chest of drawers plummeted through the fiery hole, missing him by inches.

He let go of her hand and staggered through the door.

He meant to take only a few breaths before lunging back inside to get her. But by the time he stopped choking, solid flame filled the door opening. The swelling heat drove him farther out into the yard, where Naomi had bent the sapling almost to the ground in her twisting to be away. He untied her and got into the saddle just as the roof fell in, leaving the chimney to stand wreathed in sparks and smoke.

Naomi started to bolt again, but Simon stayed her by wrenching hard on the rein.

Then he began circling the ruin, looking for tracks. He made a slow turn around the coals, saw nothing, and widened his search to take in the mud along a tiny creek that trickled down from a spring higher on the hillock.

Nearing some birches, Naomi shied.

Simon stroked her ears, then eased down to the ground so the saddle leather wouldn't creak.

He listened. The guns in the distance were still. That probably meant the Rebels had decided to call it a battle.

He inched over the sucking mud toward the birches. He was almost to them when a figure bolted out of the leaves and splashed across the creek.

Simon started to follow, but then stopped. He was unarmed. In his mind's eye, he could see a musket flash. Once again, he could feel himself being caned, and then sinking into the earth.

But his feet were moving as if of their own mind, and he was giving chase through the water and out into the buckwheat on the slope beyond.

The figure climbed out of the deep shadows of the birches and emerged into the firelight. Female.

"Wait!" he hollered.

Again, his first thought was that it was the old Dunker woman. But no compress was to be seen on her sleeve, and she was running far too fast for someone that age—despite the bundle in her arms. He realized that he was chasing a girl, and she was holding a child who'd begun to cry.

"Stop, please!" he shouted in German.

But she kept going. She topped the slope, her shawl flying off her shoulders as she ran.

He was sure that he'd lost her for good, but cresting the hillock he saw that the wheatfield plunged into a swale just below the spring. There she was sprawled, gasping for breath.

"Won't hurt you," he panted. "Promise." Then he flopped down on his shins and rubbed an aching side with his fingers. A fluttery sensation in his heart and lungs, the same one he'd felt that morning in the East Woods when the cannonade started. "Boy or girl?"

"Hannes," she said at last. "His name is Hannes."

The voice was a bit older than expected. He now guessed her to be in her early twenties. "Why's he stopped crying so suddenly?"

"I don't know. Maybe I fell on him."

"Let me see." Simon staggered to his feet and started down into the swale.

But she half-rose and fled again, scrabbling through the muck on her knees and free hand.

"Please," he called after her, "I'm a doctor."

She stopped, stood motionlessly for a long moment, then slowly faced him.

He approached, making no sudden moves. "Lift him."

She raised the child into the glow breaking over the hillock. A pair of startled eyes, green they seemed in the dying firelight, met his own full on.

Simon smiled. "He's fine. And quite handsome. A year old?"

"In a month. And he was born a month early."

Simon turned his attention to the young woman. Her head trembled convulsively as her eyes flitted from gilt button to button on his coat. Even in the dimness of the swale, he could tell that she was strikingly beautiful. Honey-colored hair parted down the middle. He finally made himself glance away; his stare was frightening her. "Who killed the woman in the house?"

Her answer was a wail, full of pain, and she was turning to run blindly again when he caught her by the arm. "A relation? Your sister?" She yanked so violently to be free of him he added soothingly, "It's all right. We won't talk about that now."

She collapsed against his chest, sobbing.

He held her. "You're safe."

He said nothing for a while, feeling the child fidget between his chest and hers as she cried herself out. Below, campfires were beginning to dot the Valley floor, another vast Union bivouac taking shape against the night, yellow twinklings divided by the dark stripes of the company streets.

"What's your name?"

Silence.

"How can I help you if I don't know your name?"

"Rebekka Zelter." She was still shuddering.

"Mine's Simon Wolfe, Frau Zelter, and no one's going to hurt you from now on. My word on it." Three more casualties to add to the tally. One slashed on the arm, one murdered in her own kitchen, and one made hysterical by what she'd seen since Philip Sheridan had brought his army to Winchester today. Fresh grief. *So this is how it hemorrhaged before turning inward, before hardening into silence.* As he held the young Dunker woman, Simon thought of his sister Leah, imagined that night a year-and-a-half ago when her husband Israel's body was returned to her. A rare luxury, getting the remains back for burial. Most went into an unmarked common pit within spitting distance of where they fell. But Simon knew that raw grief appreciates nothing but dreamless sleep.

Finally, he let go of the woman and ran his hand over the child's belly, gently probing. "Come back to Winchester with me," he said. "Hannes must eat soon."

⊰ CHAPTER 2 ⊱

8:34 P.M.

The doctor's white mare was very tired.

Somehow, feeling the slow lurch of the saddle beneath her made Rebekka Zelter tired too. It was all she could do to hang on to Hannes and the pommel. She was afraid of falling off, but fancied that if she did, Hannes and she would float on the black pillow of the night. The air felt that dense, that sultry, and the lightning bugs seemed to be locked motionlessly in its suffocating stillness. The pike was lit by the campfires of the blue soldiers, but even without them she could have made out the road cutting grayly through the tents like a moonbeam on the river. Streets of white tents, laid out just like a city. So peaceful were these men, stirring their kettles or washing the soot of battle off their faces, it was hard to believe that they could kill and raze just as eagerly as they now laughed or played fiddles.

Yet, knowing how they could change in a blink, she was ready to jump down and run into the cedar brakes.

A voice whispered from somewhere slightly behind her left ear.

"No," she said low. *Must think of something. Anything.*

The doctor was leading the mare by the rein. A shame that the war had pruned him, for he was fine-looking. He had warm brown eyes with a touch of sorrow in them. A Jew, she believed. She had known only one other Jew, a peddler who'd swung by her parents' farm in Pennsylvania twice a year, driving a wagon rattly with pots and pans. He'd pretended to be very fond of children.

"Frau Zelter," the doctor suddenly turned and asked, "does Herr Zelter know where you are?"

"Yes." False teeth with a hinge that clicked as he chewed. She shut her eyes for an instant, and the odor of his body came back to her. *"How are things with you, Rebekka?"* He was with her always. Watching, always, eyes too crowded with disappointment to ever seem warm. *"Are you well enough to make supper?"*

"Is he in Winchester?"

"No. Jacob Zelter is dead."

The doctor stopped walking, and the mare nuzzled his back. She waited for him to ask how Zelter had died.

But he didn't. And, after a moment, he led them on.

"The hand of her that betrayed me is with me on the table . . ."

She started. The doctor seemed not to have heard. She wanted to close her ears with her fingers, but she couldn't, not without letting go of Hannes. Thankfully, no more voices followed. They could torment her at any moment, even when she was happy, but she felt most powerless against them when exhausted. Like now.

The doctor and she came into town. Lights everywhere. New Orleans was the biggest city in the South, but was it as gaily lit as this? She thought she could smell the honeyed glows that were spilling out onto the street. Sweet. But then other odors hit her nostrils. Blood. Intestines opened to the air. The smells of the slaughterhouse, of making sausage. And she realized that the entire town had become a hospital. A church door was propped open in hope of a breeze, and inside she could see how the pews had been shoved aside to make room for the wounded. She tried to pray for them, but the words shriveled inside her head.

She'd seen what they could do. The blue soldiers.

The doctor turned them up a side street. He was limping slightly now. Pineknot torches shone ahead. Moaning, almost inaudible, was drifting from the building they were set before.

Then she covered Hannes's eyes with her hand.

"I'm sorry," the doctor said. "Don't look."

She couldn't help but look: a wagon had been backed up to a dock. It was full of severed arms and legs. Under her astonished gaze, they suddenly came to life. Fingers opened and closed, feet tried to pad away in naked silence. The strange sight made her want to giggle, shriek, even pitch Hannes into the rubbery nest of limbs. She hated these bursts of feeling, guarded against them every waking moment. But they came no matter what she did or thought, no matter how hard she prayed.

Then she saw that all the cut-off parts of men had gone still again. "Why so *many?*" she asked.

"The minié ball. What that bullet does to bone. No choice but to amputate most of the time." The doctor took Hannes on his shoulder before helping her down. He had a gentle touch, and for an instant it seemed that he wanted to kiss her son.

But then he said, "When we go inside, keep your eyes on my cap. And breathe through your mouth."

A scream shot above the low hum of moaning. She jumped a bit, but then said, "I'm not afraid of this place."

Smiling, he returned Hannes to her arms. "Good. Eyes on my cap now."

He took her inside.

Simon ordered the first dresser he came upon to throw some canvas over the limb wagon. Then he looked roundabout for his orderly. Pamunkey was hauling water for the three-man surgical team headed by Callender Ames, splashing their table clean between lightning-swift amputations. He happily gave his two buckets to Ames's Negro and came over.

"Have you set up my room for me?" Simon asked.

Pamunkey nodded, then stared at Rebekka Zelter.

Simon realized that even the wounded were half-rising from their cots to look at her. Her beauty could shock, it was that rare, that angelic. Men grew silent before it. Her own look was one of hurt, as if she somehow mistook their silence for dislike, but then an instant later it dissolved into that of a frightened little girl making up her mind not to cry. Her cheeks and cap were splattered with mud from the swale.

"Show us the way, Otis," Simon said to Pamunkey.

They filed out of the ward and down a gallery of small workshops, the largest of which Cal Ames had claimed for him. It had a sash window, which Simon cracked at once, hopefully. But the breezes had died. Pamunkey lit the lamp, and Simon told Rebekka to put Hannes on his cot. He took off his coat, winced at his own pungency, then went to the pitcher and basin the orderly had laid out for him.

"Otis, find the child some condensed milk," he said, washing the grime off his face. "Have the cook warm it."

Pamunkey hurried out.

Hanging his towel on a nail, Simon realized that Rebekka's gaze was on his shirt. He'd had his tailor in Washington cut off and sew shut all the right sleeves at the shoulder.

She quickly asked, "Is your man deaf?"

"No." He frowned—what he'd taken for mud spatters on her cap and face were dried blood. She had stood within a few feet of the killing, then. "Otis was a scout for us in the Peninsula Campaign . . ." As had been most of his mulatto clan, a mixture of Indians and runaway slaves. "He and his brother were caught. His brother was hanged, but the Rebels made do with cutting out Otis's tongue. Then they let him stagger back to our lines."

She gave no reaction, her face strangely impassive.

Simon slipped on his gutta-percha apron. "You mustn't be afraid of him. And he idolizes children." Simon started for the door.

"Where are you going?" she asked sharply. In an instant, the animation had come back to her face.

"I have my work."

"Must you?"

"Yes. Sleep in here. I won't be needing my cot tonight, and tomorrow we'll make other arrangements." He studied her for a moment longer. She was too desirable-looking to be left alone at the rear of an entire army. Generally, the men of the regiments were of good character. But then there were the teamsters and the quartermaster troops.

"I don't wish to be alone tonight, Simon Wolfe."

He was a little surprised, even though he was sure that fear had given an accidental meaning to her words. "You'll be fine." He paused, unable to look away from the blood spots on her cap. "You've seen the worst man in this army. You must tell me if you see him again."

Her eyes clouded, but she said nothing.

"Will you promise?"

She began undressing Hannes, who whimpered when she plucked his thumb out of his mouth.

Simon caught Dr. Twiss cleaning foreign matter from a bullet channel with a sponge. He grabbed it. "Gentlemen," he called for the attention of all the surgeons, who one by one lowered their knives and saws and looked at the sponge he was holding over his head. "I thought I'd made myself clear about this," he went on, remembering to smile. "The enemy Medical Department has no marine sponges, thanks to our blockade. So their surgeons have been making do with clean linen and cotton rags instead. The result? Half our own incidence of blood poisoning, gangrene and lockjaw. *Half,* gentlemen. You may draw your own conclusions, but I'll have no sponges in my hospitals. Particularly those for communal use. Carry on, please."

Twiss reached to take back his sponge, but Simon grimly tossed it down into a pile of used lint.

"My dear Colonel," the man said as if to a bright but headstrong boy, "there's nothing to indicate that most healing is possible without suppuration. Lacking the formation of laudable pus—"

"Nothing laudable about it, Doctor. I'm not sure how far we can take union by first intention . . ." Healing without infection. ". . . but I think that should be our aim, don't you?"

Twiss obstinately went back to work. "And where, if I might ask, did the colonel learn of the Chivalry's want for sponges?"

"My sister."

"Oh?"

"She posted me an article she cut out of the *Richmond Enquirer.*" Simon strolled on.

Heat had come to his face.

He stopped beside Ames's team, who were starting an amputation. The patient suddenly shoved the chloroform-laced paper cone away from his face, took hold of Simon's apron and pulled him closer. "You a surgeon too?"

"Yes."

"Where'd you lose yours?"

"Antietam."

"Will you look at mine?" the soldier begged, his pupils made large by an opium pill.

Simon hesitated, then probed the ragged hole with his index finger. The man was breathing thunderously. This was the worst part, lying there in an opiate swoon, realizing that there's no avoiding it but hoping against hope. It came back to him with a sickening rush—that hot tent fly along Antietam Creek under which he himself had waited for the verdict.

"Has to go," he finally said, pulling out his finger. The minié ball had left a gap of three inches in the humerus.

"But it's mine to say, isn't it?"

"Entirely yours."

"I'd sooner die," the soldier said, although he'd begun to cry.

"I understand." Simon wiped the boy's brow with a cool damp cloth, then called for some stretchermen to take him away. "Put him at the door to the dead house," he whispered to one of the bearers, "then check on him in a half hour." He turned to Cal Ames. "When'd you boys jump in?"

"When the surgeon-in-charge from Thoburn's division passed out on his feet." Assisting Ames were Carlisle, one of Simon's two medical inspectors, and Nevins, his statistical officer. Both were such talented surgeons he often regretted using them for staff work. "I sent him and a half-dozen others from Sixth Corps over to the Taylor Hotel for a nap," Ames went on in a tired murmur.

"Good," Simon said, standing back as the next wounded man was lifted onto the table. A rare hemorrhager. The minié ball usually stanched the bleeding it caused. "I want enough teams rested for an early departure south." He used the tips of his forefinger and little finger to pinch shut the mouths of the femoral artery while the surgeons took a quick stretch. "If Little Phil pushes on, we'll need a depot at Newtown, or even Strasburg by late afternoon."

Ames put the man out with a few whiffs of choloroform. "What's Sheridan have up his sleeve?"

"I've yet to catch up with him." Simon withdrew his hand as Carlisle and Nevins applied a silk-thread ligature. "Lew," he asked Nevins, "d'you have some numbers for me?"

"In my shirtwaist pocket, Simon." The young major offered his gap-toothed grin in apology. "But they're preliminary."

Simon realized that he was still clutching the cloth, so tightly he was wringing the water out of it. He dropped it and took the slip of paper from Nevins's vest. His own estimate of casualties was much higher, but he thanked the young major, then stopped Pamunkey, who was sweeping past with a pan of milk. He handed him his apron. "Bring me my coat, Otis."

Ames had paused in the midst of sawing bone and was watching Simon with his usual look of concern. He smiled reassuringly, then went back to work. He folded the dismembered leg like a jacknife and tossed it into a bushel bucket with devastating ease. "You off then, Simon?"

"Yes, looking for Sheridan." Simon's shoulders had jerked slightly at the sound of the leg hitting the bucket.

Ames nodded as he stretched the flap to close it over the exposed slab of meat and bone. "Do tell Little Phil we have enough trade for the time being." But he was still smiling.

A provost guard directed Simon up a side street to a mansion from which Philip Sheridan's twin-starred red and white flag was flying at a limp flutter. The general's old comrade from his Indian-fighting days in the Oregon Territory, Brigadier David Russell, had taken a shell fragment in the heart this morning while leading a counterattack, a desperate, stopgap sort of thing Little Phil had personally ordered. Simon half-expected to find a somber Sheridan.

Yet, the general's aide-de-camp swept open the door for the surgeon on a dining room full of bright voices. The long table was studded with magnums of champagne and tins of oysters, and silverware was ringing against china.

"Simon, find a chair!" Little Phil said, his eyes like sparks in the candlelight. No grief in them. Just the glee that where five Union generals before him had been whipped, whipped like dogs, he had triumphed. Two months ago, Jubal Early's ragtag army had been knocking at Washington's backdoor; now they were skedaddling the other way with their tails between their legs. By all accounts, the provost guard didn't know what to do with all the prisoners. "Christ Almighty, boys, will you make room for my surgeon . . . ?" Sheridan's long-waistedness hid his tiny stature below the table. He was only five feet, three inches, and all of the shortfall was in his legs. But at one hundred and twenty pounds he was the perfect cavalryman: no burden to his mount. "Make room there, dammit, before I shoot one of you to clear a chair."

Simon hesitated. "Forgive me, sir, I have a few matters to report, but I see now's not the time."

"Balderdash—sit down."

"General . . ."

"Sit down."

Simon took a chair and accepted the glass of champagne Sheridan personally poured for him.

"Thank you, sir."

Sheridan had crossed one leg over the other and was jiggling a boot. Simon realized that he was waiting for the men to start talking among themselves again. George Crook, who'd known Little Phil longer than any of them, took the cue and began telling how things had gone for his 8th Corps today. Simon found "Old Buzzard" a bit too staid and unimaginative for stimulating mess company. But Crook was also unpretentious. He wore a simple blouse without insignia and never seemed to capitalize on having been Sheridan's chum at West Point.

Uneasy with being the center of attention, Crook quickly asked a mud-speckled colonel from his staff how things had gone for him. Rutherford Hayes, a Cincinnati lawyer before the war who was as happy as an undug clam to be away from his overbearing womenfolk. Like Simon, a Harvard alumnus, and on that basis they enjoyed something of an arm's-length friendship. Hayes started telling how his horse had gotten mired halfway across a slough in the middle of the wildest charge of the day. Shot and shell so thick you could've hung your wash out to dry on it. Just the sort of story everybody was in the mood for.

Everyone but Sheridan. He listened politely for a moment, then turned to Simon. "What's it look like?"

He tried not to stare at the general's head—it was shaped like a minié ball. Cal Ames, an amateur phrenologist, said that its mastoidal prominences were proof of an excessive combativeness. A passion for destruction. Regardless of what the bumps on Little Phil's skull meant, it was whispered that he got too full of wrath and fury in a battle for his own good. A well-bred officer didn't get excited under fire, even if his excitement gave him courage. He was supposed to pretend that he was no more aware of danger than he was of vice.

Yet, Simon thought of Sheridan as being more driven than wildly aggressive. Some men found him charismatic, usually the cavalry types—but no, not magnetically so in the way McClellan had been. Little Mac had sincerely hated seeing what hot metal could do to the splendid army he'd created.

"I'd put it at thirty-five hundred wounded, at least, sir," Simon finally answered.

Sheridan's boot skipped a beat. Other than that he gave no sign of concern. "How many of theirs do we have to look after?"

"Maybe five, six hundred. And their surgeons. I trust they'll be repatriated."

"Hell yes," Sheridan said, raising his voice just enough to quiet the table. "Old Stonewall let our sawboneses go in sixty-two, didn't he?

So I'm pleased to do the same. Elias," he said to Colonel Deering, his provost marshal, the only man Simon had ignored when nodding his hellos, "see to it these Johnny surgeons are given a safe conduct through the lines."

"Very good, sir." Deering frowned, and the vein that split his forehead stood out. Then he glared a moment at Simon, who let it pass. You don't recommend a man for court-martial and expect to make a friend.

"Anything else, Surgeon?" Sheridan asked.

"I'd like to order a big field hospital set up south of here, if that's in keeping with your plans."

Sheridan nodded. "Anywhere along Cedar Creek'll do. Is that it?"

Simon felt his nerves tighten. "No, sir . . ." But he paused when he saw that Little Phil's gaze had rushed to the far end of the table, where a jangle of spurs had just gone silent. A brigadier stood there, giving the most theatrical salute Simon had ever seen. For an instant he wondered if a junior officer, in the high spirits of victory, was impersonating some ludicrous brigadier general known to them all. But that proved not to be the case. "Well, Curly?" Sheridan was beaming, his eyes full of jovial affection instead of the usual glint that some took for evil.

"The graycoats are showing us their heels all the way to Newtown." Before the applause had died, the brigadier—no more than an overgrown boy with reddish-blond mustaches and a scarlet cravat—bounced into a chair and called for "my carafe." He then toasted his own news with a gulp of what looked to be water.

"You been introduced, Colonel Wolfe?" Sheridan asked.

"No, sir."

In a flash the boy-general was on his feet again, leaning over the table to shake left hands, the gilt arabesques on his jacket sleeve glinting. "George Custer—a pleasure."

"Simon Wolfe, sir," he said, rising. He knew few of the cavalry officers well; their far-ranging missions and his own duties usually kept them from crossing paths.

Custer's eyes widened slightly at the name, and Simon was about to ask the brigadier if he'd gotten his message when the man fairly gushed, "You mean *the* Simon Wolfe of Antietam?"

Oh Christ. Here we go. "I was there, yes."

"My good fellow," Custer exclaimed, "the honor's all mine! Gentlemen—" He turned to the others. "—you are supping with the surgeon who rallied the Twelfth Massachusetts to hold the line at the East Woods!"

Simon sank back into his chair, sure that Custer had learned of this only after asking about the one-armed colonel who'd presumed to summon him to the hospital—without compliments—to answer for the outrages of his troopers.

"Wasn't at Antietam, myself," Deering said with a full mouth. As if the bloodiest single day of battle in the war so far had been a country fair. "In Mississippi that September." His vein bulged and ebbed as he chewed. "Hot."

"You've never said a word, Simon," Hayes said. "Tell us."

Little Phil was already smiling, and the ring of expectant faces made Simon's throat feel raw. He took a sip of champagne, then told them in as few words as possible. How in minutes the regiment lost 224 of its 334 men. Thirty-odd survivors managed to fend off the Louisiana Tigers—under Stonewall Jackson that morning—long enough for the 90th Pennsylvania to plug the gap in the line. Simon paused. Once again, he saw that hunched figure lofting his hand, blue eyes blazing, an apparition of cool hatred in the morning shadow of a Dunker church. Yet, the same devoutly Presbyterian ghost had been the first to repatriate surgeons. ". . . I wasn't much inspiration to the men. I went down at the edge of the trees. It was they who stopped the Louisianans."

Silence weighed upon the table.

He saw that he'd disappointed them with his matter-of-fact telling. Custer especially, who had started chatting with Deering. The officers had wanted a lively anecdote with sham self-deprecation instead of the genuine thing. Simon found himself disliking them a little, and this gave him the nerve to turn to Sheridan. "General, I have every reason to believe our cavalry's up to some barbarity."

The officers went quiet again.

Sheridan glanced up from the oyster that had just tumbled off his fork. "How's that?"

"I chanced upon an elderly Dunker woman. She'd been slashed on the arm with a saber—"

"Where was this?" Deering interrupted, looking keenly interested despite his obvious dislike for Simon.

"Just south of town." Simon caught Little Phil's eye again. "And then, while checking a farmhouse that had been set afire against your orders, I found a second Dunker woman—murdered." Simon resisted looking at Custer for his reaction.

"How?" Deering asked. As provost marshal, he was responsible for investigating this sort of thing.

"Stabbed in the abdomen."

"Once?"

"Thrice."

Custer asked with a troubled look, "By saber, Colonel?"

"I don't believe so."

"I see. Then what makes you think a trooper slashed the first woman?"

"She said so."

"And you believed her?"

"She virtually swore so."

"Excuse me, Surgeon Colonel," Deering said, "but that can't be the case."

"*Sir?*"

"I'm from Philadelphia—"

"That goes without saying," Simon said.

A few officers started to laugh, but Deering silenced them with a sour look. "I grew up on the edge of Germantown, been around Dunkers all my life." Deering's voice raised a notch. "They are self-serving to the point of criminality . . ."

Simon glanced down into his lap at his hand. Flakes of splintered bone were sticking to his index finger. He brushed them off on his trousers and exhaled. Inwardly, he was seeing hundreds of Maryland-bound Union wounded being off-loaded by Deering's provost guards and the ambulances filled with Rebel prisoners, one of whom was moved to remark what a "cruelacious thing" it was to leave shot-up men out in a killing August sun "just to make sure ol' John Mosby don't capture us back."

"Dunkers will do nothing to serve the common good," Deering went on, slapping the table, "not a damned thing!"

"But they are obedient," Hayes said.

Deering blinked at this unexpected challenge.

"Yes indeed," Hayes continued, affably enough. "I heard this from a Johnny captain who fell into our hands. Seems they caught a Dunker in sixty-two feeding one of our patrols. 'Vat vill you do mit me?' he asked, shaking to beat the devil. 'I'm going to have you shot for collaborating with the enemy,' the captain told him. The German thought about this a moment, then said, 'Vell, vatever the rule is.' "

Ignoring the laughter, Deering rattled on, "Dunkers refuse to swear oaths. So I must doubt that Wolfe's woman swore to anything." He glanced around the table for support. "They're a galling bunch, and I for one am gratified to see them take their licks. The sooner we move them out of this Valley, the sooner we starve Bobby Lee out of Petersburg!" The War Department's plan was to deprive the Confederacy of crucial farm labor by escorting all Dunkers and Mennonites north across the Potomac.

Simon quietly said, "I only meant, Elias, that the old woman seemed truthful."

"Oh . . ." Deering took his time lighting a cheroot off the candelabra. "Then you're familiar with Dunkers?"

"Not very. But I am familiar with saber wounds. And the honesty that usually comes with the shock of injury. Surprising, the confessions I've been privy to these past few years. And the sleepless nights they've given me."

"Then that," Deering said, smirking, "must make you the conscience of this entire army . . . what?"

"Not quite. But I've been thinking of applying for chaplain status with some Catholic regiment. I don't mind working Sundays."

Custer chuckled louder than anyone.

Deering stared at Simon a moment longer, then smiled grudgingly around his cheroot. "Well, whatever the case, I think you might dash off a report on this to the Provost Marshal General." He then looked to Sheridan. "Don't you think so, sir?"

The general stirred, then asked Deering to repeat himself.

"I said Colonel Wolfe ought to put this Dunker thing down for Washington."

"No," Sheridan said distantly, "let's keep it here for the time being."

"Yes, sir," Deering said, scarcely hiding his displeasure. But then, forcing another smile, he got up with his glass raised and brought the others to their feet with: "Gentlemen, a toast to the memory of our brother, Davey Russell." He fixed a hard gaze on Sheridan as he said, "God rest . . . and may he finally know who his friends were."

Sheridan paused a moment, expressionless, then drank.

* * *

The hospital was no quieter than when Simon had left it two hours before. The three-man team had finished the amputations and then split up to take care of bullet extractions, each taking a table under a lantern hung from the ceiling. The big room of the old factory stank of blood, chloroform and sweat. And, as always, underlying the noisy bustle of the surgeons and the dressers was that low, ghastly hum of damaged men groaning behind compressed lips. Few ever cried out, although Simon often wished that they all would scream to the high heavens, lament the awful damage to their young bodies. But no. Even those who eventually went to the dead house did so in manly silence, just before the end—which they realized with uncanny accuracy—breaking it long enough to ask the nurses to write their folks that they'd gone like men.

But was a brave death enough to justify all this?

Strolling between the cots, Simon struggled to put it in a positive light. He'd had enough of darkness these past years. Hippocrates had said that war is the only proper school of the surgeon. This war would end one day, and these doctors would go back to their towns and cities with ten times the skill they'd had upon appointment.

But what if the war never ended?

Simon frowned. Sometimes it seemed possible, especially late at night after a battle, like now. Field hospitals picking up and moving endlessly, wagon after wagon filled with amputated limbs, and at the smoky edges of the nightmare Napolean cackling: "You medical people will have more lives to answer for in the other world than even we generals!"

Cal Ames was working lozenge-eyed with fatigue on a neck wound. "How're you feeling?" Simon asked.

"Got a few more hours in me."

"You sure?"

Ames nodded, then glanced at his patient and gritted his teeth. "Orderly!" he barked. "Take him away!" He lowered his voice and said from the fringes of that strange giddiness a surgeon lapsed into after two nights without sleep, "He's as cold as stone, Simon. Probably been dead ten minutes. God help me, I've been trying to raise Lazarus!"

"Can you use a taste of whiskey?" A few ounces helped now and again.

Ames looked at him intently, and Simon suspected that the man was thinking about what he'd done at Chancellorsville as a medical inspector. One arm or not, Simon had bodily thrown a drunk surgeon out of the operating tent and turned him over to the provost guard.

"No thanks, Simon. No bug juice tonight. Don't want some boy spending the rest of his life telling everybody a drunkard put the knife to him—and that's why he's not worth a damn."

"I've never seen you drunk, Cal," Simon quietly said.

"Wait till we get home to Boston. Then hide the bedpans and bar the door."

The next arrived on a stretcher: cannister wounds to both legs. Simon agreed with Cal's assessment that they might be saved.

Ames poured choloroform into the sponge at the apex of the paper cone. "What's on for tomorrow?"

"We advance."

A loud sigh. "Does that damned Paddy realize what the hell we've got here?"

"I suppose so, Cal." For in parting, Sheridan had rested his hand on Simon's armless shoulder and suggested that he not overdo. *Don't go pushing yourself, Simon,* he'd said. The insinuation had been clear. An amputation was more than a loss to the body. It permanently hacked something off the spirit too. Its moral firmness, maybe. Its grit. And this invisible wound never healed. It festered for as long as a man went on testing his courage against the likes of Bobby Lee and Jubal Early.

Then Simon noticed Rebekka Zelter out among the wounded, ladling them water, brushing their faces with her fingers whenever they thanked her. She felt Simon's gaze on her and looked back at him.

Simon tried to smile but couldn't. Instead, he gave her an embarrassed wave. "God forgive us."

Ames knew what he was talking about without glancing up. "She pitched in as soon as you left."

Then Simon felt as if he were capsizing. He groped for the edge of the table to steady himself. The blood had rushed from his head, leaving a kind of sickly yellow light behind his eyes. He started to brace himself on his missing arm, but caught himself just in time.

Fortunately, Ames hadn't seen, for he yawned and then said, "Something I oughta show you." Limping more heavily than usual, he led Simon through the cots toward a dim corner of the room. He snatched a candle lantern from a dresser along the way. "This came in about a half hour ago, and the devil if I know what to do with it . . ." He knelt beside a cot and removed the bandage from the face of a Union cavalryman. Simon drew close for a better look.

"I hope he's had no chloroform," he said after a few moments.

"Nothing," Ames said, "not even an opium pill."

"Good. We don't want any blood in the air passages." The trooper had fainted, which made it easier for Simon to explore the wound with his fingers. A minié ball, he was sure, had carried away the right anterior portion of the lower jaw as far back as the second bicuspid and, on the left, to the first molar.

"When he comes around, he'll bleed to death," Ames said.

"Afraid so."

"Any ideas what to do?"

"Yes, a few." And then Simon hissed under his breath, strangely disgusted with himself, his empty sleeve. "If I still had two hands, Cal."

"Well, dammit—tell me step-by-step and I'll have a go."

"No. I need you back on the extractions. I can't let ten die for the sake of one."

"I will be your hands," a soft voice with a German accent said.

Simon stood straight and turned. Rebekka Zelter was looking squarely at the trooper's shattered face. There was no revulsion in her expression, nor any hint that she'd steeled herself—only a visible determination to be of use. It reminded him of his sister Leah's headstrong determination to keep their family together, whatever the cost to herself.

"Are you sure, Frau Zelter?" Simon asked. "It won't be pleasant."

She dipped her head.

"I'll have Pamunkey bring you your kit," Ames said, then rushed back toward his own table.

Simon told the young woman to go around to the other side of the cot and kneel opposite him. He wanted to call for two camp stools, but none of the staff was within earshot.

She whispered, "Is this man close to death?"

"Yes."

"I'll pray that we save him."

"Please do," Simon said. Pamunkey set his surgical kit on the floor beside him. "Stay, Otis, and hold the light for us."

The orderly glanced at the disfiguring wound, then let his gaze drift out over the cots. He could never be persuaded to help directly with the operations. Maybe the memory of his own maiming got in the way.

"Are your hands steady, Frau Zelter?" Simon asked.

She was wringing them together, but nodded again.

"Very good. What we must do now—at once, before this lad comes around," Simon explained as he took out a scalpel, "is close the chin so that it conforms to the fractured ends of the jaw. We'll have to ligate some arteries—that's something like fine needlework. Then we'll make some incisions, trim and suture the remaining tissue. The incisions are easily made, and I'll show you precisely where. I need them done first . . . before he rouses."

She paled as he gave her the blade.

"I'm just not steady enough with one hand," he went on. "But I can help you hold his head, and I'll be with you every inch of the way."

She hadn't moved since he'd laid the scalpel in her palm.

After a moment, he gently said, "All right, Frau Zelter. This is really asking too much of you." Particularly for the sake of a trooper—when it was the cavalry that had brutalized her and her sister Dunkers south of town. Even for a medical student, the first instance of cutting into live flesh was terrifying. "We'll just have to wait till one of the surgeons is freed up. Why don't you check on your son?"

A gurgling sound broke from the trooper's throat, and he rocked his head.

"No," she said, gripping the handle of the scalpel at last. "Jakob Zelter was our healer, and I helped him sometimes with things as bad as this. Show me where to cut, Simon Wolfe—and I'll do it, Christ willing."

⊰ CHAPTER 3 ⊱

Rebekka Zelter buttered a piece of freshly baked bread, her eyes steady on his. "How is it you speak German, Simon Wolfe?"

He paused. "My parents came to this country from Hesse." *Two countries for the time being,* he reminded himself.

"Were you born there?"

"No, in Charleston. Three years after they arrived in South Carolina." Behind him, Simon could feel Hannes walking hold-to-hold along the bench, but his mind was on the butter. Dunker, most likely. Commandeering had left the commissary well-stocked with meat and dairy goods, but he'd promised himself to stick to the usual rations during this campaign. He supposed that he'd feel less like a plunderer that way. Leah, in one of her early letters to him, had accused the Army of the Potomac of being a pillaging mob at Fredericksburg. Thieves and cutthroats. Her patriotic indignation had waned since. But still, his sister had a point. Robert Lee, both times he'd invaded the North, forbade the taking of even a fence-rail for firewood. On the march to Gettysburg, he hanged two of his soldiers for robbing and murdering a civilian.

"Then you're a Southerner, Simon Wolfe."

"Am I?"

Rebekka put down her bread. "You were born in Carolina, so how can you be anything but Southern?" Then she slowly smiled at him. It was almost seductive. These little vagaries of behavior had popped up last night too, even while she was grimly helping him close the trooper's chin. He suspected that it had something to do with the horror she'd been through, her understandable fear of Union soldiers and a desperate urge to please them for survival's sake. So he didn't let himself feel flattered.

"I've spent most of my adult life in the North," he said, looking out across a hospital mess full of dusty sunlight and the clatter of utensils. "First to Harvard Medical School. And then I opened my practice in Boston."

"Why there . . . and not your home here in the South?"

Having endured this line of questioning a hundred times before, he was relieved when Mother Haggerty interrupted: "We can't find no crutches, Colonel." The matron and three of her nurses had come in from the Berryville Canyon field hospital at daybreak, and now were busy whipping the wards into order. The stout woman had never passed muster with Dorothea Dix, the superintendant of female nurses, thanks to the rumor that she enjoyed a pipe and a drop of rye now and again in the privacy of her own tent. It was no rumor, Simon had learned. But Sheridan liked her, probably for the same reasons Miss Dix loathed her, and had seen to it that she had an unofficial posting as "mother" with his medical department.

Simon had never complained. She was a demon for cleanliness, and the boys loved her salty tongue.

Briefly, Mother Haggerty swept up Hannes into her huge bosom and kissed him, then nodded a guarded hello to Rebekka. She felt that civilian women were utterly useless. "I gone through all our wagons, sir, and not a bleedin' pair to be had."

Simon said, "I'll telegraph Sandy Hook before I head south this morning." In late July, he'd organized a 1,300-bed hospital at this Maryland village on the Potomac. He got up. "Mother Haggerty, may I introduce Mrs. Zelter. She'll be staying with us a while."

"How d'you do."

"I'm happy to meet you," Rebekka said in English.

"It's a darlin' boy you have, ma'am."

"Thank you." But as soon as Mother Haggerty had withdrawn, Rebekka pressed Simon, "Why did you stay in Boston when your family was in Charleston?"

Simon sat again, carefully wiped clean his amputee's combination knife and fork, then dropped it into his coat pocket. "Why do you ask?"

She lowered her gaze. "Forgive me, Simon Wolfe. It's just that people are always deceiving me." She said this so pathetically he felt bad for having stopped her dead in her tracks about his father. But he was sick to death of this. Then it hit him. *Deceit.* Last evening, had the soldier used a ruse to get inside the farmhouse, feigned injury maybe? Or was she talking about something else, something that went beyond the war? "I'd just like to know more about you," she added.

He rolled his eyes. "My father is Jefferson Davis's pet Jew."

She shrugged.

He wondered what had made him say it. Maybe not saying it for so long had led to this moment, holding it back when he knew full well that this is how most officers, both North and South, saw his father.

"I don't understand what you're saying, Simon Wolfe," she half-whispered, making him feel even more ashamed of himself.

"I'm sorry, Frau Zelter. That wasn't polite of me." He paused. "My father is Solomon Wolfe, the Confederate Secretary of War."

Mild surprise—it was better than the shock most people showed. "But how's this possible?" she said. "You wear blue. Does he know?"

"He knows."

"Do you write to him?" Rebekka asked.

"I write my widowed sister, who lives with him in Richmond."

Hannes began fussing. Frowning, Rebekka lifted him by his dimpled elbows onto her lap. "What about your mother?"

"Died while I was in school."

"But what would she say of all this?"

Simon fell silent, her long-absent face suddenly before him—pallid and distraught, broken by that chronic heartsick smile. She'd suffered magnificently, and he supposed he still resented her a little for that. Leah was far less artless in her pain. His sister wrote that when she learned her husband, Israel, had been killed at Chancellorsville she screamed and carried on like an Irish scullery maid.

"I believe my mother would understand," he said, pulling out his pocket watch. Time to go. Wherever up the Valley Little Phil found Jubal Early's crippled army, another massacre would follow. He now had more complete numbers on yesterday's Union wounded. More than four thousand. Including the surgeon of the 26th Massachusetts, who'd already been sent north with the first ambulance train bound for Sandy Hook. Somehow, beyond reason, he felt responsible: one of the men under his command had been hurt. It was hard to imagine what Sheridan felt—if anything at all. Different weights, different measures.

He came to his feet, and she looked up at him anxiously. "Must you go?"

"Just for a day or two. Pamunkey will stay here and see to your needs." She had washed her white cap, yet some of the bloodstains hadn't come out. An unexpected feeling of tenderness for her made him say, "I'm thankful, Frau Zelter."

"For what?"

"That he didn't take your life as well."

She paled, slightly. Seeing this, he found himself sitting again— Jubal Early could wait for the moment. He realized that what she'd just said about wanting to know more about him was a plea, not curiosity. She wanted him to find the soldier who'd come to the farmhouse. She wanted Simon to make sure that what had happened yesterday evening would never be repeated. And now he had to assure her that he could do this. "Madam, I'm not the sort of man to forget what I saw in that kitchen . . ." He went on to tell her that he'd been criticized before in his life for being inflexible, but that had never swayed him from doing what he felt was right. He believed that even his enemies—and he had a good number—would admit that he was an honorable man, and Simon saw no meaning in that word unless it meant seeing right done in all things, great and small. "Do you understand what I'm prepared to do for you and your son?"

She was staring at him, confused. "Was Leah your mother's name?"

"No, Leah's my sister. How did you know—?"

"You just called me Leah."

He reddened again. "I'm sorry. I could probably use some more sleep." But then he continued in the same insistent tone: "You alone have seen him. The beast who deserves to be hunted down. As long as he remains hidden in our ranks, we—all of us in blue—are no better than he. I accept that responsibility, Frau Zelter." Simon hesitated, briefly. "Now, can you tell me what he did in that kitchen?"

Her hand flew to her mouth and, before he could utter another word, she rushed from the table with Hannes wailing under her arm.

10:00 A.M.

ALONG THE VALLEY PIKE

The pike, paved with tar and crushed rock before the war but gone to potholes since, was bearing a double column of wagons so slow the Union infantry had found it faster going to tear down the snake-rail fences and stream alongside through the fields. Simon took their lead and turned Naomi out into the corn. Heat was already weighing on the Valley, and through its shimmers he could see the darkly forested hump of the Massanutten range to the south. The sky was clear but for a thread of smoke rising from a windrow that had been set on fire by the cavalry.

He had come up this road with Banks's army in the wet spring of 1862, but then it had been under a drizzle of doubt that the Rebels could ever be beaten. Now, Sheridan was winning, although word trickled back with couriers that Old Jube was digging in on Fisher's Hill. A billow of ridges, spurs and ravines above the village of Strasburg. It was the best defensive ground in the Valley, and if Little Phil took it head-on, the dead and wounded might pile up as they had on Marye's Heights at Fredericksburg.

Simon suddenly gave a tug on the rein and listened.

He thought he could hear the thumping of cannon. But no, it was a band, or more likely massed bands.

Another mile passed beneath Naomi's hooves before he could pick out the tune, "St. Patrick's Day in the Morning," and at that point the provost guard was dressing the ranks, relieving the men of the live chickens, melons and household goods they'd plundered along the way, before letting them slog on.

"Why the bands?" Simon asked a sergeant with a badly sunburned neck.

"Review for Little Phil ahead, sir."

"What's the occasion?"

"Abe's promoted him to brigadier in the Regulars."

Simon raised an eyebrow. Promotion to general in the Regular Army was a plum, especially at Sheridan's tender age of thirty-three.

Officers had spent their entire adult lives in the peacetime Army and been glad to retire out as arthritic captains. Either God or the Devil was being kind to Phil Sheridan.

Simon then asked the same question he'd put to every provost post along the way: "Were you men on sentry duty anywhere near Mill Creek last night?"

"We guarded the bridge, sir," the sergeant said, inclining his head toward a meek-looking private with spectacles who was standing behind him.

They'd been within sight of the house then. "Did you see that Dunker place go up in flames?"

The sergeant nodded, although he obviously sniffed trouble. The private was staring down between his brogans.

"Any of our people go up to that house before it caught fire?"

"Not what I recall, sir," the sergeant said. The private said nothing. "Does it mean anything if somebody did?"

"I should say. A woman was murdered there."

The two soldiers glanced at each other as if agreeing to say nothing more.

"Very well then," Simon said. "Know where I can find the big field hospital that's being pitched along Cedar Creek?"

"No, sir. Sorry."

Simon clucked his tongue, and again Naomi clopped on over the hard limestone soil. So this is how it would be. Nobody admitting anything more than he absolutely had to, short of winding up in the guardhouse.

Topping the next crest, Simon glimpsed the new brigadier, R.A., on his black gelding, Rienzi. Rare—a horse completely black down to its muzzle. Sheridan was waving his round little hat at the hurrahs from the passing regiments. Bright-cheeked. The best day of his entire life. Yet, he frowned deeply when he noticed Simon ride up, only to grin an instant later at an especially boisterous cheer from some Ohio regiment. His home state.

"Look at those gritty bastards," he chuckled. "They'd spark their own sisters on a dare."

Ah yes, Simon thought as he found a place in the mounted rank to Sheridan's back. During the gloryfest of the past twelve hours, he alone had brought dark news to Little Phil, violating the first rule of being attached to a commanding general's staff: always pretend that everything is going just splendidly.

Obviously, somebody else hadn't learned the same rule.

"Don't know what the hell they have to cheer about," a dour voice said. "Early's going to brush us off that hill like flies off dung."

Simon, riveted on Little Phil, had unknowingly fallen in beside Elias Deering, who was on a Morgan that was almost Rienzi's equal—the only other totally black mount other than Sheridan's that Simon could recall off the top of his head. Three horses down the line Custer watched the parade from under a great slouch hat, tapping his stirrup to the beat of the music, confident-looking, mindlessly happy, not a care in the world. He'd been last in his class at West Point.

"Morning, gentlemen," Simon said. Replies were muttered, fingers touched to hat brims. But they were not about to forget last night. Simon's gut tightened for a moment.

"I admire your brass, Surgeon Colonel," Deering said, although his smile was almost a sneer. For a second Simon thought that he was talking about Antietam, but then the provost marshal added, "Most men would simply say the devil with what you saw last night."

Simon wondered if he was being baited. "Should I do just that, Elias?"

Deering paused for another booming hurrah, then lowered his voice. "Be reasonable, Simon—look at the delicate position I'm in."

"I don't understand."

"The hell you say. You went to Harvard, didn't you? Good old Harvard logic."

"What's that supposed to mean?"

"Nothing." Deering began rubbing the forked vein on his forehead as if it ached. "Let's forget our differences for the time being . . . all right?"

Simon asked, "Then you *really* want a report?"

"Of course I do. And I swear—God as my witness—it'll get passed on to Washington."

Simon was surprised. Particularly after hearing Deering's tirade against Dunkers. "Wouldn't that violate our orders?"

Deering ignored the question and leaned forward to catch Custer's eye. "I say, Georgie—Phil's come a ways since the Terrill thing, what?"

Custer kept his eyes on the parade, but Simon could see embarrassment ripple down the line of staff officers, even though, given the bands, Sheridan was a few yards out of earshot.

"At West Point," Deering went on for Simon's benefit, "our new brigadier took offense to something his cadet sergeant said to him." The colonel lifted his cap, scratched his sparse gray hair. "Young Sheridan lunged at the fellow with his bayonet. Seems his anger takes naturally to steel, wouldn't you say?"

Then Deering gathered in his rein and galloped off alone.

Simon realized that the review was over. "Ah well," he sighed to himself, "nothing like being back in the field with the boys."

He followed Sheridan and the staff toward a distant clutch of tents. Field headquarters. The tent hospital he had ordered erected was supposed to be close by. But where? The floor of the Valley was too buckled here to see much from one spot. He'd have to find out at headquarters.

Custer came up alongside, doffing his hat. "Bulliest day since Christ was born, wouldn't you say?"

Simon just smiled.

Custer's skin didn't take the sun well, and he was chronically red-faced, but Simon realized that he was now blushing as well. The Christian remark had been unintended, then. Dead last in a West Point class that was not particularly stellar. But in all fairness, it was said that he shined in battle. He had a knack for doing just the right thing at the right instant.

Or maybe it was luck.

They rode in silence for a minute.

Then the boy-general said, dropping his voice, "I suppose poor Elias must be forgiven for all that rot."

"Must he?"

"His mother had a rather . . ." Custer seemed to grub for just the right words. ". . . unfortunate past. It was his salvation to be appointed to the academy. Socially, I mean."

"When was he graduated?"

"Sir?"

"He's senior to Sheridan, isn't he?"

Custer grinned, which accentuated his shallow chin. "Well, there's no hoodwinking you, is there now." He cut Naomi out of the line with his charger, so that they were suddenly riding on the flank of the others. For privacy, Simon realized. "Elias," Custer then went on, "was commissioned *eight* years before Phil. And he was quite the dig, you know." A studious cadet. "So today's news is more than his pride can take. I trust you won't pass on his little indiscretion. He's really a decent sort, even though I understand there's some bad blood between you two."

"I wouldn't call it bad blood," Simon said.

"Then what? If you don't mind."

"Not at all. He tossed my wounded out of their ambulances so he could transport some prisoners. I wouldn't stand for it."

"As you shouldn't have. He was wrong, and you were right. But what's the point in embarrassing him now?" Imploring made Custer look very young. "Do I have your word it stays among us?"

Simon wanted to laugh, but then managed to say, "You do."

Custer squinted up into the sun. "Ah, great day in the morning!"

"But I'll ask for something in return."

"Yes . . . ?"

"Was Deering south of Winchester last evening?"

Custer's vivid blue eyes widened. "Yes, he was." Then they turned wistful. "But we all were. Including you."

"Is that an accusation?" Simon asked, trying to smile.

"Heavens, no. I'd never accuse you of anything, Colonel Wolfe. Not after what you did at the Cornfield. A man as brave as you could never be unjust. I know that, believe me." Custer then paused so long Simon expected him to take his leave. But instead he suddenly simpered and asked, "May I trouble you for some professional counsel?"

Here it comes. Father confessor on a brevet's pay. "Of course."

"You see, I was just married this February . . ."

"Felicitations," Simon said.

"Thank you. Libbie's a real trump, and God how I adore her." The simper faded. "The Bacons are fine people . . . proper . . . I mean, Libbie once sought forgiveness for sewing on the Sabbath." He was blushing again.

"Is there some difficulty of adjustment?" Simon finally rescued him.

"Precisely. My lord, there's nothing you don't see right through. What I'm trying to say—is it usual for a girl of fine breeding to . . . well, experience some discomfort at first?"

"Actual pain, you mean?"

A humiliated nod. "So she says."

"Where's your wife now?"

"Boarding in Washington."

"She should see a physician there."

Custer gave Simon an agonized look. "Do you really think it necessary?"

"Well, it'd be prudent. To eliminate some physiological cause. But honestly, sir—how can I suggest any course of action without examining her myself? And that, of course, is impossible."

"All right, all right," Custer said weakly. "Sure."

"Can she describe her distress?"

"Like being poisoned, but not quite. Shooting pains, I suppose."

"From where?"

"The lower abdomen."

Custer said this in such a way Simon glanced to his saber. He was surprised to see that he wasn't wearing one, but rather a sword, broad and straight. Better suited for an artillery officer. It was also a blade not likely to leave an incised wound.

Custer caught him looking at it. "Took this off the first man I ever killed."

"Did you now?"

"In White Oak Swamp. A colonel. I chased him down and fired. He threw up his hands and fell to the ground. A gush of blood from his mouth." Custer drew the claymore and handed it to Simon. A gleaming trophy. No apparent afterthought that he'd shot a man in the back to win it. "Engraved. Can you read it?" Custer tested.

" 'Draw me not without reason; sheathe me not without honor.' " Simon gave it back, then wiped his hand on his saddle blanket.

"You're an absolute trump, Colonel. I had ghastly luck with Latin myself." Custer sobered again. "Then should I ask her to see a physician in Washington?"

"I think so. As a first step. And it might well clear up everything."

Custer bowed slightly. "Thank you, sir." But then panic came into his eyes. "May I rely on you to . . . ?" He didn't know how to finish with dignity.

"I'm a doctor, General," Simon said, feeling weary all at once. "What comes to me, stays with me. And I'm getting so full of confidences I fear that one day soon I shall blow up like a caisson."

"Really . . . ?" Custer asked.

12:46 P.M.

HEADQUARTERS, CONFEDERATE ARMY OF THE VALLEY

The gray-jacketed man found an overlook with some shade to break up the midday sun. Jubal Early sat with his back against a boulder. Cool limestone. Would do his rheumatism no good, but it felt nice for the moment. Below he could see dingy little Strasburg, then Middletown, Newtown and finally the church spires of Winchester in the grainy distance. The two forks of the Shenandoah River joined, then snaked down between the Blue Ridge and the Alleghenies toward the Potomac. The Valley pike, usually a white streak from this height, was dark with troops, artillery and wagons. He slowly ran his hand over his ragged salt-and-pepper beard. Had Virginia not seceded he might be marching down there with them today. Leading them, even. He'd been at least fifteen West Point classes ahead of Phil Sheridan. Prior service with the Regular Army in the Seminole War. Then, after practicing law for several years, off to Mexico as a major of volunteers. And there were those who still remembered his outspoken Unionism right before Fort Sumter. Like Lee, he'd swallowed secession with a dose of regret.

Early raised his field glasses to his eyes. The motion made his shoulder twinge: he'd taken a minié ball there at Williamsburg. "Rain coming," he muttered, then steadied the glasses.

A few of their skirmishers were already testing his pickets at the foot of the hill. But not the usual cloud of them that foretold a big push.

"Will they come this evenin', sir?" a voice asked from the side. His aide-de-camp.

"No, not tonight."

The young captain studied a fallen log for ants, then sat. He snapped off a long stem of grass and began chewing, sucking the juices hungrily. Skinny as a rail, like all of them now.

"Anything stirring?" Early asked.

"Lomax is fussin' about being stuck out all alone on the left, sir."

Early closed his eyes for a moment. Not enough troops after yesterday for an ironclad defense all along the four-mile front, so he'd have to take risks. And taking risks had propelled his little army all the way to Lincoln's doorstep in July. He had come within five miles of the White House. Picked blackberries from the Postmaster General's garden and soaked his gnarled feet in Silver Spring. A forlorn hope. That was all this strategic diversion had ever been, really. A stab in the dark to get Grant to send part of the Army of the Potomac away from Petersburg, to scare Washington into believing that the South could mount one more big northern offensive. Whatever had happened yesterday on the plain east of Winchester, Early felt that he had met the aims Lee had given him. Yet, the "Old Tycoon" expected more. He wanted a stunning victory in the Valley on the order of what Jackson had delivered in 1862. But that had been then. This was now, and the men were chewing grass to relieve their hunger pangs.

Jeb Stuart was rotting in Hollywood Cemetery outside Richmond, and Lunsford Lomax didn't like being stuck out on the left. The cavalry had failed Early so often lately he no longer cared what worried its officers. "Lomax menstruates," he grumbled.

His A.D.C. said nothing. An earnest young man, but lacking humor.

Axes could be heard ringing in the woods behind them. The meager noon meal was over, and the men were back to strengthening the breastworks.

"Any word about Mosby yet?" Early asked.

"Not yet, sir."

An unconfirmed report had the ranger wounded in the groin on a raid behind Union lines four days before. A man with an ungovernable temper, John Singleton Mosby. While at the University of Virginia he'd shot a fellow student in the throat. But Early needed him. Mosby was his eyes in the falling darkness of a last-ditch campaign. "Any of his people handy?"

"Just the Louisianan."

"The loon?"

The captain nodded.

Early shook his head, but then said, "Get the son of a bitch."

4:59 P.M.

UNION FIELD HOSPITAL, CEDAR CREEK

The hospital tents had been pitched close to the fringe of a woodlot to catch the afternoon shade. A long row of ambulances sloped away on a browning pasture toward Cedar Creek. Simon counted more of the two-wheeled kind than the four, but for once wasn't displeased. The four-wheeled ambulances gave a less jolting ride, but being heavier were no good on soft ground or chaotic terrain—and the Valley around Fisher's Hill had both. During noon mess with Sheridan's staff, he'd gathered that some sort of turning movement through the mountains was being threshed out. Faced with this troubling possibility, he'd sent for the medical director from Eighth Corps. Waiting, he watched a steward unpack a plush-lined case. Tools glinted on the blanket laid before him in the dry grass. A metacarpal saw. Amputating knives. A pair of bone forceps.

"May I help you, Colonel?" the medical director from George Crook's corps asked, dismounting.

"Yes, please. How're you today?"

"Fine, sir. Almost ready."

"Glad to hear it." Simon raised his cap and wiped his brow on his sleeve. Autumn couldn't come soon enough for him. "You have any cacolets?"

"No, sir. Will I be needing them?"

"Maybe," Simon said, recalling how Crook had been the most vigorous proponent of a climb around one of the ends of the Rebel line, either where it was anchored on the Massanutten in the east or Little North Mountain in the west. "I'll order some by headquarters courier right away." He started across the pasture toward the sycamores in which the stock had been picketed, berating himself for having forgotten cacolets. These chairlike devices hung off each side of a mule's back to carry the disabled over country too rough for ambulances. Must forget nothing from now on.

He glanced over his shoulder. The surgical tools shone and sparkled on the blanket. It was too soon for another big battle, what with the hospitals and ambulance routes to the rear still clogged with wounded. But Sheridan would never be put off by something like that. McClellan would've been. But not Little Phil.

Naomi was spent after the twenty miles from Winchester, so he picked out a steady chestnut gelding named Rex he'd ridden before.

"Bad air be risin' tonight, Colonel," the black groom solemnly warned as he heaved the saddle over Rex's back. The lowliest member of the hospital gang felt it his duty to report the onset of any miasmas.

Simon was too weary to argue that the cause of disease and infection still beggared explanation. "Thank you," he simply said, then spurred Rex toward field headquarters.

It was one of those drowsy late afternoons in which tens of thousands of men wanted to freeze the sun's descent, forestalling tomorrow. Simon saw a soldier in one of the bivouacs strolling around with a handful of earth, contemplating it, trying to squeeze it into something fathomable. He halted. Eternity, he seemed to suddenly realize. This was eternity. Dirt. The remains of countless eons of plants and animals. The eve of battle turned ordinary men into philosophers, yet mute philosophers—it was bad form to talk about one's fear. And tomorrow's horrors grew even more monstrous in this shell of silence.

Simon was well along a narrow, sandy road through some pines when a bespectacled private, walking toward him, hailed him with a wave that quickly became a salute. "Colonel . . . ?"

"Yes?" Simon said, reining up. "Oh, it's you." The mild-faced private from the provost detail he'd seen at Sheridan's review. "What is it, soldier?"

"Sir, I was a divinity student before the war," he explained, utterly mystifying Simon.

"So . . . ?"

"Just wanted you to know." The man paused, looking pained. "Somebody did go up to that house before it caught fire."

"You know who?"

"Yes, sir. Colonel Deering."

Simon let go of the rein and raked his fingers through Rex's coarse mane to keep from making a triumphant fist. "Are you absolutely sure?"

"I swear, sir—I held his horse for him."

"Why didn't he ride up to the place?"

"He said he didn't want to spook off the folks inside. Most Germans run when they see a blue uniform coming on horseback. They know it's an officer ordering them off the property."

"Did you see him enter the house?"

"No, sir—he went around back."

Just as Simon himself had. "How long was Colonel Deering up there?"

"Three, four minutes, maybe."

More than enough time. "All right," Simon said, "I do appreciate your telling me this. I'm Colonel Wolfe, Medical Department. What's your name?"

The soldier hesitated, but then said, "Private Woodworth, B Company. You know the outfit, sir."

Deering's, of course.

"Is your company posted to headquarters tonight?"

"No, sir. We're marching east to guard some crossroads near Little North Mountain. Least that's what I hear."

"Thank you again, Woodworth. I may be in touch."

Simon rode on.

At headquarters, he scribbled out his message for a courier impatient to be on his way. While he wrote, he sensed eyes on the back of his neck. "Here you go, Lieutenant," he said to the courier, then looked around.

Sheridan was staring down at him from Rienzi.

"Simon," he said amiably enough, "care to view the ground with me?"

It wasn't a request. "Yes, General."

They rode southwest through the deepening twilight. The length of Fisher's Hill crest was glittering with orange beads. Rebel cook fires, Simon realized. Only two outriders formed the escort, and Sheridan signaled for these troopers to keep their distance. "Well, Simon," he asked, "you ready for the next push?"

He wasn't. But Sheridan didn't want to hear that. "Yes, sir. When?"

"Day after tomorrow. And knowing you, I scarcely had to ask about your readiness." Sheridan said this with such warmth Simon was left mystified: he'd been virtually ignored at noon mess, and now suddenly he was being treated as one of the congregation again. "Have you . . . ?" The general started to ask, but then waited until both their mounts had cleared a fence—Rienzi with the grace of a deer and Rex with a clumsy vaulting that left the top rail in the grass. "You been following the national hullabaloo?"

Simon decided Sheridan could only be referring to the election campaign. "Somewhat."

"What d'you think?"

"I—" Simon flinched when a minié ball whirred overhead, but Sheridan seemed to take no notice. "—I'd imagine the President's pleased by the fall of Atlanta, sir. And now your victory at Winchester."

Sheridan didn't respond. They had come to a knoll. It was covered with ground laurel, but the growth rose little higher than the fetlocks of the horses. Yet, the general galloped to the exposed summit. More bullets sizzled through the air, but he refused to dismount. "Come up, Simon, and have a look," he called down. A jaunty voice.

Simon hesitated. Wisely, the outriders had made themselves scarce. He told himself that it was only long-distance sniping—and in failing light as well. Still, butternut sharpshooting had astonished him before.

"Are you coming up, man?"

Then Simon's own vanity leapt to his heels. He jammed them into Rex's flanks. Bloody Antietam. Once a hero, always a fool.

Sheridan, smiling, handed him his field glasses. "I'm sure Old Jube thinks he's done just dandy."

Working the lenses along the bluff, Simon would have agreed: it was a labyrinth of rail-and-earth barricades that the troops called bull pens. Early's could pour shot and shell right down the throats of the advancing Federals. Five or six thousand casualties, easy.

"Early left the Army to become a lawyer," Sheridan said. "A prosecutor, they tell me. Well, he hasn't prosecuted this one worth a damn."

"Sir?"

Sheridan started to point, but then decided to just lift his chin at Little North Mountain, a densely wooded ridge choked with boulders. "We'll turn his line there." He then indicated the north end of the Massanutten. "Or there." Approaches far too steep and tortuous for a flank attack. Simon kept silent, but his doubt must have shown in his face, for Sheridan added, "Oh, I'll win here." All the Irish affability had run away from his darkly brilliant eyes. "D'you know why, Wolfe?"

Simon gazed back in silence.

"Because I must. Unless *you* stand in my way, Wolfe." Sheridan paused. "I didn't think one man could matter much to how this war turns out, not with Lee still on his feet after the thousands I've seen plowed under. But I was wrong." Before Simon could digest this, he snapped, "You a Lincoln man?"

Simon hesitated. Feelings too complicated for the quick answer Sheridan wanted. Like most abolitionists, he'd groaned at Lincoln's election. And then the long-awaited Emancipation Proclamation, which had come only after the Pyrrhic victory at Antietam, the loss of his own wholeness in the Cornfield, proved to be a halfhearted document, freeing just the slaves in the Confederacy so as not to offend the border states. Yet, now that Simon had tasted the ferocity of Southern arms, the fragility of Union resolve, he thought of Father Abraham as something of a firebrand.

Then he realized that he'd hesitated too long.

"Are you for *focking* McClellan then!" the general cried.

"No, sir. I mean to vote for the President."

"Good," Sheridan said without satisfaction. "Because I'm putting it all in your lap, the whole glorious mess."

"Sir?"

"Well, if I make a wrong step here, *Lincoln* loses in November. The election will be that close, they tell me. With no Abe at the helm, the Union's as good as pissed away. But it's more than just winning, Wolfe—" A round came close enough to Rienzi's ears to make him skitter, and Sheridan gave a yank on the rein. "Even if I beat Jube Early, the Union can still be pissed away at the polls. McClellan and the Democrats are desperate to have the White House. They'll say anything to give the South peace. Even that Phil Sheridan's boys are murdering womenfolk in the Shenandoah to get a twist on Early. You want that news ringing from every pulpit in the North?" Then Sheridan whipped off his hat and shouted, "D'you think I can be responsible for every thing my boys do in the heat of a fight!"

"No, sir," Simon said evenly. "I'm just saying that somebody's responsible—and must answer."

"What if we can't find the bastard?"

"I think we can, sir."

"The hell you say. We might be damned glad she burned up. That's what happened, didn't it?"

"Yes, sir."

"Good—then Mosby can't dig up her poor corpse and ship it off to Richmond so Jeff Davis can sell peep show tickets at the door!" Sheridan glared at him a moment longer, then shut his eyes. When he opened them again, they were blank, and he was smiling. A pointless smile, for his hands were still clenching the rein. "I know I can rely on you. Right, Simon?"

"You can, sir. To do my duty."

"Dandy." Sheridan exhaled. "Now all my boys are with me on this."

Simon wanted to point out that, while attached to Sheridan's staff, his true boss was the Surgeon General in Washington. But at that instant the man started down off the knoll.

Simon gratefully followed.

The outriders materialized out of the trees to join them. "There's Johnny vedettes all through these woods, Gen'ral," one of them reported breathlessly.

Sheridan was joking that it would take more than a few mounted sentinels to get him—when a flash touched the top of the knoll. The shellblast was followed by a shower of laurel leaves through which the horses spun and crowhopped. Rex bucked once, twice, and Simon almost jumped off before the gelding began to settle down again. "Easy, boy." Then he looked up at the knoll. A scorched place marked where they'd been viewing Early's fieldworks. He felt the color drop out of his face.

Sheridan glanced at him, then burst into laughter. "Never look where you've just been, Simon. It excites the imagination. And the last thing a soldier needs is imagination. Let's go. We can both use a drink."

No more minié balls creased the air around them on the ride back. It was finally dark, except for a violet afterglow behind Little North Mountain, and both armies had quit popping at each other. From the heights drifted the strains of a waltz. A Rebel band of only a half-dozen instruments serenading. Their bands had sounded better at Cedar Mountain—before all the horrific casualties. The Union ones were getting more accomplished every day. The progress of the war in a nutshell.

By the time they reached his tents, Sheridan's mood had swung back to irritability. He shouted for a rider and, when none appeared right away, snapped at Deering, who was squatting on a campstool before the fire. "Find me a courier, Elias."

Deering didn't turn from the flames. A whippoorwill filled the silence between the two men.

"Elias?"

"Perhaps the general can make use of my humble services," he finally said, still not turning.

"Can you be spared from your other duties?"

"Undoubtedly."

"Very well, Elias, ride to Torbert . . ." The head of the cavalry corps had departed earlier in the day with Custer to break through the enemy horsemen at Front Royal and dash up the Luray Valley east of the Shenandoah to cut off Early's escape route. "My compliments. See how he's doing. Impress upon him once again that he get behind the bastards. I want Old Jube to see nothing but a wall of blue standing in his way when he tries to run south."

"A wall of blue." Deering picked up a wood chip, flicked it into the flames, then slowly rose. "Very good, sir."

⊰ CHAPTER 4 ⊱

1854

SPRING

ADAMS COUNTY, PENNSYLVANIA

The sky at dusk was a windswept blue except for a pink and white cloud that showed through the window. Like all the openings in the Hartz's farmhouse, it was curtainless. The main room had a low ceiling but was large enough to have seated the entire congregation before the Marsh Creek meetinghouse was built. In its middle, five hardback chairs were arranged in a circle. The one closest to the window and its square of light was notably empty, as if waiting to be occupied. Rebekka Hartz squirmed in the next chair to its left. Beside her sat her ten-year-old brother, Peter, and then her mother and father—all with eyes shut, lips silently moving.

Rebekka tried not to fidget.

She focused on the cloud as it inched over the wooded hill that separated the Hartz's fields from the market town of Gettysburg. She wished that she might become that cloud—cool, moist, airy, tied to no single place. A cloud kept changing shape all the time, but didn't seem to mind.

"Rebekka," her mother said, her voice dry and cold.

She looked at the woman, the ridges of tired flesh under the eyes, then dropped her gaze and prayed. She prayed that it might suddenly be night, with this ordeal hours behind her. As much as she wanted, she didn't feel sorry. Just confused and nervous.

Now her father was scrutinizing her. A faint unease crept over his face as he watched.

Then, suddenly, it happened. The break-apart thing.

For a split second she saw not the whole of him—but just his foot-long beard curling down from his chin, hanging in the air like part of a costume that had been cast off. The rest of his body was there, but no more substantial than a shadow or a mist.

Then, thankfully, it passed, and she could take all of him in again.

He was older than her mother by almost a generation, but Rebekka had heard both her parents agree that this was good. Admittedly, Emma Frans had been a prideful young woman, given to bursts of temper and grandiose dreams prior to her baptism and marriage at age twenty-one. She'd even plaited her hair once. Emma had needed the firm hand of an older man.

Her father urged Rebekka back to prayer with a forceful nod.

And she prayed for a moment or two, prayed that the feelings that left her so frightened would go away and never return. But it was so hard to keep her mind on one thing; especially over the past year, her thoughts seemed to be forever tumbling along like wind-blown leaves. The most awful things occurred to her and then stayed trapped inside her for days on end. Her heart, her mother had warned her, was becoming a cage of evil.

It had all started, she believed, last winter with a bad dream. The nightmare itself she couldn't recall, but she distinctly remembered awakening with the light of the full moon falling across her bed. She stood, still trembling from the dream, toes cold on the bare floor, and sensed that something dreadful was about to happen. Then, with a gasp, she saw that it already had: her moonlit hands were not her own. They were somebody else's, shaped and complected differently. Her arms and feet as well. The truth was inescapable. She was no longer inside the body she'd been born with. She screamed, waking the household, and could be comforted only when her mother showed her in the hand mirror that she was indeed Rebekka Hartz.

Peter, she now saw, was avoiding her eyes.

He was ashamed. And his shame gave her pleasure. He was a beautiful boy, rosy-cheeked and golden-haired, but he'd brought this upon her by telling their mother *everything.* Yet, Rebekka could forgive him. He'd been scared, and she understood that. She felt scared nearly all the time now, even though her father told her that there was no reason, that they were all safely in God's hands.

But he couldn't see things through her eyes, feel what she felt. Something was happening to her, something vile jailed up inside her was worming its way out. None of her family believed her when she described the things she saw, let alone understood what was unraveling at the center of her being. She herself didn't understand, not in the way that one could link a draft to a cold.

She heard hooves and iron wheels on the York Pike, which ran through the apple orchard out front. She liked to watch the English come and go on it in their proud carriages, the women with ostrich plumes in their hats, the men with bright knots of silk at their throats.

Her father quickly said "Amen," then rose and went to the window.

Beyond him, Rebekka saw matched brown mares trot into the dooryard and then the deacon himself sitting tall, gripping the lines with one hand and holding down his flat-brimmed hat with the other.

"Whoa," he sang out. The tail of his plain frock coat was flapping in the wind.

Rebekka looked down into her lap. She felt her heart beating. Cage of evil.

Her father opened the door and went out to the deacon, who was tying off the lines.

Grimly, she watched them share the holy kiss, then stroll inside

side-by-side, chatting about the new corn. But she could tell by their eyes that their minds weren't really on the crop. They were thinking about her.

Their heavy shoes drummed over the wooden floor toward her.

"What wind, yes?" the deacon said. He offered Emma Hartz a brotherly right hand, then forced a smile at Rebekka and Peter. He had a pasty skin and darkly hooded eyes. Rebekka found him repulsive even though everybody in the congregation spoke of him as being kindly and just.

"How old are they now?" he asked—as if Rebekka and Peter couldn't speak for themselves.

"Peter is ten," her father said, "and Rebekka thirteen."

"How very good," the deacon said, although she had no idea what he meant by this. He loosened the single row of buttons fronting his coat and eased into the chair that had been left empty for him. "Oh yes indeed," he murmured, then studied Peter and her for what seemed an eternity, not looking angry, exactly, but grave enough to bring water to Rebekka's eyes.

Still, she smiled. She wanted to please him so he'd go away and not come back for a long while.

When the deacon finally spoke, it was to her parents, not her. "I have talked to Sister Griebiel—"

"Yes?" Her father interrupted, hopefully.

"The widow's satisfied with the price you'll give her for the cow. She was an old cow, almost past giving milk, and yes—twenty bushels of corn is fair."

"It's fair," her father echoed, reassured, nodding at her mother.

"All is reconciled," the deacon went on, "so you and the widow can go to the table of the Lord in peace. This is good, and I rejoice." But then he paused, no longer rejoicing, the skin around his tight mouth curdling. "However, I don't understand how this came to pass. Young Peter and Rebekka have always been so obedient."

Her parents looked expectantly to Rebekka, but she shifted in her chair and stared off as if the room had far regions.

"Rebekka . . . ?" her father insisted.

She hated him passionately at that moment. He was no better than the deacon's pet dog.

"Rebekka, speak."

What could she say? She knew that it'd make no sense to them—

how she'd seen Sister Griebiel on that chilly afternoon two weeks before. Peter and she had been in the widow's pasture, searching for the fresh green spikes of wild onion—when the old woman flew out her kitchen door and shouted for them to go away, that their being there upset her old cow so badly she refused to give milk. And then the most incredible thing happened. Sister Griebiel turned into a figure of ice. She glinted in the pale sunlight, then turned stiffly and smiled down at Rebekka. And that smile, showing big teeth as white as salt, froze Rebekka to the spot on which she stood. Slowly, the individual features of the widow's face glided apart from one another—the teeth, then the nose, then the cheeks and finally the sharp chin. It was like looking at a face in a shattered mirror. That the features refused to come together again terrified Rebekka more than anything. She couldn't recognize Sister Griebiel even though she knew who she was. The familiar had become the strange. Finally, she was able to run. She and Peter ran all the way down to Rock Creek, then hid along the bank.

"Peter . . . ?" Her father's voice snapped Rebekka back to the present. "If your sister's too full of herself to yield to God and our deacon, will you?"

Peter nodded, miserably.

"What happened, my boy?" the deacon asked.

"I stabbed Sister Griebiel's cow with a pitchfork . . ." Then Peter's lower lip began to tremble, and he was unable to go on.

"All right, all right now," the deacon said gently. "These tears are good, Peter, and God rejoices in them. They are washing away what you've done in the ignorance of childhood. And you are feeling sorry for the cow, yes? For isn't it said in Ecclesiastes that in death all living things are equal? What more do you have to say, Peter?"

"I . . . I don't . . . I . . ."

Her father grew impatient. "Tell our deacon why you did this."

Peter glanced at Rebekka, gave a tiny shrug, then faced the deacon again and said, "Rebekka said Sister Griebiel would send the cow against us—unless I killed it first."

"*Against* you?" the deacon asked.

"To hurt us."

"But how could the widow do such a thing?" The deacon glanced to her father with a puzzled grin. "And we're speaking of an old cow, not a bull. I've been chased by a bull, but never by an old cow."

"Rebekka told me that Sister Griebiel's a demoniac," Peter said, his voice reduced to a whisper.

The deacon raised an eyebrow. "Truly?"

Peter lowered his head once. "And they can make animals do bad things."

Rebekka felt that the deacon was resisting the urge to look at her as he asked, "Whatever gave her such an idea?"

"The gospel of Mark. When Jesus put the demons into the swine, and they fell into the sea. She said Sister Griebiel would put the demons into the cow, and it'd come after us."

Suddenly, Rebekka was furious with all of them. They were fools, really. Anybody with half a brain knew about demoniacs, even if they didn't constantly see them as she did. She glared off through the window, her chin upraised. The pink and white cloud was almost gone, and she wanted ever so much to go with it, sailing noiselessly over the countryside until she might drop down into some great city, shining with gaslights.

The deacon made a thoughtful noise, a kind of murmur deep in his throat, then said to Peter, "So Rebekka convinced you that the Widow Griebiel was a demoniac and that she'd set her cow against you—unless you killed it. Is that right?"

"Ja," the boy said, then broke down, sobbing.

Rebekka saw that her mother was now weeping, holding a fist against her lips to keep down the sound.

"We are greatly sorry," Rebekka's father said in a stricken hush. "We know that the tree is judged by its fruit, and we give ourselves up to God in our failing."

The deacon held up a hand as if her father had spoken too soon, then turned to Rebekka. "Truly, my child, do you believe that this pious old woman is possessed by demons?"

"I do," Rebekka said adamantly. But secretly she wasn't sure. She wanted to tell the deacon how the widow had turned into ice; that is what this was really all about, the awful way things looked now and again. But she knew that he'd understand no better than Peter would have—that is why she'd decided to say that the widow was a demoniac. It was something from the Holy Book, something understandable to everyone. Even if she weren't one, Sister Griebiel meant her harm, that much was clear, and Rebekka had desperately needed to do something to make the old woman keep her distance.

"Rebekka," the deacon said, "you have bent another to your will—and that is prideful. You must never lure someone into wrong-doing again. Especially one who loves you, as your brother does. Do you hear me?"

She said nothing, her eyes slitted against him.

"Now, Rebekka—the widow is not a demoniac. There are no such evil spirits among us here in Marsh Creek."

"Did our Lord cast them all out of the world?" she hurled back at him.

"Well . . . I don't know, child."

"If He didn't, they're still among us—aren't they?"

The deacon watched her for a moment, then said, "Perhaps."

⊰ CHAPTER 5 ⊱

1864

8:47 P.M., SEPTEMBER 20

NORTH FORK OF THE SHENANDOAH

Deering splashed across the river and began melting into the growth on the far bank.

Simon waited as long as he could without losing him to the moon-less woods, then followed.

He didn't know these shallows—unlike the provost marshal, who rode as if he'd forded this way before—and drew up his legs as the black waters lapped the saddle skirts. Rex was flexing his haunches as if thinking about bucking Simon off and making for dry ground alone. Hooves suddenly slipped on the bottom. Simon braced for a soaking to the waist, but after a few lunging strides the horse was standing on a gravel bar, shaking himself so loudly Simon was sure the dripping could be heard above the rasp of crickets.

Ahead, Deering was standing on his stirrups, listening.

His charger neighed, and Simon gave a snap on the bit to keep Rex from answering. Brigadier Torbert had no doubt strung vedettes behind his advance to give warning if Rebels stole down off the Massanutten. Simon suspected that Deering's mount had smelled the horses of these sentinels and not Rex—the breeze was in his face, faintly warm.

Deering sank back down into the saddle, then moved on.

Simon silently counted to ten before spurring Rex.

The provost marshal kept to a stock path through the rolling cedar thickets. Simon was sure that he was headed for the Front Royal pike, but still felt a squeeze in his belly whenever Deering dipped out of sight. Mustn't lose him. He soon led Simon out of the cedars and into an apple orchard, then slowed the gait to a walk.

Ahead, two panes of lamplight were floating on the darkness. A farmhouse.

Simon drew rein when Deering did. The blood was thumping through his neck arteries, and he ignored a mosquito whining around his face.

A penned cow lowed, and Deering seemed to start a little.

From the curtainless kitchen window a face appeared, skin golden in the lamplight. A young woman wearing a white cap.

Simon expected Deering to wait a few minutes more, as if to sharpen the thing within him Custer had hit upon: *"His mother had a rather unfortunate past . . ."*

Yet, the colonel then wheeled away from the house. Simon followed, confused. Would Deering approach it from the darker side?

No, he galloped off toward the southeast.

An image filled Simon's head as he rode on. He couldn't forget how Deering, risen from his fire at headquarters, had glowered up at Sheridan. The look had been intestinally cold. Withering. Shot from a face as hard as granite.

Simon began trying to make sense of it all, building on what Private Woodworth could attest to: Elias Deering approaching the farmhouse south of Winchester alone, on foot. He had to come up with a well-knit argument he could confidently take to Sheridan, or even Washington, if it came to that.

First off, there'd been the provost marshal's tirade against Dunkers last night. Yet, Simon asked himself—did any of the other officers present at that supper feel the same scorn for German Baptists? Maybe, but they didn't hold an apparent resentment against both women and Dunkers. And a *Dunker woman of middle age* had been stabbed to death.

Might she have resembled Deering's mother?

Simon blew the air out of his cheeks.

But then, dammit, this morning at the review, Deering had done something curious. He'd tried to deflect blame when nobody was blaming him of anything. Insinuations against Sheridan. And in doing so, he hadn't dredged up just any scandal out of Little Phil's past—of which several were rumored—but had chosen one that was keyed to the very instrumentality of the woman's death. Young Sheridan had gone after his cadet sergeant with *steel.* A bayonet.

Simon suddenly stopped.

Deering had come to the pike—but then cut across it without pause. Simon had a glimpse of him disappearing into the tall woods below a spur of the Massanutten on which the Rebels had a lookout. No sign of the signalmen above, not even the blush of a cook fire.

He picked up the pace before losing Deering for good.

It made him feel better that the man had turned away from the most direct route to Torbert's headquarters. Another hint of guilt?

But, all in all, wouldn't a guilty man have settled upon a less risky scapegoat than Phil Sheridan? No. Maybe Deering had to satisfy his envy as well as any murderous impulse he hid behind his sarcasm. Officers like him, regulars, comfortable with the humdrum of army life of the fifties, had seen the slow but steady progress of their careers derailed by the war. Cowards by no means, they still lacked the dash others like Sheridan and Custer had shown under fire. At Chattanooga, Little Phil had blazed up Missionary Ridge, colors streaming, and out of obscurity forever. And Custer had stopped Jeb Stuart dead in his tracks at Gettysburg.

That was it, then. Deering's revenge.

Philip Henry Sheridan—Irish upstart, former dry goods clerk from some backward town in Ohio—stood poised to save Lincoln's tottering presidency, the Union itself, by crushing Early's Army of the Valley. Yet, that victory still could be tarnished, and how better to do it than slaughter innocents? The New York press, pulling for McClellan in the upcoming election, would jump on such a report even more eagerly than the *Richmond Enquirer.*

Simon halted again.

Fog was sifting up from the river. It had already choked off the crickets and frogs, and was beginning to muffle the other sounds of the night. He couldn't hear Deering's horse ahead.

He dismounted, ran the flat of his hand over the earth and felt a track that seemed freshly moist. Then he got back in the saddle. But Rex soon slowed of his own will, and Simon could dimly see where the path ended at a brook. He hesitated, then urged the gelding across the water and into the dense brush beyond, a wall of briers that clawed at his trouser legs.

Rex backstepped out. A frustrated snort.

The brook tumbled so steeply off the mountain Simon couldn't believe that Deering had kept to it.

He led Rex by the bridle down over the stony ledges to a pool, where he let him drink. The moon had risen. While he couldn't pinpoint its place in the sky, there was now a bluish cast to the fog.

Suddenly, a drumming of hoofbeats made him pull Rex into the willows. From the dripping leaves he watched a rider stretch his mount over the brook, hang suspended against the blue mist for a split second, then land with a thud and gallop away. Two more horsemen followed.

And then there was silence, except for the little dripping noises.

Rebel or Federal—Simon had no idea which, but he knew that Torbert's vedettes would've been just as quick to shoot him as Early's. And Mosby's rangers were lurking out here somewhere, a trooper with a broken ankle had solemnly warned at the tent hospital this afternoon. Shot their prisoners outright, he added. It hadn't seemed as likely a threat as it did now.

He gave the three riders a few minutes to move on, then took the slit in the brambles they'd shown him.

The fog had gotten worse, and Rex was picking each step with care.

Then a low-hanging branch flipped Simon's cap off his head, nearly catching him on the eye. Enough, he made up his mind. No sense losing an eye and an arm in the same war.

He got off, fumbled for his cap in the grass, then walked the horse away from the narrow path and out into a clearing. From the saddle valise he took a length of rope and used it to hobble Rex. He thought to throw the blanket over the ground as a cover, but then decided against it. Saddling and cinching were cumbersome for him, and he needed to set off at once if more horsemen came upon him.

He buttoned his coat to the throat, then lay down on the chilled earth with his knees cocked and his arm bent over his face.

An hour or so passed in chilly discomfort. Sleep refused to come. His watch was softly ticking in his trouser pocket, but he dared not light a match to read it. A present from his father on his thirteenth birthday. Not really for a bar mitzvah, as Simon passed into manhood without ceremony. Solomon Wolfe had always been careful to distance himself from Charleston's more observant Jews, and in society otherwise he was accepted as that "gentlemanly Levite," known to enjoy shellfish and even ham now and again. Oddly embarrassed— Solomon Wolfe's expression whenever he ate ham. As if he'd just broken wind in a crowded parlor.

Simon suddenly sat up and rubbed the dew off his face.

He was fully awake again, suffocating with bleakness. The fog seemed to slowly whiten in the east, or what he took to be east. But after a few minutes this dawn proved false, and the darkness grew deep again. He lay back down.

He stopped hearing his watch after another hour.

12:40 A.M., SEPTEMBER 21

HEADQUARTERS, UNION ARMY OF THE SHENANDOAH

George Crook waited at the table set before Sheridan's tent, smoking. All through the trees a low fog was drifting, filling the hollows. The campfires were long since dead, and the only light seemed to be a kind of glow within the vapor itself.

A sentry floated through the stuff, just his head and musket visible.

Two hours before, Sheridan had ridden out of headquarters without escort. East. That meant he had gone to mull over a turning movement around the right end of Early's line. That would call for either 6th or 19th Corps, which were much larger than Crook's own 8th, to scramble up the face of Three Top Mountain, the northernmost spur of the Massanutten range on which Old Jube had a signal station. Crook had argued against it, sensing that Early was strongest on the right and weakest on the left, where his line was apparently anchored by some cavalry spread thinly along the base of Little North Mountain. It would still be a hard scramble up a rocky slope. But, with no signal station on that side, there was more of a chance to take Early by surprise.

The sentry challenged a noise out in the night, and Sheridan answered in a tired voice.

A moment later he walked from the fog, leading Rienzi. His groom trotted up and took the horse away. He slumped onto a corner of the table. "Dark out there."

Crook had risen and now eased down again. "That it is, Phil."

Most of the men who had fought Indians before the war were not afraid of a little reconnoitering in the dark. Dave Russell, who'd soldiered with Sheridan and Crook in the Far West, had been one of them. Now he was in darkness forever. A strange comfort to think that he was used to it. Still, it was a shame how Little Phil had been forced to use Russell as he had yesterday, desperately plugging his division into a gap the Johnnies had punched through the line. But Davey would've been the first to understand that a good commander would throw in his own mother to reinforce a breached line.

"You know," Sheridan finally went on, "I don't scare worth a damn, but it finally got to me tonight . . ."

Crook knew that he wasn't expected to say anything. It was an old ritual born of their boyhood friendship in Ohio, and then carried on at West Point in strolls along the Hudson; the talking out of that bottomless black mood Sheridan fell into now and again.

"Did I tell you what Stanton said to me?"

"No," Crook softly lied. He'd already heard the tale about the Secretary of War. Twice.

"Took me to the White House to meet Lincoln. On the way back, he told me—no unexploited victories. Unless I wanted McClellan calling the tune after the election. Put it all on my shoulders, Stanton did. He made me look at the dead cock in the pit. And that cock was the Union." Sheridan took a cheroot from his waistcoat pocket. "We've got to do it this time, George."

Crook knew it was a faint rebuke. His corps had been detailed to pursue Early through last night's darkness. But with his men exhausted, he'd called a halt to the chase less than a mile south of Winchester.

"We can't keep letting them slip away." Sheridan began patting his pockets for matches until Crook offered the coal of his own cigar. He sucked his cheroot to life, the glow pulsing on his youthful face. It was oddly flushed, as if he'd taken a fever. Yet, he was never sick. "Relaxing out there tonight, George. I like the smell of a river at night." Then, as if it were an afterthought, he said, "I think I'll go ahead and swing your corps around their left."

4:27 A.M.

Simon bolted up from the sopping grass.

He could hear noises. The chafing of canvas knapsacks. The clink of canteens, rattle of bayonets in scabbards. Infantry on the march. There'd been no talk at headquarters about foot soldiers supporting the cavalry attack on Front Royal. These troops had to be Rebel, then. Yet, their steady tramp meant they were in brogans, and much of the Chivalry's infantry went unshod until winter, when they made do with rags.

He unhobbled Rex and climbed up, shivering from the damp that had seeped through the back of his coat. But he didn't dig his heels in right away. He absently stroked one of the gelding's ears.

If they were Rebels, he had to confirm it.

That meant risking capture to get close enough to see their uniforms or hear them talk, and these gaunt, long-haired men had earned his wariness. God willing, if they were Federals, they could point him back toward Cedar Creek. He had finally admitted to himself that he'd never find Deering in this murk.

He rode toward the sounds, but they were quickly fading into the east.

At the very least he expected to find the road on which the infantry had just marched. But he didn't. A patchwork of woods and pasture plunged unbroken all the way down to a slow, wide creek. The surface was like quicksilver. He glanced skyward: the fog was brightening. Dawn, for sure.

Upstream, he found some shallows and forded.

Pausing atop the weedy bank, he was baffled to hear limbers or caissons rumbling behind him somewhere. A cavalcade of horse artillery. Believing now that the Massanutten's cliffs or the swirling fog was playing tricks on his ears, he refused to cross back over the run. Instead he pushed on through a muddy slough. It sucked at Rex's hooves, but ended with promise: an embankment littered with bits of coal, rusted spikes. "Manassas Gap Railroad," he grunted with satisfaction, topping the bed. The rails had been bent by fire and the ties scattered, though it was the line without a doubt. But both ends were swallowed by the fog within fifty feet, the two horizons equally bright. How had he gotten so turned around?

He had owned a compass, a Swiss one, and made good use of it as medical inspector for the Army of the Potomac. But then he'd lost it and much of his baggage when the Rebels overran the forward hospitals at Chancellorsville. He'd almost bought another in Washington recently, but at the last minute told himself that after campaigning with Nat Banks in sixty-two he knew the Valley of Virginia.

"Well, I'll leave it up to you, boy," he said, dropping the rein.

Rex turned left as surely as if warm mash and a rubdown were only a couple bends away.

The fog to Simon's back slowly turned lustrous. "Good boy."

At last confident that he was safely headed for Cedar Creek, he slumped over the pommel. Rex's hooves clopped hollowly over a stretch of ties that hadn't been uprooted. Simon dozed, but then dreamed of falling out of the saddle. He snapped awake only to realize that Rex had stopped and was nickering.

Then he saw why.

A bay charger was standing astride the bed, his ribs showing through his coat. On his back sat a young man in a faded gray-brown tunic. He was glaring from beneath a felt hat with one side pinned up by a rosette—glaring over the sights of the revolver he was holding steady on Simon's chest. His pale jade eyes seemed to be waiting for Simon to say something—when suddenly one side of his face convulsed. For those few seconds his eyes were glassy and vacant, and then they started to burn with irritability as he motioned for Simon to raise his hands.

"This is the best I can do," Simon said, obeying, struggling to keep the fear out of his voice.

The Rebel glanced at the empty right sleeve, seemed to commiserate. But his face quickly hardened again, leaving Simon to wonder if he'd only imagined the flash of sympathy. He no longer had an emerald sash, relying instead on the "MS" on his cap patch to mark him as medical staff. But the meaning of this insignia was lost on the Rebel, for he waved his Colt for Simon to get down.

"I've got no weapons," Simon said.

The Rebel rode around him to make sure. His dark brown hair hung down to the small of his back. Even in the dawn coolness he stank of sweat and cook-fire smoke. Just above his right ear was a scar, either an old depressed fracture or a healed-over penetration through the temporal bone.

"I'm a surgeon," Simon added.

The man reined up, visibly mulling this over. A handsome face, although badly thinned by hunger. He raised his chin in doubt at the empty sleeve.

"Medical director for this army," Simon explained, understanding the man's skepticism that an amputee could function as a line surgeon.

The Rebel holstered, and Simon thought that was that. But then he drew his saber and swung it toward Simon's kidneys.

He half-turned and stiffened, waiting for the blade, but it stopped short of him, and the Rebel used the point to cut the straps to the saddle valise. He reached over and took the small medical kit Simon carried with him. Leaving him nothing but the bottle of morphine crystals he kept handy in his coat pocket while in the field.

The man's left palm was bandaged with a handkerchief, and fresh blood was seeping through the cotton. He touched the blade to the brim of his hat, smiled faintly, then spurred his horse down the embankment and into the fog.

Simon watched the break in the trees where he had vanished, unable to move for a few moments. It was a delicate calm he was afraid to test. Then his shoulders jerked once, violently as if from a deep chill, and he put his heels to Rex. The gallop was shuddering, and Simon had to clench his teeth to keep from biting his tongue. But he didn't slow for over a mile.

Until a musket barked.

He heard the minié ball pass through the air a few feet above his head. Rex might well have been grazed before—Simon had no trouble turning him sharply off the bed and down into a ditch. Horse and man breathed heavily, waiting for the next round.

When it didn't come, Simon cried, "Don't shoot!" toward where he'd seen the puff of smoke squirt out of some rocks.

A voice rolled out, asking him who he was. Down-easter accent.

"Colonel Wolfe," he answered, trying for his life to sound Northern-born. "Medical Department."

He must have failed, for the soldier asked, "Which army?"

"Little Phil's, for godsake!"

Several men laughed. "Well, come out slow, Surgeon Colonel, and let's see if your orderly put you in the propuh uniform this mornin'."

Pickets for some Maine regiment, fishermen and lumbermen with florid complexions. They shared their coffee with him. He had to skim a few weevils off the surface, but it was good. Their corporal was bundled up in his bedroll at the bottom of a rifle pit, complaining of fever and diarrhea. Simon suspected fruit and green corn to be the culprits, but then he felt the man's face. Fever. Fearing typhoid, Simon ordered him taken to the hospital on Cedar Creek. He had no sooner picked up his tin cup again than he noticed a halo out in the fog. He thought that it might be the risen sun, but then realized that this strange aurora was more to the south than to the east.

"What's that?" he asked around the campfire. The blank, astigmatic faces of veterans. Whatever it was, it didn't endanger them, so to hell with it.

"Farm's over there someplace, Colonel," a private finally said. "Wolverine cavalry rounded up their livestock last night."

"A Dunker farm?"

"I believe so, sir."

The cup slipped out of Simon's fingers. "Did you see our troops set it afire?"

"No, sir," another soldier said. "I seen nobody up that ways since the cavalry."

"Couriers . . . any couriers ride through here?"

"Ayuh." The soldier pointed. "That's the main road to Front Royal on the other side of that stone wall."

Simon untied Rex and began hiking up a field of flattened corn toward the glow. A section of the wall had been razed to let artillery pass, and he led the horse over the pile of stone rubble and then across the road. He could now hear the roar of the flames as they curled orangely up into the fog. They were were rising from what had been the barn, for across the yard the twin chimneys of the house could be seen poking up out of a heap of embers.

Rex shied. "Easy, boy." Had he smelled something other than the smoke?

Simon turned around, slowly. His eyes swept along a worm-rail fence that had been pulled down, over a wooden trough shot full of holes, and into a blackberry patch filling a ravine—and then back to a small roof peaking above the tangle of vines. The springhouse. Its plank door was ajar, and the mud at the threshold had been scored by a long streak that snaked all the way back to the barn.

He let go of the rein, and Rex began nibbling at some oats spilt across the ground.

Cavalry trumpets were bleating in the east, dozens of them. As if Torbert were having trouble assembling his troopers in the fog. Understandable.

Simon stepped into the musty darkness of the springhouse.

A glint on the wall told him where the lamp hung. He lit it and shook out the match. The flame guttered up, and shadows of cobwebs filled the cavelike room like haze. The pillaging that had left grain strewn across the yard hadn't reached here: apples, turnips, and stoneware crocks of butter were undisturbed, although a white cheese had fallen from its rafter hook and been crushed underfoot.

Simon knelt.

Fingers had left stripes in the mold on the grate over the spring. And a smear of blood. He lifted it with effort, leaned it against the wall, then peered down into the depths.

Opaque depths.

He seized the lamp and held it close to the surface.

A face gaped back at him. Thousands of tiny silver bubbles were trapped in the beard. Before Simon could recoil, he saw a second face deeper than the first, the astonished eyes of a woman shrouded in the red billows of her hair.

❧ C HAPTER 6 ☙

The fog had lifted, and the Blue Ridge Mountains could be seen rising
steamily behind Front Royal. Another long day of heatstroke cases in
the hundreds—Virginia broiling to death those who would dare invade her. It was hard to believe now that spring in the Old Dominion
could be so soft and balmy, but maybe that was only Bobby Lee's annual lure to draw the great northern armies down to destruction.
Simon rode into the village behind the ammunition wagon he'd commandeered; the two corpses were strapped atop the crates and
shrouded with canvas. The Negro driver slowed for the wagon park,
but Simon waved for him to go on to the common. There, he found a
handful of wounded lying in the shade of an oak being treated by the
local practitioner. The old man, used to little more than delivering ba-
bies and spooning out a dose of calomel now and again, was clearly
overwhelmed. A gray-jacketed horseman was sobbing so loudly from
his gut wound the physician couldn't hear Simon. "Sir?"

Dismounting, Simon repeated, "Have you seen any of our surgeons?"

"Afraid not. You a—?"

"Yes." He offered his left hand, even though the practitioner's
fingers were wet from suturing a saber cut. "Simon Wolfe, Medical
Department."

"Dr. Lazelle." The old man's eyes grew watery as they rested on
the trooper, who went on sobbing as if nothing short of the grave
could ease his pain. "What in heaven's name d'you do with something
like this?"

Simon leaned over the man, who beseeched him with a loud wail.
It was doubtful the trooper felt much pain through his shock; he'd

probably just realized that he was dying. The wound was from a minié ball. A musket. And that meant infantry had gotten him. The phantom company Simon had heard tramping last night? Lord, how nice it'd be to grasp the full picture of a battle just once, instead of constantly feeling as if he were bumbling around the smoky fringes of the thing. The Rebel on the rail line had taken all his opium pills, so he slipped the bottle of morphine sulfate from his coat pocket and removed the cork with his teeth. He licked his forefinger, dipped it into the white crystals, then plunged his finger all the way into the bullet entry hole and dusted the torn nerves.

"That's all we can do for him," he said, lowering his voice.

"I've got no opiates." Dr. Lazelle shrugged apologetically at the medicine bottles he had set in the bloody grass. "I made a tincture of jimson-weed—"

"Please stop giving it. Here now," Simon said, handing him the morphine, "use this up."

"How much?"

"Quarter grain per man. More should be coming any minute." Simon then turned and ordered two passing troopers to help the driver unload the corpses. A warm breeze, stinking of gunpowder, rose out of the south and strewed dressing lint and tatters of uniform cloth across the lawn.

Dr. Lazelle was staring at the bodies being hoisted down from the crates. "What's this?"

"Is your office nearby?" Simon asked, going to the next man.

"Why, yes . . ." Dr. Lazelle pointed at a two-story brick house across the common. His hand trembled.

"Kindly tell those soldiers for me that I want the bodies carried inside your office." Simon glanced up from a carbine bullet wound that could await treatment. "With your permission, of course."

"Of course, Dr. Wolfe."

"And I must find out something—" Another man howled before gnashing his teeth; all of these Rebels had probably been hit early in the day, and one by one were coming out of shock.

"Sir?"

"Who these two people were. I believe they were Dunkers."

Dr. Lazelle had no sooner walked off than the surgeon from Custer's brigade rode up. He looked surprised to find Simon so far east of headquarters, but went to work without taking the time to satisfy his curiosity. His assistant surgeons arrived with his wagons a few minutes later, more than enough staff to handle the casualties trickling out of the Luray Valley. It was up this, the south branch of the Shenandoah, that Torbert's cavalry was rushing to cut off Early's escape, should Old Jube be pushed off Fisher's Hill by Sheridan's main force tomorrow.

Simon washed in a rain barrel, then led Rex to the brick house and tethered him to the porch railing. A cicada skirled from a lilac bush. An elderly woman in an apron answered his knock, and he doffed his cap. "Dr. Wolfe for Dr. Lazelle, ma'am."

A moment's hesitation, as usual. His accent and the blue uniform. Then she said, "This way, Doctor." Her hands were white with flour. "I'm Mrs. Lazelle."

"Charmed."

"I don't ordinarily bake on Wednesdays." She smiled over her shoulder, although her gaze was red and moist. "But it does so nicely take my mind off things."

"I understand," he said quietly. For a fleeting moment he was reminded of his mother, but then admitted to himself that—except for the eyes like running sores—the practitioner's wife little resembled that frail ornament to Solomon Wolfe's political career. This woman had never suffered heartbreak, or, if not that fortunate, had learned to live graciously with it.

"Will you have some tea?"

"Only if it's no trouble."

"No trouble . . . and no sugar, I fear. First door on the left, Dr. Wolfe."

"Thank you."

The sense of stepping back into the familiar persisted. Perhaps it had been evoked by the parlor he'd glimpsed as he followed her down the hallway, the lace and other feminine touches around the darkened room. And then it occurred to him: except for hospital matrons and refugees, he'd been around few women in the past three years, women as he'd known and enjoyed them in Charleston and Boston. Women whose emotions had not been hardened or dulled by war, as he privately suspected Leah's had been, despite her breezy letters. The cynical undercurrent in her writing went beyond grief; part of her, it seemed—her faith in mankind possibly—had perished along with her husband. Maybe it was fortunate, his finding Mrs. Zelter at the critical moment in which that part of her, the best part of her, might be lost forever to bitterness. He hadn't been able to soften that time for his sister—and he regretted it.

He went through the door.

The female corpse lay on the examination table, and the male on the floor of the cramped office. Dr. Lazelle stood grimly at the foot of the table, his hands clasped behind him.

Simon shut the door. "Sorry to distress your wife like this."

"The war's come here before. She's used to it."

Simon nodded, unconvinced, then asked, "Did you know them?"

"Yes. The Hostedlers. Josef and Chlora. And you're right, sir, they were Dunkards."

"Will you help me take off her clothing?"

For the first time, it seemed, Dr. Lazelle glanced at the empty coat sleeve. Then his fingers tugged at the bow in the strings to Chlora Hostedler's black bonnet, which had floated off the top of her head in the springwater. Inside it was the same kind of white muslin cap Rebekka Zelter wore. Again, an attractive victim, although gray was just beginning to invade her thick red hair. Still, at least fifteen years younger than her husband.

Dr. Lazelle shook his head while staring at her. A tinge of blue had come to his lips in the last few minutes. "Who'd do such a thing?"

"I've been trying to find out."

Then the practitioner raised an eyebrow. "Not the first?"

"No. Sadly."

"Your boys . . . ?" Dr. Lazelle tossed the sopping cap into a tin basin and began unbuttoning the homespun dress. "Ours?"

"Federal, I think." Simon saw the question taking shape in the practitioner's eyes, and decided to cut it short before his father's shadow fell over the room. "I was born in South Carolina"—he took the heavy dress from the practitioner and put it in the basin—"but had my practice in Boston when the troubles started. All my friends were there, my fiancée."

"I see," Dr. Lazelle said after a moment. "Then these years have been hard for you too."

Simon realized that he'd sounded overly defensive. "Yes, thank you. May it soon all end."

"You've been listening to our prayers, Dr. Wolfe," Dr. Lazelle said.

The body was finally bared. Simon took a slow breath and began the examination. He searched for less apparent signs of trauma before turning to the abdominal stab wounds he'd already noted at the farm. "What kind of woman was she?"

"She . . . well, what can I say? Dunkards keep to themselves."

No wounds to her hands or forearms; she had died without a struggle. Religious conviction more powerful than instinct? Or had she known, even trusted her murderer?

"Why're they called Dunkards or Dunkers?" Simon asked, even though he knew the answer. He just didn't want a silence to set up between them: Dr. Lazelle might suddenly realize that he was communicating with the enemy.

"From how they baptize. Full immersion. I'm afraid they're not much liked around here, Doctor. Their men won't serve, so their farms have prospered while ours have fallen into ruin."

Simon glanced up. "Till now."

Dr. Lazelle pressed his lips together, then said, "Don't think me unkind, sir. Mother and I lost our only boy at Sharpsburg." The Confederate name for the Battle of Antietam.

"I'm sorry," Simon said, hoping that it hadn't been in the Cornfield.

The give of human skin made gauging the width of the blade used impossible, but Simon guessed from some hints of incising that the point of a saber might have been used this time. The woman in the burning kitchen had probably been knifed. Yet, like her sister Dunker, Chlora Hostedler had died from three deep thrusts to the belly, and it was possible that the same instrument had been used on both women.

Tea arrived, and Dr. Lazelle took the tray from his wife at the door. Simon and he drank a cup each, then lowered the woman onto the floor and covered her with a sheet. They lifted her husband onto the table, Simon supporting the stout legs. As they undressed him, cavalry stormed past the window in sets of four, carbines held at the ready. When it was quiet again, he asked, "Was Josef Hostedler an elder? He looks like a patriarch."

"No, it's just the beard. He was a rather meek fellow. She was the one."

"You mean she preached?"

"No, Dunkards don't hold truck with their women preaching, far as I know," Dr. Lazelle said. "But they can prophesy, and she did plenty of that."

"Oh? Like what?"

"Disaster on all our prideful heads. Satan roaming the land with blood on his horns. That sort of thing."

"She may've been on to something there."

"So it'd seem." Dr. Lazelle brushed some moss out of Hostedler's thin white hair. "What d'you hope to learn?"

"Well, obviously he was shot in the chest and abdomen." Simon folded down Hostedler's upright coat collar; it was blood-stained. "And grazed along the neck. I'd guess the . . ." What to call him in the midst of a war? ". . . the murderer . . . he meant to shoot him in the throat first . . ." He glanced toward the sideboard. "I'll need a large scalpel and a Nelaton's probe." Dr. Lazelle took them from a drawer. "Let's see what kind of bullet killed him."

"But the lower projectile passed cleanly through him, and the one to the chest . . . well, it'll have been flattened by the ribs, yes?"

"True, but still possible to tell." Simon sliced open the abdomen and revealed the intestines which, even after Hostedler's submergence in cold water, gave off a bit of warmth. "See here," he said, sifting, "the bullet didn't perforate any of the viscera. Just pushed them aside."

"What's that tell you?"

"Roundball ammunition. A minié ball, being conical, would have caused perforation. As in the case of that poor lad outside you were trying to help."

"Will we look for the same thing in the chest cavity, then?" Dr. Lazelle asked, keeping up with Simon by handing him a saw.

"Just the opposite."

"Really?"

"Yes. Please hold him steady . . ."

Five minutes later Simon had his answer. Even though the round bullet had shattered and the pieces were like nuggets, it had disclosed itself by bruising and lacerating a large area of lung tissue.

The minié ball, swifter, would've left a clean-cut wound.

Simon put the saw on the sideboard and drifted over to the window. He looked out onto the common, which was crowded with troopers, loud with bantering voices, but his eyes were turned inward. He saw Elias Deering at Sheridan's table, the vein in his forehead distending as he chewed and carried on against the Dunkers. *"They're a galling bunch, and I for one am gratified to see them take their licks."*

"What is it, Dr. Wolfe?" Dr. Lazelle asked from behind. "What've you determined?"

3:39 P.M.

UNION SIXTH CORPS, NEAR STRASBURG

Simon watched Philip Sheridan from the edge of some woods.

The general was sitting astride Rienzi. Before him a half mile of wheat stubble, golden-orange in the flat sunlight, swept up to a knoll at the foot of Fisher's Hill. He kept fixing his field glasses on it. There, gray specks could be seen even by the naked eye, working antlike on what appeared to be piles of matchsticks. Hastily built fieldworks. Through the trees to Sheridan's back sifted a tide of blue. Infantry moving into line to the long drum roll. The colors were being uncased when a round of solid shot warbled through the air.

Simon hunched in the saddle as it crashed into the top of a big locust tree a hundred yards to his right.

Splinters, glistening with sap, showered the line. Two men dropped and didn't get up again. Simon thought to save his report to Sheridan for later and help the wounded. But then he saw the stretchermen trot forward. An assistant surgeon waited back in the dusty shade of the dressing station, arms crossed over his apron. He'd hung his sash from a branch.

Another ball hit the trees.

Rex skittered. It was no time to be bucked off, so Simon tied the rein to a bush and walked the last few yards up to the general. He must catch Sheridan while he could. Might not see him again for days. "Sir, beg to report."

Sheridan gave him a distracted nod, then went on glassing the knoll. Union artillery was now answering the Rebel battery that was hidden somewhere behind the brow of the hill, and the air over it was suddenly peppered with tufts of smoke.

"Afternoon, Simon," Sheridan muttered after a moment. "What d'you have?"

Simon hesitated, asking himself for the last time since leaving Dr.

Lazelle's office if there was another way around this. Yes. He simply had to arrange for Rebekka Zelter to see Elias Deering when the provost marshal got back to Winchester. That would settle it at once.

But there was no time for that now. The army was advancing, and—with three Germans dead within that many days—he had no reason to doubt that more Dunkers would die unless he gambled on their behalf. The murdering soldier was using the confusion of battle to kill the innocent, and he'd keep on killing until he was put under guard.

But what a gamble this was. Simon knew the unspoken rule: you accused a brother officer only when his guilt was too blatant to be ignored. Never before. In the army, justice was always weighed against its effect on cohesiveness and morale.

"Sir," he said at last. "I believe an officer on staff should be questioned . . ."

"About what?"

"Dunkers."

Sheridan gave no reaction.

"There've been two more killings," Simon went on, that old feathery feeling in his chest making him short of breath. "I believe Colonel Deering should be questioned about them, sir—and given the chance to absolve himself as soon as possible."

There. Done. He waited for Sheridan to tell him to go on, but at that instant bugles turned his head, and the line hurrahed and started across the stubble at a mechanical walk. One hundred paces to the minute.

Sheridan watched as if the men were on parade, a ruthless ease in his face.

The Rebel cannoneers had ceased fire, probably to limber up their guns and flee before they could be captured. Early was short of artillery, along with everything else.

Over those last miles from Front Royal with the sun hot in his face, Simon had asked himself how Sheridan would react. Surely, after Deering—in a wallow of bitterness and self-pity—had volunteered for courier duty last night, Sheridan had some idea of how his provost marshal felt about him.

Whatever, Simon hadn't foreseen a scowl. "What're you accusing him of?" Sheridan asked.

"I'm not accusing, sir."

"Could've fooled me, then."

"I'm just saying that he should be questioned."

"By whom?"

"Not my prerogative to say, sir."

"I know that," Sheridan said. "Answer me, dammit."

A quick breath. "The Inspector General, maybe."

"Somebody from *Washington?*"

"Well, it's an awkward situation. We can't ask our own provost marshal to investigate himself."

"What's your accusation?" Sheridan repeated. "You're making my goddamn head spin, Wolfe."

"I'm not—"

"Say what you've come to say!" Rienzi pranced at the bark of his voice.

Simon held his eyes for a few seconds to let him know that he wouldn't be cowed, then began telling him about the corpses in the springhouse. Hard to keep his mind on the telling, for the infantry was halfway to the knoll and the Rebels had yet to open fire. He suspected that Little Phil, under the same expectation of horror he himself felt, had stopped listening. But then the general interrupted, "And when were these Germans killed?"

"I can't tell precisely, sir. Their bodies were dumped into a cistern of cold water."

"Then you have no idea?"

Simon felt his own temper flare, but waited a few seconds before answering. "The onset of rigor mortis would indicate to me that they were murdered, say, two to four hours before I came upon them—"

The Rebel volley—muskets—came at last, making Simon start. He shut his eyes for an instant, then looked across the field. The right end of the Federal line had borne the brunt and was dissolving into ragged flight even as the bulk of the regiment genuflected and hurled back its own salvo. Just before smoke enveloped the scene, Simon saw a colonel topple out of the saddle, grasping his throat. Foolish to go in mounted: he'd probably been trying to impress Sheridan.

He hadn't. Little Phil yawned.

A few seconds later, the entire line came jogging out of the smokebank. It wasn't a rout, but they were done for the day, trailing their colors.

"Rider!" Sheridan boomed. Simon expected him to give an order related to the failed sortie, but instead he said to the trooper who galloped up, "Find Colonel Deering—I saw him at our tents not an hour ago—and have him report to me at once."

Simon felt somewhat vindicated, even though Sheridan glared at him as they waited. "How you feeling, Simon?"

"General?"

"Not too tired?"

"No, sir."

Sheridan pointed toward Rebel-held Fisher's Hill. "You still want to whip these traitorous sons of bitches?"

"You know that, sir." Simon faced forward again, seething under a pale, sweaty face. The smoke had rolled away, and the stretchermen hurried out to the wounded, whose cries could now be heard over the rustling of a fresh regiment going forward. Simon glanced at the colors: the 6th Maryland. He told himself not to focus on the faces; he'd supped at Willard's Hotel on Passover last with a young officer from this regiment. Captain . . . ? How had he forgotten the name so soon? Benjamin something. Simon looked up. The sky was still white with heat. As it had been at Antietam while he waited for someone, anyone, to take him off the field.

"You know," Sheridan said, breaking the silence between them, "death isn't the maximum punishment you can inflict on an enemy population."

"Then what is, sir?"

"Poverty. It'll bring prayers for peace more surely and quickly than killing, any day—so don't think I see a military use to what's been happening."

"I wouldn't presume, sir."

Sheridan sighed. "And as long as we're being high-toned and picayune, let me ask you something. Day before last, nearly two thousand boys on both sides were *murdered* along the Opequon. God only knows how many more'll follow before I push Early off this goddamn hill. Now sure, I've got a sense for the distinction here, these three Germans didn't have a side in this foolishness, like the rest of us. But by Crimus, Simon—is the distinction really that great? Is it worth standing my entire army on its ear!"

Simon looked squarely at him. "Yes, sir. It's that great. And if we forget the distinction, or pretend it doesn't exist, we've just taken a step back toward the darkness."

"Who—you and me?"

"All of us. Mankind."

"Oh, piss on mankind," Sheridan said. "Mankind will still be clubbing one another with the jawbone of an ass, or whatever the devil they got handy, when you and I look like something that belongs in a snuffbox. We're stuck in this dung heap forever, as far as I can figure." He paused. "No, Simon . . . I'm asking why this Dunker sideshow means so much to you, personally."

Simon hesitated. *My sister,* he was thinking. But he could never bring himself to reveal what he feared as much as anything about this war: the coming day he'd have to stand before Leah and explain why he had gone against their home state, their father, and her husband, killed by Union counter–battery fire at Chancellorsville. He'd have to convince her of the righteousness of the cause that had taken Israel from her. And he couldn't do that if the army he served left a trail of dead civilians all the way to Richmond.

Finally, he heard Deering's voice at his back: "Reporting as ordered, sir."

Turning, Simon tried to glimpse something in the colonel's eyes. Murderousness, maybe. But they just looked weary. Even the forked vein on his brow seemed deflated.

"Your revolver please," Sheridan said to Deering.

"Beg your pardon, sir?"

"Give me your sidearm."

Deering glanced over at Simon, then surrendered his Army Colt.

"Come help me, Wolfe," Sheridan said, and Deering shot him a second glance, this one sharper.

Sheridan snapped out the cylinder, inspected it, then tossed it to Simon. All six chambers were loaded with unexpended cartridges and caps. Simon ran the tip of his thumb over the roundball bullets, the same kind of ammunition that had felled Josef Hostedler. He could feel Deering's stare on him, but didn't return it.

Sheridan peered down the eight-inch barrel, and then passed the revolver to Simon for him to do the same. The barrel was clean but for the usual dust that came with life in the field. "You familiar with what a freshly cleaned weapon smells like, Wolfe?"

"I am, sir."

"Does this one smell of solvent?"

Simon sniffed, then put the cylinder back in. "No."

"May I ask what this is all about?" Deering asked with a flat tone that somehow reassured Simon: the man almost seemed relieved at being found out.

Sheridan ignored the question. "Your saber, Colonel."

Deering looked off, blinking fitfully, then drew his blade and presented it hilt-first. A minute later, Sheridan lowered it so Simon could see the point. Nothing to indicate that it had been blooded or washed of late.

"Anything else, Colonel Wolfe?" Sheridan asked.

"No, sir," Simon said, his voice tinny-sounding to his own ears. There was no way to really tell if Deering had fired his revolver or used his saber in the last day. But still, Simon's certainty was beginning to flag, and he felt as if he were sinking under the weight of Little Phil's stare.

Sheridan handed Deering his weapons back. "Colonel Wolfe says you may've had something to do with the deaths of a German farmer and his wife along the pike to Front Royal . . ."

At this point Simon wanted an outburst from Deering—however feeble, it would be his last gasp at innocence. The natural thing for a man to do just before confessing. But the colonel didn't rant. Instead, he smiled out across the field from which the wounded were still being carried. "And when, if I may ask, did these killings happen?"

Sheridan turned to Simon. "Between two and four this morning?"

He straightened himself. Nodded.

Deering continued to smile, although triumphantly now. "I just left a Captain Browne of Torbert's staff in the mess tent. I ask only that he be sent for."

"Very well." Sheridan dispatched the same trooper back to field headquarters, and the three men waited in silence as the hoofbeats faded into the trees. The sun was close to dropping behind Little North Mountain, but felt as fierce as it had at noon. Simon longed to unbutton his coat and open his perspiration-soaked shirt to the breeze; he blamed the heat for a sudden lightheadedness. Sheridan was jiggling his boot for the 6th Maryland to be off, and Deering kept swiping at some gnats that had drifted over him. All at once, the Marylanders gave a throaty roar and rushed out into the field. The Rebels didn't wait long to take this assault on. Above the rip of musket fire Simon heard the thwack of a bone being splintered by a bullet. He started to wince, then realized that Deering was looking at him as if vaguely amused. He gazed back at the man, who then looked off into the smoke.

A blue soldier on a black gelding had slashed the old woman on the pike, he reminded himself to ward off another wave of dizziness. Elias's outburst against Dunkers at the victory supper. And blast it all—there was a witness, Private Woodworth, who'd held Deering's horse for him. Simon meant to save that until the official inquiry if only to protect the former divinity student. The man was under Deering's thumb, after all.

Captain Browne arrived and reported, a boy no older than twenty years. Blond wisps of mustaches. He was bug-eyed at being summoned by Little Phil himself.

"Go ahead, Elias," Sheridan said, although he was training his glasses on the 6th Maryland. The regiment was fighting well enough, yet had begun to show the first sign of faltering: standing but not advancing.

The air was positively vibrant with bullets.

"Captain," Deering said, sounding as cocksure as a lawyer, "will you kindly acquaint the general with the circumstances of our meeting last night?"

Browne paused for a quick breath. "Well, sir, I met you on the road to Front Royal."

"And from there?"

"I guided you through the fog to our headquarters."

"After we met on the pike, were you continuously in my company until we were interrupted at mess a short while ago?"

"That's right, sir," Browne said. "Brigadier Torbert sent me back with you should General Sheridan need to send any further orders to him. You know, sir, with a courier who'd know the way up the Luray Valley."

Deering had left out the most important fact of this encounter. "What time last night, Captain, did you meet Colonel Deering?" Simon asked.

"Around ten o'clock, sir."

Simon looked to Sheridan. "About nine-thirty I saw the colonel leave the road. Strike out across country."

"That's true," Deering quickly said. "I hoped to save some time with a shortcut along the foot of the Three Top Mountain. But when the fog set in, I decided to backtrack and resume my ride along the road." He turned to Simon. "And what were you doing following me?" He flashed a weak smile at Sheridan. "I must admit—for a while there I was sure Mosby's men were on to my trail."

Simon said nothing.

"I demand an explanation," Deering went on.

"Answer him, Wolfe," Sheridan said.

Simon knew that what he would say next was improper, but he had to find Deering's anger, to use it against him. The truth was slipping through his fingers. Nothing was going as he had planned on the ride from Front Royal.

"Did you hear me?" Sheridan said crossly—the 6th Maryland was slinking back through the stubble.

"Sir, Colonel Deering said some things in my presence that led me to believe he didn't want things to go well for you on this campaign."

"This is too much!" Deering cried, and Simon felt an inward squeeze of gratification. With anger came carelessness.

"How has he wronged me?" Sheridan asked. "I want something more than words, Wolfe. Words don't mean a goddamn thing to me." Before Simon could answer, the general turned in the saddle and shouted at his aide-de-camp, who'd ridden up in the last minute, to have the full brigade that was coming forward to fix bayonets. "Steel will break the bastards," he added.

Simon said, "If Colonel Deering has done this—and I say *if,* for I've only asked that he be questioned—he makes that wrong step for you, General. The one you fear will put Lincoln out of the White House."

This struck a chord, for Sheridan's expression slowly turned thoughtful.

Suddenly, Deering spurred his horse at Simon. He reined up within inches of bowling him over.

But Simon stood his ground.

"I demand an apology," Deering said with an incensed grin. "An end to this before Harvard logic makes bloody fools of us all. Otherwise, I must demand satisfaction . . ." He paused to press his fingers to his forehead, then asked Sheridan, "For godsake, how do we know these killings even happened!"

Simon stepped around Deering's horse and handed Sheridan an envelope. "My report on the postmortems. Attested to by the Front Royal practitioner who was present."

Deering laughed. "Are we to take the word of Confederates now!"

Simon reeled on him. "I am not a Confederate, sir! Damn you to hell for saying so!"

"Whatever you are, Colonel Wolfe," he said just loud enough to be heard over the gunfire, "I believe it my duty as provost marshal to look into why you alone, by your own admission, are the only officer known to have been at both the Winchester and Front Royal killings."

Simon lunged at him, seized his horse by the bridle as he shouted, "Not quite! I have a witness that you went up to the house near Mill Creek before it was torched! Alone! And yes—you shall have your satisfaction!"

"Stop it!"

Simon let go of the bridle and slowly faced Sheridan. Beyond the general he could see—with no interest now—that the bayonet charge was spilling over the knoll. The Rebels were abandoning their fieldworks and loping back toward Fisher's Hill.

"I'll shoot the first bastard who agrees to a duel!" Then Sheridan lowered his voice again. "Did you go up to that house, Elias?"

"Most likely, sir. In obedience to your orders."

"How's that?"

"I was searching the area for Dunkers and Mennonites, preparatory to evacuating them north under escort."

Sheridan then asked, "Did you go inside the place?"

"On my honor, no. The latchstring was pulled, and the door barred." Deering glanced at Simon. "I refused to force an entry. These people, who aren't in revolt against us, still have the protection of our laws."

Sheridan fell silent, and Simon began to feel amazed with himself. He'd been ready to do the unthinkable. For the first time in his life he saw how fatigue and anger could conspire with some chain of events to make a man do what he'd never do on a better day. *Must watch my emotions. These aren't the best of times.* But there was also a faint echo of pride in this. He was a hot-blooded Carolinian, after all.

"I've heard nothing here that makes me accuse either of you of these . . . these happenings. So the matter's closed. Any communication to Washington—without my approval—and I'll leave guts on the tent ropes. Elias, look to keeping good order behind the army. And Simon, see to you wounded—period. D'you both understand me?"

Deering nodded, and Simon did the same after a pause.

Sheridan sat erect in the saddle. "These boys have just won me a decent view," he said with sudden good cheer, "and I mean to enjoy it." But then, as he began to spur Rienzi toward the lingering smoke, he drew rein. He turned slightly toward Simon, but didn't meet his eyes. There was an air of pensiveness, almost distraction, around him. "Surgeon," he said at last.

"Sir."

"Present yourself with my compliments to General Crook. Eighth Corps has a tough march and a hot fight ahead of them. Your services will be appreciated, I'm sure."

Then he set off across the field at a gallop.

⊰ CHAPTER 7 ⊱

11:00 P.M.

UNION EIGHTH CORPS, HUPP'S HILL

Simon hiked up into the timber on the north side of a hill overlooking Strasburg. Haversack and canteen were slung over his shoulder. No moon yet. And no bivouac fires to break up the sultry darkness. He walked in a kind of numbness, his ears ringing as if a shell had burst next to him earlier in the day, leaving him dazed. Slowly, the trees closed around him, and he became aware of a vast human presence sprawling over the forest floor. Mingled smells of urine and sweat. Around him more than five thousand infantrymen squatted on their heels or lay on the shoals of dead leaves, quiet but for an insectlike hum of talk. Crook's entire corps. At its middle stood a wall tent, the canvas glowing like honeycomb held up to the sun.

An aide led Simon through the flaps.

The inside of the tent was stuffy, like the feeling inside his head. He took a deep breath. Had to stop thinking about Deering. Nothing to do for the time being. Rebekka Zelter, back at the transfer hospital, would settle it all with a glance. And at the court-martial Private Woodworth's testimony would clinch it. Philip Sheridan couldn't sidetrack justice forever, not with a witness like Woodworth waiting in the wings.

Crook was poring over a map at the table. "Why, Simon," he said, looking up for only an instant, "good to see you." Leaning over him were his division commanders, Rutherford Hayes, whom Simon had last seen at the victory supper in Winchester, and Joe Thoburn, a physician before the war. Thoburn poured a splash of whiskey into a mug for Simon. His deep-laired eyes never seemed to brood over putting down the scalpel and taking up the sword. Still, a decent man. They were all decent men, which made their unconcern over the Dunker murders that much more infuriating.

"Thanks, Joe." Simon took a sip, then reported to Crook. Sheridan's compliments.

The general swatted at a moth that was spinning around the candle lantern. "To go with us on the march, Simon?"

"Yes, sir."

Crook and Hayes exchanged a quick look.

Ignoring it, Simon went on, "I've taken the liberty of ordering up a train of mules with cacolets to pack out your wounded—here within the hour, hopefully."

"No," Crook said sharply. "No mules. Total surprise." His eyes blazed at Simon a moment more, then drifted back to the map. Lines and squiggles of deceptive simplicity: farm boundaries, creeks, a back road, a mountain. Little North Mountain. But there wasn't even a bridal path up its eastern face. Then he said with a worried smile, "I'll do all the braying this trip."

Thoburn softly laughed, but Hayes was stroking his nose with a finger in thought. Eighth Corps, also grandly called the Army of West Virginia, was no more than two divisions. Did Hayes think his brigadier was chewing off too much? At Antietam, Crook had reportedly gotten lost while trying to get around the impasse at Burnside's bridge. Not that he was anything but a solid, battle-tested officer. But still.

Thoburn suggested that, after the attack was launched, an ambulance depot be set up at the base of the mountain, say the fields near St. Stephen's Church. From there, the mule train could be guided the rest of the way up to the battlefield. Reasonable enough.

Crook looked to Simon.

"That'll be fine, General."

"Why don't you tag along with Joe's division? His column will be bringing up the rear."

"Very good, sir." Simon was downing the last of his whiskey when a young captain ducked inside through the flaps. A blandly handsome face. His eyes found Crook first, but then fastened on Simon, the empty sleeve.

"What is it, Will?" Crook asked.

"Message from General Sheridan, sir," the captain said. "Confidential."

Simon was taking his leave when Crook interrupted, "When's the last time you ate?" He tried to recall, but before he could come up with an answer Crook barked for his aide. "Lieutenant, see that Colonel Wolfe gets something inside him. He looks like he's going to blow away."

Outside, Simon asked the aide, "Can you spare a courier?"

"I'm sure, Colonel."

Simon rattled off a verbal message for the head of the Ambulance Corps, who, unfortunately, had already readied a mule train. Don't set off for Little North Mountain until ordered sometime tomorrow afternoon. Had he told the grooms to send Naomi up with the train? He wasn't sure. Maybe he *was* hungry enough to blow away.

"I'll get it off at once, Colonel." The lieutenant left him at the head of some soldiers lined up for corn dodgers.

Simon took one and shuffled off a short ways, sat down cross-legged at the edge of a company. The haversack slid off his shoulder. Stuffed with dressings and morphine. "Surgeon Colonel Wolfe," he said between voracious bites, for the men had quieted themselves.

"Evenin', Col'nel," a West Virginia twang answered.

The fireflies were thick among the trees. Here and there they lit up ghostly white faces. Antietam's dead, their last evening in bivouac. All at once, Simon had no appetite.

"Never had us a surgeon colonel taggin' along before," somebody said. "Things gonna be that bad tomorrow, sir?"

"No," Simon said, "Little Phil just wanted me out of his hair."

The men started to laugh, but then a solemn, older voice said, "It'll be plenty bad. We'll be played out when we come on them. Creepin' up the mountain most the day in this heat. They'll get a twist on us, you wait and see."

"It'll be all right," another said. "We got woods most the ways."

"There's clearin's," the older voice went on. "The Johnnies got themselfs a watchtower across the valley on Three Top Mountain. See a hundred miles from up there. Like an eagle. 'Upon a watchtower I stand, O Lord, continually by day, and at my post I am stationed whole nights. And, behold, here comes riders, horsemen in pairs!' "

"We ain't comin' on horseback. 'Cept Hayes and Old Buzzard, maybe." Crook—the soldier meant, made bold by the darkness. But it hadn't been completely lacking in affection.

"Colonel Wolfe?" a figure called out.

Simon rose. "Here."

"Captain McKinley, sir," he said, approaching, his boots raising a dust Simon could taste but not see. "General Crook has a change for you . . ."

"Yes?"

"He wants you to attach yourself to the Twenty-third Ohio instead of Colonel Thoburn's command. The color company."

"Where will I find the Twenty-third?"

"Tonight? Who knows, sir. But they'll be first to move into column in the morning," McKinley said, then paused. "They'll have the lead."

1:58 A.M., SEPTEMBER 22

WINCHESTER

Crying kept drifting from Colonel Wolfe's room. There, Mother Haggerty found the German baby wet, but no sign of his mother. "Come now, darlin', can't be that bad . . ." She changed him, then was looking for the woman in the main ward when Dr. Twiss needed help treating a suspected skull fracture. Opening the scalp confirmed it. Bleeding from the incision was already copious, but Twiss said, "More purging."

After applying the leeches and making the poor lad as comfortable as possible, Mother Haggerty continued her search for Mrs. Zelter. At last she found her in the room set aside for Rebel inmates too bad off to be moved north.

Just as she'd feared: the young widow had formed an attachment.

Frankly, she wasn't plain or mature enough for the work, unlike the elderly Mennonite widow—Mrs. Bohn, wasn't it?—from town who'd just volunteered her services. There was a woman who knew how to nurse without stirring the snakes, even though some of the boys were left blinking by her German accent. After Colonel Wolfe had gone yesterday, Mrs. Zelter turned sulky as a grass widow; but now it was clear that any fine-looking man would do.

"Now madam," Mother Haggerty said from the door, "this'll never pass muster round here, don't you know."

The woman ignored her, went on holding the Rebel's hand. A young Georgian with a slender nose and firm lips. The loveliest man in the entire hospital, now that Colonel Wolfe was gone.

"Mrs. Zelter," Mother Haggerty said, closing on her through the stark light that shone down from the rafter lamps. "This here's a bleedin' military hospital, and the rules of—" She stopped short of the cot.

The toes of the Rebel's stockings were pinned together: he'd been made ready for transfer to the dead house.

Mrs. Zelter stared loweringly up at her.

Never had Mother Haggerty seen someone so destitute of joy, so hopeless-looking. "I'm sorry," the matron said, shame fuming over her like ether. She'd been unchristian. Still, she had to say, "Madam, your child needs you."

But Mrs. Zelter turned her face and went on caressing the dead man's hand. " 'You come to me with a sword and with a spear and with a javelin; but I come to you in the name of the Lord of hosts,' " she said, almost whispering.

"I come to you with a baby, ma'am—whose soil I'm sick of handlin' for you."

" 'The stone sank into his forehead, and he fell on his face to the ground.' "

Mother Haggerty paused, her eyes narrow, then asked, "What are you sayin', child? Who fell on his face?"

"Goliath," Mrs. Zelter said. "Little Goliath."

The poor woman was off her head, but that gave her no right to go muddling up the Holy Book. "The Philistine was a great giant of a man. There was nothin' little about him."

"Not this time."

"What're you *talkin'* about?"

She looked at Mother Haggerty again, hatefully now. " 'When the

Philistines saw that their champion was dead, they fled. And the men of Israel and Judah rose with a shout and pursued the Philistines as far as Gath and the gates of Ekron.' "

Once more, Mother Haggerty started to ask what she meant, but then decided to let it pass. Instead, she backed off with a frown, then hunted up a couple of orderlies and told them to remove the corpse to the dead house—"before that poor, daft woman makes up her mind it's her long-lost husband, boys."

4:35 A.M.

HUPP'S HILL

Noise all around. Simon snapped awake.

Crook's thousands were already on their feet, rolling up their blankets, putting on their knapsacks. Officers drifted through them, whispering. A gibbous moon had risen. Simon shook off his sleepiness, took a swallow from his canteen, then stood. Men milled all around, walking off their stiffness, then settled down to wait in silence for the order to march. After a minute, two mounted figures led a group of them toward the west. Simon hurried to catch up, then asked in a hush, "Twenty-third Ohio?"

"Yes."

A loose, shambling column of fours materialized around him. Route step. Muskets were shouldered, barrels gleaming bluely in the moonlight. He felt a spasm pass through his chest, an unexpected thrill as he watched the corps unravel off the hill and flow westward behind the horsemen. Crook and Hayes, he believed, although he was scarcely able to see them through the dust being churned up. It was dimming the stars, yellowing the lopsided moon.

The column wound along a wooded ravine, trampling the undergrowth. Simon stumbled on a shallow root, and a hand reached out to steady him. "Thanks." But then a sapling, bent by the man ahead of him, whipped back against his arm. Like a cane.

"Oh, thunder," someone said low, "ain't this just jim-dandy?"

They snaked out of the trees and up onto a grassy rise. The dry grass whished around their trouser legs. Both Crook and Hayes rose in the stirrups to gaze south. Simon looked too.

On the far left, backdropped by first light, was Three Top Mountain with its Rebel signal station. Then the long, broken ridge that was Fisher's Hill, pricked orange here and there by the enemy's breakfast fires. And then dead ahead, spinelike Little North Mountain, along whose eastern face this corps would have to climb throughout the coming day—without being seen.

Impossible, Simon thought.

The Union Army, for all its merit, moved with the stealth of a traveling circus. A soldier in the ranks was thinking the same thing, for he said, "Old Jube's gonna lop the head right off this ol' buzzard. And we're that naked little head, boys."

"We done somethin' wrong to wind up here."

"Yeah, we didn't catch Old Jubilee the other night and bring him to Lil' Phil in chains."

"*Quiet.*"

Strange to imagine that the Jubal Early who had once come to his father's house in Charleston might kill him today. A lawyer with a caustic wit, he had revealed an irreligious bent Solomon Wolfe had found refreshing in a Virginian. Yet, Early had been tenderly polite to Simon's mother. And in parting he'd presented Simon with a volume of Thucydides. "Don't believe a word of it," Old Jube had said in his squawky voice, winking. "History's just a passel of lies nobody's alive to set straight."

Simon adjusted his haversack strap. It was already chafing his shoulder.

He wondered if Early would still hold the same opinion about history if he thrashed Phil Sheridan today and sent the Army of the Shenandoah reeling back to the Potomac, if he somehow damaged the Union war effort enough to topple Lincoln's presidency and fill the White House with the peace candidate.

Ahead, the column went on cresting the rise, the jutting rifles making it appear to be some quilled black serpent rolling along the land. South. Ever deeper south.

9:00 A.M.

CONFEDERATE ARMY OF THE VALLEY HEADQUARTERS,
FISHER'S HILL

A message had finally come from Mosby. He was recovering in Loudon County over the Blue Ridge and promised to be back in the field within the month. Good. Get him back hitting Sheridan's supply lines. Only real good he did.

Jubal Early was thinking this about Mosby over breakfast when John Gordon came riding up with one of the ranger's lieutenants. The loon, Claude Tebault, a Louisianan with the bad habit of staring too keenly at his superiors. He'd been cracked in the skull at Sharpsburg, but Early doubted that a bullet could change a man that much. He'd probably been a loon before the war.

The two men, both thin and erect, both accomplished riders, dismounted, then strolled through the morning light and shadow to Early's table. General Gordon was tall, but the lieutenant had a few inches on him. Before they could salute, Early rose arthritically from his camp chair and motioned for them to walk away from the tents with him.

No use letting the whole damn army know.

He led them through some waist-high cedars to a ledge with a view to the north. Winding up Fisher's Hill from below was the Valley pike. Then Tumbling Run, the first serious obstacle to a Union frontal assault. And finally, a hazy mile away, the blue 19th Corps, just beginning to send its skirmishers into the golden fields west of Strasburg.

Today it might get serious.

"General," Gordon drawled, the shadow deep in his sunken cheek where he'd taken a bullet at Sharpsburg, his fifth wound that day, "Lieutenant Tebault came across something of interest on the Manassas Gap line. Near Passage Creek." He nodded for the Louisianan to go ahead.

"Their medical director, sir." An uncommonly soft voice, kind of spooky.

Early waited for more, but Tebault just stared back at him.
"And . . . ?"

"Well, sir," Gordon said for him, "their senior medical officer was
looking over the ground. For ambulance routes, no doubt. It can mean
only one thing—Sheridan's getting ready to turn our line."

"I see." Early shook his head, smiling. Gordon had been a lawyer
before the war. Nothing against that; he was one himself. But the
Georgian had no military training, no Mexican War experience, regardless of Lee's high opinion of him. And he insisted on taking his
wife on campaign with him. The Yankee cavalry had nearly snatched
her in the flight from Winchester. No such luck. "The dwarf will try to
turn our right then?"

"Maybe," Gordon said. "But I rather think our left's more vulnerable. One side or another, sir—Sheridan's getting set to flank us."
Then he added with that grave, hound-dog look of his, "Again."

A cloud of gnats had drifted over them. Early and Gordon
stepped back, waving their arms, but Tebault continued to gaze north,
unaffected. Crazier than hell, but a whirlwind in a scrap, they said. At
it again lately, for his left hand was bandaged.

Early glanced over the Union positions once more. Keeping an eye
on them throughout the morning, he'd changed his mind on how the
battle would unfold. Sixth Corps, their strongest, was arrayed squarely
along the middle of Fisher's Hill. The 19th was just to its left, anchored on the big oxbow of the river. The 8th was unaccounted for,
alarming if that corps were anything more than two divisions. No,
nothing serious was coming on the flanks; Early would bet his life on
it. "That mick dwarf will demonstrate against our flanks, then hit us
head-on," he concluded.

Gordon didn't look convinced. To hell with him; he could go back
to camp and bellyache to his wife about it.

"Anything else, Lieutenant?" Early asked.

At last Tebault strode out of the living cloud. "No, sir." He rested
his hands atop the hilt of his saber. The picture-perfect chevalier, but
for the dent in the side of his head.

Smirking, Early asked, "Why'd you keep your blade?"

"Sir?"

"Don't most of you rangers make do with two revolvers?"

"All but me—yes, General."

"What's different about you?"

"A saber best expresses my honor, sir." Followed by that vapid green stare.

Early snorted. "Well then, give me a meat cleaver, son."

11:10 A.M.

LITTLE NORTH MOUNTAIN

Word came back through the 23rd Ohio: drop knapsacks and blanket rolls, muffle gear. Mounds of packs were soon piled up, and each company chose a man to stay behind in the skirt of woods beyond St. Stephen's church and guard its equipment. Simon hiked forward through these caches to Crook, who was sitting on a stump in the shade, telling a courier in a conversational tone to have Thoburn bring his division up alongside Hayes's. Form two parallel columns.

Well, Simon realized, here are *horsemen in pairs* the voice in the bivouac darkness had prophesied last night. A weak feeling came over him, that old sense that he was trapped into going forward no matter what. But then it passed. The heat, he told himself.

The courier rushed off, and Crook absently broke a daisy off its stem. His fingers began kneading it into white pulp.

"Excuse me, sir," Simon finally interrupted. Crook's eyes flared a little, but he said nothing. "About my mule train . . . when may I get it going?"

Crook stood and took out his watch. "Another three hours. But no ambulances on the Back Road till four. My aide's off to Cedar Creek in a minute. I'll send word to your depot with him."

"Thank you, sir." Simon started back for the 23rd Ohio, but Crook's voice stopped him short.

"Surgeon Colonel?"

Simon turned. Crook had never been so formal with him.

"Did General Sheridan order you to go all the way up with us?"

"That was my understanding, sir."

Crook nodded, frowning.

Simon walked on, convinced that the brigadier's eyes were on him until he reached the regiment again.

The veterans, sensing what lay ahead, were napping in the rhododendron. Downslope, Thoburn's division was coming up, a noisy blue millipede. The dew had been warmed off, and the men, crashing over dead branches and last year's leaves, raised dust into the slanting rays. Hearing Thoburn's approach, Hayes's men got up, brushed themselves with their caps, and started marching as well.

The two columns plunged into a glade. Ferns. Shadowy and cool. But from there it was all climbing, not for the summit of Little North Mountain, but creeping ever higher along its face. Boulders forced Crook and Hayes out of the saddle, and they led their horses by the bridles. The colonel had borrowed an ungainly-looking plug from a teamster for the march, but it was Crook's handsome charger that suddenly side-slipped. Both officers had to pull him back up onto the level.

At one o'clock a rest was called near a creek that played over the slope in several tiny branches. The men stooped with their hands and knees pressed into the mud, drinking straight from the flow. A sergeant filled a tin cup for Crook. As the brigadier drank, his eyes fixed on Simon. He murmured something to Hayes, then came down the slope.

"Stretch your legs a minute, Simon?"

He had been stretching them for seven hours now, but followed without a word. Crook took him to a parting in the trees, then halted well back in the shade and trained his glasses on Three Top Mountain. "Good," he said after a few moments, "no signal flags yet. Have a look?"

Simon accepted the glasses. Hard to hold them steady with just one hand. No hint of the Rebel lookout.

"Two years ago," Crook said quietly. "Almost to the day, isn't it?"

"Sir?"

"You were wounded."

Simon lowered the glasses. "Yes, that's right."

"I took an arrow in the hip out West. Most of two years to get over that. And that was just a bit of stone. Not a bullet."

"I was back in the field at Chancellorsville." Six months after Antietam, as one of the Surgeon General's medical inspectors. But Simon didn't add that he'd then spent the following summer at a special hospital in Philadelphia. Neuralgia. Although the official diagnosis was listed as exhaustion.

"Big wound," Crook said, almost in a whisper, "losing an arm. Some say it's so big there's no sensation. That so?"

"Maybe if the limb's carried away on the spot. Mine wasn't. I felt it."

"Arrow's like a hot poker," Crook said. "How's a minié ball feel?"

"Like somebody taking a cane to you."

"Pretty much what Hayes said."

"Was he hit?"

"In the arm at South Mountain. Just like you—" Carbine fire to the northeast made Crook snatch back his glasses. "Our cavalry screen," he said, scanning below, "has just bumped into their vedettes. Better hurry now, what?"

"Yes, sir."

"But rest whenever you like, Simon," Crook said, leading him back. "And no need to march with the color company."

Simon was about to say that the view was better up front when Crook asked over his shoulder. "Two more Dunkers?"

"Yes, General."

"Just like in West Virginia, I'd say."

"Sir?"

"Bushwhackers. Took advantage of the war to rob and kill. I had to hunt the bastards down."

"I don't believe these Dunkers were robbed."

Crook was silent for a moment, then said as he turned for his horse, "Don't push yourself, Simon. A tired soldier feels every rock in the road. Loses sight of the big picture."

Simon angrily watched Crook lead his horse forward. Little Phil's message last night. It had concerned himself, Simon was now sure of it. Before he'd only suspected. Damn. Was he to be tested then? Hell of a way to treat a man who'd seen everything he had. But Sheridan knew that.

The column stirred again, a wave from front to rear of men using their muskets to rise. Arms were slung. Blue uniforms were now almost black with sweat. No breeze was penetrating the crowded trees. The woods tumbled away into a ravine, and Simon slid down the scree on his heels, but then found it impossible to climb up the other side with just one hand. The color-bearer scrabbled past him, then offered down the staff to pull him up. A cedar thicket followed, buzzing with deerflies, and then another steep ravine. "Here, Colonel," the color-bearer said, again offering the end of his staff. "Almost don't need the colors today." The flags were being trailed so as not to draw attention. Simon had seen nothing of Thoburn's column in several minutes. And where was Crook? Had he ridden downslope to see what was holding up Joe? His own column staggered into a steep clearing, a rockfall tufted with dry grass. He watched Hayes, hoping a rest would be called before they plodded back into the breathless woods. Out here, the sun burned the back of his neck, but the stirring of air through his sweat-soaked uniform was blissful.

Hayes signaled a halt.

Simon gratefully faced the breeze. As he turned, his gaze swept over the lower end of the clearing.

A half-dozen mounted figures lurked there, motionless, some in gray, some in butternut, blending almost perfectly into the sunbaked brush. Then the Rebel vedettes raised their carbines and revolvers—and charged the column.

Simon was about to shout a warning when the volley passed overhead. Cringing, he felt as if he could have reached up and lost fingers to the mass of bullets. A few men of the 23rd Ohio knelt to return fire, but the Rebels had already wheeled behind their own smoke and vanished.

"Anybody hit?" a voice cried. It was Hayes, coming at a gallop. He looked down from the saddle—strong, vigorous, whole. Wounded in the arm, but the arm had been saved. "You all right, Simon?"

He slowly got up. Only now did he realize that he'd dropped to his belly. "All right."

"Anybody else?" Hayes asked.

None. And all of them had stayed on their feet during the attack.

The van of Thoburn's column trudged into the clearing just as a round of a solid shot howled across the sun. It collided with a pine higher on the mountain and split the trunk in two. The top heaved over with a splintery sound and crashed against the ground, shattering branches, filling the air with a sweet, resiny smell. Simon dropped again, but then saw the rest of the regiment double-quicking past him toward the covering gloom of the woods.

A hand grabbed his collar and half-carried him along. The color-bearer.

Shrapnel shells came next, a string of sunbursts across the sky that turned into patches of smoke, dirty little thunderheads that were carried off by the breeze. Simon felt saliva well in his mouth as if he'd just taken a big dose of calomel. And then percussion shot plowed up the earth all around him. The ground shuddered, and dirt rained down in a torrent of clods. Between bursts, the Dunker church, incandescently white across the years, flickered before him, and the gray figure held up his hand and urged Simon to cross the Cornfield toward his belching cannon. The figure wavered like a mirage, then became Crook, who'd materialized beside Hayes at the edge of the woods and was waving the men on with his hat. The shells chased the 23rd Ohio into the trees, showering them with splinters.

A surprised yelp.

Simon found the soldier on his back in some brambles, his forearm lanced by a sliver as big as a bayonet. Yet, he squirmed backward as Simon approached and shrieked, "Don't touch me! You leave me be, you son of a bitch!"

Simon slapped him once, hard, then pulled it out before he could recover from the shock of indignation.

The man gripped his arm a few inches above the wound and started to cry. "Will I lose mine too?" he whined, his eyes on the empty sleeve.

Simon shook his head as he dusted the wound with morphine. He asked for the man's help in tying off the compress, then hurried on through the smoke.

The barrage suddenly stopped, and then ear-ringing silence fell over the mountain. Simon thought it'd go on forever, a hot, dreamy stillness, when a smattering of musket fire erupted ahead. Word filtered back that skirmishers were overrunning a Rebel picket outpost—still no enemy in force.

The men, of their own accord, began dog-trotting.

The trees had thinned, and far below Simon could see a gray courier dashing over a field toward the southeast, whipping his mount with the ends of his reins.

Both columns were halted, Thoburn's some distance farther back than Hayes's, and Simon fumbled for his watch. Later, years later, if he lived, he would want to remember the time.

Seven minutes to four.

He snapped shut his watch, pocketed it again.

The shelling began anew, tinny thunder that made his ears ache. Explosions sprouted among Thoburn's men as they moved into line on the left of Hayes's division. Caps and swatches of blue cloth and canteens were tossed into the sky. Solid shot visibly arced overhead, stitching through the puffs of smoke, smashing into trees. Through all this, Simon heard movement to the rear: a regiment of Hayes's second brigade was forming about twenty paces behind the 23rd Ohio. He now saw how it would be: two divisions in two lines, one brigade behind the other.

He was in the first line, then.

Next to him the colors were unfurled. Stripes billowed; on two of them were embroidered in gold thread: Twenty-third Regiment, Ohio Volunteer Infantry.

"Ohio!" they were shouting up and down the line, "Ohio!" And some of them were crying as they shouted—from terror or patriotism, Simon wasn't sure. A man was never sure, even when he himself was overwrought. So much raw and shapeless feeling. He remembered being chosen to read the Declaration of Independence at a Fourth of July celebration when a boy in Charleston—and bursting into tears after the first few lines. He hadn't realized that he'd been sobbing until his father led him by the hand down off the bandstand.

A horse snorted behind. Simon turned. Rutherford Hayes was staring at him from the saddle.

Simon stared back a long moment, then asked, "What did Sheridan's message say?"

"My wife made that flag," Hayes said, pointing. "Biggest one in the whole corps." Then he slowly lowered his hand and frowned. "How well do you understand Phil Sheridan's burden, Simon?"

"What—?"

"The eyes of the world are on this campaign. So many ways for us to fail, and if we go down the Republic goes with us."

The men started hurrahing, but Crook, on his horse a few yards down the line, hollered for them to save it for the charge. *"Then* give it to them, you sons of bitches!" His gaze skated over Simon without seeing him. A lustrous calm in his face.

Simon caught Hayes's eye again. "The message. What did it say about *me?"*

The man hesitated, looked ashamed even, but finally said, "General Crook was ordered to reacquaint you with the moral fiber you showed at Antietam."

"Moral fiber," Simon echoed, stung. "Are those Little Phil's exact words?"

Hayes nodded. Then Crook bawled for him, and he galloped over to the brigadier.

Simon gazed down on Fisher's Hill, but saw only Sheridan's swarthy face. Contemptuous. He felt a heavy thud nearby, then found himself floating in light. A searing heat passed through him, followed by an airy sense of sky and coolness and crushed green leaves. As it all faded, he thought he could smell bromine, which had been sprayed around the ward in which he'd recovered from the amputation.

He was down on his chest.

Unhurt, he believed.

The soldier to the left of him had a shrapnel wound to the knee. Simon was seeing to him when someone grabbed the tail of his coat. He turned slightly and saw the colors shredded on the churned, smoking ground. He quickly wrapped the knee and crawled to the color-bearer, who had just let go of his coat. The man's neck was awash with bright red arterial blood. Simon thought he was already dead, but then the sergeant blinked sleepily. Simon swiped the punctured neck with his sleeve. No use. The carotid artery had been clipped, the esophagus perforated. The sergeant began to squirm, probably more from the sensation of slow drowning than his drowsy, helpless fear. Reaching up with both hands, he seized Simon by the hair. Simon yielded to the clutch, and his forehead came to rest against the gaping mouth. Breaths coppery with the smell of blood. Then the man let go. Gone.

Bugles. A hurrah from more than five thousand throats. The men were going forward.

Simon looked around for someone to take the colors. No one noticed that they had fallen. Except Hayes. He grinned expectantly at Simon, who could scarcely move. Sheridan had put a dunce cap on him, set him in the hottest corner of this awful classroom. And why? Because he couldn't stomach the murder of innocents. Little Phil would have him believe that there were no innocents in this new war, that a Dutchman wielding a scythe for Bobby Lee's commissary was as dangerous to the Union as an infantryman with a rifled musket.

Hayes drew rein, clenched a gloved hand in the air.

Moral fiber. Courage was the measure of everything else in a man, and by doubting Simon's courage Sheridan was doubting his integrity. It was that simple with these men.

Suddenly, Simon threw off his haversack and canteen, and picked up the colors.

Hayes gave a cheery salute and spurred his mount.

Simon started down the mountainside, the flagstaff resting on his shoulder. It felt nothing like a charge. Nothing like the Cornfield. Strangely lonely. No enemy in sight. He caught up with two privates and filled the gap between them. Were they ahead of the rest of the line? Or behind it? The three of them, seemingly alone in the shifting smoke and racket of Rebel shells, plunged down the slope and thrashed through the evergreen scrub. Bayonets tilting forward. Simon lofted the flag so it might be seen. Waved it a bit. But no one cried, "Ohio!" After the scrub came ankle-turning rocks, and he could hardly keep from falling, so when he finally fell it was no surprise. He slid a ways on his chest. The two privates helped him up. "You all right, Colonel?" Solicitous faces. Farmboys.

"Yes, yes," Simon said breathily, but he used the staff for support the rest of the way down.

Eighth Corps reached the open field at the foot of the mountain a mob, lines dissolved, the trailing brigades mixed in with the leading. But no regiment stopped to put itself in order, and the men surged on toward a twinkling of carbine fire from the far woodline. Rebel cavalry. They were fighting dismounted.

Simon's lungs were burning, but he was afraid to let the colors drift back into the crowd running at his heels.

"Charge'm!" somebody bawled—but hell, each man was already running as fast as he could.

A cheer flew up around him.

For what? He asked the private on his right, who pointed: the gray horsemen were clearing out, many on foot. Unbelievable. And why hadn't Early shifted troops left to meet Crook? His vedettes had been aware of this threat for over an hour.

The advance, of its own accord, had finally slowed to a fast walk.

A sergeant held his canteen to Simon's lips, then drank himself. Simon wiped his chin on his shoulder.

Somebody cried, "Here they come!," just as inhuman Rebel yells broke the short-lived calm. More cavalry. But these troopers weren't pulling back. Their mounts cleared a rail fence with grace, a roll of horseflesh curling endways like a comber, and came on at a trot. A moment's hesitation followed in which the Rebels seemed to be awed by the Yankee horde trampling down the sunbrowned grass toward them.

No matter, their captain seemed to say with a wave of his revolver, and they charged.

Musket locks clicked.

Oddly sublime: the sparking of the Rebel carbines against the shadowy green wall of the woods. Simon knelt and dipped the colors so the men to his back could shoot over him. The volley left him awash in smoke. Another salvo was pumped blindly into the acrid fog, gashing and swirling it. And then a third.

A riderless horse stampeded into the ragged Union line. The Rebel captain's, Simon believed. He tensed, waiting for troopers to gallop over him. But no other hoofbeats came.

The charge had been repulsed, and 8th Corps was marching again before the smoke had cleared.

Simon began seeing gray-coated dead and wounded in the grass. A Rebel with a bloodied mouth was begging for water. A corporal paused over him, glaring. For an instant Simon's heart froze: he thought the corporal was going to bayonet the trooper. He was moving to stop it, hopelessly slow as in a nightmare, when the corporal suddenly offered the man his canteen.

"Thank you," the Rebel said, then rinsed his mouth and spat. He'd lost several teeth, but looked otherwise unhurt. He even smiled as he said, "For that I'll give you my Colt."

Simon strode past. He helped kick down the rail fence the Rebel cavalry had just jumped. They marched clear of the smoke. A lovely, bright late afternoon. Except for the smoke. Ahead was a ridge, and Simon knew at once that the antlike scurryings atop it were enemy infantry settling in behind a stone wall.

"Goddammit . . . *Napoleans,*" the private closest to him said, and yes—on the left end of the ridge Simon could see twelve-pounders being hand-wheeled into place around the blue flag of Virginia. Cannister. They would fire cannister shot if they had it. The weak feeling came over him again, and he sensed that the entire corps had slowed a beat. They marched out of Little North Mountain's shadow and into sunlight. The flat rays were hot on his back, but a sensation of cold, of pulpiness, was spreading throughout his guts. Cannister.

"Double quick!" a familiar voice shouted. "Take those guns, boys!" Simon glanced over his shoulder and saw that it was Crook, mounted, vulnerable, rearing out of the sea of blue.

They ran.

Muskets flamed along the stone wall. A volley to give their artillerists more time to set up. Simon braced for the swarm of minié balls, but they whistled overhead and fell into the rear of the brigades. A solitary shriek.

"Keep running!" Crook again. Still up.

The ridge spewed little blossoms of smoke. Their cannon, at last, leaping off the ground as they let go double loads of cannister. Simon stiffened for them. Skeins of lead marbles.

Thoburn's division took the worst of it. Sudden gaps. Flags down. The foremost men stopped, and those behind them began stacking up. From that moment it was only natural that those in the rear began turning back for the sheltering woods of the mountain. Yet, Crook, dismounted now, stood in their path, chucking rocks at them, screaming, "Back, you bastards! Turn around or I'll shoot you myself!"

Simon faced forward again. Keep running. If you stop for even a moment, you'll take to your heels too. The wall. Focus on the wall. Nearly there.

Another cheer. What was it this time?

The Virginians were limbering up their cannon before they could be captured. No more artillery. Just musket fire. And then these stabbing flames were gone behind the smoke. Pretend that the smoke is as solid as granite. Yet, he could hear the minié balls all around, and each passing whisper made him flinch a little. Wounds. He knew too much about them for this sort of thing, anymore.

Then it was there, coming out of the murk: the stone wall.

He jumped on top. He thought to wave the colors, but his arm was too tired. A sprinkling of dead lay behind the wall, a few draped over it, but the living had broken and run. Hayes's division swept over and began enfilading the Rebels who were still blocking Thoburn on the left.

But Simon sat on the wall, out of breath.

Hayes rode up, hatless. "Why, Simon," he said with an admiring laugh, "your face is aflame. Wait till Little Phil hears about this!"

"Please don't tell." Simon didn't want to give Sheridan the satisfaction.

Hayes sobered. "You're as brave as they come, Simon, and I find it hard to believe that a brave man would care about something that doesn't matter." Simon started to argue, but the colonel stopped him by raising a hand. "I'm no longer doubting your wisdom in looking after this Dunkard madness. On the contrary—please call upon me if you need some legal advice."

Then Hayes snatched the colors from him and galloped on.

⊰ CHAPTER 8 ⊱

1860

LATE SPRING

ANNUAL MEETING OF THE BRETHREN

LIMESTONE, TENNESSEE

Dozens of sisters from the Shenandoah Valley congregations, Virginians with a slovenly accent to their German, closed around Rebekka Zelter, laughing, touching her, offering her their felicitations. But she began shoving them away and then broke out of the circle of dark dresses, shawls and white caps. She hiked up her own homespun skirt and hurried into the grove behind the big house in which the meeting had been held these past days.

She felt a little better in the gloom of the locust trees, a little safer in her solitude. Clusters of white blossoms dangled off the branches—liked hanged angels, she thought.

She leaned her back against a trunk and stared through the foliage, the low-lying smoke from the cook fires, at the gathering.

"Rebekka . . . ?" her mother's voice drifted to her, but from the far side of the house.

She didn't answer.

As the hour of departure grew nearer, the long-bearded men strolled the grounds in the hundreds, talking, some walking hand-in-hand with brotherly affection as they took their leave of one another for another year. The only stationary figures seemed to be the sisters from this part of the country, cooking the noonday meal at several fires, and a cluster of men on the porch of the house. They were listening to a thickset elder with a gray beard that almost reached his paunch. He spoke vigorously, his stern brown eyes flashing. He'd created a stir at the meeting, arguing for the church to remain united against both slavery and the war many believed was coming—even though he was from Virginia, the upper Shenandoah Valley, where the Brethren were resented by the English. His name was Jakob Zelter.

He was her husband of three days.

She'd first laid eyes on him at the Annual Meeting of the year before, which had been held in Pennsylvania. At that time, he'd been a widower of only a few months—and had struck her as a grave, unpleasant man, who'd stared at her during the hymn singing with what she'd thought to be disapproval. But then in January, her parents had received a letter from Jakob Zelter, proposing a "holy union" with their eighteen-year-old daughter, "whom I understand to have reached the age of accountability for both the sacraments of baptism and marriage." Her father wrote back a brotherly missive, but put off the decision until they all might meet again in person to discuss the matter.

"Rebekka . . . ?"

She knew that her parents had secretly delighted in Zelter's offer. They had despaired of her finding a husband in the Marsh Creek congregation—or any of those in Adams County, where her condition was widely known. Consolingly, they urged her not to believe that she was a demoniac, as she sometimes did—for in the New Testament were not those possessed by evil spirits so constantly bedeviled that they had to dwell apart from others, such as the man of Gadara, who had to live among the tombs near the Sea of Galilee? Rebekka's affliction wasn't constant. It could come as suddenly as it went, and when she was free of it she was almost herself again: obedient, loving and devoted heart and soul to living as simply as Christ did on this earth.

From this her parents took hope. They reassured her that with time, prayer and maybe the steady hand of an older man to guide her, she'd be eventually delivered from this trial.

However, the decision to marry Jakob Zelter, they said, was hers entirely.

So she went to Tennessee with them not having made up her mind, yet with the listless feeling that she was a condemned prisoner, trapped in the breathless space between sentence and execution. The clacking momentum of the train bearing her south became her own momentum—speedy, inexorable, irreversible. She knew that she'd never see her brother, Peter, who'd stayed behind to mind the farm, again on this earth. She'd never see her home again.

"It's through God's goodness that I see you once more, Sister Rebekka," Jakob Zelter had said, gaping at her from beneath his unruly white eyebrows, the hinge in his false teeth clicking as he talked. He'd met the Hartz family at the train station in Jonesborough, then driven them in his farm wagon to the site of the meeting in Limestone. Somewhere over those jolting miles Rebekka told her parents that she consented. They rejoiced, as did Zelter. But she herself felt nothing. And within the next twenty-four hours she changed her mind several times. But she said nothing about this to her parents, for she sensed that they'd be mortified if they had to take her north again. In the end, she was married to Jakob Zelter, and the ceremony was held by many to be the high point of an otherwise somber Annual Meeting. Painfully uncomfortable, Rebekka had been unable to eat any of the cakes, gammon and cheese set out for her wedding feast.

Now, on the porch, Zelter interrupted himself and smiled across the grounds at her. She knew that he'd intended to give her a look of warmth, of tenderness even, but she found it menacing. She also felt a twinge of repugnance.

Moaning, she bolted through the trees and into a pasture, where a square of buggies and market carts penned in the horses. She was thinking of melting into the animals, vanishing into the eddies of horseflesh—when she heard her mother's voice behind her. "Rebekka, your husband asks you to ready yourself."

She turned.

Her father was standing a few paces to her mother's back, his eyes on the grass. It was in their faces—the shame of having given her to this Virginian with gray hair and false teeth that clicked as he talked.

They had betrayed her as Judas had the Lord, and she wished that she had pieces of silver to fling at them. But she had only words. "I will go with him," she said defiantly, "and I will be happy."

Her mother's face started to brighten, but then she caught the look in Rebekka's eyes. "I pray you will," she said.

Two hours later, she was perched on a wagon seat beside Jakob Zelter, who, with a flick of his snakelike whip, started the team toward Virginia. Other Brethren families from the Shenandoah fell in behind him, and the grind of all the iron-shod wheels on the hard road set her teeth on edge.

She didn't look back at her parents, not once.

"Ah," Zelter said, giving her hand a squeeze, "we know that we've passed unto eternal life from death because we love the Brethren."

Yet, the opposite seemed to be true to her as the wagon train climbed into the mountains. With each mile, she was passing deeper into death. The daylight seemed far off in the west—and dimming, quickly. It was a strange land, nothing like home. Ledges of dark, mossy stone loomed over the road at every turn, and the hollows were choked with mist. The trees were crowded and bent and deformed. Once, as they forded a stream, she saw a hideous creature slithering down among the rocks, a demon with such a bright red skin it seemed to be engorged on blood.

She described it to Jakob Zelter, who chuckled and said that it was nothing more than a salamander. "Don't worry so."

But her life was mostly worry, and assurances such as Jakob's only seemed to mock her. Just once, she would like someone to say, yes, there are demons all about and one must fight them constantly. What a true companion such a person would be.

When night came, they camped in a clearing.

Rebekka kept her distance from the other women as they built a fire and cooked supper, for she knew that they were whispering lies about her. One especially meant her ill—she just knew it. The woman's eyes spoke hatred. This redheaded sister was said to have the gift of prophesy, and Rebekka was sure that she was foretelling a bad end for her.

"Come, Sister Zelter," this woman said, waving a wooden spoon for her to approach the warmth of the fire. "Join us."

"No thank you, Sister Hostedler."

It was then that Jakob Zelter stepped in, rubbing his hands together, and encouraged her to help the others. "Idleness is Satan's workshop, no?"

But Rebekka ran out into the cedars and wept. She wanted to die, but then again she was half terrified that she already was dead, that this lingering horror would last forever. Unless, of course, the Savior intervened. That warm-eyed Jew of Galilee who knew demons so well.

Nightfall brought her back to the farthest reach of the firelight, for she'd seen shapes in the darkness, shapes not of this world. And when Sister Hostedler turned from her pot and glowered at Rebekka, she cried, "I can't stand it!"

Jakob Zelter put down his tin plate and came to his feet. "Stand what, my dear?"

"They won't leave me alone!"

"Who?"

"Your demoniacs!"

"What—?"

"Send them away!"

She must have fainted then, for when she had possession of her senses again she was lying on a blanket and Jakob Zelter was leaning over her, his face severe with worry and something else, too—disappointment. It was only then that she realized that her parents had told him little, if anything, about her affliction.

"And they cast out many devils," he was quietly saying, "and annointed with oil many that were sick." He dipped some sweet oil from a jar and applied it to her head. Then another elder joined him on the blanket and they piled their right hands atop her hair before calling upon God, through Jesus Christ, to forgive and pardon whatever sin that had brought this sickness upon Rebekka Zelter, their beloved sister.

Rebekka felt the warm oil drip down into her eyes. She was sure that it was blood.

She screamed.

CHAPTER 9

1864

11:36 P.M., SEPTEMBER 22

MARTINSBURG PIKE, NORTH OF WINCHESTER

> "We're the boys that's gay and happy,
> Wheresoever we may be;
> And we'll do our best to please you,
> If you will attentive be—"

Cal Ames stopped singing.

The rumblings of a thunderstorm were drifting to him on the southerly breeze. At first, he'd imagined them to be cannonade, but eventually he caught the scent of rain, sweet like cut hay, and then a breeze as soft as velvet wrapped around his face and made him long for home, for Boston, on a night like this, the wet cobblestones shiny under the gaslights. But no use getting homesick, so he turned his mind to speculation. The thinking man's solace. Maybe all the firing this afternoon on Fisher's Hill, the choking clouds of smoke billowing up to heaven, had set off the storm. Rain always seemed to follow the big massacres—Fredericksburg and Gettysburg, especially. Rain by the bucketfuls, washing the bloodstained corpses clean only so that the next day's sun could blacken them beyond recognition. Artillery fire and then a drenching. Perhaps a scientific possibility worth investigating.

But not tonight.

> "So let the wide world wag as it will,
> We'll be gay and happy still,

Gay and happy, gay and happy,
We'll be gay and happy still."

He rode up onto a rise and gazed over Winchester's rooftops and belfries into the starless bowl between the Massanutten and Little North Mountain. There, lightning jinked within every few seconds. Dead souls desperately trying to twist back to earth, maybe, and take up their shattered bodies again. Was life so sweet that it was worth risking a second death? Not likely.

How many more gone today? A thousand? Two? Five?

And what of the wounded already pouring down the Valley toward him? Estimating no longer made him feel sad. Just drained. He'd been asking himself all afternoon what the numbers would be like if Sheridan tried to push on to Charlottesville with Early standing up to him every twenty miles, tooth and nail.

Too big a question. You needed a fifth of brandy and three cigars to tackle a question that big. And then you still might wind up blubbering like Grant did the night after Wilderness when he got a look at the butcher's bill Lee had sent him. Besides, there probably weren't enough boys in the world to get Philip Henry Sheridan where he wanted to go. Not that the son of a bitch would ever realize it. Little Phil figured that what Yankee wombs couldn't provide the immigrant boats would deliver.

Ames touched a heel to his horse and turned back for the pike.

"We envy neither great nor wealthy,
Poverty we ne'er despise;
Let us be contented, healthy,
And the boon we dearly prize."

Simon had ordered him to start looking for a site for a tent depot. Flat, well-drained, an ample supply of fresh water nearby. Hard to find. It'd be a virtual canvas city, four thousand beds, bringing together all the far flung hospitals in the lower Valley. Under Simon's thumb.

Ames smiled to himself. The medical director might be a mystery to some of his cohorts, but not to a student of the science of phrenology. When Simon's head got wet, there they were for all the world to behold—the bumps for cohesion. Ames had never seen such a marked propensity for unity on a skull that could also be read for ideality. *Excessive* ideality. A personality that labored to bring everyone together, yet under a strict and unyielding morality. Oh, young Simon Wolfe had belonged to the Harvard Freethinkers' Club, but his cranium betrayed his true bent: he was about as freethinking as an Old Testament prophet.

Unity versus ideality. It was one hell of a contradiction, for sure, and no doubt the reason for Simon's troubled spirits now and again. Ames had recognized a complicated nature the first time the dark-eyed prodigy from Charleston pulled up in Oliver Wendell Holmes's carriage to perform surgery at Boston City Hospital. Holmes, dean of Harvard Medical School, had so touted the skill of his teenage graduate a number of surgeons convened in the hope of seeing the boy fall flat on his face. Dr. Callender Ames, included. Young Dr. Wolfe had been given a depressed fracture of the cranium that called for trephining, devilishly tricky—unless you didn't care if you turned out an inmate for the state insane asylum.

But Dr. Wolfe had not failed. Far from it. For when he was done, his critics rose one by one and applauded, none more vigorously than Cal Ames. How much had he come to admire that skill? He'd wept when he heard that Simon had lost his right arm. Less for Wolfe than for mankind. It still hurt when he thought of it. That damned minié ball might as well have blinded Michelangelo or torn away Daniel Webster's tongue.

> "The rich have cares we little know of,
> All that glitters is not gold,
> Merit's seldom made a show of,
> And true worth is rarely told."

Ames was waved through a torchlit outpost of provost guards—they'd challenged him on the ride out at twilight. "Evening again, boys."

"Find anything out there, Surgeon?"

"Just a few odd arms and legs. You boys missing any?"

The guards didn't know whether to laugh or not, and Ames went on into the darkness, chuckling to himself.

> "So let the wide world wag as it will,
> We'll be gay and happy still—"

Unity *versus* ideality.

It was just like Simon to spoil now the good relations he'd built up with Sheridan and staff by going headlong after this Dunker thing. He'd done the same with much of Boston's medical society by taking up abolition to the point of neglecting his hospital duties. It'd put off his family as well, no doubt, for a month before the war broke out he returned from a Charleston visit so grim and distracted he'd scarcely been able to hold a conversation. He'd also picked up the curious habit of massaging his upper arm as if it ached. The one he later lost. Something had happened down there, the sort of thing to destroy a family forever, and Ames suspected that Simon had precipitated it.

Damn him—his sense of right and wrong was almost Biblical in its intensity. Once, he'd caught another surgeon stealing from the hospital dispensary for the benefit of his private practice. Simon hadn't been satisfied with the man's dismissal; it almost seemed as if he wanted to see him stoned outside the city gates, that only a punishment that severe could put the universe on a proper kilter again.

Yet, he was no easier on himself.

He'd insisted on resigning after an Irish girl, a charity case at that, died under his scalpel. This had been during the pioneering days of anesthetics, and she'd probably gotten a whiff too much of ether. Nobody had a sure idea how much of the stuff to administer, and the experimentation—or the blundering, as it really deserved to be called—went on for years. But it'd been all that Holmes could do to keep his young marvel in medicine.

Simon Wolfe was the most honest man in the blue crusade (forget Honest Abe—he was a politician, through and through). That was both admirable and an enormous pain in the ass, particularly when you were second in command to one.

> "Gay and happy, gay and happy . . ."

But Ames supposed that without men like Simon, humankind would eventually slink back into the caves. Not that mankind didn't have a perverse desire to do just that—it was what this war was all about. Not Union. And sure as hell not slavery. A lot of boys of the ilk of Phil Sheridan and Curly Custer could still feel the warmth of those ancient fires on their blood-daubed faces. Otherwise, everybody would've had a bellyful of this nonsense after Bull Run and gone home like sensible fellows to write inflammatory letters to the editor.

"Gay and happy, gay and happy still."

Curious. He'd received a message from Simon this afternoon, asking him to call in a Private Woodworth of the provost guard for an eye examination. Detail. That's what was wrong with Simon Wolfe. He could let nothing slip by. Some guard popped his musket off at the Johnnies, missed, and Simon ordered him to the transfer hospital for an exam.

"Oh pus," Ames sighed.

Supply wagons were clogging the main street, the mules braying impatiently, so Ames had to take another. It was lined with mansions, windows lamplit, rocking chairs on the verandas, everything customary-looking—except for the cavalry horse-lines and Negro grooms in blue uniforms on the lawns. Not much in the way of slave country, the Shenandoah. No cotton to tend. No plantations. Winchester had been occupied so often it was no longer an occasion for panic. Wealthy families such as these simply withdrew to a back room and quietly waited for their Yankee boarders to be driven back across the Potomac. Bobby Lee's Army of Northern Virginia had yet to disappoint them.

What was this now?

Pamunkey, Simon's man, had jumped down from the hospital loading dock and was running up Amherst Street to meet him.

Damned ideality. Otherwise, Simon would have chosen a more suitable orderly from the Invalid Corps, at least one who could talk. "Yes, yes, Otis—what is it?"

Pamunkey pointed south, toward Fisher's Hill, his face so anxious Ames thought for a moment that Sheridan had been routed. But then, grabbing the bridle, the orderly pulled him on horseback down an alley. "If you insist," Ames sighed, dropping the rein.

Pamunkey stopped before a big tent pitched between two darkened houses, and Ames suddenly came close to groaning as he flew out of the saddle and limped through the flaps. A thin, marblelike corpse lay nude on a cooling board. Shrapnel wounds peppered the thorax, but the face had been spared disfigurement. Half-shut, dreamless eyes and a sparse brown beard. The Jesus of a thousand Renaissance oils.

Ames could breathe again.

He'd somehow expected to find Simon. But it was too soon for any dead to have arrived from Fisher's Hill.

When Ames burst inside, the embalmer had stopped wheezing fluid into the corpse with a hand-pump. He now asked, "Have you come for her then?"

Ames shrugged. "Her?"

Half the space was partitioned off by a blanket, and the embalmer reached back and whipped a corner aside. Ames's gaze passed over a row of several naked bodies, then swept back to one that was female—and still had the blush of life.

Rebekka Zelter's hands were folded over her soft, pink belly, and her eyelids were scrupulously clenched as if she had every intention in the world of being dead and staying dead.

The scene might have seemed humorous, had not it been so shocking.

Ames sidled past the embalmer, who gave him a bewildered smile, and knelt at her feet. He took her dress from where it was bundled in the straw, unfolded it and covered her.

She jumped as if he'd pricked her with a needle.

"Mrs. Zelter . . . ?"

She made a throaty noise, but said nothing.

"Scared me to death," the embalmer murmured from behind. "She must've come in while I was at supper."

Ames tried not to sound as if he were scolding her. "My dear," he said gently, "why are you here . . . ?"

4:42 A.M., SEPTEMBER 23

THE VALLEY PIKE NORTH OF STRASBURG

A deep blueness hovered over the Valley. First light was filtering through drizzle as Simon led the ambulance train north toward Winchester. The pike was thronged with vehicles heading south to catch up with Sheridan, sopping horses lashed by teamsters in black oilskins. The ammunition wagons had priority, and within a few miles of having left the field hospital at the foot of Little North Mountain he had only to hear the snap of a whip to wave his ambulances over to the side. He carried a lantern for this purpose, and it had grown as heavy as a skillet during the long night.

There was a clatter of wheels ahead. Another ammunition train. And another drenching squall was coming. He could hear it moving through the woods toward him. He turned Naomi under a wide oak, but the rain went on popping against his cape and trickling down his neck. There was no getting away from it.

Behind his closed eyes he could still see the confusion at the field hospital, the strings of mules coming and going off the mountain, the wounded in the hundreds, lying out in a cloudburst, opening their mouths like baby birds to the drops.

Simon looked up. The last ammunition wagon had clattered past. He rushed out to take the road. His ambulances began to follow, but then stopped within a few yards of having crept out of the mud. One of them was mired axle-deep, and the other drivers tied off their lines and came running to rock it loose.

The light was now strong enough to make out faces. Infantry was marching against him, but Simon refused to budge, forcing the musty-smelling column to break ranks and stream around him and among the ambulances. They were green troops in unfaded uniforms, too shocked by the sight of bloody bandages and missing limbs to gripe. Often, this was harder to bear, coming upon the wreckage and carnage of the last collision with the enemy, than going into battle line oneself.

"Lookee here, fellas," one of the wounded said, chortling, "here's you by t'morrow . . . shoot yourself now and save your feets the walk!"

"Leave the poor veal be," another voice groaned. "They're just boys."

"Christ Awmighty, *we're* just boys."

Finally, the stuck ambulance was jostled free, and the train moved on again. Other than that one taunt, the wounded had been quiet. Before departure he'd given them each an opium pill to help bear the jolting, but they were more tranquil than usual. Maybe the rain pelting the canvas tops of the ambulances was calming them. For himself, the soft pattering against his cape was lulling his mind into an almost irresistible drowsiness.

His vision slowly grayed.

"Colonel!"

Simon swiveled his head toward the voice. It took him a moment to realize that the driver of the lead ambulance was hailing him. "Yes?"

"You just 'bout fell out of the saddle back there."

Simon blew out the lantern and hooked its handle through the cantle ring, then looped the rein tighter around his fist. "Did I?"

"I swear, sir."

Possible—he'd had only snatches of sleep in the last three nights. No trooper, he couldn't safely doze in the saddle. Rest soon or collapse. Somewhere away from the pike noise.

"I'll make room in the back, sir," the driver offered, "and you can tie your mare to the tailgate."

"No." Simon didn't want to relive that jostling trip from Sharpsburg to Frederick, wedged between a corpse on one side of him and a ten-year-old drummer boy, foaming with lockjaw, on the other. "I'll catch up in an hour or so."

The train was so lumbering he was sure he could rejoin it long before Winchester. "Come on, Naomi."

Away from the pike the rain was loud in the leaves. Touches of autumn were yellowing the tops of the oaks. A coolness was seeping into the land; the South's "General Summer"—dysentery, malaria and typhoid—was finally quitting the field. And no more sunstroke. Or prickly heat chafed raw by wool. But soon influenza and pneumonia would prowl the muddy camps. Bronchial coughing would echo down the company streets, awaken everyone hours before reveille.

Simon followed a creekside pasture up to the mouth of a ravine, where he hobbled Naomi under an overhanging ledge. He was soaked to the skin. Still, he sat with his back against the cold limestone, closed his cape around his doubled legs and rested his forehead on his knees.

He had taken the colors forward again. What a buffoon. It would've served him right to lose his other arm.

Still, secretly, he wanted to be there when Rutherford Hayes told Sheridan about the charge. Yet, as much as Simon tried to imagine an approving look on Little Phil's face, he could only visualize the general as he'd appeared the night of his victory supper in Winchester, minutes after Deering had forced a toast to the memory of David Russell. Sheridan had settled back into his chair, then quietly slipped into a funk that was relieved only when Custer knelt before him, bright-eyed. In either a spirit of odd hilarity or equally odd intimacy—Simon wasn't sure which—the young brigadier took Little Phil's hands in his own and asked, "Do you remember, sir, what General Kearny always said in times like this?"

Sheridan, smiling faintly, shook his head.

" 'I love war,' " Custer quoted. " 'It gives me indescribable pleasure, like that of having a woman.' "

Little Phil stared into Custer's gleeful eyes for several long seconds, his own expression profoundly sober, then suddenly kissed the brigadier on the brow. "It does, Curly! God rot us, but it does indeed! And now we're going to make Lady Secessa grab the hot end of the poker!" Beaming at the laughter and applause that followed, he had shouted for more champagne, more tins of oysters.

A gust of rain found its way under the ledge. Simon began to shiver, but then stopped. He was too tired even for the involuntary, he supposed.

Just before sleep, or maybe halfway down the fitful slide to it, he saw the cane. Shiny black with Japanese lacquer, topped by a silver lion with fangs exposed. Whistling through the air, it struck his right arm just below the shoulder joint. Smarting, confused, humiliated, he gazed down and watched his sleeve fill with blood. He could see where the minié ball had gashed through the blue material of his sack coat. And then, once again, as on that morning in the Cornfield—mothering darkness spared him the worst of the pain.

Naomi whinnied.

The day was brighter than before, although still misty. Had it stopped raining?

Yes.

He waited for eyes to make sense of the bleary shapes a few yards in front of him. Vaguely human. And then he realized that they were definitely human.

Three men stood grinning down at him, ragged and wiry men in threadbare butternut. One of them had trained a revolver on him.

Simon slowly raised his hand.

The Rebels laughed. "That *MS* on your cap?" one of them drawled, a man with cold black dots for eyes and a chin tuft that had almost blended into several days' growth.

"It is," he answered with more relief than he'd ever care to admit, although this Union insignia had meant nothing to the lone Confederate on the Manassas Gap line two days before.

"You got a lil' somethin' to dry up chancres, Surgeon?"

"I beg your pardon?"

They laughed even more uproariously, but then—without warning—the man with the chin tuft swept the barrel of his revolver skyward and fired three times.

Simon's lower jaw jerked with each blast.

"What you think of that, Surgeon?"

He was speechless. The Johnny vedette was out of his mind. He and his men were miles behind Federal lines.

Then, from the direction of the pike, came three shots in reply.

"And how 'bout that crowin', Col'nel?"

Simon stared back at him, more confused than ever. Had Early outwitted Sheridan with a flanking attack of his own? Or was Mosby about to pounce the supply line, as he had in August?

Hoofbeats in the lower pasture: a blue-caped major burst from the belt of trees and rode calmly toward them.

No use two Union officers winding up in Richmond's Libby Prison. "Go back!" Simon cried.

Howling, the Rebels slapped one another with their forage caps.

"What's that?" the major asked, continuing to bucktrot toward them.

Simon tilted his head toward the Rebels, but he already sensed that he'd been made a fool.

"Oh yes," the major said brightly, his voice shaking from his mount's bone-shuddering gait, "yes indeed." Another cherub-faced adolescent delighted to be chasing up and down the backside of Virginia. He stopped not ten feet from the men and returned their indifferent salutes.

Simon stood, his temper rising. "What's this about?"

The major caught Simon's look, and his eyes sobered. "Forgive us—Colonel Wolfe, isn't it?"

"Yes."

"Lanced a boil on my thumb at Harpers Ferry, remember?"

Simon shook his head.

"Didn't mean to alarm you, Colonel."

"*We?*"

"Yes sir, Seventeenth Pennsylvania Cavalry."

"All of you?"

"Quite, sir. Sergeant Pettigrew here"—the man with the chin tuft—"is in charge of our special detachment of scouts."

"Been cuttin' off some mischief behind Old Jubilee's back," Pettigrew added. "We seen you dozin' from up on the ridge. Just a speck from up there. Figured you might be the major come for us. Tricked out this way, we're kinda shy 'bout where we meet folks."

"Are you Northern born?"

"Yes, sir. And ain't that a trump, though?" Pettigrew gave a wide grin. Horrid teeth. "How 'bout you, Surgeon? Where was you born?"

Simon didn't answer. It provoked him. The relish with which the Pennsylvanian had taken up rural butternut mannerisms. Pettigrew's r's were as hard as Appalachian flint, and his breezy military courtesy befit a Johnny private, but all this was only skin-deep, and beneath it Simon sensed a deep contempt for things Southern. Yet, as he stared back at Pettigrew, it came to him that these men had probably ranged farther than any other Union forces. "How far south have you been?"

Pettigrew glanced to his major, who nodded. Then he said, "Harrisonburg."

"Come across any Dunkers?" Simon went on.

"A few."

"Any murdered?"

Pettigrew looked as if he had been asked something intensely personal, but then chuckled. "Hell, Surgeon, me and the boys seen a little mischief done to everybody. Dunkers. Quakers. Runaway darkies. It's just the way things is on the edge of the fightin'. See, folks don't naturally harmonize, don't you know, and they figure a war's the best chance they'll ever have to get even."

"Even with whom?"

Pettigrew just smiled.

Simon studied the man's belt: like Rebel irregulars, he carried no saber, but wore a bayonet in a leather scabbard. "You didn't answer me, Sergeant."

"Sir?"

"Did you come across any Dunkers . . . slain?"

Pettigrew stopped smiling, and Simon realized with a twinge that the man hadn't put away his Colt. He was resting it in the crook of his left arm. "Found nothin' in particular, " he said in a low voice, holstering at last, " 'cept the same old war, the same miserable folks usin' it however they see fit."

"You use the war as you see fit?" Simon asked.

The major broke in. "These men serve at great risk, Colonel. If captured, they're shot as spies. So you must forgive them if they seem a bit gritty."

"Nothing to forgive," Simon said, taking out his watch. Quarter past eleven. He started to move toward Naomi, but the major stopped him.

"If you're looking for cutthroats, Colonel—why don't you see Brigadier Custer at Front Royal?"

"What d'you mean?"

"He captured six of Mosby's boys this morning."

"Were they molesting Dunkers?"

The major hesitated, but then said, "No doubt. The sons of bitches'll do anything."

"Maybe you can tell me something . . ." Simon stooped to unfetter Naomi. "What enemy outfit wears a gray felt hat with the side pinned up?"

The men exchanged glances before Pettigrew asked, "You come across a prisoner like that?"

"I was the prisoner. He held me captive for a few minutes two mornings ago."

"Where, sir?" the major quickly asked.

"Manassas Gap line between Front Royal and Strasburg."

Pettigrew dropped his nonchalance. "What happened?"

"He let me go."

The sergeant's eyes narrowed and then widened. "What'd he say t'you?"

"Not a word."

"Which way'd he ride out?"

"South."

"Toward the Massanutten?"

"Yes."

"You saw him ride up into the range?"

"No," Simon said, "I simply saw him head that way. It was foggy."

"Sir, you came across the Forty-third Virginia Partisan Ranger Battalion," the major said. "Count yourself lucky."

Pettigrew added, "Mosby's Rangers usually shoot their prisoners.

Not let 'em go on their own sweet way." He pantomimed shooting Simon with a revolver. To the throat, chest and belly. "You're damn lucky."

"Maybe," Simon said, although he could still feel those pale green eyes on him, "but he didn't seem a murderous man."

"Nobody is, sir," Pettigrew said, "till there's thunder to pay. You might remember that."

"I might. Good day." He mounted Naomi and rode down the pasture.

He reined up at the pike. More troops were flowing toward Fisher's Hill and the fleeing enemy beyond. Steam rose off their rain-darkened uniforms, and the entire column seemed to be smoking as if it had just ascended from hell to maraud the Valley of Virginia. Simon looked away, afraid that something irreversible had happened to him in that burning farmhouse: that from now on he'd see these soldiers only as killers and thieves.

His ambulance train had already reached Winchester, no doubt, where he knew he should go straightway to help Cal Ames speed the transfer of the wounded north to Sandy Hook. That was his job, and it seemed one of the few inarguably worthy things to do in this war.

An evil instinct was at large in the Shenandoah, but Simon Wolfe—an insignificant cog in the huge martial clockwork—was not empowered to use the law to stop it. In fact, he had orders to do the exact opposite.

Yet, wasn't it in the Talmud somewhere: *The law does not ignore the evil instinct?*

Damn Philip Sheridan—this had nothing to do with military law. Or even the law of the land. Slavery was still the law of this land. No, it was an outrage against that greater law, the immutable one brought out of the desert so long ago that said: *He who murders a man shall be put to death.* Period. And on that authority a *Revenger of Blood* would come forth and cleanse the world, lest the evil spread and poison the soul of every man who had, quite sensibly, declined to put his career on the chopping block.

"Damn you, Phil Sheridan," Simon said, almost shouting. "You've gone and made an Old Testament Jew of me!"

Then he struck out across country toward Front Royal.

⊰ CHAPTER 10 ⊱

1862

In the beginning, there was blackness. But it wasn't absolute. He had a mote of awareness. He was aware that it engulfed him, that he dwelt within it, drifting on its silent tide. And after a while he realized that this darkness, suffocatingly hot at first, stinking of ether and rust, was slowly cooling down, hardening, like a piece of tar taken from the sunlight and put into the shade.

Then the torch winked on.

It was far off, fuzzy and dim, and kept bobbing as if gripped by an invisible hand in motion.

He moved toward it, swimming more than walking, for the blackness was as thick as molasses. But whatever distance he covered, the flame always shone that much ahead of him. It would not be approached. Still, he knew he had to follow the light and join it if possible, for he sensed resolution in it, an end to his vague suffering.

Once, a voice, surprisingly nearby, said quite clearly, "The power of articulation . . ."

Was it God commanding him to speak?

He tried, but only a dry rattle broke from his mouth. He tried to tell God that his heart was filled with love for Jesus, that he regretted the lives he'd taken on the field of battle.

But it was no good.

"He's goin'," another voice said. "By ginger, he's givin' it up."

Then the torch was very close and the blackness brightened to a uniform gray much like fog. Off to his left side a figure materialized. Its shape confused him till, quite abruptly, he realized that it was praying mantis, one as big as a man, poised to devour him.

But minutes passed in awful expectation and nothing came of this monstrous threat.

Then, while he strained to see the figure more clearly, it wavered, took on color and became, at last, Corporal Oughiltree, his orderly.

It was morning, he believed, for there was that fresh quality to the light.

He blinked, his eyes teary from the glare.

A ray of sun was blazing down from a high window at the far end of the long, brick-walled room in which he lay. A tobacco warehouse in another time, he figured from the smell, although now its floor was thick with cots. On each reclined a wounded soldier scarcely able to lift his head. All except Oughiltree. He was sitting upright, looking his usual chipper self—even though both his forearms were missing from the elbow, and fluids the color of tea were seeping through the bandages on his stumps. He was originally from Indiana, but Fort Sumter had caught him working on the docks of New Orleans, so—like most men when it came to war—he threw in lots with his friends. He joined the Louisiana Tigers, the "Wharf Rats," as they called themselves, and had served the brigade well.

It struck Tebault with a queer, sad feeling: this was life again.

Oughiltree's homely face was filled with wonder. "Lieutenant Tebault?" he said. "By ginger, I think he can see me!"

"I can see," Claude Tebault croaked. He began flexing his left hand, trying to work a strange tingle out of it. There was a general ache all over his head, but one spot especially seemed to be on fire. He wanted to explore it with his fingers, but the orderly stopped him.

"Don't touch now, sir—you'll go and knock your poultice off. They don't like it. That ol' sawbones, Finch, he'll give you thunder for touchin'." Oughiltree giggled shrilly as he raised his abbreviated arms. "I ain't got the problem, myself. The temptation, yes, but not the problem." Then he turned on his cot and shouted down the aisle, "Doc, come back. He's with us agin'." The orderly dropped his voice and said to Tebault: "Ol' Doc Finch's been talkin' to you, wavin' matches in your face—tryin' like the devil to bring you 'round."

"Where am I?" Tebault asked.

"Culpeper, sir . . . it don't come up to the Delta in my eyes, but dern if you'n me din't make it back alive."

From where, though? Tebault had no idea. His first solid recollection went back only as far as that torch winking on in the blackness. "Was the battle in Virginia?"

"Virginia?" Oughiltree giggled again. There was something demented and unhappy about it, as if he'd lost more than his forearms. "Great Jerusalem, sir—Marsa Robert marched us all the ways up into Maryland. We was givin' it to 'em in Sharpsburg when we ran out of steam late in the day. September seventeen. Don't you 'member, Lieutenant?"

A bit. A cornfield. "How's the company?"

Oughiltree's face grew solemn. " 'Bout the same as the brigade, sir. Just a third could walk home when the battle was done."

A disaster. The Louisiana Tigers scarcely existed, then. But Tebault was too exhausted to feel much about it. "Where's the enemy?"

"Warrenton, settlin' in for the winter."

Less than twenty-five miles to the northeast, Tebault calculated—in Fauquier, the neighboring county. McClellan was back on the soil of Virginia. "My cousin . . . is he here someplace?"

Oughiltree gazed off, then scratched his chin on the point of his shoulder.

"Corp'ral?" Tebault prodded.

"No, sir—Cap'n Philippe's still up there in Maryland. The boys crossed his hands on his breast and left him in the shade."

Tebault closed his eyes. "What happened?"

"We was pushin' across the corn with some Georgians when a shot slapped you bang on the side of the head. " 'Member that, sir?"

Tebault shrugged. Just some cornstalks lying shredded on the ground. A low smoke pressing over the rolling field. Green woods beyond.

"Well," Oughiltree went on, "you know you're a big man, sir, and I was havin' trouble with you, so Cap'n Philippe come over to help. He fetched you back to a hollow under that little white church there, then went down hisself. Same shell what got him took off my arms, so clean they din't even bleed." He gave out with that unsettling giggle again. "I could see 'em lyin' in the dirt there, like a pair of gloves I'd took off after a day's work on the wharf. No more stevedorin' for me, and I'm damn glad, if the truth could be known. I'm gonna be an idler now—and proud of it. Finch says I got a pension comin'."

A Negro set a stool beside Tebault's cot, and a few seconds later a man wearing a rubber apron sat upon it and gave out with a tired, breathy grunt. He had a grizzled beard, and his lids half-drooped over eyes inflamed by sleeplessness. "Good morning—Lieutenant Tebault, is it?"

"Claude Tebault, Sixth Louisiana."

"I'm Surgeon Major Finch."

"Sir."

"Good to hear you talking. I feared you'd lost the power of articulation. How d'you feel?"

Tebault had no idea. It was all too much—the light, the colors, the babble of voices in the ward.

"Can you move your extremities, Lieutenant?"

"I don't know."

"Try, please."

Tebault gingerly lifted his arms, then his legs.

"Good," the surgeon said. "Have you ever been rendered unconscious before?"

Tebault paused, remembering. "Yes."

"How long ago?"

"I don't know—five years, maybe."

The surgeon scooted closer on his stool and began removing the bandage that held the poultice in place. "How old were you then?"

"Seventeen."

"What happened?"

"A quarrel. It was nothing."

The surgeon smiled faintly. "Over a lady?"

"Yes," Tebault said, returning the smile. But then it faded. He couldn't recall her face. "What's wrong with me? Why am I here?"

"You've suffered a gunshot fracture of the mastoid process of the right temporal bone." The surgeon wrapped the poultice in the bandage, then dropped them to the floor. He bent close to examine the wound, his breath whistling softly in his nose. "Oh, much better," he finally said.

"Is there a ball in my head?"

"No, not now. But I removed an irregular piece of one—and four little chips of skull."

"Will there be a hole . . . ?"

"I don't think so, or at least not much of one. The opening in the cranium is being closed by a new deposit of bone. God has been kind to you, Lieutenant. Brace yourself a moment, and I'll get a better idea how it's mending." The surgeon took a mental probe from his shirt pocket.

Tebault tensed, readying himself for pain. But it was anger he felt when the probe touched his wound, a burst of rage almost indescribable in its intensity. He wanted to smash his fist into the surgeon's face, to kill the man even. But then the probe was withdrawn and the feeling vanished, leaving him awash with shame. He'd never felt hatred like that.

"Hurt . . . ?" the surgeon asked.

"Yes," Tebault lied.

"That's from the temporal muscle, not the brain itself." The surgeon turned toward a steward, who'd just appeared at the foot of the cot. "Discontinue the drops of muriated tincture of iron. But apply a fresh flax-seed poultice. Check daily to see that cicatrix over the cavity stays firm. A diet of milk and beef tea for the time being, nothing more."

"Yes, Major." The steward hurried off, and the surgeon began to rise, but Tebault held him by the tail of his apron.

"What'll come of this?"

Frowning, the surgeon eased down again. "We can never be sure, Lieutenant. But you must be wary of bodily and mental exertion. Exposure to the sun as well. I hope you're not overly fond of stimulants."

"I like my brandy."

"Avoid drink at all costs."

"But why?"

The surgeon hesitated. "This is a special wound. Those hit in the head where you've been, they must exercise a kind of moral restraint . . ."

"Sir?"

"They must guard against their own anger and fear."

"Are you saying I'll be mad?"

"I don't know. There may be times you'll think so."

"Then it'll just be a bad dream?"

"Perhaps. But I know this much for sure—you're out of the war and on your way home soon. Where's that?"

"New Orleans."

"Oh," the surgeon said with sympathy.

The city had fallen to Union General "Beast" Butler and his swaggering Ethiopian brigades that spring. There'd be no going home for Claude Tebault.

"Well," the surgeon went on, "I'm sure the good people of Virginia will offer you every kindness till Louisiana's back in the fold. Good morning, now. God bless you."

The first of these kindnesses was to move him each day, cot and all, out of the airless, overcrowded hospital and into the autumn sunshine. The trees were turning in that muted Virginian way, going to yellowish browns and dull reds, and an old slave at the mansion across the road was already burning piles of leaves. The smoke drifted over Tebault as he gazed up from his pillow. Watching it, he thought of that misty morning near Sharpsburg, his last conversation with his cousin, Philippe—which had been inauspicious, as best he could recall, the sort of things one says to anybody on any morning. There'd been no premonition.

Then, in an inward flash, he saw the face of the enemy colorbearer coming at him across the Cornfield. The man was screaming as he ran, but his eyes looked uncommonly mild, almost Christlike. All at once, his right arm suddenly jerked and his entire body spun around as he went down. Another Yankee scooped up the colors, but he was cut down too. And then Tebault must've taken his own bullet, for he could remember nothing of the battle after this.

In mid-November, when the Union army was on the march from Warrenton to Fredericksburg, Tebault moved out of the hospital and into a small room he rented from an elderly widow. Her son was serving with Mosby somewhere behind enemy lines. Mrs. McRae, as most ladies did, found favor in Tebault, his gentle manners, and took an eager hand in his recovery. He, in turn, came to adore her. He'd been raised mostly by his widowed mother and three affectionate older sisters; it was good to be in the world of women again. Soon, he was feeling much better, with most of his vigor restored.

But he was also at a loss what to do with himself for the remainder of the war. Surgeon Finch wouldn't release him for duty, insisting that his wound had left him permanently disabled.

Secretly, he had no desire to go back to the infantry—being locked shoulder-to-shoulder in a long line, sweating like a field nigger and choking on smoke, waiting helplessly to be ripped apart by minié balls and cannister. He'd set his sights on a commission with some cavalry regiment, but so far a rash of letters to the Louisiana delegation of the Confederate Congress had gotten him nowhere.

To worsen matters, his funds were dwindling with no hope of getting more from home. His mother and sisters had been turned out of their house by the Union occupiers and were destitute themselves.

On Christmas morning, he came downstairs to find three young men at the Widow McRae's kitchen table. Their mud-splattered gum coats hung on the backs of their chairs as they ate. It was all they could do to tear themselves away from their plates and stand to be introduced.

"Edmund, gentlemen," Mrs. McRae said from the stove, where she accepted a peck on the cheek from Tebault, "may I present Lieutenant Claude Tebault of the Sixth Louisiana Infantry . . ." She was quite proud of her familiarity with regiments and ranks. "Claude—my son, Lieutenant Edmund McRae, and Corporals Andy Walker and Bill Cutts, Mosby's Partisan Rangers."

"Mosby's *Regulars,* Mama," McRae said, winking at Tebault as they shook hands. Like his companions, he was a slight man, a foot shorter than Claude. He had lank blond hair parted down the middle. "The Yankees shoot *partisans* if they have the blind luck to capture one."

Tebault realized that the rangers were sneaking glances at the side of his head. He decided to tell them outright. "I was hit at Sharpsburg."

They nodded appreciatively, then sat again, their spurs lightly jangling.

Tebault took a chair. In his unease, he stared out the window. It was an overcast day with a promise of rain or snow. Suddenly, he turned to Mrs. McRae. "Is something burning?"

She came over and gave him a playful slap on the arm. "What manner of cook d'you take me for?"

"Sorry, ma'am. Didn't mean that." Tebault paused. "Your only equal as a cook is my own dear *maman.*" He'd smelled something for a moment. Strong. Maybe it'd been more like smut or mold than smoke.

"Are you soon back to your reg'ment, sir?" Walker asked, reaching across Cutts with his fork and stabbing a thick slice of ham off a platter. His face, otherwise agreeable, had been badly scarred by smallpox.

"Perhaps," Tebault said. "But I may be looking for other duty."

"Of course," McRae said with a hint of pity in his voice.

"I meant field duty, sir. I've just purchased a horse. A sturdy bay gelding."

McRae glanced to his two comrades, then said, "That's what I assumed, Lieutenant. Field duty."

They ate in silence for a while.

It slowly dawned on Tebault that he'd been brusque in the society of others, something he was sure that he'd never been before. Lately, after improving so marvelously, he was prone to bouts of irritation. Was Surgeon Finch's warning to be taken more seriously than Tebault had thought? He now sought to make amends to the rangers. "I've heard many good things about your Captain Mosby."

"Have you now?" McRae said, chewing.

"Yes. I consider him to be the only true knight of this war." Tebault realized that McRae and Walker were suppressing smiles; Cutts was pretending to stifle a yawn. "Something wrong, gentlemen?"

"No." McRae sobered. "Not at all."

Tebault asked, "Is Captain Mosby here?"

"Afraid not," McRae said. "He's in upper Fauquier, someplace, with the rest of the battalion. I'll be sure to mention your kind words to him."

"I'd prefer to do that myself."

McRae stopped chewing. "Sir?"

"I'd like you to take me to him."

McRae took a slow drink of buttermilk, then said, "For what purpose . . . if I may ask?"

"So I might enlist in your battalion." Tebault couldn't recall having come to this decision. Quite suddenly it was there in his head, settled, and he was completely satisfied that it was the most natural end to all his desires.

"But your *injury*, Lieutenant," Walker blurted.

"If I can take a Yankee ball in the head and still be sitting here—how serious can it be?"

"There's another matter," McRae said. "Your size."

"I don't understand."

"Your horse will—at the end of a hundred miles in two days."

Tebault smiled. "Then it'll be up to my horse to complain, won't it?"

McRae grinned, as did Walker and Cutts after a moment. "All right, I'll take you to the captain. But I promise nothing more than that."

"When do we leave?" Tebault asked, trying to hide his excitement.

"Now."

"So soon?" Mrs. McRae whined to her son. "Why d'you always do this?"

"So you won't get your hopes up, Mama."

By four o'clock that afternoon a steady, cold rain was falling. The three rangers and Tebault rode in an Indian file ever deeper into Fauquier County, with Edmund McRae leading on a coal-black stallion. The easy gallop of that morning had given way to a cautious walk, and now they suddenly halted in some low pines on a ridge above the glistening pike. McRae left Tebault to wait with Walker and Cutts and went on alone to find a bridle path through the Yankee vedettes. The pike was no good, he said before going—there was bound to be a Yankee picket post on it within the next few miles.

The rain fell harder. The men lowered their heads to keep the drops out of their eyes. Tebault had only the cape of his greatcoat for protection, but he didn't mind getting wet. Nor did he mind the unctuous Virginia mud that was quickly tiring the horses. His spirits were higher than they'd been in months. The freedom of the ride was exhilarating.

Cutts whispered, "Name your bay yet, Lieutenant?"

"I have," Tebault said. "Coeur de Lion."

Smiling, Cutts winked at Walker, who then pointed at Tebault's saber. "We don't sport blades, sir. Not much need for 'em, the way we fight."

Tebault didn't argue, although he had no intention of giving up his saber. It had been his father's in the Mexican War.

Hoofbeats were coming. Tebault assumed that it was McRae, but Walker and Cutts took no chances. They drew their revolvers. Tebault did the same, but tardily.

They all holstered a few seconds later when McRae trotted into the pines. "Yank cavalry," he said breathlessly, struggling to keep his voice down, "at least a squadron. They moved through here 'bout ten minutes ago, heading west."

"What we gonna do, sir?" Walker asked, his eyes bright with fear from this new threat.

Thinking, McRae dipped his head, and the front of his hat became a waterspout, soaking the stallion's mane. Tebault half-expected him to turn back. This part of Fauquier sounded awful busy for a Christmas day.

But McRae didn't sound the retreat.

Instead, he led them farther north into the county, which was fine with Tebault. Rangering was risky, for sure, but the chances were yours to take or not to take—unlike the infantry, where a whole regiment was reduced to a pawn moved by a general who was just as blind and confused as the lowliest private when the smoke rolled in like fog.

Twisting around in the saddle, he cheerfully said to Cutts, "This is very good."

The ranger shrugged that he didn't understand.

Tebault chuckled to himself. Very good indeed.

They crossed the tracks left by the enemy cavalry and broke into a trot for the next stand of covering woods.

Tebault took pleasure in the sounds of the ride: the creak of saddle leather, the splash of hooves on the flooded trail, the patter of rain against the rangers' gum coats. By now, he was drenched to the bone and his poor horse was as bedraggled as a drowned rat, but he couldn't recall a finer day for sport. He felt excitement at the prospect of a brush with the Yankees, not the dread that had filled him before a set-piece battle like Sharpsburg. Most everything about this jaunt seemed perfect, even the storm—everything except the nagging tingle in his left hand. The sensation had started while they were waiting for McRae in the pines, a kind of buzzing along the nerves. And now and again he thought he could smell smoke again—or whatever that unpleasant odor was.

He let go of the rein and shook his hand. But the feeling persisted. He slid his fingers under the saddle blanket, hoping the warmth would help.

An icy wind started blowing out of the northwest, and with that the rain turned to snow. It melted as it hit the mud, but a half hour later began to whiten the ground in earnest. McRae halted them. He murmured something about this being no time to leave a trail as plain as a pikestaff. Not with half the Federal cavalry on the prowl.

"I know a friendly place, sir," Walker volunteered.

"How far?"

"Mile. No more."

"Can they be trusted?"

"I'll swear on it," Walker said.

McRae let him take the lead.

Big, fragile flakes began spinning down. Tebault tried to catch one on the tip of his tongue—but stopped when he saw that Cutts was staring at him. Snow was still a novelty to him.

The twilight was almost gone when they rode up to a farmhouse, their hats and shoulders dusted white. The glimmer of a lamp showed through the kitchen window. Walker dismounted and went up to the stoop alone. Some long minutes passed before his knocking was answered, and then the aged man inside opened the door just enough to speak through the crack.

Walker caught McRae's eye and gestured sharply toward the barn.

The lieutenant nodded, then said to Cutts and Tebault, "Let's get out of sight, boys."

The inside of the barn smelled of rotten hay.

McRae finally decided that it was best to unsaddle their mounts— after a moment's hesitation, worrying what the delay might cost them if the Yankees suddenly appeared. Then the three men lay down in a pile of moldy straw.

Tebault realized that he was shivering.

"You may not live to see Mosby," McRae said with a halfhearted grin.

"I'm already dead," Tebault said, tapping his scar with a forefinger. "You can't be killed twice. I have that on good authority from the adjutant general."

Cutts snorted.

Walker pulled his weary horse by the bridle through the barn doors and shut them. The abrupt darkness was almost total.

"Should we light the lantern?" Tebault asked.

"Don't," said Walker. "These folks're scairt enough as is. Big Yank cavalry bivouac in the next valley over—you can smell the smoke when the wind shifts. I promised 'em we wouldn't come near the house and would be long gone before first light."

"Any chance of somethin' to eat?" Cutts asked.

They'd had nothing since breakfast at Mrs. McRae's.

"Nope," Walker said. He could be dimly seen leading his horse into a vacant stall. "They have nothin' themselves. The Yanks been usin' them for their commissary."

Walker plodded over and flopped down beside McRae, who simply said, "Sleep."

Tebault slept soundly, but awoke before the others. He had no idea what time it was; his pocket watch had vanished somewhere between Sharpsburg and Culpeper. No doubt the nigger ambulance drivers had gotten it.

Quietly, he went outside and took several muffled paces into eight inches of fresh snow. He stopped and looked up. The sky was clear and starry with the barest possible flush of dawn just beginning to show. He was very happy—strangely happy, for no reason sprang to mind. He felt as if he were free of something that had long oppressed him. No, it was more than that. He sensed that some grand purpose would soon reveal itself to him. What exactly, he couldn't say.

Then he noticed a string of mounted blue figures charging out of a belt of leafless woods and into the snowy pasture before him.

He ran back for the barn, reaching the doors just as the first carbine bullets thudded against the boards over his head.

"Yankees are coming," he said more matter-of-factly than he'd realized, for McRae sat up and asked him to repeat himself.

"Yanks." Tebault tossed the bridle over Coeur de Lion's head. "They're spreading out to hem us in."

The three rangers bolted for their horses. "Son of a damn bitch!" Walker cried when his skittish gelding pranced out of its stall and began trotting free around the inside of the barn.

"Scatter as soon as we break," McRae ordered, cinching his saddle girth with a furious yank. "Meet up again in Culpeper."

"What about Cap'n Mosby?" Cutts asked.

"I sure as hell can't lead the whole goddamn Union cavalry to him, can I now?"

Tebault mounted and rode to the doors, peered through the crack: one squadron was already at the corral gate; another was splitting up out of a column of twos to line the fences on either side of the barn. "We're bottled in," he said calmly.

"What?" McRae said, sounding more exasperated than frightened.

"I'll clear the way."

"Wait, dammit."

But Tebault had already kicked open the doors and spurred his horse into the corral. Scattered shots whistled at him from both flanks, but he crouched over the pommel and trained his Army Colt revolver on the troopers massed near the gate. He fired two quick shots. An officer stood in the stirrups, clutching his belly, and a trooper's horse went down on its knees, screaming.

"Wait!" McRae cried.

Tebault glanced behind just as McRae's arms spread out to the sides and he tumbled back over his stallion's rump and down to the snow. He immediately rose, gripping a bloody shoulder, and Cutts helped swing him back up into the saddle. But then a flurry of bullets put the ranger lieutenant down again, and he stayed down.

Growling, Tebault turned and emptied his revolver at the Yankees blocking the only gate out of the corral.

Another horse toppled.

Then he felt something jerk his right foot. He was sure that he'd been hit, but glancing down he saw that the stirrup strap had been clipped. For some reason, it made him angry—that a Yankee bullet had come that close to maiming him again.

Nearing the gate, he drew his saber. He wanted heads. He decided to take only heads. He saw blades glinting at the ends of blue coat-sleeves, but the sight did nothing to check the wide, heavy swing of his own saber at an officer who, quite absurdly, was pointing a small riding whip at him and bawling for his troopers to fire. The blade slashed into the man's neck, slowed from an impact with bone, then passed completely through on a spray of red.

In a blink, Tebault was beyond the enemy throng and out on the clean white expanse of the pasture.

His sword was bloody.

He ducked as a ball whirred close by. And then another.

Walker was dashing a little ways behind him, looking amazed, stunned. And farther back was Cutts, but he was dangling from one of his stirrups, dead, his corpse stirring up a cloud of powdery snow. His mount finally quit running.

"I'll go southeast!" Walker shouted. "You go south!"

Tebault nodded.

Walker grinned. "You keep that goddamn sword, sir! It got us outta this one!" Then he veered off.

A squad of Yankees chased Tebault all the way back into Culpeper County. But eventually they reined up, fired a meaningless parting volley, and turned back. Either their mounts didn't have Coeur de Lion's stamina or the troopers were afraid of ambush the deeper south they pushed.

Tebault rested his horse in some cedars for an hour, then continued on toward Mrs. McRae's.

He knew that he'd arrive at her house before Walker and didn't look forward to telling her about her son. But he'd do it—and remain with the old woman all through the night, as he had with his own mother when news came that his father had died in a steamboat fire while returning from business in Memphis. He knew how to help a woman grieve, what things to murmur and not to murmur, how to play silence like an instrument. He was comfortable with the sadness of women.

Suddenly, a wave of lightheadedness made him lurch and grab for the pommel with both hands. Something white-hot was flashing behind his left eye. A steamboat, loaded with cotton and turpentine, burning far out on the darkened river. It exploded with a roar, and the night was freckled with bits and pieces of fire.

Blinding agony.

When it had passed, he could taste blood in his mouth. He explored his tongue with a finger, but came away showing no color.

Then he noticed his left hand, the one that had been tingling so annoyingly since yesterday. Shock made him reel in the saddle, sending Coeur de Lion into an aimless trot—the hand was three times its normal size and puffing up larger with each breath he took. Had he been shot or slashed, and was the injured flesh swelling? No—he couldn't find a wound. Before his eyes, his hand was simply turning into a thing as shapeless and ugly as a pig's bladder.

He put his heels to the horse.

He needed to find someplace warm and safe quickly. Someone to care for him. He trusted that if he could find a woman, she would help him.

Painful lightning was coursing up and down his spine, and something was sweeping through his brain with a howl, skipping like a tornado over one region only to ravage another, dropping him into actualities as real as anything he'd ever experienced. One instant he was in Mrs. McRae's parlor, sitting across from her, telling her about her Edmund's last moments, watching her cry into a dishcloth—and the next he was somersaulting through a deep-blue twilight swirling with voices, his father's foremost, baying at the edge of drunken incomprehensibility.

A splash filled his ears and liquid cold wrapped around his waist. He found himself on his knees, squatting in a slough with thin pieces of ice floating all around him.

He slowly leaned forward, trying to catch his reflection in the rippling surface. His face was little more than a shadow, but he could tell that its left side was horribly misshapen.

He cried out, and his horse whinnied and churned past him, a chaos of spindly legs.

He staggered to his feet and then over to the nearest bank, into some willows that, despite being winter-bare, chirred with angry-sounding bugs. He held himself in his arms, resisted the spasms racking his body.

"Mon Dieu," he hissed through chattering teeth, *"mon bon Dieu!"* Then he wailed, *"M'aidez!"* But there would be no help unless he could find a woman. One as kind as his mother, as lovely as his sisters.

He spun at the slow, dry slither of a snake on dead leaves, but saw nothing but wind-driven snow, undulating over the drifts like lines of skirmishers.

A menacing hum made him stare up into the sky.

He gasped in amazement.

The heavens, so bright and blue just moments ago, were unraveling into an abyss, a maelstrom of voices, angrily sibilant, that accused him of things he couldn't quite make out. These tongues began to pull on his body like sticky ropes, and he spun along with them even though his head was about to burst with rage. Why must they accuse him so? What had he ever done to deserve such ridicule? Faster and faster his boots stamped over the snow. Rage turned his brain into molten glass. His wild pirouette lit everything—the serpentlike willows, the overhanging branches of the trees, the lightless well of the sky—into a towering plume of fire.

Sparks twisted up all around, trapping him like a rabbit in a pit.

The rage seemed now to be driving splinters into his brain. Finally, he could take no more. He screamed and dropped. As he fell, he saw something stealing up on his left side, a dark and wild blur that glided toward him like a gust of oily black smoke, wafting outward on tentacles of charred hands, then curling in on itself like a ball of snakes, and at last becoming something sadly reminiscent of a man, a fire-blackened corpse risen from the murk of the Mississippi, arms spread in grisly affection, or even a Yankee private, his death wounds still gaping with accusation.

Whatever, its approach was freezing Tebault's blood, leaving him weak and prostrated.

He fumbled for his Colt before it was too late and the thing had him—but his holster was empty. Crying out in horror as it loomed over him, he took hold of his saber.

◄ CHAPTER 11 ►

1864

SEPTEMBER 23

FRONT ROYAL, VIRGINIA

The village was full of Union cavalry. Tobacco juice was beaded in the dirt everywhere. Hundreds of cook fires smoldered among the shuttered houses and out in the damp pastures, sending up pillars of smoke that quickly blended into the heavy sky. A pig, found running loose, was shot by a half-dozen troopers with their revolvers, then left to die in the street, its legs jerking spasmodically until the final stillness came.

"Blood 'n *dee*-struction," one of them said gleefully, holstering.

Farther down the street, Simon asked a mounted corporal where he might find Custer, but the man said, his face lost in the shadow of his hat, "Hell if I know," and rode on.

Simon started to wheel after him, but then decided not to waste his time. He was more surprised than anything: horse soldiers were usually a cut above the ruck when it came to discipline.

He cantered into the village common—and suddenly reined in.

Across a throng of milling troopers he could see the roof of a brick house in flames. Cedar shingles popped loudly as they split, and smoke flecked with sparks gushed from the smashed-out windows. Dr. Lazelle stood in front of this house—his house, motionless, arms slack at his sides. He watched the fire grow with no visible emotion.

Simon spurred toward him. "Doctor . . . ?"

The practitioner slowly turned, his skin pale and wrinkled as if he'd bathed too long. "Dr. Wolfe," he finally said. "Our home . . . our *home.*"

Simon glanced around for an officer, and at last spied one perched on the lip of a water trough across the common. "Captain!" he cried. "Buckets here!"

The officer took the cigar out of his mouth and cupped a hand behind his ear just as an artillery train blocked him from view. When it had rumbled past, he was gone.

"It'll do no good, sir," Dr. Lazelle said. "No good."

Simon dismounted. "What d'you mean?"

"He's the one who smashed our lamps against the walls."

"What?"

"He dropped the matches." The practitioner started to weep, but then held his lips together and made himself stop. "The look in mother's face, Dr. Wolfe . . . our *home.*"

"Where is she?"

Dr. Lazelle pointed at a neighboring house. The curtains were pulled.

Sheridan would have Torbert's head for burning houses. At least Simon hoped that he would. But something was happening to this army, something that would've been incomprehensible to the soldiers of the first two years of this war, and there was the possibility that Little Phil—with his relentless drive to smash Jubal Early's Army of the Valley into flinders and terrorize all who might support that force—had set the tone for it. *"Why?"* he asked Dr. Lazelle, watching the flames curl around the eaves with a roar.

"Mosby, I think."

"Was he here?"

"His rangers," the practitioner said, "early this morning. They attacked your supply trains. One of his boys was hit . . . the abdomen . . . made his way to my house. I'm afraid I couldn't save him."

"If he was hit in the belly, nobody could've."

Dr. Lazelle lowered his head. "He no sooner passed than your soldiers broke in and found him on my examination table. They took me, chased out mother and . . . and left the boy in my office to burn." Grimacing, Dr. Lazelle buried his nose in a handkerchief. "Dear God, I think I can smell it."

Simon tried to ignore the smoke. It had shifted and was pouring over them, stinking of charred flesh. They moved, and a provost guard, who'd been leaning on his musket a short distance away, moved the same number of steps.

"*You* were arrested?" Simon asked. This was unbelievable.

"I'm accused of helping the partisans. Collaboration, they said."

Simon raised his voice so the guard could hear. "Medical service isn't collaboration!"

"Don't make trouble for yourself, Dr. Wolfe. It'll do no good. They're bent on vengeance." Dr. Lazelle paused. "They say Mosby's men shot one of your lieutenants after he gave up."

"Did they?"

"No."

"Are you sure?"

"My honor on it. The ranger told me as he lay dying—your man's rein was cut by a bullet. His horse bolted into our ranks. He drew his saber and was shot only then."

"What about the Dunkers?"

The practitioner looked confused. "Sir?"

"I heard that the rangers've been molesting them—God knows how. But that's what brought me here."

"Why'd—?" Dr. Lazelle cut himself himself short, then asked, "You acquainted with John Mosby?"

"No."

"Well, let me tell you—he's a man of the law. An attorney. This is our country, and he can be trusted to abide by its laws. Who'd say otherwise?"

The entire Federal Army with Father Abraham to second the motion, but that was beside the point.

A hoarse cry went up, and the troopers began swarming toward the south end of the common. Bound prisoners were being marched under escort, five men in sun-faded gray, two of them bareheaded, three in felt hats with one side pinned up. The sixth captive, several years younger than the others, was dressed in a calico shirt. A gawky stride. There was nothing military about him, not even by Confederate standards.

Simon looked for the ranger who'd spared him on the rail line: he wasn't among them, thankfully.

"No!" Dr. Lazelle exclaimed. "They've got young Henry Rhodes!"

"A ranger?"

"*Look* at him, Doctor—he's just a boy. Seventeen. I delivered him myself."

"Why's he with Mosby's men?"

"I don't know. I . . ." A bewildered shake of his white head. "The rangers came through town at dawn. He must've gotten excited and gone after them. Do something, Dr. Wolfe. I beg you!"

Simon started into the mob, but then stopped and turned. "Swear to me—the boy's innocent."

"Yes!"

Simon tried to push forward. Shoulder straps meant nothing. The troopers jostled him and one another, trying to close on the prisoners, to scream in their faces, to get near enough to throw a fist. The cords stood out on necks flushed red; teeth were bared and spittle whitened lips. Some men had drawn their Colts, and a feeling of helplessness came over Simon as he realized that there was no one to order them to holster—except himself.

"Stand back," he bawled, "put away your weapons!"

A cheer flew up, covering his words, as one of the rangers was booted in the backside.

Then the press of bodies gripped Simon, and he could go no farther. Six inches taller than most of the troopers, he gazed over their caps at the file of Rebels. Haggard, sweat-streaked faces. The boy was the worst off; his head was hanging between his thin shoulders, and he was sobbing. These weren't murderers. Simon could see it at once. They were ordinary men waiting for someone, anyone, to step in and save them. A ranger with smallpox scars had grown sick of his own fear and was now spitting at the Yankees.

Simon realized that he was being squeezed against a sergeant major's back. "Sarn't major!"

The man turned a bulging eye. "Sir?"

"Stop this!"

"Stop what, sir?"

"This lynching!"

"Order for execution's been approved."

"By whom?"

"General Merritt."

Division level. Not a good sign. "Who requested it?"

"Brigadier Custer."

Suddenly a gang of troopers fell upon two of the prisoners and dragged them, kicking and clawing, away from the common and into the yard behind the Methodist Church. Most of the men stampeded that way, flattening the picket fence around the graveyard and streaming among the monuments. Simon was swept along with them, but then saw a corporal make the captives to kneel before him. Simon began flailing his arm to get away. He didn't want to see. It would stay with him forever, like the Cornfield, like the ambulance ride away from Sharpsburg.

But too late.

The corporal thumb-cocked his Colt, a nervous hatred making his eyes small. Two quick blasts, a mist of blood and smoke, and the rangers flopped down out of sight. Other revolvers joined in, pumping bullet after bullet into the corpses.

"Bastards!" Simon cried, "I saw. I *saw!*"

"What'd you see, Colonel?" a trooper demanded.

Simon shoved him aside and plowed back the way he'd come.

Dr. Lazelle stood where he'd left him, clinging to Naomi by the bridle. His face was blanched, his lips the color of oyster shells—he too had seen. "God in heaven," the old man whispered, "are these Christian men?"

His guard had been carried off by the excitement and was nowhere to be seen.

"Come with me," Simon said, taking the rein and starting north on foot, away from the square.

The practitioner followed, huffing for breath, mopping his face with his handkerchief. "How can these men be Christians?"

Simon looked back: the surviving captives were being herded in this direction. Must keep ahead of them.

A provost guard was walking post at the junction with the Strasburg pike.

"Headquarters!" Simon demanded. He was shouting. Control yourself. Can't shout at Custer. Sheridan's fair-haired boy.

"Colonel?"

"Where are brigade headquarters?"

"Sir, the wagon yard."

"I know where," Dr. Lazelle said, panting. "Toward the river." Then he almost wailed, "Is this war? How can this be war, Dr. Wolfe?"

It was. Philip Sheridan and his boys were reinventing it. But Simon said nothing as he hurried on.

He saw Custer's red and blue swallow-tailed banner, and asked Dr. Lazelle to stay back from the spacious tent with Naomi. Out of earshot.

Two hunting dogs scampered out of the parting in the flaps and nipped at Simon's trouser cuffs. An aide called them off. "May I help you, sir?"

"Colonel Wolfe to pay his compliments to General Custer."

"The general's given orders that no one—"

"Let him come," a listless voice said from inside the tent.

Simon entered. Custer was slumping at a field desk. He didn't return Simon's salute. In his large, bony hands was a slip of paper. The execution order? A candle lantern had been lit against the gloom, and the man's eyes were glistening, his nostrils moist.

Simon realized with a mild shock that the brigadier had been weeping. Slow down. Don't accuse. Remorse might be taking hold here. But his heart was hammering.

Custer spoke first—with disarming kindness. "It's always a pleasure to see you, Simon."

"Thank you, General." A cautious pause. "Are you well?"

"Passing well . . . passing well." And then he hid his eyes behind a hand, his shoulders racked. "Thank God you've come."

Simon stared down at him, stupefied.

Custer sat up, snuffled loudly, and gave Simon the paper.

He glanced at the writing: a woman's hand. *My Dearest Husband,* it began. Simon hesitated. "You sure you want me to read this, sir?" Custer nodded.

Simon scanned, expecting the news of a death in the family. But nothing even close to that. He read it more carefully, and the only thing he saw that even remotely justified Custer's reaction was the final paragraph: *I must now confess, Autie, that that terrible day in Monroe lives on in my memory. It consumes me with fear, loathing even, and I must beg for your reassurance that it shall never be repeated.*

Simon handed back the letter. Custer had finally collected himself enough to be embarrassed. "I'm not sure I understand, sir."

"I was drunk that afternoon . . ." Custer's voice broke, ending a brief, awkward smile.

"Yes?" Simon thought of the captives and his heart raced again. But he struggled to look attentive.

"And now it turns out she saw me. I never knew. Till now, Simon. I was walking from a friend's back to my sister's home." Then he added with a self-detesting growl, "Fairly *staggering,* I'll admit. Staggering past Libbie Bacon's window." He glowered up at Simon in sudden wonder. "Then why'd she consent to marry me?"

Simon didn't know what to say.

"It was the last day I ever drank spirits," Custer went on, snuffling again, "for I made the pledge to my sister the very next morning. Not a drop since. Not a drop. But I never knew that Libbie . . . my God, what a humiliating courtship . . . I . . ." He suddenly pressed his fist against his lips as if something disastrous had just occurred to him. "Simon, tell me—is this the cause of her . . . discomfort?"

"I don't—"

"God let me rot in hell if it is!"

A gunshot to the south. Simon flinched. "General, your troopers are murdering their prisoners. Two were just shot to death in a churchyard. These are prisoners of war, sir."

"Oh no." Custer's wet blue eyes slowly hardened. "They're partisans, Simon. Rabble. Last year, they gunned down one of my poor orderlies. Stripped everything off him but his trousers."

"Sir, just this morning a major of cavalry assured me that Mosby's men are duly enlisted as the Forty-third Virginia Battalion."

"One of our majors?"

"Of course, sir."

"He was wrong," Custer said coldly. His transformation of the last few seconds was jarring. "There's no such unit in the Army of Northern Virginia. You may ask your father, if you enjoy the occasion."

Simon ignored the insinuation, even though it angered him. He knew at last that there was no hope for the three surviving rangers. Save the boy. Save Henry Rhodes from his stupid dream of glory. Do whatever you must. A short silence, then he calmly said, "May I venture an opinion in regards to your wife's condition, sir?"

Custer's face brightened at once. "Why, yes . . . *please.*"

"It's likely an intelligent young woman of good breeding—"

"Yes, that's Libbie."

"—might show her distress over your drinking in some unexpected morbidity. An influence of the mind upon the body."

"All right, all right, all right," Custer rattled, "but what's the cure, Simon?"

"I believe she's already recommended it."

"Has she?"

"Your pledge. You made it to your sister, yes?"

"Quite."

"And I trust that you've kept it?"

"To the letter. Not a drop."

"Then make the same vow to your bride."

Custer rubbed a knuckle over his sun-skinned nose, then asked, "In person?"

"What?"

"Should I ask Phil for a leave of absence?"

Simon thought for an instant that he was joking. They were in the middle of a campaign. One that might yet be lost, for why wasn't Custer's brigade up the Luray Valley, helping spring the trap on Early's retreating forces? "I'm sure a letter will do, if it's heartfelt."

"It shall be!" Custer seized his pen and dipped it in his inkhorn. In a blink he seemed to have forgotten Simon.

"Sir—"

"Yes, yes."

"There's a boy from this village among your prisoners . . ." Simon waited for Custer to lift his pen from the paper. "Henry Rhodes, his name. He's no partisan. And I have that on good authority."

Custer frowned and went back to writing.

"General, at the very least, can his execution be stayed until the fact's proved to your satisfaction?"

"Very well, if you insist."

"What about a written order to that effect?"

"Unnecessary. Simply tell my A.D.C. that young Rhodes is to be spared for the time being."

Simon hesitated, but then withdrew. Outside, he couldn't find the aide.

"He just rode off," Dr. Lazelle explained. And a few minutes before, a detail of soldiers had marched two of the rangers past Custer's tent and into the wagon yard.

"Was Rhodes one of them?" Simon asked.

"Dr. Wolfe, please—Henry's *not* a ranger."

Simon was sure that, if they had not made it this far, Rhodes and the unaccounted ranger were dead. But he got back in the saddle and started toward the village.

Dr. Lazelle caught up, wheezing. "What'd your general say?"

"He'll stay Rhodes's execution for now."

"But I heard a shot a while ago."

"So'd I."

Simon noticed a fat Negro boy clinging to a tree limb that arched over the road, and Dr. Lazelle called him down. He boasted that he'd seen everything: a ranger dragged off toward Perry Criser's farm and Henry Rhodes taken up the lane to Rose Hill. The shot had came from the direction of Criser's.

"You sure, boy?" Dr. Lazelle asked.

He was sure.

Dr. Lazelle swiftly decided that Simon should ride to Rose Hill without delay. He would follow on foot. Simon waited only long enough for directions, then put Naomi into a gallop.

At least the troopers were admitting their shame by how they were dealing with the captives: herding them away from public view.

He overtook a woman on the lane. She had pulled up her hoop skirts and was running as best as she could. "Madam?"

A bruising look, then she turned her face.

"Are you Mrs. Rhodes?"

Her disdain turned to pleading. "Yes!"

"Where's Henry?"

She pointed up the lane toward the house at its end.

"I have orders to stay his death!"

"Hurry!" She stumbled and collapsed to her knees, yet she urged Simon on by clasping her hands together from the ground.

He charged ahead into the yard. A dozen troopers stood around Rhodes, taunting him because he was crying. He suddenly fainted, and they grabbed him by the shirt, held him upright until he came around again.

Simon glanced at sleeves for two or more stripes, but there were no noncommissioned officers among them.

"Brigadier Custer's orders—no harm's to come to this boy. Unhand him." They swore at him, called him a son of a bitch, and he stiffened. "If you murder him," he said gravely, "there will be witnesses. More than I." He gestured at an upper-story window of the house, where a woman's face had appeared.

A trooper unholstered his Colt.

A shriek turned Simon around: Mrs. Rhodes had come into the yard, and behind her Dr. Lazelle was lumbering up the lane.

Mrs. Rhodes tried to embrace Henry, who moaned at her brief touch, but a trooper held her at bay with his saber. "Should I take off their heads?" he asked around, not joking.

"Do it, and I'll see a rope around your neck," Simon said, dismounting. He'd found them at last. Men capable of butchering Dunkers. And then a spark went off behind his eyes: the dead ranger had been left in a house to burn. Like the woman south of Winchester. "You," Simon told the trooper with the drawn saber, "are under arrest . . ." He was about to order him to throw down his weapon when something metallic tapped against the back of his skull. The muzzle of a revolver, he knew without turning.

"Bad day to jerk on my bit, Surgeon," a whiskey breath said in his ear.

Dr. Lazelle was repeating, "Dear God, dear God in heaven," but Simon could barely hear him. The trooper's voice had convinced him that he was going to die, and filling his head was a sound like cicadas shrilling. Suddenly so weary. He closed his eyes. The revolver snicked as it was cocked. Faint curiosity: would a gash of light rip through his brain along the track of the bullet? He could see Leah at the far end of a shadow that seemed to compress his imagination into a tunnel, the Leah of his youth trying to comfort him after he'd run up against their father again. Leah, the peacemaker. Leah—

The shot came. Three more. There was no pain, as expected. And no darkness.

Then there was band music on the humid breeze.

Simon opened his eyes.

The troopers were running for their mounts, which they'd tethered to a fence. One man kicked down the rails, and they rode through the gap into the pasture and disappeared into the trees beyond. Faces. Simon tried to sear the faces into his memory, but it was no good: they were already blurring together into the face of an entire army. Sunken blue eyes and drooping mustaches. Long, thin Anglo-Saxon noses.

Dr. Lazelle was crouching over Henry Rhodes, murmuring encouragement to the boy, who lay perfectly still on his back, arms outstretched, chest bloodied in three patches. Mrs. Rhodes had passed out.

Simon realized that he himself had sunk to his knees. He crawled to the practitioner's side.

"I think there's a pulse," Dr. Lazelle said with a kind of giddy hope. Simon felt the carotid. Nothing. The old man had mistaken his own wild pulse for the boy's. "Find it, Dr. Wolfe?"

"He's gone," Simon said, then looked at Dr. Lazelle more closely. Minutes before, his face had been blushed and running with sweat, but now it was clammy-looking, and his lips were a deep, sickly blue. "How're you feeling, sir?"

Dr. Lazelle ignored the question. The band could be heard thumping and woofing in approach, and he gazed down the lane with an odd smile. It didn't appear right away, and the smile faded as he said, "Let's see to Mrs. Rhodes." He rose dizzily and, halfway to the woman, suddenly cradled his left arm in his right. "My dear God," he gasped, then retched.

Simon rushed to catch him, help him to the ground. Grimace of horrible pain. "Breathe deeply in spite of it," he urged.

Dr. Lazelle cried out, then his eyes clouded. Simon slapped him. He roused and grimaced again.

Slippers drummed down the wooden steps from the veranda, and the woman who'd shown herself in the high window knelt beside Simon with a rustle of crinoline. "What do you need?" she asked.

"Some salts, quickly."

She ducked back into the house, and Simon held the old man's gaze to make him feel less alone. Smiling, he said, "Looks like you'll be bedfast for a while." Then he realized from the man's easier breathing that the episode was almost over. He'd come through the worst of it. "Better, my friend?"

Dr. Lazelle nodded, then tenderly grasped Simon's hand, his lips moving.

"Don't try to speak."

The mounted band broke into view. Custer's cavalcade, led by the brigadier himself. Simon recognized the tune, "Love Not, The One You Love May Die," and studied Custer's face, looking for a hint of the savage irony that would have called for it—of all songs—to be played. There was none. Custer looked happy and graceful and self-possessed on his charger, fully restored from his depression of less than an hour ago.

"Simon," he said lightly, "what's happening here?"

"Your troopers just shot Henry Rhodes."

Custer glared back at him, then threw the rein over his horse's head and waited for an aide to take them. "Well, I've learned since our talk that he was indeed one of Mosby's men. Sorry." For the first time he seemed to notice Mrs. Rhodes. She had stirred and crept wide-eyed over to her son's corpse as if fearful of waking him. Simon waited for her to scream, the lull was like that between lightning and thunder.

Custer started to speak, but then his eyes misted. "The poor mother?" he asked.

Simon gave a wooden nod. Nothing solid or sharp left inside himself. Just pith.

Custer jumped out of the saddle. "Who let her see this!" he shouted at his staff.

The officers looked sideways at one another, or stared off at the Blue Ridge. They'd obviously played this before.

Custer swept Mrs. Rhodes up in his powerful arms just as she keened and began sobbing. "Now, now," he cooed and carried her up the steps and past the woman of the house, who was rushing out the front door with smelling salts and a tumbler of water for Dr. Lazelle. "The parlor," she said to Custer. He dipped his head respectfully.

The salts were no longer needed, but the practitioner took a long draught of water. "I'd like to sit up."

"In a moment," Simon said firmly.

Cows were filing out of the gap in the fence, hooves thudding around Henry Rhodes's corpse, barely missing the outspread arms.

Custer bounded back outside and shooed the cattle away with his hat, then glanced down at Dr. Lazelle. "Has he been shot too?"

"No," Simon said, rising. "His heart."

"Weak?"

"It couldn't stand up to witnessing murder."

Custer looked surprised. "You're serious."

Simon just stared.

"Surgeon Major!" Custer bellowed, and the brigade medical officer dismounted and strode over. "Major, see to this gentleman's care. Nothing less than a full recovery."

"Yes, sir."

Then Custer took Simon's arm and drew him aside. Eyes mischievously bright. "Finished it."

Simon stole a look at Custer's scabbard. It held a sword, not a saber. And Chlora Hostedler had died by saber. Yet, the Dunker woman in the burning kitchen had probably been stabbed with a knife. His head was spinning. "Sir?"

"The letter to Libbie." He handed Simon an envelope, then slipped the rein from a captain and swung up onto his horse. "Come along, I'd like you to read it. See if it does the job." He took off down the lane, but halted after a few yards to wait for Simon with an impatient grin. "Got to hurry, Simon—time to get back up the Luray."

Simon silently shook hands with Dr. Lazelle, who tried to reassure him with a faint wink, then he caught up with Custer.

Apparently, something had gone wrong with the endgame to Little Phil's plan. "Torbert isn't behind Early?" Simon asked.

"Afraid not," Custer said. "Leastways not yet. Had some trouble yesterday, so we're going to try again this afternoon." He grinned once more. "Don't worry, Simon—Jube's still going to find out there's a God in Israel."

Simon gazed south, where the sky seemed a shade darker. By now Early's fleeing army must be farther up the Shenandoah Valley than New Market Gap, where Sheridan had ordered Torbert's cavalry to cross over from the Luray Valley on this side of the Massanutten and cut off the Rebels' escape. Crook's march on Little North Mountain yesterday, the charge against cannister, had decided nothing. The battle would go on. Repeated on some other ridge, along some other creek. The war was deathless. This generation would pass it on to the next, like a biblical curse. He wanted to lie down in a place dark and hidden, and sleep for a long, long time.

"What d'you think?" Custer asked. His staff was closing on Simon and him, but he backed them off with a glare. The band was bringing up the rear, tooting out "Yankee Doodle."

Simon had opened the envelope and been holding the letter with the rein for some minutes. "I'm sorry, I—"

"Please, Simon—*read.*"

He read. Florid drivel. Phrases popped out at the eye like chrysanthemums, but any meaning . . . Simon glanced up. "What happened to the last two rangers?" He already knew without asking that the man taken up to Criser's Farm had been shot dead.

Custer frowned. "Being interrogated at the wagon yard. If they tell us where Mosby's hiding, I'll spare them. Go on, man."

"I'm finished." Simon gave back the letter and said without conviction, "It'll do nicely."

"But does it seem sincere?"

"Yes."

Custer beamed. "It is, isn't it? Utterly." He took a deep breath and looked around with intense satisfaction as they turned onto the main road. "All right, all right, all right," he muttered happily, letting out the breath. "On with it then."

The morning rain had left behind a warm, clinging haze. A view of the river came and went like a mirage. They trotted into the wagon yard, where the rutted and hoof-churned ground steamed.

Two figures in gray were hanging from a walnut tree at its edge, heads drooping.

"Ah, yes," Custer said, not slowing, "commendable. Brave fellows, despite it all. How very sad. But I mean to return evil for evil till these scoundrels quit their depredations." Then he half-twisted in the saddle to smile at Simon. "Well, a clean shirt and I'm off up the Luray. Care to tag along?"

"No, thank you," Simon said, almost whispering.

"Are you sure? It'll be fine fun, Simon."

"I'm sure." Simon peeled off from the cavalcade and started northeast alone, feeling as if he were falling from a tremendous height and had just dropped far enough to accept what awaited him at the bottom. No explicable solution. Just a swift nothingness to end his puzzlement. In seeing how the rangers and young Henry Rhodes had died, he may have glimpsed the way of all the murders, which might not be the work of one man, or two, or even a dozen. The whole thing might not be laid intrinsically to men, but to a contagion that suddenly had seized them on campaign, like camp dysentery or any other disease. And like dysentery, it would spread, run its course, then vanish, the contagion as mysterious as ever.

"Simon!" Custer called after him. "Where are you headed? What's wrong!"

≺ Chapter 12 ≻

9:51 A.M., September 24

Winchester

Callender Ames lowered himself onto the stool Simon had set beside his field desk. A stool instead of a chair to discourage lingering. "Morning, Cal," Simon murmured, leafing red-eyed through the pile of reports left during his four-day absence by Nevins, his statistical officer. Lots of Confederate inmates. The hidden price of overrunning the enemy. No civilian casualties had been reported, other than the Dunker woman in the house south of town, and Simon himself had recorded that for Sheridan's eyes only. In obedience to Little Phil's orders that Washington remain in the dark for the time being.

"You look like holy hell," Ames said between sips of coffee. "Smile some, will you?"

"I am."

"D'you honestly fancy so? Your mouth looks like a wagon track in a cow patty."

"How gracious."

"Your eyes like a couple of day-old navels. Get any sleep at all this trip?"

"Not much," Simon said, rubbing his face with his hand. The skin was prickly with sunburn. "You find me a site?"

"Maybe. Shawnee Spring just outside town. I'll take you out later for a look." Ames paused. "Not easy to find one spot for four thousand beds, Simon." He looked off into a corner of the room; not quite himself today, Simon finally realized—he'd been too busy putting up his own front of quiet determination to notice.

"Something wrong, Cal?"

"Wrong?" Ames said. "I was about to ask you the same. You looked like death warmed over when you dragged in last night."

Ames and he had rubbed elbows too long to hide their moods from each other. But no, things weren't as hopelessly muddled as they'd seemed to him on the ride in from Front Royal yesterday. Upon awakening this morning, Simon had reminded himself that everything would be settled soon. Elias Deering would come back to Winchester, Rebekka would see him from a safe distance, and that'd be that. Meanwhile, Simon would bury himself in his old reliable sedative. Work.

Yet, there was a new fly in the ointment: the strange look in Custer's face when he admitted that he'd had a humiliating courtship, the effect his wife's abdominal distress was having on him. And then there'd been that peculiar moment during the Winchester victory supper when the young brigadier and Little Phil communed rapturously over the late General Kearny's observation that war was like having a woman. Based on his own limited experience, in which only genuine affection had led to sex, Simon saw no similarity—at least none he would ever want to claim for himself.

But even if he were so disposed, he couldn't ask Sheridan to have Custer questioned—not after that public disaster involving Deering.

"Oh," Ames said, "that boy from the provost you wanted me to order in for an eye examination . . ."

"Yes, Woodworth—did you do it?"

"Of course. But he's missing."

A sinking feeling came over Simon. "How can that be?"

"Don't ask me. But his company commander presumes it was Mosby's work. Scooped up Woodworth's whole picket post the night of the twenty-second." Ames paused. "Care to tell me what it's all about?"

"Later, Cal."

"What was this boy, the eyes of the entire army?"

"In a way, yes." Simon shook his head. Woodworth might even be dead. Damn. Now it would come down to the word of a Dunker woman who was still in emotional shock. He started to pick up his ink well, wanting to toss it against the wall, but caught himself just in time. "The devil can take this war!"

"Damn straight. Never met a nigger worth tramping all over Virginia for. Especially at the height of summer."

"You don't mean that," Simon said—but without reproach. He was too tired to argue.

"I'm just saying I never was one for politics."

"Neither was I when I first came north," Simon said after a moment. "Scared to death somebody'd ask me if my family owned slaves. Just wanted to learn to heal, to be a good surgeon . . . to be useful . . ." He suddenly thought of the standard line he'd penned so often in a disability report so some poor bastard could get a pension: *His wound is so severe and disfiguring he will ever be an object of pity, and unable to gain a living, except in seclusion from society.* It applied to Simon Wolfe as well now—didn't it really?

"It was a good life, Cal. Esther and her folks on Friday evening for supper. You for a milk punch on Saturday night. The hospital, my work."

Simon realized that he'd sounded despondent when Ames asked with care, "What *will* you do when it's over?"

This was Ames's first admission that he felt the end was in sight. Maybe it truly was, no matter how interminable the war had seemed yesterday with Custer murdering his prisoners. Lee was bottled up at Petersburg, and Early was licking his wounds far up the Valley. Heartening to think about. Peace. But really, Ames's point was well-taken— what could a one-winged surgeon do? More than enough whole ones would flood back into civilian practice, and the Regular Army wouldn't keep on any brevet colonels who'd come out of the Volunteers and never taken to calcified military ways.

Simon tried not to sound overly hopeful as he said, "Maybe Holmes can use me at Harvard."

"Yes, that's it—lecturing," Ames said too quickly. "I'm sure Oliver'll take you in a minute. He thinks you're the second smartest son of a bitch in the universe." He paused again. Waiting his turn.

"All right," Simon said, "now tell me what's got a twist on you."

"Mrs. Zelter."

"Mrs. Zelter," Simon echoed, a little surprised. "What's wrong?"

"Dementia."

Simon sat erect. "Chronic, you mean?"

Ames nodded, then averted his eyes, apparently still uncomfortable talking about mental disorders with Simon.

Months ago, during a quiet moment, Simon had told Ames the real reason he'd gone into the special hospital in Philadelphia after Chancellorsville. A severe depression that may or may not have had something to do with a transitory paralysis of his remaining arm. It'd been a test of his recovery, he felt: to be able to discuss his case with someone other than the physicians at Turner's Lane Hospital. But there was a risk to that. Even the most sympathetic fellow officer would probably see the reason for such a convalescence as a loss of manly comportment, proof that an amputation did indeed take away mettle as well as flesh and bone.

Rebekka. Simon turned his thoughts back to her. Coming in late last night, he'd found her withdrawn but apparently pleased to see him, almost affectionate. He had been heartened enough to believe that she was coming out of her low spirits. "How d'you know it's dementia?"

"Well, I should've seen right off. A general malformation of skull shape—"

"What has she *done?*" Simon interrupted, before Ames got into phrenology. Bump witching. "She seems reasonably normal to me—given her circumstances."

"And she is again. But you should've seen her before."

"Starting when?"

"As soon as you left. She turned quite melancholy."

"That's all?"

"Dear Jesus, no." Ames locked his fingers around his cup. This really had upset him. "One afternoon I saw her rush from the hospital. I followed her out. She was standing in the middle of the street, watching the troops come and go as if her life depended on it. I asked the poor dear what she was doing, and she said she didn't want to miss him."

"Miss whom?"

"I thought you, maybe. But she wouldn't tell me. Her head kept lurching as we talked. Devilishly strange."

"Twitching?"

"No, more like a hand shoving the back of her head."

"Did she try to explain it?" Simon asked.

"Not then. But next evening I had the shock of my life. Otis was in a state, all but dragged me down to the embalmer's tent. There, I found her . . ." Ames paused. ". . . lying naked among the corpses." Simon said nothing for a while. "Did you ask her why?"

"She said sometimes she feels fingers digging into the back of her neck, pushing her along. She said these invisible fingers made her go down to the dead. Where she belonged. Well, I said, 'Dear child, you're too young to think about dying.' Know what she came back with?"

Simon slowly shook his head. Dammit—one murderous bastard was causing all this. He was sure of it again. Hearing of her suffering convinced him.

"She claimed she was forty years old," Ames said. "What the hell is she? All of twenty-four?"

"If that."

"Finally I got her to admit she wasn't forty. 'Why would you want to be forty, child?' You should've heard her, Simon. She sounded so pitiful when she told me that forty's better because it's closer to death." Ames sighed. "So young, so pretty—and self-slaughterous."

Another silence hung in the small room, broken only when a man's sobbing drifted in from one of the wards. Simon said at last, "I think I'll have Otis move my desk out into the main ward. More accessible, wouldn't you say?"

"You might get an earful out there."

"How's that?"

"Staff's wondering why you've taken Mrs. Zelter in. I told them it's none of their goddamned business. The medical director can take in Mrs. Jefferson Davis, if he wants."

For all his bluster, Cal was too kindhearted to be caught in the middle of something like this. Maybe that's why Simon had held off telling him. But now it was time for Ames, his only ally against the gossips in the hospital, to learn enough to justify his loyalty.

"I suppose I expected her to . . ." Simon didn't know how to finish. Expected her to what? Accept murder as the usual fare of Union occupation? "There was no time to explain before I left for Fisher's Hill, Cal, but somebody's killing Dunkers."

"Oh damn," Ames said. "Our boys?"

"I think so."

"Just in cold blood?"

"Yes. First a woman outside town here. Stabbed in the abdomen. No doubt she was known to Mrs. Zelter. Related, even. I don't know how, or much of anything else. She still can't talk about it."

"Pathetic," Ames said.

"I found two more. A Dunker couple on a farm near Front Royal. The husband shot, the wife stabbed. And there will be others . . ." Simon thought to go into his suspicion of Deering, but then turned against the idea. He might have confided in Ames about the provost marshal had he not seen Custer yesterday. Best to keep everything to himself for the time being. Rebekka would end all speculation with a glance *and* a spontaneous reaction. He would trust her reaction more than her words. Deering or Custer—her face would tell which, if either. But what if Custer stayed out in the field for weeks? It happened with the cavalry.

"I see then, Simon." Ames had come to his feet. "She'll come around again. What if it's from a single bad jolt."

"I think so, Cal. This kind of dementia usually passes, given a little time and sympathy."

"I'll let you get back to work." Ames gripped Simon's armless shoulder. "Be careful, boy. I don't like the sounds of this one bit." Then he limped out the door.

Simon sighed and took the next report off the stack, but over the next five minutes couldn't keep his mind on the figures. Nor could he sit still. He got up and went out to the loading dock for some air.

A fine autumn morning. Clear light, but not dazzling. A few swift white chunks of cloud, iridescent around the fringes. Pamunkey was stooped over a wooden tub near the well, washing dozens of surgical knives and saws. He glanced up, nodded somberly, then went back to work. Simon focused on the deft brown hands, loosening the dried blood and gore in the pinkish water. Then, for a split second, he saw a heavy, engraved sword in Pamunkey's hands instead of a knife. And he knew with a dull, tired feeling that he wouldn't be able to concentrate on his duties until this was settled.

"Christ," he said, turning back for his room.

Chlora Hostedler's wounds had been incised. A saber, then. The woman's in the burning kitchen hadn't been. A sword, maybe. And Custer had just ridden through the area that night, his own admission. He wore a sword, not a saber. Mustn't fixate on Deering.

Perhaps there was a way to question the boy general with Sheridan being none the wiser. And a mute might do it best.

He sat again at his desk and scrawled out a note to Custer, apologizing for his curt departure from Front Royal, blaming it on fatigue. It was still awkward to write left-handed. He restated his belief that the vow of abstinence would ease Mrs. Custer's distress. Best wishes and all that. Simon sealed the envelope and hurried back out to Pamunkey. He motioned for the orderly to walk with him away from the grooms. "You know General Custer, don't you?"

Pamunkey dipped his head—as expected. In the Peninsula Campaign, Custer had been an aide to McClellan, and Pamunkey had served as one of Allan Pinkerton's scouts on the same staff.

"I want you to take this to him."

Pamunkey stuffed the envelope down the front of his uniform blouse.

"He's somewhere up the Luray Valley. Twenty or thirty miles from here, at least. Take what time you need. Don't push your mount." Simon paused. "It's bound to be more interesting than cleaning up for the surgeons."

The patient, watchful Indian eyes flickered agreement.

"Find Custer. Deliver my message. Then stay with him for a day or two. No need to explain to him. He'll think you're just resting your horse."

A questioning smile.

"It may come to nothing, but I want to know if he washes his sword during the time you're with him. If he does, find out how he blooded it. Against the enemy? Or somebody else?" Simon forced a smile. "Like working for Pinkerton again, what?"

A faint nod. Lost his tongue for no less.

For a second, Simon felt that he was no better than Sheridan, risking human life so that he might get a "decent view" of things. "It's for me, Otis, not the Army, so this isn't an order. It could be dangerous. One never knows. I'm leaving it up to you." He paused. "D'you still want to go?"

A more vigorous nod.

"Good. Well, be off then. And keep safe."

Pamunkey trotted toward the horse-line, and Simon went back into the hospital. Mother Haggerty was waiting for him inside his room, stone-faced. In no mood for the usual complaints, he felt his defenses tighten. "Madam."

"The colonel don't look well."

"So I've already been told by the poet laureate of our little band." Simon sat. "Anything else?"

"About Mrs. Zelter . . ." The matron's breath smelled of tobacco. "She's—"

"After all this woman's suffered," Simon cut her short, "we can forgive her a quirk or two. As we forgive any other casualty of war for not quite being himself."

"Agreed, sir," Mother Haggerty said huffily, "but it's her care of the child that bothers me."

"In what way?"

"Well, she either clings to him or ignores him like visitin' kin she wants out of the house. Nothin' in between. I try to remind her of her motherly duties and she spouts holy verse at me like thunder and blazes . . ."

Simon was staring toward the door frame when Rebekka suddenly stepped into view. Behind Mother Haggerty's back. The matron started to go on about Hannes, but Simon cut her short by coming to his feet. She turned and noticed Rebekka, then frowned at Simon as she excused herself, and went out.

"Hello, Simon Wolfe," Rebekka said.

"Hello."

Dark circles under her eyes. And the eyes themselves were spiritless. But then she gave him a relieved smile. "You're back."

"Yes, I'm back."

Her smile died in sudden panic. "And you're angry."

"Angry?"

"About Hannes."

He felt peeved at Mother Haggerty for talking so carelessly with the door open, but then he realized that Rebekka meant something else.

"He woke you last night," she went on.

"No, I woke him. When I struck a match for the lamp."

"They told me to put him in your bed."

"I know."

She smiled again, but tentatively. "It was nice to find you holding him."

"Nice to hold him." And it had been. The warm, sleepy baby's head nestled against his neck as he paced the floor. Maybe that's why he'd gotten up this morning less despairing. "Where's Hannes now?"

"Outside with some soldiers. The sunlight."

"It'll be good for him."

"But I prefer a small room," she said with extreme pointedness. "Like this one. They can't all fit in a little room."

Simon studied her, wondering what she meant, but then saw that his staring was making her uncomfortable. She'd begun to wring her hands in the duck cotton apron the staff had given her.

"Will you a take a stroll with me?" he asked.

She blushed, and he was thinking that he'd suggested something unseemly when she said, "I'd like that, Simon Wolfe."

Smiling, he gestured toward the door. "Come."

Two troopers were giving Hannes a ride on a draft horse. One man, with a facial wound, held the child up on the broad, lurching back, while his comrade used his unbandaged left hand to lead the animal by the bridle round and round the well.

Hannes noticed his mother, but didn't whimper for her to take him. And she looked back at him without expression.

"They're not all bad," Simon said, watching her closely. "These soldiers."

"No," she said, but then her head rocked forward slightly and she started down Amherst Street toward the center of town, lips pressed together and clenching her skirt in her fists.

Simon caught up with her, but didn't know quite what to say.

She pointed at his boots. "Your feet hurt, Simon Wolfe."

"They do. Lot of marching this week. Not used to it."

"Do you want to go back?"

"No," he said.

"I like to walk."

"I too."

"It quiets the head," she added.

"Rebekka . . . ?"

She avoided his eyes.

"Rebekka, are you feeling the fingers on your neck right now?"

She abruptly stopped at Loudon Street, the pike, and visibly strained against some force that made her stutter-step a few feet more.

"Yes," she said with fear in her eyes, "they won't just leave me alone sometimes."

"Who are they?"

Her lips tightened.

"Can you see them, Rebekka?"

A wrenching headshake, as if upset with him for asking.

"All right . . . we won't talk about that." This was more than he'd bargained for: it went far beyond melancholy. Perhaps Ames was right about her dementia being chronic, although Simon had stronger doubts that it wasn't. He set off south if only because the warmth of the sun drew him that way. But he soon realized that he was alone; he'd left her at the corner.

"What is it, woman . . . ?"

Then it came to him. South on the pike led to the ruin of the farm where he'd found her.

She stood grinding a heel into the pavement.

"You want to go another way?"

"Please," she begged as if her life depended on it.

They walked east through town, and then out along Senseney Road and into some low, wooded hills.

She blinked fitfully whenever they burst from leafy shadow into sunlight, but gradually her stride became less urgent and a tenderness played over her face. The tenderness he'd glimpsed last night as she had taken Hannes from him. They didn't speak at length. So long Simon finally felt moved to say something. He cleared his throat, startling her. "I once saw a Dunker church in Maryland—"

"Where was this?" Sharply. She was still fighting something inward.

"Near Sharpsburg. I wondered about it at the time—you know, a church with no steeple."

"It'd be prideful to build a steeple."

"Why's that?"

"To poke it in the eyes of God?"

"I see." What then would she have thought of the Second Temple?

"And you mustn't call us Dunkers, Simon Wolfe. It's vulgar. We're the *Brethren."*

"I'm sorry. I don't know much—"

"I've been to that meetinghouse," she said. "Once."

"Have you?"

"On our way to an Annual Meeting in Tennessee. Mumma's meetinghouse, it's called."

Simon asked, "Isn't Maryland the long way around, going from Virginia?"

"I'm from Pennsylvania."

"Your husband too?"

"No," she said, "Jakob Zelter was from this country."

"Where in Pennsylvania are you from, if I might ask?"

"Marsh Creek."

"Where's that?"

"Near Gettysburg."

Simon had thought that there was a slight difference in her German dialect from what other Dunkers in the Shenandoah spoke. "Are your parents well? After the battle, I mean."

"I don't know." No visible emotion.

The woman in the burning kitchen had not been her mother, then. Perhaps an in-law. Certainly a friend. Prepare her to see Deering. And Custer, possibly. "Rebekka, I know this is unpleasant for you, but we need to talk about the evening I found you."

"Not now, Simon Wolfe," she said hollowly. "I'm very happy." She didn't look it. At the moment, she appeared to be devoid of feelings and attitudes, a hauntingly beautiful marble whose sculptor had nevertheless lacked the rare talent to convincingly animate his work.

"Did the soldier ride or walk up to the house?"

"Not now." The same plodding tone, no more or less insistent.

He vacillated for a moment, then gazed off toward the gap along the Berryville pike through which the Army of the Shenandoah had spilled onto the plains of Winchester. Already seemed like years ago. And if five Union armies had never tramped up this Valley, what would her life be like now? Remarried, probably, to some pious farmer, bringing him his noon meal in a basket out to the fields at this hour.

"Are you married?" she asked. Out of the blue.

"No."

"Star of Bethlehem," she said, stripping some white flowers off an almost leafless stem. "Death. Do you call on a lady in Boston?"

Simon had begun to hobble slightly. On both heels were blisters the size of silver dollars. "Not in a long time."

"Because of the war?"

"No, we parted before that."

"What happened? A quarrel?"

"No." He suddenly realized that he'd never quarreled with Esther Monis, and that nearly all his memories of her—except the last—were entirely pleasant. Even now, he thought warmly of her sitting in her father's parlor on a sofa, a smile on her face—olive-complected from the Spanish sun burnishing generations of her Jewish ancestors. Her legs would be drawn up beneath her so she might conceal her malformed left foot under a woolen shawl. Although he'd proudly considered himself a freethinker at the time, he accompanied her father and her to temple on Friday evenings. Marriage had seemed a certainty, particularly after they unexpectedly consummated their love one August afternoon when her father was away on business. And then the shock of that last Friday.

As usual, Simon showed up an hour before sunset at the Monis's fashionable house just a few blocks off Beacon Hill. A March gale was driving wet snow down the street, but Mr. Monis stepped outside his door in a light coat and invited Simon for a stroll. His open and friendly Sephardic face was taut for once, and some moments passed in awkward silence before he could say what he had to say. Esther had expressed a desire not to see Simon again.

He was dumbfounded. *"Why?"* he blurted.

"Please, my dear boy," Mr. Monis went on, "I'm as shocked as you. She confesses the tenderest possible feelings for you, but . . ."

"Yes?"

"She thinks you pity her."

"Nonsense," Simon said, although a spark of realization went off behind his eyes. He also knew that he'd protested less forcibly than he might've.

"That's what I told her, dear boy. But she's firm on this. She says you confuse love with pity—whatever that means, and she can't bear it any longer . . . the way she feels about you."

"Let me talk to her, sir."

"Just what I suggested. But she refuses."

"Ask her again. Tell her that I want only the chance to explain myself in the most precise and affectionate terms."

Mr. Monis smiled sadly. He'd begun to shiver. "Of course. Go now, and I'll have another try with her. I'll send word to you as soon as she consents."

Word had never come, and a month later Fort Sumter was fired upon. Fletcher Webster's offer to march away with the 12th Massachusetts—although only as assistant surgeon, as the surgeon's spot had already been filled by one of the governor's cronies—had been irresistible. On the soft, rainy night before Antietam, it suddenly hit him that both Esther and her father had expected him to call without waiting for consent, and he vowed to do just that as soon as he could return to Boston. But by the next sundown he was damaged goods.

"Simon Wolfe," Rebekka now said adamantly, "please—what happened to you and this lady?"

"She and I just decided we weren't for each other. No bad feelings."

"You seem saddened by that."

"That we parted?"

She sprinkled the Star of Bethlehem petals on the road behind her. "That there were no bad feelings."

He looked at her, surprised. "Do I really?"

"Yes. You're like someone else I know."

"How's that?"

"A good man of strong feelings. Handsome men are said to feel less for women than plain men, but that isn't true. You are quite loving, Simon Wolfe." She slowly smiled, expression coming back into her eyes, her face. "And you're also very footsore."

"That I am."

They had come to a shallow stream. Abraham's Creek. The shady banks were littered with spent paper cartridges and bits of scorched lint. There had been heavy fighting along it earlier in the month, but Simon could smell no corpses that had been overlooked in the brambles, only the rain-damp foliage going sour with autumn.

"Take off your shoes, Simon Wolfe."

"There's no need—"

"Please."

He sat on a rock and removed his boots, his shoddy gray socks, then dipped his bare white feet into the creek. "Oh yes," he groaned with pleasure at the coolness. She waded in and knelt before him, the water flowing over her legs and rising to her hips. His gaze lit steady on hers. "Rebekka . . ."

"Yes?"

God, he hated this. "We have to talk about the other evening, that house south of town. And what happened in the embalmer's tent. I need to know. To help you and Hannes."

She went still and waited, eyes large, the stream rippling around her waist.

"Why'd you lie with the dead, Rebekka?"

She stared at him, then smiled mischievously. "Why do you hate your father so?"

"What makes you think—?"

"You called him Jefferson Davis's pet Jew."

"I didn't mean to say that."

"Yes, you did."

"It didn't reflect my true sentiments."

"Oh? Then why won't you even live in the same country with him?"

"I don't hate my father, Rebekka."

"Yes, you do." Snippy, now. Humming softly, she began washing his feet.

"We have differences. That's not the same as hate."

"Slavery?"

"That's one, yes."

"No, it isn't. There are things you won't talk about, Simon Wolfe."

"And how d'you know that?"

"They fly out your ears and turn into insects . . ." Then, mimicking him, almost laughing, she said, "All right, we won't talk about that."

If only he knew what to expect, he might get ahead of her. But it was disconcerting, this sense of never quite catching up with her flights of fancy. One thing was certain: she had a knack for finding the sore spots in others—like this suspicion about his relationship with his father. She knew exactly where to put the knife, if he displeased her in the least.

He winced: she'd brushed a puffy heel. "What're you doing?"

She looked up at him, her face milk-white but very much alive. "We Brethren have what's called a love feast . . ." Her hands worked more softly over his blisters. "Bread and wine are set on the table, water and aprons beside the elders. We sing, then the elders put on their aprons and begin what Christ himself did in obedience to love . . ." Then, firmly grasping his right foot, her eyes fastened on his, she kissed it. A sweet unease washed over him. "You'll be blessed by your own charity, Simon Wolfe," she said. "Help me, I beg you. Help me." He tried to withdraw his foot, but that only made her cling to his legs more insistently. "Help me, please."

It struck him that she was talking about her infirmity. He touched her face, and she clasped his hand to her cheek as if it were a compress. "I'm trying, Rebekka. But I know so little."

"I must go home," she said.

"Of course you must." He paused. "To Gettysburg, you mean?"

She drew back and stared intently at him. "Yes, that's it. Marsh Creek. Do you know what it is to have nothing?"

"No." First his father's wealth and later the profits from his own practice. Never. Maybe after the war he'd learn. He dropped his hand from her face.

"The others aren't as kind as you, Simon Wolfe."

"Who?"

She turned her face, exasperated.

"Name those who've been unkind to you."

"Demoniacs."

"Who're you talking about?" The troops?—he wondered. Lord, what had they done to her? "The blue soldiers?"

"You know who they are. You've been up and down this valley, all over this country."

"*Who?*"

"I won't go back among them penniless."

Her face was suddenly so full of venom it was a moment before he asked, "The Brethren here, your people back in Pennsylvania?"

"All of them."

"These *demoniacs*," he said carefully, "tell me about them."

"What's there to say? You Jews had them in Israel, didn't you? And we have them here. Why're you pretending not to know, Simon Wolfe?" For the moment he thought she was growing angry again, but then her tone turned soft and conspiratorial. "Before the war . . . can you keep a secret?"

"Yes."

"Before the fighting, Jakob Zelter hid all our money on his brother's farm. Gold coin. The English neighbors knew he had some, so he didn't hide it on our place."

"Where's your place?"

She shushed him with her wet fingers. "I must get back up the Valley. There's nothing down here. It's mine."

"*Where* are you from?"

"My brother-in-law's farm. Near Staunton."

Why this secrecy about her own home? Did she believe that once revealed it would be put to the torch? Whatever, she was talking about a distance of eighty miles to her husband's cache of gold. Most of those miles were still in Jubal Early's hands, and what neither army could positively claim belonged to John Mosby and his irregulars as soon as the sun went down.

"Take me there," she pressed when he said nothing.

"It wouldn't be safe."

"What's safe for any of us in these times?"

"Listen . . . another woman of your church has been killed."

In a blink, her voice was toneless again. "Where?"

"Near Front Royal."

"Did you hear the name?"

"Hostedler. Josef Hostedler was killed as well."

She gave no reaction, and Simon assumed that she hadn't known the couple, especially when she went on with the same doggedness, "Take me to Staunton."

"What about Hannes?"

"Frau Haggerty can look after him. The soldiers. Take me, please, Simon Wolfe."

"I can't."

"I'll share my gold with you."

"I don't want your gold," Simon said. She was recalling that he was a Jew; it hurt him to think that she was making this offer for that reason. "I want to see you happy, with a peaceful mind. Your money's of no interest to me."

She smiled caressively, radiantly. "I knew that." Then her face snapped toward the metallic whirring of a meadowlark, and she shuddered for a few moments. At last she seemed convinced that it was nothing harmful—although she apparently saw her world as one of almost constant menace—and turned back toward Simon, imploring him again with her entire being. "Staunton's not so far. And I know the back roads. I walk them all the time, always in darkness. Never the pike."

He decided to keep after her about the particulars of this menacing world. "These fingers you feel—"

"The fingers try to make me go one way, but I go the other. So I'm lost, but I never get lost." She crawled out of the water and lay on her side next to him, unmindful that she was soaked from the bosom down. Her cap slid off, and her luxuriant hair coiled down over the sand as she gazed up at him. "You're like one of the Brethren, Simon Wolfe."

"How's that?"

"So quiet, so plain . . . so determined to be good."

He wasn't sure if it'd been a compliment. Something in her voice said otherwise, something utterly puzzling.

"You never boast, do you?" she went on.

"I try not to."

"I thought all soldiers like to boast."

"I'm not a real soldier."

"Yes, that's right . . . you put the soldiers back together so they can go on killing."

It was brutally true. Stripped of patriotic claptrap, that was his place in the scheme of things. He didn't know where to take the conversation next.

She scooped up some sand and let it trickle out of the bottom of her fist. Her honey-colored hair, free at last to frame her face, made her all the more strikingly lovely.

"Tell me about your husband," he said. But, when distress flickered in her eyes, he quickly added, "Some recollection that gives you pleasure."

She took hold of some more sand, sprinkled it over the back of Simon's hand as a child might. "When the war began, the gray soldiers came and told the Brethren the younger men had to go into the army. Jakob Zelter told them that, as Christians, we didn't have the right to use carnal weapons. But the officer with the gray soldiers said it was no matter, all the younger men would have to go with him when he returned . . ." She brushed the sand off her fingers, then laid her hand beneath her cheek. "The Brethren decided, rather than be disobedient to our Lord, who commanded us to love our enemies, the young men would leave Virginia. Go out to the West until the war was over. Brother Zelter, even though he was too old to go into the army, would lead the others to this safe place . . ." Her eyes fixed dreamily on a point in the stream until—

"Why'd your husband lead them, if he didn't have to go?" Simon asked.

"Because he was an elder. And he'd traveled all over the mountains on church business. He said to me before he went, 'You may never see my face or hear my voice again.' " She sat up, found her cap and began tucking her hair beneath it. "They were captured, all of them, and taken to prison. What follows I heard from the others. Brother Zelter told them to stand fast and see the salvation of the Lord. They were sure they were going to be hanged. Still, they prayed for their captors and remained trustful in the Lord, Simon Wolfe."

He nodded that he understood.

"After some days in this prison," she continued, "the Brethren were taken in chains before a judge. He asked Brother Zelter, who spoke for the others, if he was fearful for his life. He said no, God had given him enough grace to suffer any kind of persecution, even death. He was asked what he'd do if put in a battle. Brother Zelter said he would fold his arms and open his shirt to the bullets of the blue English. The judge thought about this for a while, then asked if the Brethren would feed the enemy if they came to their farms. 'Yes,' Brother Zelter said, 'for we are commanded by Jesus Christ to feed our enemies.' This moved the judge, for he told the Brethren to go home and tend to their fields in peace. They were free to go as long as they paid a fine . . ." She smiled again, and Simon was sure that this was the happy memory he'd asked her to resurrect. But then her smile went out. "They were waiting for him three miles from our farm," she said, hushed—then nothing more as her gaze was drawn to the flowing water once again.

"Who, Rebekka? Who was waiting for Jakob Zelter?"

"Our English neighbors. The worst of them, I mean. They'd set out on their own to rid the county of traitors. They didn't care what the judge had ordered. They shot Jakob Zelter in the darkness, and rode away. There were nine holes in his body when it was brought to me to be washed. I buried him in the graveyard of our meetinghouse at Pleasant Valley." Then, as before, she filled her palm with sand and watched it dribble out. Dust to dust.

Simon turned his head and stared up the Valley. The crown of the

Massanutten was just showing above the treetops. "I'll get this savage," he said. "I promise, Rebekka. For you. And for Jakob Zelter."

"Be careful, Simon Wolfe," she said. "I care much for you."

Then she embraced him.

He could tell from the play of her hands on his back that it wasn't from fear. Nor was it another plea for him to take her to Staunton for her gold. She lightly kissed his neck, and he shut his eyes against the chill-like sensation that followed. Intoxicatingly, he recalled both the shame and elation of making love to Esther, how each emotion had only intensified the other, and he told himself that this act now, however wrong for this time, would clean the stench of hospital wards out of his nostrils and let him breathe freely for a while. Lying with Rebekka Zelter would be a step back from the dead house. He closed his arm around her, drew her more tightly against himself. A whole and undamaged body. He'd nearly forgotten that there were such bodies in a world where shot and shell reigned. And to think that the human body was an instrument for pleasure as well as pain nearly made him dizzy. He had forgotten the possibility.

"You are so good, Simon Wolfe," she whispered. "So much better than other men."

He froze, then let go of her.

"Simon . . . ?"

He rose and said, "We must be getting back."

⊰ CHAPTER 13 ⊱

SEPTEMBER 30

NEAR HARRISONBURG

It was a fine autumn dusk, the air as clear and cool as springwater. Sister Christena Leibert gazed down the long slope upon the broad stretch of valley she'd first seen from her mother's arms. Several plumes of smoke were rising from where she knew farms to be, some belonging to the English, some to the Brethren. She sighed. To her back, she could feel the heat of her own house burning, but didn't turn and face the flames.

They and all the other fires were only proof.

This morning, while harvesting the corn she'd managed to plant and tend by herself—the little bit that hadn't already been carried off by the blue English—it'd come into her mind and stayed there, repercussing, the line from an old Brethren hymn: "I soon shall see His lovely face at home."

The coming of the soldiers, the fires, made sense after that. Everything made beautiful sense. Soon she would no longer be alone.

And now, down in the lower pasture, she could see two tiny male figures, dressed plainly, walking up toward her. She shaded her eyes against the last of the sunlight with a dirt-stained hand. One of the men, of course, was Martin, her husband. He wasn't far from where he'd dropped dead the year before, his heart giving out from grief and overwork. He was no stranger to her in death, although he'd come back to her from the grave in a gradual way. First, his voice. As she sat up night after night, watching the armies march up and down the pike, he whispered for her to sleep. Then, after she neglected to eat for days on end, he left a loaf and the bread knife out on the table. Finally, while she wept hysterically and pulled at her hair, he appeared bodily in his rocker and began amusing her with recollections of their courtship, how her father, Papa Hostedler, had scolded him for visiting too late on Saturday nights: "No wonder you doze in the meetinghouse, Brother Martin!" Laughing through her tears, she tried to embrace him, but he warned her never to try, as the Lord had commanded Moses not to come near the burning bush. The two of them had then chatted away the long night.

So it didn't shock her in the least to see Martin coming up through the pasture, his body more lifelike than ever. It was one more sign that she herself was starting to die. How sweet it would be to die.

But who was that beside her husband?

She squinted for a better look, for at that instant the blue soldiers galloped past, blocking her view. They whooped like men possessed by demons, fired their guns skyward, then tossed their last torches into the barn through the hay door before riding down to the pike and turning for Harrisonburg.

Big red flames shot out of the hay door, and the two old cows trapped within began lowing.

I soon shall see His lovely face at home.

Eagerly, she gazed down again at the two figures, now midway up the pasture, coming at the same purposeful stride. She had hoped against hope that the other one might be her son, but it wasn't so. Nor could it ever be, really, for Andreas had gone into the presence of his Judge with the blood of his fellow man dripping from his fingers. He'd run off with the gray soldiers from this country—the sons of the English neighbors he'd always envied for their splendid horses and smart clothes—and died up in Pennsylvania last summer. She'd written to the Marsh Creek congregation, asking them to find his grave, but their deacon responded that most were marked unknown.

No matter. *I soon shall see His lovely face at home.*

Was the stranger her cousin, Josef Hostedler?

She'd just learned that he and Chlora had been taken by the war. How exactly, she didn't know.

No, she decided, it wasn't Josef.

Finally, she could make out the bearded face of the stranger walking beside her husband—it was Jakob Zelter.

"Joy!" she said, pleased that Martin had found her distant in-law on the other side. And it was reassuring to see the elder vigorous and whole again. She'd heard from the Brethren up in Staunton how Jakob's corpse had been found brutally stabbed, bloody, doubled over the lip of the well in his own dooryard. But now death was conquered.

The two figures stopped ten paces short of her. A passing sparrow flew right through both of them without the slightest pause.

"Sister Leibert," Jakob Zelter said, giving the brim of his hat a squeeze.

"My good wife," Martin said warmly.

The elder looked roundabout at the fires. "This is nothing to be feared. It will pass."

"I know," she said.

"And your poverty will soon be ended," Jakob Zelter went on.

This confused her somewhat. Was he talking about the inheritance? Last spring, she'd gone to Staunton with the expectation of receiving some property that had belonged to a cousin. Things hadn't worked out, and she'd come home even more penniless than before. "I have no wish for the provender of this world, Brother Jakob."

His eyes turned solemn, and he asked, "Are you entirely sure?"

"Entirely—for soon I shall see His lovely face at home."

The two men glanced at each other.

"Then go, my dear wife," Martin said, "go and feed the stock."

She turned without another word and started for the corncrib, which the blue soldiers had somehow overlooked. Another sign? Humming the hymn to herself, she filled the bucket with some green ears, but then dumped them back into the crib—the barn roof had just come down with a crash.

Martin and Jakob must've intended something else by sending her up here.

Then she saw Him.

He was radiant, on horseback, looming against the pillar of fire roaring up from the collapsed barn. His face was aglow; she knew that His features would never be revealed to her, so she stopped looking for them. He gave off the unmistakable air that He was in pain, and He seemed to be favoring His left hand as if it'd been injured.

"Sister, I need a place to rest," He said in a voice as soft as a breeze. "Somewhere I can be alone for a while."

"Of course you do," she said. "Come." And then, smiling rapturously, she held her hands out to him.

OCTOBER 1

LURAY VALLEY

Claude Tebault chased the blue-coated rider toward Front Royal along the west slope of the Blue Ridge. The tops of the peaks were still sunlit, but the floor of this smaller valley running parallel to the Shenandoah was already deep in the shadow of the Massanutten. The wind slipping past his face felt clammy, promising a night of dew dripping off the laurel, fog scrolling up from the river. He broke from a belt of pines on to a field of trampled wheat and put the spurs to Coeur de Lion.

Faster, before he lost the Yankee.

But the poor beast was used up. And hungry. Nearly two hundred miles had passed under his wafer-thin iron shoes in four days. Still, no backing off now: in the last minute Tebault had lost sight of the rider.

Thankfully, the ground was moist after the recent rains, and the hooves of the Yankee's mount cut a bold line, ever northward.

He was a courier, no doubt. And a shrewd one. Near Flint Run, he'd suddenly veered off into the trees—skirting the ambush Tebault and two fellow rangers had laid for him along the pike. From that point, Tebault had to take after him alone.

Le secret de la guerre est dans la sureté des communications. Napolean. Tebault had copied that into his notebook during the first months of the war, between drilling in that hot and malarial camp outside New Orleans.

Falling on the enemy's communications.

That's what this was all about. The farther up the Valley of Virginia Sheridan pushed, the more men he had to string behind him to safeguard his lines of communication, his supply trains. And the job the rangers had before them, Colonel Mosby had explained at their last rendez-vous, was to cut down the number of troops Sheridan could throw against Early's front. When the blue army was pulled thin like taffy, Early would attack and roll it up all the way back to the banks of the Potomac. When Sheridan least expected.

Tebault lifted his eyes. Far to the north, a black scarf of cloud was trailing rain. Nightfall was coming fast now, but not as fast as it did in the Louisiana latitudes. The brasswork of a steamboat would be glinting out on the Mississippi, and then in a split second the only sign that it hadn't been swallowed by the river was the plume of sparks from the smokestacks. Hell's own chimneys, those stacks—at least he'd thought so as a small boy, gazing out from the veranda of the big house on a summer evening.

And then he found himself recalling another veranda, the one in Culpeper where he'd met John Mosby for the first time. "So," the slight ranger had said, "Andy Walker tells me you're a demon with a saber."

Tebault shook himself.

His mind had been drifting, one aimless thing after another.

He was more tired than usual. Exhausted, really. Most of yesterday was a shadowy blur to him. He'd been sick again, he supposed. It happened more frequently now than ever before. He'd always been careful to go off by himself as soon as he felt the sickness coming on, but he knew that eventually Mosby would find out and order him to some hospital in Richmond. If Tebault lived that long. It didn't seem likely, not the way things had been going these past weeks, a scrape with the Yankees nearly every day. So what was the use in taking himself out of the fight? He'd be gone soon enough. In peace.

He slowed the gelding to a walk.

The courier's tracks had faded over a limestone ledge. Tebault was afraid that he'd lost the trail until he noticed a broken sprig of cedar dangling off a bough. He rubbed the top of his head, which was aching, then picked up the pace again.

Coeur de Lion stumbled once before breaking into a heavy-footed gallop.

"I find myself without a lieutenant for Company A," John Mosby had gone on, smiling in that half-mocking way of his. "You doing anything for the remainder of the revolution, Mr. Tebault?"

Ahead, the blue-coated rider showed himself, out of revolver range, at the edge of some burnt trees. He'd apparently stopped to listen for other horsemen boxing him in on his front. Canny.

Tebault halted and waved at him.

The man just stared back—as if to show that he hadn't lost his nerve.

Then he urged his horse over a rail fence and a thicket of charred branches. Shellfire before the rains had left scorched pockets in the woods. As if the maze of blackened tree limbs wasn't enough to frustrate Coeur de Lion, the land fell steeply away, creased by gullies.

But all this slowed the Yankee's mount too, and Tebault began to close the distance between them. The man tossed a look over his shoulder, and Tebault saw his face clearly. A Negro. Maybe some Indian blood as well.

Time to stop him.

He drew his Colt. Coeur de Lion started to leap over a fallen pine and Tebault quickly decided to use the smooth glide at the top of the jump to squeeze off some rounds. He fired twice, and the smoke sheeted back over him, blinding him while he kept expecting to feel the gelding's forehooves thud against the hard ground. Instead, there was a glancing ring from a horseshoe, and then Tebault was crashing headlong through the dead growth. He remembered to let go of the rein before he pulled the horse down on top of him.

He landed on his shoulder, bounced over onto his chest, and then lay still for the few seconds it took him to make up his mind that he wasn't hurt.

His Colt was beside him in the ashes.

Taking hold of it, he blew the grit off the cylinder, then eased back down and listened for the Yankee's horse. Had he hit it? That's what he'd been aiming for.

But Coeur de Lion was neighing too loudly to hear anything. The gelding was on his side, his head upraised, eyes crazed. "What is it, *ami?*" Tebault crawled over to him, then swore.

The right foreleg was broken just above the fetlock.

He knew that it was his fault, for having pushed the poor beast so hard these past days. No horse in the world could stand up to such punishment. Yet, without a moment's hesitation, he pressed the muzzle of the Colt to the wet, bay-colored forehead and pulled the trigger.

Holstering, he saw that the green corn had spilled out of his saddlebag. He brushed the ashes off an ear and began gnawing. He'd eaten three ears when he noticed a piece of paper tumbling along the ground in the languid breeze. Quickly, he got up and retrieved it—the title page to a German Bible with a hand-drawn map of the Valley on its backside, the place names in a lacy, feminine script. It'd come out of his saddlebag with the corn.

He pocketed the page, then slumped down beside his dead horse again and ate.

OCTOBER 2

WINCHESTER

The week before, Simon had ordered the Taylor Hotel turned into an officers' hospital, yet only this morning had he found the time to inspect it. He made his rounds, spent ten minutes trying to reassure a young captain who'd lost an eye and a hand at Fisher's Hill that there was a life beyond injury, then went downstairs to the dining room. The officers paid for their own food, so the room seemed more like a restaurant than a hospital mess. He settled in at a table next to the front window and ordered coffee from the Negro attendant. The only other men in the room were at a far table, two colonels with round, fleshy faces who'd been visiting a wounded comrade. They wore 6th Corps badges. Simon knew neither of them.

His coffee came. Drinking leisurely, he let his gaze drift out the window. A low mist hung in the street, staining the cobblestones. He was reminded of spring mornings in Boston, and all of a sudden he missed Esther Monis, badly. Invariably, he'd gravitated toward her on overcast days, or when he'd lost a patient, regardless of the weather. Maybe he'd get a letter off to her tonight, even though so many attempts before had gone into the fire. And really—what was there to say? *I've found another to pity with all my heart and soul, so you're safe from the humiliation of my attention.*

Enough.

He put his mind to the Dunkers again.

Pamunkey had arrived back from Custer's headquarters last night—and simply shaken his head.

So that was that.

The boy-major general, as he'd just been promoted again in the Volunteers, hadn't blooded his sword in the time the orderly'd spent with him.

From that instant Simon's thoughts snapped back to Elias Deering. But where was the provost marshal? Most of his staff had returned to garrison in Winchester, but the man himself was reportedly still in the upper Valley.

Perhaps just as well.

Rebekka Zelter had grown worse: argumentative, desperately confused. Earlier in the week there'd been a frightful moment he couldn't forget. She had turned so poisonously spiteful toward him he walked away wondering if *she* had killed the woman in the house just south of Winchester—the look twisting her face had been that murderous. Yet, the idea was quickly dismissed; it was ludicrous: the Hostedlers had been slain shortly after the Winchester woman, twenty miles distant, and all the while Rebekka had been at the transfer hospital under Cal Ames's or Pamunkey's watchful eye. And then another thing: she'd given absolutely no reaction to the news that the Hostedlers were dead. Surely, a murderess, hearing of her crimes, would've at least steeled herself, but Rebekka obviously hadn't cared in the least.

The Negro filled Simon's cup again.

But those moods of hers—only doses of calomel seemed to bring her out of them, and then he couldn't bear to watch the extravagant salivation the mercurous chloride triggered. Maybe if she saw the killer put under guard . . .

The 6th Corps colonels had raised their voices a notch, and

Simon, despite himself, couldn't help but to eavesdrop. "No, Charles—Manassas is an Indian word," one of them was saying.

"Oh drivel. It's from an old Shylock named Manasseh. Had a lodge at the crossroads there."

Simon caught his own reflection in the glass. Uneasy-looking. Nothing, he told himself. Nothing was meant by this, just a manner of speaking.

They began murmuring again, laughed suddenly, and then Charles said in a bright voice, "D'you know the biggest quandary of army life for a Hebrew?"

"Why no, can't say that I do."

"*Free* bacon."

In the reflection on the window glass, Simon could see the washed-out faces of the colonels. They'd gone as still as tintypes, staring across the empty tables at his back. He came to his feet.

The colonels exchanged a glance, then mocking smiles.

Simon had started toward them when the door rattled open and Pamunkey stepped inside, bringing the damp chill of the street in with him.

Simon frowned. "What is it?"

The orderly crooked a forefinger and began tapping in the air.

Simon nodded, then started for the telegrapher's office at head-quarters. But he paused at the door. "You're misinformed," he said to the officers without turning. "The biggest quandary for a Jewish soldier is whether or not to *salute* bacon. Damned if it doesn't smack of idolatry." Then he went out, slamming the door behind him.

As he strode through the mist, Simon looked straight ahead. *You're more surprised than hurt,* he told himself. Nothing like this had happened in a few years, not since Grant had put out Order Number 11. The general, believing that "Jews and other unprincipled traders" in Tennessee were peddling information to the Rebels, prohibited their travel. Simon, although only a month past his amputation, joined in the outcry of Jewish officers—and gritted his teeth against a few petty humiliations such as this before Lincoln stepped in and revoked Grant's edict.

A sudden thought—Sheridan had been serving in Tennessee during this affair, hadn't he?

Simon realized that Pamunkey was following him. "Go back," he said. "Check on Mrs. Zelter."

A message from Washington was waiting for him at Sheridan's headquarters. Little Phil himself was somewhere in the field.

From the Surgeon General to the Medical Director, Middle Department. Simon read the order twice, then crumpled the yellow flimsy in his fist and hurried out.

The maneuver was clear. And admirably clever. Philip Sheridan, unlike Jubal Early, had sniffed a threat coming around his flank—and moved quickly to thwart it. But how had Little Phil known that Simon hadn't given up on the Dunkers?

He nearly ran, darting through a column of platoons to reach Amherst Street.

Twiss.

Yesterday, the contract surgeon had asked Simon how long he intended to afford the young Dunker woman "his private care." Had he somehow passed word on to Sheridan? Damn him to hell if he had, although any one of a dozen officers could've dropped a line to Little Phil.

Simon rushed into the hospital and found Ames just back from a ward inspection throughout the town. "Come with me, Cal," he said on the way to his room.

He sat on his cot, tried to gather himself. Blame no one. Rise above it. He remembered his mother rising above worse.

Ames came in. "What's wrong?"

Simon took a few seconds to steady his voice. His smarting eyes he could do nothing about. He felt so young. Maddeningly young. "I've been sacked."

"Oh pus—who says?"

"Have a seat. The Surgeon General. He's pretending it's temporary. But I'm to turn my command over to you."

"Simon, I never wanted—"

He held up his hand. "That's not it, Cal. I can think of nobody I'd rather have take over . . ." Another pause, longer. He couldn't let his eyes tear up, even out of anger. Ames was watching him closely.

"You all right, Simon?"

"Here. Have a look." He gave over the balled-up telegram.

Ames smoothed it on his knee, read. "I don't understand," he said after a little. "It's just a furlough order."

"That's right."

"Aren't all Jewish troops being given the same?"

"Troops—yes." Simon snatched back the flimsy. "But I'm the chief medical officer of a field army. We're in the middle of a campaign, Cal. You were at Fredericksburg—did the M.D. for the Army of the Potomac go home for Christmas?"

"No," Ames said quietly, "of course not."

"Sheridan's having me sacked. Plain and simple."

"How can you be so sure?"

"I'm sure."

"But it could be—"

"*Cal,*" Simon said, "this is how it's done. You know that as well as I. First Washington temporarily relieves you, tells you to go home and await further orders. Then they never come." Then, despite himself, he cried out, "You can grow senile waiting for those orders!"

After a moment Ames asked, "When's Rosh Hashanah begin?"

"Tomorrow at sundown." Simon let out a breath. Maybe it was indeed time to go. He was making a fool of himself—and solving nothing. Innocents in the Valley of Virginia would go on being butchered no matter what he did. "I'm sorry, Cal," he sighed.

"What for?"

"Shouting at you."

"Were you shouting at me? Well, boy—you can go to hades in gum boots if you were."

Simon was trying to simmer down when it hit him like hot water. His dismissal was common knowledge in the Army of the Shenandoah, and he was the last to know. The incident in the Taylor Hotel fell into place with a mental click. Of course. The two bastards from 6th Corps had been on to it. "There's been talk against me, hasn't there?" he asked. "Generally, I mean."

Ames glanced away, obviously to come up with something to buffer the truth.

"Come on, Cal. Will *anyone* square with me?"

"Some," Ames admitted. "Just don't think too much of it, Simon. You take everything so goddamn hard. You put together the medical department for a brand-new army in two weeks. Two galloping weeks I'm glad I won't have to live through again. You're a man who gets things done, and doers always wind up—"

"*Why* are they talking against me?" Simon interrupted.

"I only caught drift of this yesterday—a rumor about Deering and you. It's said he made some remark about Little Phil, and you repeated it to Sheridan."

"No rumor, it's true."

Ames looked stunned. "Dear Jesus—you blew on Elias. That was bound to stir up bad feeling, Simon. You know the etiquette here."

"I'm afraid I do. Ignore anything unpleasant that crops up on campaign. Even homicide."

"Oh—come on, man."

"Cal, they're treating murder like chicken stealing!"

"What if they are? Who appointed you to look into this?"

That gave Simon pause. "Nobody."

"Then why are you?"

Simon stood and went to the window. More ambulances were coming in. From a cavalry skirmish somewhere. It never ended.

"Talk to me, Simon. I'm trying to understand why you're driving yourself out of a command you moved heaven and earth to get. I'll daresay that if this war lasts long enough, you could wind up Surgeon General, despite being a volunteer with no political ties to speak of. You're just that competent." His tone turned less strident, more pleading. "Explain to this simple old Yankee cynic how even a dozen dead Germans are worth *you,* your services to the boys of this long-suffering army."

"If these murders go on, there'll be no meaning left to any of our services."

"Oh laudable pus. Try again . . . I'm listening."

Simon struggled to keep his voice from breaking, infuriated with his own rise of emotion. "If I were standing here whole, Cal, that'd be easier to accept—no real meaning. But not like this."

"Is that it? Then you're just damn lucky a runaway cart on Beacon Hill didn't lop off that arm. Then where'd you be, my noble young friend?" Ames shook his head. "You can't fool me, Simon Wolfe— you're looking for a cause. And a holy one at that. Well, there hasn't been anything close since Moses quit Egypt in a huff. Unless I'm mistaken, nobody rolled back the Potomac for us to cross into Old Virginny. So you can forget about this bluebelly romp being divinely blessed. Now, tell me, Simon—why *you?"*

Silence, but for the clatter of ambulance wheels, and then Simon said, "I'm in no mood for this, Cal." Suddenly so weary. Too weary to talk about Leah, the day he'd have to face her and justify everything this army had done.

Then Ames suggested, "Why not go to Sheridan? Apologize and tell him you'll let God look out for the Germans from now on."

Simon glared. "Are you joking?"

"See it another way, man. This army, however ruthless it's become, is going to wipe out slavery. If let alone to do its work. Abolition, Simon—isn't that what you've wanted all these years? Stick it out here, and you will have helped put an end to the nigger question once and for all. Then we Americans can fight over something else, something more serious."

"I didn't ask for this, Cal," Simon said angrily, "and I'd gladly hand it over if somebody with half a brain would take charge and do *something.* But that's the rub, don't you see? Nobody will!"

Ames shot to his feet. "What do I do? Once more unto the breach, dear friend! Is that it?"

"What are you saying, Cal?"

Ames briefly shut his eyes, then lowered his voice. "Nothing."

"Please—what are you talking about?"

"Ancient history."

"How ancient?"

"Boston City Hospital . . . forget it."

"No."

Ames took a moment. "When you came back from Charleston that last time, so out of sorts . . . the board wanted to bar you from the place . . ." Simon was stunned. He'd never imagined. "I wound up taking personal responsibility for an improvement in your sociableness. Thank God for milk punch. Otherwise, you might never have come around." Ames belabored a smile. "Didn't mean to bring it up, Simon. Whatever happened down in Carolina remains your business. I'm sorry."

"No, I'm sorry. And thank you for steering me straight. I had no idea." Simon paused. "I'm not asking you to risk anything for me, Cal. You're free to disassociate yourself, starting this minute."

"Like pus I am," Ames said, limping for the door. "I'm a putrid old cynic, and we both know it. But I'd never turn my back on a friend—so I'll be keeping this room for you."

Simon gave a distracted nod, and Ames went out.

Well, he thought, from noble purpose to a deficiency in personality—all in five minutes.

What to do now?

Pack, certainly. But just the essentials. The rest could follow. And it would surely follow. Ames was just being kind: Simon would never come back to Sheridan's army or any other Union army. He must impress upon Cal, who had his reservations, the urgency of setting up the big tent depot. Too much staff time was being wasted riding between the wards scattered all over the Valley. Then he caught himself. It was no longer his prerogative to tell Cal what to do. He'd bungled the job, and now he was going on the shelf with all the other stunted careers of this war. No parting instructions, he decided. Just a few handshakes and be gone like a gentleman.

He was taking his valise from the corner when he saw Rebekka standing in the doorway, her face stark and perplexed. "What're you doing?" she demanded.

"I've got to go away."

"Up the Valley with the army again?"

"No, I'm leaving the army."

"When will you come back?"

"I doubt I will."

She fell into a long, seemingly vacant pause, but then said, "You came back before."

Simon sidled past her into the corridor and, as expected, found Pamunkey leaning against the outer wall, keeping watch. "Have a wagon hitched at once. And Naomi saddled." He turned back to Rebekka. "You and Hannes are going with me, at least as far as the Potomac."

"Potomac . . . ?"

"Yes." Quietly going back to Boston to await further orders was the last thing he'd planned for this contingency. He would go to Washington and report the killings to the Surgeon General, or to the Inspector General if his own boss refused to see him. Forget the Provost Marshal General—he was too busy enforcing the draft. Unwittingly, Sheridan had freed him to act by conniving with the Medical Department for his dismissal—Good Lord, what officer was told to go home on furlough and await further orders? How far into Maryland he would travel with Rebekka depended on the state of the railroad. As usual, Mosby was making a mess of the Baltimore and Ohio, burning bridges and ripping up track. But after Simon boarded a train for Washington, Pamunkey would continue north with Rebekka and Hannes. "Otis'll then take you into Pennsylvania," he went on, gently taking her arm, "the village where you grew up."

He had hoped the prospect of going home would calm her, but she stepped back from him.

"What is it, Rebekka?"

She refused to look at him.

"Don't you want to see your mother?" he asked.

"No."

"Why not?"

Her expression turned even more sullen, and her head had begun to rock, as if the fingers were at her again. "Don't you want to see your father?" she asked. When he said nothing, she raised her voice. "Tell me, Simon Wolfe—you, so full of questions! Don't you want to see him!"

"No, I don't. Not right now."

"Why not!"

"Very well," he said, making an attempt at self-control, "if we might step inside I'll tell you."

Wild-eyed, she swept into his room, and he shut the door behind them. He gestured for her to sit in the chair, but remained standing himself.

How to explain this? Was it possible for her to understand even part of what had happened? He was sick of bartering information with her, but how else could he learn anything?

"Just before the war," he carefully began, afraid that it would all slip from him as easily as the pit from a rotten piece of fruit, "I went home to Charleston. My father and I got into a quarrel. A very bad one. Reckless things were said on both sides, and then . . ." Again, vividly, he heard the cane whistling through the air. He almost braced to keep himself from flinching. ". . . my father took his cane to me."

Rebekka's look softened. Sympathy—he hadn't seen it in her face for days. "Was the quarrel over slavery?"

Simon hesitated. "It concerned a slave, yes."

She suddenly dropped from the chair to her knees and clasped his legs. "Forgive me, Simon," she said miserably, pressing her forehead against him, "sometimes I don't know who I am, and my heart is horrible . . . such a cage of evil."

He reached down, meaning to cradle her face in his hand. But her expression, so tender just a few seconds before, had become a scowl.

"You're lying," she said. "There's more. There's always more with you."

"Please . . . not as you are now."

"And how's that, Simon Wolfe?"

"Afraid. Unhappy."

"Only because you hate me!"

No use arguing. He waited close-mouthed for another long outburst, one as abusive as several of the past few weeks in which she'd accused him of deceiving her and trying to steal her property—which amounted to no more than the clothing on her back, as far as he could tell. But then, without warning, her scowl faded and her eyes turned more cunning than hostile. She looked as if she was on the verge of hissing at him. As with each of her jarring shifts of mood, he had no idea what had brought it on.

"The burning house," she said.

"What?"

"You know what I mean."

Then he believed that he did. She was now willing to talk about the Dunker woman in the kitchen.

But he'd just begun to ask when she cut him off, "Will you take me to Staunton if I tell?"

Make haste slowly, he cautioned himself. "Eventually," he said. As soon as the Valley was secure, he'd see that she was safely delivered into the hands of the Dunkers there.

"And you won't make me go back to Pennsylvania?"

"Not against your will, no."

"Those people up there are vile. They tried to kill me when I was little. They put demons in a cow and set it against me!"

Simon tried not to look doubtful. He'd come to think that her talk of demoniacs was nothing more than some religious belief of her sect. But no, this was different, something personal and far more troubling. "If the people up there are so bad, why then have you been coming north—?"

"Do you want to hear about the woman or not?" She waited, but he said nothing. "You're my friend, and I'm *trying* to save your life . . ." He was sure that there was no threat against him; this was just part of her general fearfulness. "Don't be like the others, Simon . . . I beg you."

He eased down onto his cot and asked, "Who was she?"

"A sister."

"*Your* sister . . . a blood relative?"

"No, a sister in the church."

"Had she taken you in?"

A moment's pause, but then Rebekka whispered, "Yes."

"Who killed her?"

"I did."

Simon looked as if he'd been slapped. Only after several moments did he move slightly. "What d'you mean?"

"I let the soldier in. The door was latched, and I let him inside."

He relaxed a little. "A blue soldier?"

"Yes."

"Can you tell me what he looked like?"

She got up from the floor, tottered briefly as if having trouble with her balance, then turned so that her back was to him. "Small," she said, "a small man."

"Shorter than I?"

"Yes. Much. Smaller standing than you sitting. And his eyes had a shine to them."

"A shine?"

"Yes, yes—an evil sparkle."

"What color?"

"Dark, I don't know."

"Did he come up to the house on foot? Or on horseback?"

"Um . . . yes. Black."

"A black horse?"

"I think so." Her eyes clouded for a moment, but then cleared again. "No, wait—I don't remember a horse. I just remember him. His eyes."

Simon found himself rethinking all his plans. If she could stay this lucid, he might take her with him to see the Surgeon General. Far more convincing than his own words could ever be, the visible torment of this beautiful young woman. He was tempted to mention the prominent vein on Deering's forehead, but then decided it was best to suggest nothing to her at this point. Save it for the Surgeon General. He must see all this in its startling freshness. "I'm sorry, Rebekka. I

know this is painful, and I wouldn't ask unless I absolutely had to."
But a new point had just occurred to him. Sheridan's army had yet to
reach Staunton, so what had driven her north? "I must know—why'd
you come to Winchester?"

"Stop it!" she said, spinning on him. "Why are you trying to trick
me!?"

"I'm not—"

"You *are*. The woman in the kitchen. You wanted only to know
about her."

"That's true." He took a breath. "What was her name?"

"I forget," she snapped.

This wouldn't do for the Surgeon General. Perhaps after she
rested a while in Pennsylvania, he could bring her to Washington.
"Rebekka . . . ?"

"You look so faraway," she said. "So cold."

"Why do you say that?"

"So cold. So flat."

He rose to comfort her, but she shrank from him.

"You're not going to take me up the Valley, are you?"

Best not to lie. The only guidepost through all this he trusted. "I
will, Rebekka. But not now. Not till it's safe."

"I see. Then we're staying here. We can live here while I wait."

"No, we have to leave. North."

"North?"

"Yes."

Simon thought that one more outburst had been avoided—when
she fumbled for his desk lamp. She missed it on the first swipe, as if she
couldn't quite judge depth.

He resisted grabbing her. "What are you—?"

She seized the lamp, clung to it briefly, spilling coal oil down her
dress, then hurled it through the window. The crash and tinkle of falling glass shook Simon out of his shock. But before he could stop her,
she picked a knifelike shard out of the frame and clenched it with grotesque fervor, slicing open her palm. A trickle of blood shot out the
bottom of her fist.

"What're you doing?" he cried. "Stop it!"

Then she joined both hands together and raised the shard over her
head. She was looking down at her abdomen. Almost toppling, he

reached out and caught her at the wrist, but his single arm could only slow the downward plunge of both of hers.

"Otis!" he shouted toward the closed door.

The blade of glass passed inches from his face on its way to her belly. An outward flick almost opened his cheek.

"Otis!"

"Deceiver!" On her face was a grimace, almost primal in its ferocity. "Thief!"

The door boomed open, and following a quick scuffling of boots Pamunkey was at Simon's side, reaching for her hands. A second later, the shard broke against the floor, and Rebekka let out a long scream.

Ames rushed in, gape-mouthed. "My God!" Mother Haggerty was two steps behind, and he ordered her, "Calomel and some trusses, rope, anything—quickly." The matron turned on her heel, and Ames helped Simon and Pamunkey carry Rebekka to the cot and restrain her on it.

" 'Let them be turned back and confounded who devise evil against me!' " she cried, the right side of her face being pressed into the blanket. " 'Let them be like chaff before the wind, with the angel of the Lord driving them on!' "

Simon began rubbing the back of her neck. "Rebekka—"

" 'Let their way be dark and slippery, with the angel of the Lord pursuing them. Let ruin come upon them unawares!' "

"What gibberish is that?" Ames asked.

"Psalms." Simon saw that a courier was standing out in the corridor, his face ash-streaked, watching the struggle with Rebekka with some amusement.

He brought his heels together. "Is Colonel Wolfe still hereabouts?"

Simon hadn't realized how breathless he was until he said, "I'm Wolfe."

"Good," the trooper said in obvious relief. "An urgent message from General Sheridan, sir. Verbal."

Ames, pinning Rebekka's arms against her sides while Pamunkey managed her legs, looked questioningly at Simon.

"Go ahead, soldier," he said.

"The colonel's to disregard previous orders and proceed to headquarters near Harrisonburg with all due haste." The courier paused. "D'you want me to repeat it, sir?"

⊰ CHAPTER 14 ⊱

The Massanutten loomed out of the darkness. The range seemed silent and empty now that the Rebel eyes on Three Top Mountain were gone. The signal station had been abandoned by Jubal Early in the rout following the battle of Fisher's Hill. Except for John Mosby— who sometimes seemed more like a ghost than a flesh-and-blood enemy—these fat, rolling lands were Philip Henry Sheridan's satrapy, his to rule as he saw fit. He was the only law left in western Virginia, the only voice to say that this was murder and this mere death. And all death was now blameless in the Valley, a happenstance of war.

God forgive an army that believed all death was equal.

"Enough rest, Rex?" Simon softly asked, patting the horse's thick neck. Then he put his heels to the gelding and started down the pike from the overlook, the same hill on which he'd bivouacked with Crook's 8th Corps the night before Fisher's Hill.

Strasburg came into view through the cedars, a sprinkling of window lights, a black steeple set against a bright glow. It was breaking over the ridge that lay between the village and the winding slit in the trees that marked the river.

He was too far gone to wonder what it was.

The grinding weariness of the miles—twenty of them since Winchester—had left him numb. Rebekka's face had haunted him all the moonless way, sweaty and convulsed, grimacing as Ames force-spooned her calomel. Simon had rushed from the room before the horrid salivation started.

Then, just as the grooms were finished saddling Rex, the town provost marshal pulled up in a carriage seized from a local wealthy family. Elias's adjutant stepped down and, handing Simon an envelope, said gravely, "On behalf of Colonel Deering, who relies on your reputation as a gentleman . . ." All done with such ceremony Simon was sure that the letter was another offer to trade pistol shots at ten paces.

But Simon had said, "Give the colonel my compliments," then stuffed the envelope in a coat pocket and started south.

Now, at the first crossroads in Strasburg, the provost guard challenged him. He gave the countersign, then asked which way to the division hospital.

The corporal pointed toward the glow Simon had first seen from the hill.

Simon rode on.

Damn Callender Ames. For reminding him why he couldn't let go of this thing, why he had to find the killer, no matter what. Leah. It always got back to his sister and the coming moment in which they'd come face-to-face after these years of separation. Israel's ghost would pass between them like the long screech of a shell—unless Simon could justify the army he served.

He'd hoped only to down a few ounces of whiskey, to bring on sleep quickly, and then tumble into a spare cot. But the hospital encampment was blazing with torches long after tattoo had been sounded, and the strong fecal smell lingering in the tent streets told him why. Camp dysentery. It was filling all the beds. Even the wounded recently brought in from the upper Valley had been stricken, and the surgeon-in-charge, a young major, was rattled by finding so many men in violent distress on his hands. "Should I start some of them north by ambulance, Colonel?" he asked.

"No, treat them all here . . ." Simon then turned to the head steward and ordered those cases who'd seemingly improved only to suddenly pass brick-red discharges in the past few hours, to be set apart from the others. These would die soon. No use disheartening those who might survive if their spirits were kept up.

Grabbing a lantern, he made a sweep through the camp.

The sinks had been well dug, eight feet deep, and the day's waste had been covered with six inches of soil. But within a few feet of the spring used for drinking water, he came upon a furrow of cracked earth. "Oh hell," he muttered. An old privy—which army's God only knew.

Poor ventilation in tents, damp uniforms and eating fruit were generally blamed for the first appearance of the contagion, but Simon had found these absent in several epidemics, while invariably the water source had been tainted. Worth a paper after the war, maybe.

Whatever, the hospital had been pitched on old ground, a violation of the general order for sanitation. But Simon knew that, with massive armies having shifted up and down the Valley all summer, it was almost impossible now to find a fresh site.

He went back to the surgeon-in-charge and, without upbraiding him, ordered the entire hospital struck and moved by noon tomorrow.

Then he looked in on the dying.

There were eight of them in the tent. Most were in low delirium, murmuring nonsense, but one boy watched Simon's entry with intent, sunken eyes. His ears were waxy-looking, almost translucent in the candlelight, and his lips had shriveled back from his teeth as if the skull were already working its way through the skin.

Simon held a cup of rice water to his mouth. "Drink."

After taking a sip, the boy tried to talk, but his tongue was too badly furred.

"Lie still," Simon said. He started to reach for the descriptive list on a nearby chair, but the boy was clinging to his sleeve.

"Want me to stay with you a while?"

A nod, although it was more like a spasm.

"All right. Let go, then." Simon carried the list and the chair back to cot-side. "Who do we have here?" he said, turning the list into the light. "Private John Sparrow. First Company, Twenty-third Ohio." The color company Simon had marched with up Little North Mountain. He glanced at the face again, but couldn't recall it. His own mother probably couldn't recognize it at the moment. Sparrow had survived the charge only to die now from his own mucus-clogged bowel. Another fine irony of this noble conflict. The private's age was given as eighteen, but he was probably closer to sixteen. Simon felt for the neck pulse. Weak and irregular. But the boy liked being touched; his whitish lips formed a smile. "Sleep now, John Sparrow," Simon said, knowing that it was an invitation to oblivion. Death was that near.

The eyes half-closed, turned glassy, but then flickered as Simon eased back in the chair. Something crinkled in his coat pocket. The letter Deering's adjutant had given him. Frowning, he opened it.

Headquarters, Middle Department
28 September 1864

Dear Colonel Wolfe:

I will make the first move to reconcile our relations by apologizing for my behavior of 21 September. You must understand—and you will understand by the close of this letter—that I was flabbergasted to hear you accuse me of the killings, particularly in Sheridan's presence. Until the shock of that moment I had counted on you as an ally in my efforts to continue the inquiry regardless of the consequences to my own safety.

While your motives may have been sincere, your suspicion was far from credible—and dangerously hasty, I must add.

A rustling of straw from one of bedsacks made Simon lower the letter.

One of the men had bolted up as if with the urgency to stool, but then his head lolled and he flopped back down onto his cot.

Simon went to him—and saw at once that there was nothing to be done. The features seemed to flatten, and the lower jaw drooped almost to the chin. Simon covered him entirely with the blanket.

The boy, sleeping, hadn't seen.

Simon held Deering's letter up to the light again.

Even during that unfortunate hour between us, I was in possession of information pertinent to the affair, information that has dangled a sword above my head on a string. Only now, having heard from those I trust most that you have stuck to your guns, do I feel safe to write it to you.

In August while at Harpers Ferry, I enjoyed the society of David Russell. Over a number of pleasant evenings I earned the confidence of the late brigadier, who one night was comfortable enough with me to make light of Sheridan's habits. As you probably know, Russell was Little Phil's captain out in Oregon and had no shortage of amusing anecdotes about our glorious "Sherrydan" on the frontier. Yet, as the hour grew late, Russell's mood turned somber and then, unexpectedly, he shared something quite shocking with me.

I now share it with you.

One nightfall in Oregon, Sheridan returned to Fort Yamhill from a ride alone, his face radiant—as you and I know it fairly shines in the heat of battle. However, he was indisposed to conversation and turned in early without supping. Russell thought nothing more of it until the next morning, when an excited party of Rogue River Indians galloped in. A doctress of their tribe had been slain while out gathering herbs the afternoon before, and the character of the wounds you will doubtless find alarming. The witch had been shot several times, but also stabbed in the belly. Sheridan was quick to blame a family of renegades who had previously accused the woman of driving one of their number mad. Little Phil soon rounded up the males and brought them to justice.

Although Russell approved the sentence—ball and chain in the stockade—he was left with his doubts. Frances, the squaw Little Phil kept as his mistress during this time, was known to fear the doctress and had complained bitterly against her in Russell's presence.

He was never satisfied as to what truly happened, but in all the years since the memory of Sheridan's exalted face that evening left him with an unsettled feeling.

Now I too am unsettled.

I fear that the brigadier and I were less than discreet in choosing the location for our discussion, as it took place with nothing more than tent canvas to separate us from eavesdroppers, and I will now confide in you in what I honestly believe to be the fatal consequence of that palaver over brandies: Sheridan somehow became aware of it and murdered David Russell as surely as if he had cut him down with his own saber.

"Oh come now," Simon said aloud.

As you perhaps know, Russell's division was held in reserve behind Getty's and Rickett's at Opequon. When the Rebels rushed to break through between the right flank of the 6th Corps and the left of the 19th, Sheridan ordered a brigade of Russell's division forward to plug the gap—not both brigades, which would have been more prudent, but the single brigade Russell had personally accompanied most of the morning. As one might expect of a man so dauntless, he died spearheading the counterattack.

Simon paused. That much was true.

And then there was Bill Terrill, the cadet sergeant Little Phil came close to bayoneting at the Point. Did you know that Brigadier Terrill died suspiciously at Perryville close in the line to Sheridan? So very much for you and I to discuss. May I suggest that we meet in confidentiality as soon as I can return to Winchester?

Certainly, Simon thought—someplace open where Rebekka Zelter can get a good, long look at you.

Unfortunately, I don't know when that will be, for Little Phil has made it his amusement to keep me ranging over the far reaches of the Valley on useless but dangerous appointments. In the last week, especially, he has shown nothing but contempt for my person and office; but, whatever his demonstrations against the truth, I trust in God that you and I, combining our evidence, can bring this matter to a just conclusion.

Respectfully yours,
Elias Deering

Simon pocketed the letter, then looked at John Sparrow.

The boy's gaze seemed to be locked on his, but then he saw that it was only an accident of position. Simon shifted in his chair, and the eyes stayed vacantly the same.

3:12 A.M., OCTOBER 3

SHERIDAN'S HEADQUARTERS, NEAR HARRISONBURG

Fires winked through the smoke. Hundreds of them all over the Valley floor. Here and there, licks of flame would spurt up into the morning darkness, curl in on themselves like tongues and then fade. A rain-damp hayrick down near the pike burned with a cold blue throb, while the farmhouse beyond was melting skyward into cinders. Limned against a sheet of blazing orange from the barn were two troopers, stripped down to their drawers, dancing like Indians. Drunk, the bastards. An idle trooper could find a way to get drunk quicker than hell would scorch a feather.

Sheridan lowered his field glasses.

His scouts told him that Jubal Early had pulled back with what was left of his army to Rockfish Gap in the Blue Ridge, Stonewall Jackson's old resting ground when not scattering the Union armies sent against him.

Would Early try again?

Sheridan knew that he couldn't afford to miss the guess. He had thought of little else these past days, turned it over in his mind a hundred times.

Yes—he'd finally decided. Early was just too proud to admit to Lee that he was whipped.

But Old Jube wouldn't come stealing down the Valley again until March at the earliest. Most of his men were shoeless, in tatters of butternut homespun or even captured Federal blue. The scouts said that not more than five thousand of them were left, moping around their fires, hungry and discouraged, in that misty hollow south of Waynesboro.

And if they advanced now, what would they have to eat?

Sheridan was close to making good on his promise to Grant: soon, crows flying over the Shenandoah would have to carry their own provender with them.

Yet, the past dogged Sheridan. He hadn't utterly destroyed Early, and Rebel armies had the galling habit of rising phoenixlike from their own ashes. All Lee had to do was to send more troops to the Valley from Petersburg. That would ease the load on Grant—but not on Phil Sheridan.

He'd had enough of watching the fires. He started back up the sloping pasture on which his headquarters had been pitched. He walked with care; little starlight was filtering through the smoke, and his aides had doused the campfires at dusk for fear of drawing sniper fire.

What to do tomorrow? he kept asking himself, walking, the dry grass rustling around his shins.

Early wouldn't give battle anytime soon, that was for sure, and pillaging would eventually turn Sheridan's army into a disobedient horde. He'd seen it before. Grant still wanted him to drive on Charlottesville before linking up with the Army of the Potomac at Petersburg. But his supply lines were already too long, what with John Mosby getting brasher by the day, and Old Jube might have enough fight left in his boys to pounce on the Union flank if Sheridan risked the long march southeast.

Must sleep.

But first, once again, he needed to see if it was as real as it had been this afternoon. The fires and the smoke were making everything seem unreal. A brimstone nightmare.

He called for a candle lantern—was that dim enough to suit his aides?—and continued up the rise from his tents to the ruin of the Dunker farm. Just a pair of chimneys left to memorialize the house. And where the barn had stood nothing more than a pillow of charcoal from which cow bones jutted.

No crickets tonight for some reason, but a groan of saddle leather drifted down to him.

Pettigrew was where Sheridan had posted him hours before to keep away the curious. The scout was still mounted, although he had tossed the rein over his charger's head, and the horse was softly champing on clover. Smoke was wreathing around both man and beast. Had Pettigrew dozed off? Sheridan couldn't make out his eyes, and the scout didn't salute much. Time to trim him a bit, remind him that while he might well be the eyes of the army, he sure as hell wasn't its brains. Nor its testicles. Like an actor who'd played kings for decades, the man had taken on airs that had nothing to do with his origins. James Pettigrew was actually the son of a Universalist preacher. He'd studied for the cloth himself before the war came along. Now he'd probably killed more men than the Bible had books.

When things got hot, it was time to turn cold toward one's underlings. Sheridan had invariably gotten more out of them that way than with warm praise. Besides, it was fun pretending that he was on the verge of sacking them all. Watching them squirm as they waited for the hatchet to fall. Grovel.

His boots crunched over an expanse of dead coals to the corncrib.

He stopped and slowly raised the lantern.

The ears were still green and had resisted burning. The singed kernels were giving off a burnt, sugary smell—or was it the other thing?

He lifted the cravat he himself had put atop the pile, and it was revealed. The blackened claw of a hand reaching for the sky.

It was still there, real, just as when he'd first found it earlier while taking a stroll alone.

4:39 P.M.

Beyond Harrisonburg, Simon rode into a desert of ashes, a wasteland shaded by a dirty brown sky. The wheat, unharvested for lack of hands, had been put to the torch, and the hooves of his mule raised all that was left of the crop, a fine gray-white powder. It coated the pike like talcum. He'd exchanged a foot-sore Rex at the ambulance depot in New Market for the jack, the only animal that could be spared. But, with forty miles already in the saddle, the plodding gait had seemed merciful to him, although by now even that slight comfort had worn off.

A Quartermaster Corps wagon slipped past. He glanced down into the bed and saw that it was filled with skinned and gutted pigs, enough like human dead to make him start. And then, under provost escort, a family of Dunkers trudged by, the men in sooty beavertail coats, grim-faced, the women in bonnets, keeping their eyes on the macadam. Houses. Simon could see no houses. Just chimneys. And no barns. He waved for a passing trooper to rein up. "What happened here?"

"Sir, Little Phil's burnin' everything within five miles of Dayton."

"Why?"

"Mosby bushwhacked somebody on staff."

"Who?"

The trooper shrugged. "Not sure, sir. Engineer, I think." His stallion sidestepped and neighed. "That be all, sir?"

"No, where are army headquarters?"

The man pointed through the hazy twilight at distant tents, canvas so ash-stained the cluster almost blended into the hillside beneath it. Simon left the pike and cut through an apple orchard. The trees had been girdled with axes and left to die, and the gristmill straddling the nearby creek along with its log dam had been blasted into pieces—the bite of black powder still hung around the splintered wreckage.

The first officer he came upon was Custer. Grinning, the major general sprang from his camp stool at fireside and came down the slope to Simon nearly at a run. His hussar jacket was streaked with char. "It *worked*," he announced, then blushed under Simon's confused stare. "I mean, I'm sure it'll work . . . when I see her."

Then it hit Simon. "Your letter."

"Right. Libbie was enormously relieved. Really. Just as you said, Simon. Right on the button. God, how you've learned women—must go along with being a doctor, I'd think." Custer helped him out of the saddle. "Some ride?"

"Some ride." Simon had to take a moment before he could walk. His legs felt like they were full of termites. "But I'm glad about your wife, sir."

"Well, she didn't *precisely* address the issue."

"Did you expect her to?"

"Of course not. But her words had that flavor . . . it's been lifted. I just know it. And all thanks to you, my dear Simon. I'm in your debt always. Anything I can do—"

"Water," Simon said, grinning with his upper lip sticking on his dry teeth, "and we're even."

Custer barked for his orderly, and within the minute Simon was guzzling from a dipper.

"They do take some getting used to," Custer said. "Long rides."

"Yes." Simon denied himself a second dipper; his stomach was already churning from the first. Custer's gaze was steady on him. He realized that he was being measured. Or was it some lingering suspicion over the true reason Pamunkey had been sent up the Luray? "I understand congratulations are in order, sir."

Custer raised an eyebrow.

"I hear they've given you Third Cavalry Division," Simon went on. A quick nod as if it were nothing more than his due. "I'm going to miss my Wolverines, though." The Michigan Brigade was part of the 1st Division.

Simon handed the dipper back to the orderly, then asked Custer, "One of our engineers killed?"

"Oh no," he said after a pause. "Worse than that. It happened yesterday morning not far from here—"

"Simon Wolfe . . ."

He faced upslope toward the commanding voice. The small figure was set against the reddening sky: Sheridan looked almost like a boy, round-shouldered from an afternoon of hard play. But the brilliant eyes were anything but young. They cudgeled. And something in them made Simon think of Rebekka, the instructions he'd given Ames to send Hannes and her north with Pamunkey at the first hint of danger. Cal had asked what that might be, but Simon hadn't been able to say, and that had made leaving Winchester all the harder. "Sir?"

"Come with me, please."

Custer started to follow, but Sheridan stopped him dead in his tracks with a look.

The boy-general simpered, then gave a flap of his arms and went back to his fire. He slumped on his stool and poked at the coals with a bent musket ramrod.

Simon half-expected Sheridan to turn for the privacy of his tent, but instead he hiked up through the pasture toward a razed farmhouse, his boots stirring the ashes. "Have a good trip?" he asked pleasantly, although his hands were fisted.

"Long, sir."

"Too damned long from Winchester. That's what worries me. And it'll keep worrying me till I put a bullet in John Mosby's head."

Simon inwardly saw young Henry Rhodes. On the ground. Full of bullet holes.

Little Phil stopped beside a corncrib, turned and stared at Simon, his swarthy face blank. Then a smile tugged at the corner of his mouth. "What d'you say we take off the kid gloves?"

He'd never imagined Sheridan wearing them.

"You think I'm unreasonable, Simon?"

He expected this to work into a tongue-lashing, so he said nothing.

"Go ahead—speak frankly, goddammit. We're alone. That's why I chased off poor Curly."

This was it, then. The showdown Simon had played out in his mind a dozen different ways since leaving Winchester last evening. "Yes. I think you've been more than unreasonable in one regard."

"This Dunker fuss?"

Simon nodded, then waited for the storm.

But astonishingly Sheridan smiled and clapped Simon on the armless shoulder. "Now let me be frank. I don't admire Jews worth a damn, but I suppose I admire you. You don't scare, and you don't curry favor. Oh, you wouldn't last ten minutes in the peacetime Army with those fine qualities, but you're the bulliest medical director I've ever had, bar none."

"Then why'd you ask the Surgeon General to relieve me?"

Sheridan blew air out of his cheeks. "The truth?"

"As long as we're being frank, sir."

"I figured this Dunker business would end of its own accord if only you quit whipping it up." For the first time ever, the brilliancy went out of Sheridan's eyes, and Simon could see that he was genuinely worried. "I was wrong." The general took hold of a red kerchief on the pile of eared corn and pulled it aside.

Simon looked briefly, then glanced away, but the hand was everywhere. "Has it been disturbed?"

"Only enough to see that it's a woman under there."

Simon took off his coat, hung it on a fence post. Then his eyes roved.

"What d'you need?" Sheridan asked.

"A shovel. And some lanterns. It'll be dark soon."

Sheridan bellowed down for his A.D.C., who then roused the enlisted tents for lanterns and a work detail.

Simon began scooping the ears away from the forearm. "Who found her?"

There was no answer for a long moment, then Sheridan finally said, "A lot of us were milling around. Came up here myself for some quiet yesterday morning. I can't think down there in all those tents."

"Then somebody on staff informed you, sir?"

Sheridan nodded absently.

Simon studied the arm. Only the hand, folded down over the wrist, had been blackened. That meant she'd been buried in the crib, and then the corn had been set fire with what smelled like sperm oil. He bent the hand straight again, and it yielded with the slightest bit of resistance, stayed for a split second in the position he'd left it in, then slowly flagged.

Sheridan started rocking from foot to foot, but then quickly stopped. "What're you doing?"

"Testing for rigor mortis."

"And?"

"She's coming out of the very last of it, I think."

"Meaning what?" the general asked.

"She died sometime between sixty and seventy-two hours ago."

"Can you be more specific?"

"No, not positively."

"Grand," Sheridan muttered. Oddly, he sounded relieved, despite some exasperation.

A shadow inched over them, and Simon saw that the sun had sunk behind the Alleghenies. Rosh Hashanah had begun, he realized. The new year. A bugle, shofar-like, echoed retreat over the sprawling bivouac. Below, standing with his hands on his hips, Custer was peering up at them. He gave an uncertain wave, which Simon answered after a moment with a casual salute.

Two privates came jogging up from the tents with spades over their shoulders. "Easy there," Simon cautioned as they began shoveling the corn aside.

More men arrived with lanterns. They stood silently behind Sheridan, their breaths misting away in the chill air.

A white prayer-covering appeared, and then the face, swollen and heavy with death.

Simon wanted to catch Sheridan's expression, but didn't.

"Want her laid out on the ground, Colonel?" one of the privates asked.

"Yes . . . on her back."

As soon as this was done, Simon noticed the mahogany-brown stain at midriff. But it was the legs he needed to see first.

Kneeling, he lifted the woolen skirt, but then covered her again and met the gaze of each man encircling him. Even Sheridan's. Their expressions were curious, but not lewd. Veterans, they'd seen so much death on the battlefield it no longer seemed mysterious to them. But this was different. It was death as they'd known it before the war.

Simon went ahead and slid the stockings down to the ankles. To his back, a soldier grunted at the sight of the empurpled flesh. It was blanched with designs of corn ears.

Sheridan had lit a cigar and was shaking out the match. "What's that mess?"

"Livor mortis," Simon said. "Gravity pulls the blood into the lowest portions of the resting body."

"Then she died in that position?"

"Maybe, sir, or was moved here shortly after death."

Sheridan let out some smoke over Simon. "No drag marks I can see across those cinders. These German gals can be stout. It'd take a big man to carry her, wouldn't you say?"

Simon didn't say. He took out his pocket knife and slit the dress open at the belly. Two puncture wounds, incised.

Sheridan asked, "The weapon?"

"Saber."

"You sure?"

"Fairly."

A visible tension passed through the men: they were cavalry.

Simon saw that his own hand was shaking.

Sheridan noticed too, for he said, "When'd you eat last?" It seemed that generals were forever asking this. At least the patronizing types who prided themselves on shows of concern for their men.

What little appetite Simon had had after Rebekka's attack had been taken away by the hospital in Strasburg. "Yesterday, sir."

"Come," Sheridan insisted, "you can finish this after we sup."

Without protest, Simon followed him down into the tents. A hopeless feeling washed over him. The Valley below was as bleak as Moab. It was the Jewish year 5625, and the murdered were still being left to rot in the desert, the survivors walking away with the taste of ashes on their tongues.

God surely must've given up on man by now.

Custer bounced up, obviously hoping to be included. But, to his chagrin, he was ignored by Sheridan, who opened the flap for Simon before stepping inside himself. A bottle of whiskey was waiting uncorked on the table. Sheridan flipped his little round hat onto the cot, then poured them each a glass. "How old would you say she was?"

"Forty."

Sheridan nodded reflectively, then said, "It's all yours, Simon."

"Sir?"

"The inquiry. Go after this son of a bitch as you see fit. You're the man of science here. Maybe it should've been yours from the start. Hell, I don't know. Sit down."

Simon held a sip of whiskey in his mouth to warmth, then swallowed. "Is this an order, sir?"

"Christ Almighty, I thought you wanted it!"

"I wanted justice."

"Then who better to get it?"

Simon thought a moment. "Inside this army?"

"Of course. Nobody from Washington. You have somebody more capable than yourself in mind?"

"Colonel Hayes. He's an attorney, knows the law."

Sheridan exhaled more smoke. "Simon, we're on campaign. I can't be detaching division commanders for this sort of thing."

"But you can your medical director?"

"You tell me."

Simon knew that he didn't have long to decide. But this was all coming too quickly.

Thankfully, at that moment, Sheridan's orderly came inside with plates of boiled beef and turnips. Sheridan fell upon his food, but Simon lingered over his whiskey. Why did he have the feeling that Little Phil was just obstructing him in some new, unknown way?

"How exactly d'you intend to proceed?" Sheridan asked around a mouthful of food.

"Sir?"

"What procedures, man?"

"I don't know . . ." Simon paused. "There's a book I'd like to have as soon as possible . . ."

"Name it."

"Taylor's *Medical Jurisprudence.*"

"I'll approve your requisition myself." Sheridan took a gulp of whiskey, then wiped his lips on the back of his hand. "What became of the bodies of those Dunkers over in Front Royal?"

"I don't know," Simon said.

"How's that?"

"I left them with the local practitioner."

Sheridan frowned. "What's to keep him from shipping them off to

Richmond?" Simon didn't reply, wondering if he might be joking. He wasn't. "No more slip-ups like that, Wolfe. Promise me."

"Sir, my aim would be to find the man. Not cover up what he's done."

But Sheridan seemed not to have heard. "Tell me . . . can you say for sure if a particular saber's been used after the fact?"

"No."

"How about a revolver?"

"Again, no."

"Then why'd you ask to see Elias's Colt?"

"Just to determine if it'd been recently fired. Nothing more."

"Oh."

Simon had never seen Sheridan so distracted. He was leaning on his elbows, staring at his reflection in the dark green glass of the whiskey bottle when he suddenly shot up and began pacing the confines of the tent. "Damn this rot for happening!" He stopped and held his thumb and forefinger an inch apart in front of Simon's face. "We're this close from bringing those rebellious sons of bitches to their knees. And now this!" He trooped to the far corner where the woodstove stood, halted and kicked the cast-iron with the heel of his boot. "You question whomever you must," he said in a quieter but no less intense voice. "Just keep it discreet for the time being, all right? I want nobody to know what's really up except the two of us. Is that understood?"

"Quite honestly, General, maybe I'm not the man to question Colonel Deering, given our past history."

Sheridan froze for an instant. "Say what?"

"You heard me, sir."

"Indeed you're not the man, Simon. But I wouldn't take it personally." A whiff of irony?

"Sir?"

A silence fell, after which Sheridan said, "My God, you really don't know, do you?"

And then Simon realized, even before Sheridan said it.

"Elias is dead."

Simon went still in his chair. Sheridan looked far off. After several seconds, Simon heard his own voice ask hollowly, "What happened?"

"Thursday, I sent him to Port Republic to take charge of some contrabands. He never came back. Yesterday afternoon, my scouts found his body in a barn near Dayton."

The reason for the fan of destruction within five miles of that village. "How . . . ?"

"Shot." Sheridan paused, then sat again and took a bite. "I honestly thought you knew. Eat something, Simon."

"Where is Deering's body now?"

"Buried. Near the barn."

"I need to examine it," Simon said.

"Why?"

"First off, to see if he killed this woman here."

"I'm surprised you have any doubt," Sheridan said, reaching for his glass.

"I do, sir. And I shall till it's proved." Damn him, Simon thought. The man was willing to accept nearly anyone as the culprit, as long as neither Richmond nor Washington caught drift of the inquiry.

Sheridan took a lengthy sip, then shouted through the canvas, "Sergeant!"

Waiting, he smiled knowingly at Simon.

A wiry man in butternut ducked through the flaps and stood by without saluting. The Vandyke beard and cold black eyes helped Simon place him at once: Pettigrew, the irregular scout from the 17th Pennsylvania who'd awakened him in the rain the morning after Fisher's Hill.

"Sergeant," Sheridan said, "Colonel Wolfe wants to dig up Colonel Deering. Take him out there and see that he gets it done safely."

Pettigrew clamped his nostrils shut with his fingers, then laughed nasally.

⋈ CHAPTER 15 ⋈

6:39 P.M.

George Custer sat stripped to the waist at the table in his tent, toasting bits of steak over a candle flame. He'd lived on nothing but coffee, green corn and a few raw onions for the past two days, and now it was time for meat. Drops of juice ran down the cutting edge of his knife, plopped off the handle onto a worn map of the Valley, where they congealed. He clenched the piece between his teeth until cool enough to chew, then wiped the grease off his lips with one of his red cravats.

The flame drew his gaze and held it.

On his ride in from Waynesboro this afternoon, with the bridges of the Virginia Central Railroad sending up plumes of smoke to his back, he'd looked forward to reporting to Sheridan. He wanted to see the look on Phil's face when he heard about the swath of destruction 3rd Division had cut from Staunton to the Blue Ridge. The Confederacy, at least as far as the Valley went, was torn and bleeding in a thousand places.

But when Custer arrived at headquarters, Sheridan coolly took him aside. "Pettigrew's just back from the Reb camps," he said, fairly growling. "He picked up something that may interest you . . ." Then Phil actually spat into a pile of ashes.

"Sir?"

"Six Federal soldiers—yours if possible, others if not—will be hanged by Mosby when captured. Tit for tat for what you did at Front Royal."

Then, without another word, the general had walked away, leaving Custer baffled, humiliatingly close to tears. He'd always believed that Sheridan wanted Mosby's gang treated in the sternest possible way. And now this. There had to be a deeper reason. Over this past week he'd sensed Phil drawing back from him; there'd been none of the old joshing affection, calling him Curly and such.

Outside, someone was talking to his guard.

It took Custer only a second to realize that it was Simon Wolfe, and he hurried from the table and threw open the flaps. "Simon," he said, feeling more hopeful than he had all evening, "come in, come in . . . *please.*" But the surgeon looked so unstrung Custer had to ask, "What is it, my dear man? What's wrong?"

The hounds came over from the pile of straw in the corner, sniffed Simon's boots, then went back to their bed. The surgeon sank into Custer's chair. No matter: Custer took the other.

"Elias," Simon said.

"Oh yes. Awful, really. Mosby's work, I'm sure."

"Are you?" An odd edge to Simon's voice.

"Quite. His men are like fleas up here, hiding most the time but biting hard when they can." Custer was desperate to find out if Phil had mentioned him over supper, but decided not to rush into it. Besides, he'd never seen Simon at such a loss, his sad, handsome face almost sickly-looking. He'd had no idea that Deering's death would affect him so. A truly noble nature. And the best head in this army, Sheridan had said at mess a few days ago—thank God he'd taken up medicine instead of military science. They'd all be in his shadow.

"I'm going out to exhume him," Simon said.

"*Tonight?*"

"Yes, as soon as Pettigrew gets together a wagon and some colored teamsters."

"Strange that wasn't done in the first place, wouldn't you say? I mean, you'd think poor Elias would've been carted off to the embalmer in Winchester. For the sake of his mother." Simon looked at him so sharply Custer was left wondering if he'd stumbled on something that'd just been argued with Sheridan. Threading a fallen suspender over his bare shoulder, he went on, "But I'm sure Phil had his reasons."

"Such as?"

"I don't know, Simon. I'm just saying." Custer picked up his knife and skewered another little hunk of raw steak, then touched it to the flame. "How was supper?"

"I don't know . . ." Simon seemed to look inward. "Not sure I ate anything."

"Then you really should."

"I suppose."

Custer offered him the piece, and Simon moistened his fingertips before taking it. "Go on, down with it. Nothing like meat to get your spirits up again." Custer paused, smiling. "Do you think I'm a McClellan man?"

Simon gave a disinterested shrug, then ate. He really wasn't himself this evening—where were those exquisite tidewater manners?

"See," Custer plunged on, "my people are Democrats, and I'm just curious what's said about my politics."

"I've never heard a thing."

"Oh, fine . . . fine then." Custer started toasting another piece. "Because Phil's people were Whigs. God only knows why a bunch of papists fresh off the boat would see it that way. And I thought maybe . . . you know . . ." He purposely didn't finish, hoping that Simon would spring to it for him, but the surgeon just licked his lips and stared off. "What'd you think of Little Mac?"

"I liked him," Simon said of McClellan in that soft Carolina accent. "For all his caution, his vanity—I liked him." Then for the first time his eyes seemed to snap to life. "May I ask something in confidence, sir?"

"Of course." Just what he needed to foster between Simon and himself. Confidence.

"How'd Sheridan and Deering get along these past weeks?"

"Bit frostily. I'm afraid."

"D'you know why?"

"No," Custer admitted, "although Phil spoke glowingly of you. How principled you were. Solomonic. All that. Maybe he's taking your side now."

"In what?"

"Well, that bad blood between Elias and you. Here, have another. I've had my fill."

"Thank you." Simon accepted the knife, bit the piece off the tip of the blade.

"Hungrier than you thought, aren't you?"

"Yes." Simon said after swallowing. "Would you say Deering was given grittier jobs than others?"

"Not at all. I don't think Elias was ever in the thick of it his whole career."

"Until now."

"That's right . . . till now."

Then Simon asked, "How well did you know David Russell?"

Something in Wolfe's voice made Custer say with a shrug, "Passing well."

"What'd you make of his death?"

"Tragic," Custer said, "simply tragic."

"I mean—is it possible he was sacrificed at Opequon?"

"I'm not sure I catch your drift, Simon."

"Was Russell unnecessarily put at risk? Is that even remotely possible?"

Custer paused. Apparently, there'd been something of a row between Phil and Simon; he realized that this new situation might prove useful to him. "Perhaps. Whatever, David's loss was an awful waste."

"What'd Russell think of Sheridan?"

Dangerous waters. Simon was known to repeat things, even if for the best of reasons. "I have no idea." Then Custer added, chuckling, "Did Little Phil tell you he chased off the *Herald*'s correspondent?"

"Why'd he do that?"

"Well, he didn't actually chase him off. He invited him to accompany his adjutant to Mount Jackson to view Mosby's corpse."

Simon looked stunned. *"Mosby's dead?"*

"Of course not. But you can't have the New York press on hand with expired Germans lying about your headquarters, can you? It's all an outrageous sham. But you know Phil by now, I'm sure."

Simon visibly thought about this, then asked, "Who found the woman's corpse here?"

"Why, Phil did—didn't he tell you?"

"When?"

"Oh, I don't know. Day before last. When he picked this hill for his headquarters."

Simon turned silent and reflective again, and Custer asked himself if the moment had come. The surgeon had seen a way out of the problem with Libbie, and now might well figure out some clever plan to slip Custer back into Phil's good graces. Jews made splendid go-betweens, in case the situation had deteriorated even more than Custer had imagined. Simon could patch things up. "It's Luray," he said at last, trying not to sound as hurt as he felt.

Simon stirred. "I'm sorry?"

"I'm being blamed for Luray when it wasn't even my show."

"What're you talking about, sir?"

"Torbert didn't get us behind Old Jube in time to trap him. And now, for some insane reason, I'm catching the brunt of—"

A rustling outside cut Custer off, brogans sifting through the matted grass. Several men, more than a dozen by the sound, were closing around the tent.

Simon was sitting stiffly, the knife jutting from his fist. His eyes were quite anxious.

And then a voice whispered, "One . . . two . . . ," and the 1st Brigade band broke into the "Home Again Serenade."

Custer laughed, and Simon smiled awkwardly. He'd seemed on the verge of bolting from his chair. Whatever Sheridan had said, it had shaken up the surgeon.

"They come by every evening this time to woo me," Custer said over the tune. "Nice way to end the day, what?"

But Simon was examining the blade where it met the handle.

"Something wrong with the cutlery?"

"No." Simon put down the knife and came to his feet. "I must get going. As always, thanks for your hospitality, sir."

"It was nothing . . ." And then, after a hesitation, Custer asked helplessly, "Did Phil say anything about me?"

But Simon had already gone through the flaps.

Custer sat quietly for a few minutes, listening to the band, rubbing his chest hair with his fingers. Then he reached across the table for the knife. A plain enough one, picked up here in the Valley. He could see nothing of interest about it except maybe the city of manufacture, stamped on the metal near the handle.

Essen.

In Germany, of course. What of it? The Germans made the best, and nothing but the best for Libbie. But this was too plain for her, really. All at once, his face clenched and he buried the knife in the tabletop. He twisted the handle. The blade snapped.

9:05 P.M.

EAST OF DAYTON

The two Negroes climbed out of the shallow grave, shouldered their shovels and walked back to the wagon without speaking.

The corpse had been shrouded in a bright red saddle blanket.

"Why was Colonel Deering left here?" Simon asked Pettigrew.

The sergeant stroked his chin tuft as he peered down at the body. He was wearing a shabby blue cape over his Rebel uniform. "Lil' Phil didn't fancy us bringin' him back to the tents. It was goin' on suppertime, sir." He flashed a hard grin. " 'Sides, our niggers'd be out in a day or two to dig him up."

"Where exactly did you find him?"

Pettigrew hooked his thumb at the barn to their backs. The only one left standing within miles. "Inside, laid out on the straw. Hands folded on his breast just like he'd been looked to by his own mother."

"And what time was this yesterday?"

"About one."

"Where was his horse?"

"Down by the crick," Pettigrew said.

"Where's the animal now?"

"Don't know."

"Any blood on it?"

"None I seen."

Simon noticed that the sergeant had a soiled bandage wrapped around his left hand. "What happened?"

"Leather burn."

"From your rein?"

Pettigrew nodded. "Can't have too good a horse if you're passin' yourself off as a Johnny. And this new one don't like the sound of bullets whistlin' in his ears."

A neigh came from the darkness. Pettigrew had picketed his men around the farm. Just in case. The night was Mosby's.

"More light," Simon said, and Pettigrew grabbed one of the lanterns the Negroes had left in the mound of earth.

Simon stepped down into the grave and straddled the corpse. "How's he smell dead, sir? I'm told you thought he stunk livin'." "Quiet." Simon parted the blanket. The loss of vivification turned some faces serene, saintly even, but not Deering's. His just seemed empty. Even the forked vein in his brow was gone.

He'd been shot in the throat.

Simon unbuttoned the frock coat and then the shirt. Both were stiff with dried blood. Two bullet wounds, one to the chest and the other to the abdomen. The same pattern of fire that had taken Hostedler's life, although Josef's killer had managed only to graze his neck.

Simon bent Deering's hand at the wrist. Completely flaccid.

He looked up at Pettigrew. "This a Dunker farm?"

"Don't know, sir . . . nobody 'round to ask." The sergeant knelt, bringing the lantern closer to Deering's pressure-quilted face. "Only Germans left in this country . . ." Then he paused, smiling as if Simon had almost wheedled something out of him.

"Yes?"

"Well, there ain't many left, sir. We're movin' them north as soon as we find them. Good farmers, Germans."

Simon looked at him, full on. "Where are these Dunkers?"

"Oh, just a handful of 'em out along Cross Keys Road. They'll be run out 'fore tomorrow night."

"How far from here?"

"Two miles, more or less."

"Which way?"

"Southeast . . . but they won't be 'round long."

Simon leaned over the corpse once more, unbuttoned the trousers and parted the drawers. The lower abdomen and genitals were a putrescent green. "Dammit," he said under his breath, then flipped the blanket back over the face and stepped out of the grave.

"What'd you see?" Pettigrew asked, his ease slipping for the first time. His eyes seemed a bit glassy, as if from a recent fever. Maybe it was just exhaustion. This entire army was exhausted and ready for winter quarters. But tell that to Little Phil.

Simon started for the horse he'd borrowed from headquarters. "Get the colonel out of there," he said over his shoulder. "Put him on the wagon."

The stallion was nervous. The smell from the grave, no doubt. Simon stroked the animal's blazed forehead and looked up. He wanted stars. Beacons. But the sky was dark and woolly with smoke, and flakes of ash were jinking down like the sparse, glittering snow just before and after a heavy winter storm in Boston.

Somehow, he'd reached a point where virtually nothing was known again. All this distance for nothing.

Pettigrew's mount stood nearby.

Twin glints reflecting the lantern light showed where the sergeant had looped the strap of his field glasses around the pommel.

Simon checked on Pettigrew, who was cussing the Negroes to hurry as they lugged the body toward the wagon. Then he slipped the glasses off the saddle. He was dropping them into his coat pocket just as rapid-fire hoofbeats thudded out of the darkness.

One of Pettigrew's men raced in and dismounted on the fly. He said that he'd heard something—and that another of the scouts had seen several horsemen in Indian file on the hill above the creek.

Pettigrew dog-trotted over to his horse and swung up into the saddle. "The horn just blowed retreat, Surgeon." The wagon was already rolling, the lanterns extinguished.

"Go ahead," Simon said. "I'll be along in a few minutes."

"I'd make it damn few, 'less you fancy holdin' your sick call in Libby Prison."

Simon waited, holding his bay by the bridle, while the knock of the wagon axles faded in the northwest. Soon, the heavy air of the night erased the last sound of Pettigrew's detail.

Simon mounted and rode southeast.

11:45 P.M.

WINCHESTER

Rebekka tested the cloth straps that held her to the cot, then screamed. She was sure that in the last few minutes the straps had turned into bony hands, gripping her wrists, fingernails cutting into her flesh.

She screamed again, louder.

Two pairs of footfalls, maybe more, came at her from the corridor and scraped to a halt.

Yes?

A match sizzled into a yellow pinprick, and the lamp was lit.
Yes?

She expected swatches of loud color—it seemed that they had
been spooning color into her all these month-long days, but the huge
room, Simon Wolfe's room, was a blur, everything dimly bleeding into
everything else.

"Let's try laudanum for a while," a gruff male voice said. "She's
dehydrating too badly on the calomel."

A woman said, "Very well, Colonel Ames."

"Who are you!" Rebekka cried, afraid that the voices were the
demons pretending to be others.

"Mrs. Zelter . . . dear?"

She was surprised by sudden tenderness in the woman's voice.
The demons were never gentle with her. "Who . . . ?"

"Mother Haggerty, darlin'."

"Mother . . . ?" Rebekka could see only a fat tangle of arms. No
face.

"D'you want some water?"

"Is this the hour of temptation?"

"No, but it's late enough, and you're wakin' the lads in the
wards."

She felt a hand stroking her hair. For an instant she thought maybe
that it was her own. But no, it belonged to the woman, and her touch
was kindly.

"Take this, darlin'—it'll help you sleep."

Rebekka swallowed from a tin cup. Anything to sleep.

"What makes you carry on so?"

"Nothing's ever the *same,*" Rebekka said, rocking her sweaty head
from side to side.

"How's that?"

"You know, Mother. You know everything I'm going to say
before even I say it."

"I don't, darlin'. Truth is—a bleedin' soul never knows what Mrs.
Zelter'll say next."

Rebekka felt the blanket being tucked under her chin. *"What* do
you know about me?" she asked, suspicious now.

"Not a wisp. Listen here—I want you to stop thinkin' of those
wretched things what make you scream. Think of somethin' lovely.
The loveliest thing you can. All right?"

Rebekka started to protest, but then a strange warmth began to radiate out from her stomach. She could feel her blood drumming warmly through her veins.

"All right," she murmured sleepily.

A little time passed in a dreamy sensation of floating, and then she found herself in Jacob Zelter's farmhouse near Staunton. She was sitting alone at the window in the barren main room. A flat, almost black cloud was dusting the fields with snow. Out in the kitchen garden, which she'd neglected all summer, a raven was perched on a dried stalk of pigweed, bending it almost to the earth. The bird pecked savagely at the seed head, then twisted its neck with a jerk and settled a malignant eye on her.

"What do you want?" she whispered.

Squawking, the raven flew off, becoming a dot of purple against the cloud. She felt that it'd stolen something from her, something related to her spirit, but she wasn't sure what.

Then she heard Jakob Zelter walk ponderously into the room and stop several paces behind her. He took a moment to clear his throat. He came in from the barn each afternoon at this hour to put the same two questions to her. "How are things with you, Rebekka?"

"I'm fine."

"That is good." He cleared his throat again. "Are you well enough to make supper?"

"No, I'm not well enough for that."

After a few seconds, she heard him walk back out.

In October, before the roads turned to mud, Jakob Zelter had taken her in his wagon to Lexington. They'd finally agreed that she would enter the state insane asylum there. She had imagined that she'd have a small but comfortable room, a flower garden and maybe even a patch of woods in which to stroll. Life there would seem less threatening that it did among these Virginian Brethren, their sour-faced, carping women who'd let her know from the beginning that Jakob Zelter could've done better by marrying in his own congregation. Life would be simpler in the state house.

But then, coming into that hellish building that stank of urine and worse, with the beastlike shrieks of the imprisoned demoniacs echoing off the stone walls—she'd turned and clung to Jakob Zelter as she never had before. She begged him not to leave her in such a vile place, and when he stammered that they'd already agreed, hadn't they?—she shouted from Matthew, " 'Tell it unto the church!' " He gravely nodded. He knew at once that she was within her rights: she was demanding that the issue be put to the church. He had no choice but to take her back to Staunton. The Brethren then decided: "If a poor sister becomes insane, void of all reason, dangerous and very troublesome, still she should not be put in the state house." Jakob Zelter accepted the judgment, and nothing more was said about Lexington.

But whereas he had enjoyed a vigorous middle age before, he was suddenly old, with an old man's walk and an old man's morose silences.

Through the window panes, she could see him plodding across the dooryard, leaving prints in the light snow. He was almost to the well when he stopped in his tracks. She could tell by the stiffening of his shoulders that he'd met someone unexpectedly.

She shifted in her chair so she could see farther around the edge of the barn.

Someone was indeed there.

But when the demons were upon her, as they were now, it was impossible to take in an entire person at one grasp. At these times, people seemed to be made up of separate parts that never quite pulled together to form one being. The shattered mirror. But she could tell that the stranger was a man, and that he was holding a horse by the bridle, even though the beast was mostly defined by its thick black mane and tail. There was a fevered glint to the stranger's eyes, but those brilliant eyes seemed to have no fixed position in his swarthy face.

She knew that he wasn't a brother. There was no plainness to him. But he stood in the middle of flashes of light, a shifting cloudlet of diamonds and crystals that kept her from seeing his clothes.

Jakob Zelter turned toward her and hollered something she couldn't quite make out.

She threw open the sash. "What is it?"

"This English is ill. Bring me my medicines!" Jakob Zelter was renowned as a healer, and often even the English neighbors called upon his services. Most of his medicines he made himself from plants that grew in the hills and glens.

She grabbed his leather bag and ran outside, stumbling at the bottom of the porch steps as she always did when the demons were upon her. The air was cold on her cheeks.

Jakob Zelter screamed.

At first she thought it was at her for something that she'd done, for not coming fast enough, but then she realized that he was in pain. It was so hard to see, and now there was a thick snow falling to make things worse.

"Rebekka," Jakob Zelter cried, "I am *all!*" Finished. Gradually, he appeared before her through the flakes, holding his belly in his bloody hands. "Run!" He reached back and braced himself against the well. His hat was off, and the snow was melting on his big bald spot. "Run, girl!"

But she felt no fear, only fascination as she watched Jakob Zelter struggle to remain upright. "Get away!" He made one last desperate gesture for her to flee, then collapsed over the lip of the well.

After a few moments, his back stopped rising and falling.

Rebekka turned and tried to bring the stranger into focus. He was on his feet, behind her, gripping his sword in his hands.

OCTOBER 4, 1864

NEAR CROSS KEYS

Simon sat on a stone fence, waiting for dawn to clear the Blue Ridge. It was coming grayly through a haze. Below, at the foot of a long sweep of wheat, lay the hints of a farm: the square shadows of buildings, glimmers off windows, sparks gusting now and again from a chimney.

It was settled.

Elias Deering had not killed the Dunker woman in the corncrib. The provost marshal had himself already been dead at least twelve hours before she was stabbed to death. The onset of decomposition had told Simon this.

So much for Sheridan's all-too-convenient suspect.

Simon lowered the glasses and exhaled.

The light was coming more strongly now. He could tell that it was a well-kept farm. German.

But who, then, had shot Deering? The Dunkers in whose barn Pettigrew had found the body?

No.

The Brethren would go to the gallows before they'd spill blood.

Was it possible that some passing Rebel partisans had jumped in to help them? Maybe, but Simon couldn't imagine guerrillas leaving a murdering enemy with his *"hands folded on his breast just like he'd been looked to by his own mother,"* as Pettigrew had put it. And, as hard up as their cavalry was for horseflesh, they would've taken Deering's sleek Morgan.

In a sense, none of this was as puzzling as Sheridan's about-face over his provost marshal.

That hot afternoon below Fisher's Hill he had stymied any thorough questioning of Elias. But last night over supper he'd been more than ready to blame the man for the vilest crimes of the war. At best, it was convenience: Deering was dead, of course, and even his allies on staff wouldn't go out on a limb to defend his name. But at worst—it threw a new light on the commanding general.

Why had Little Phil been so evasive about admitting that he had found the woman in the corncrib? Of course, that was George Custer's version, and the boy-general was famous for picking up on which way the prevailing wind was blowing. He was unabashedly mercurial, and that quality had no doubt helped him survive McClellan's downfall, then jump from captain to brigadier in a single bound. But still—

Suddenly, Simon dropped behind the fence, waited a bit, then peered over its top through the glasses.

Blue-clad cavalry scouts, three of them, were riding up to the farmhouse. Two of them went through the gate while the third stayed outside, waiting. The pair split off from each other at the well. One trotted up to the barn, kicked open the door and charged inside, gripping his carbine at the ready. The other jumped down from the saddle and barged through the back door of the house.

Nothing happened for several minutes.

Crows cawed in the yellowing woods behind Simon.

Then the two men emerged from the buildings and waved to the man at the gate. He wheeled his horse and streaked back the way they had come: out of the west. Simon glassed him as he kept to the road to Harrisonburg—and then halted. Just ahead of him, a column of fours cantered around the bend, Custer in the lead, his scarlet tie marking him at a mile.

Simon crouched behind the wall again: the two troopers at the house were scanning the ridge lines if only out of habit.

He found himself in strong light. The sun had finally topped the

mountains and was streaming through the haze. He stayed hidden for
a count of ten, then trained his glasses on the column. A single troop.
About eighty men, given recent casualties. A tiny fraction of Custer's
division.

The general peeled off at the gate, watching the column of fours
split into twos and pincer around the farm. Reaching the far field, the
troopers fanned out across the stubble and blended into the shadow
that was slowly inching back toward the Blue Ridge.

Simon focused on the gate again. Custer was no longer there.
Shifting higher, Simon could see the two scouts, the butts of their carbines braced against their hips, and then Custer. He had reached the
house and dismounted. A man and woman—in dark, plain clothes—
had stepped out onto the porch, and he was talking to them, hat
doffed.

Simon fixed on the woman's face. Too far to tell if she was comely,
yet he was sure of it. The man was middle-aged, bearded, giving off a
guarded air even at a quarter mile.

"Good God," Simon whispered. The three scouts were now galloping eastward to catch up with the rest of the troop.

George Custer was alone with the Dunkers.

Then Simon heard a scuffle of hooves to his back. His own horse
was hobbled, he remembered with a jolt.

He was just beginning to turn for a glance behind when he saw
three mounted figures looming against the sun on the crest across
from him. Shades of gray and butternut—the morning rays were dazzling, but he could tell that the men were in Rebel colors.

He'd expected this all night: Sheridan had sent Pettigrew out
again to find him.

"Sergeant Pettigrew?" he hailed the forwardmost rider.

"Afraid not, dear Colonel," an English accent startled him from
only a few feet away, "but I'm familiar with that troublous devil."

Simon began to spin on the man who'd crept up on him, but then
felt a sharp point jabbing against his ribs. "Far enough," the voice
whispered.

Simon automatically sucked in a breath, which made the man add,
"A cry or such will only loose my knife. Do you understand me, sir?"

Simon nodded once.

"Care to surrender your own handkerchief for a blindfold—or
hazard the use of mine?"

CHAPTER 16

2:45 P.M.

ROCKY MOUNT, IN THE BLUE RIDGE

Several hours into the climb, the rangers halted.

Simon could hear one of them walking back down the file to him, sword clanking in scabbard. He'd noticed during the first minutes of his capture that only the Englishman wore one. Captain Hodgkins, the man had whispered an introduction at the last rest stop, late of Her Majesty's Forty-fourth Regiment of Foot—as if to suggest, *Isn't most everybody in western Virginia these days?* That had been in mist almost heavy enough to be rain, and now Simon could feel the warmth of the sun on his back. They'd passed up through a cloud, then.

"Blindfold chafing you, sir?" Hodgkins asked.

"No," Simon said, "but I'd like some water."

"Of course. How's your wrist binding?"

Simon's forearm was tied to a saddle ring behind him, and his rein was being held by one of the rangers. "All right."

Hodgkins raised a canteen up to Simon's lips. The water tasted of mud: that probably meant that the rangers had been shadowing Sheridan's army these past days of burning and pillaging, filling their canteens from creeks already stirred by the passing of Federal troops. Sheridan's gray shadow.

"Thank you." Simon said. He decided not to ask what a British officer, hollow-eyed from hunger, wearing a faded red jacket and butternut trousers, was doing with the Rebel partisans. And Hodgkins had yet to ask what a Carolina accent was doing in Abraham-blue. Simon assumed that the captain knew he was a surgeon, but wasn't sure. Self-preservation told him to say nothing for the moment.

"Ready, Colonel?"

"Ready."

Simon lowered his head, and his horse began rocking wearily under him. The bypath was so narrow the scrub whisked his legs, and from time to time the ranger leading his horse would call for him to duck. He felt no temptation to wrench his arm free and bolt, instead trusting that once they could talk above a whisper his branch of service would be realized, and that'd be that.

Over the next two hours the air turned brisk. Sunlight no longer filtered through his blindfold. Dusk? He caught a whiff of woodsmoke. After a few minutes more, the sounds of a bivouac echoed down from above. Hushed talk and a little laughter. A spoon scraped a tin pot.

His horse dug in its hooves.

Once again, Hodgkins came back to him. "Going to unbind you now, sir."

Simon's arm was freed. He tried to shake some feeling into it.

"Please get down, Colonel."

Simon dismounted, but then had to steady himself by gripping a stirrup. Impatient hands unknotted his handkerchief and whipped it off his head. He squinted, trying to bring the captain into focus.

"Have your balance yet?" Hodgkins asked. A hooked nose and brooding eyes—it wasn't the sort of self-amused face Simon had imagined. "Not easy to ride blind. Follow me—"

"A moment," Simon insisted.

The scene before him was wavering. A Blue Ridge hollow in late-afternoon shadow. Smoke was drifting lazily in between tree trunks scabbed with lichen. One by one, men in grimed uniforms got up as if out of the leaf-strewn earth itself, rose as stiffly and dumbly as the resurrected, and started crowding in on him.

He found himself standing very straight, meeting each pair of eyes set against him. It was hard to think of them as the dashing young cavaliers of the Northern press; they seemed more like mangy, half-starved dogs—even the officers. The "weather-bronzed faces" described in the *New York Herald* were like old chamois. Most of the men had hair that hung in dirty, twisted locks to their shoulders, and a quick scratch here and there told of body lice.

When the rangers had closed a circle around him, they halted. A scuffling of boots soon made them part, and a slim, frail-looking man continued up to Simon alone. His slight stoop didn't fit the cape he'd rakishly turned back to show off the scarlet lining. Piercing eyes, a stark blue. And a new beard the same sandy color as his hair. "You are . . . ?" he demanded.

"Colonel Simon Wolfe." Hodgkins had never asked him.

The man opened Simon's saddle valise and glanced inside. "You're a surgeon, of course."

"Yes."

He'd taken out the pint of whiskey Simon had packed as an anodyne and was inspecting it with a frown. "No strong spirits in my camps. War's temptation enough." He uncorked the bottle and poured the rye out onto the ground. Then he looked at Simon again. "Know who I am?"

"John Mosby, I believe."

Mosby nodded. "And you must be Solomon Wolfe's errant issue."

"I suppose."

"Well, Captain," Mosby said to Hodgkins, "you've gone and bagged our own Secretary of War's son."

The captain started to shake his head, but then turned without expression and led his mount toward the horse-line.

"So, Colonel Wolfe—you took the other tack."

When Simon said nothing, Mosby went on, "It's a wonder you didn't kill him."

"Sir?"

"You heard me."

"My father's and my differences are our own, *sir,*" Simon said.

A quick smile, almost feminine. "I meant no offense." Then Mosby gestured toward a canvas lean-to pitched out in the ferns. "Join me in a simple repast, Colonel?"

Supper yesterday with Sheridan, this evening with Mosby—Simon suddenly felt as if he had no country.

But he was famished, so he followed Mosby down a gauntlet of rangers. It was unsettling. They watched his passing as if he were the first prisoner they'd ever seen.

"Is this it now?" one of them asked, eyes savage.

But Mosby didn't answer. He walked gingerly, short steps only. Nearing his smudgy fire, he lowered his voice to Simon. "I was shot lately. In the groin." The same soft, high-toned smile. "Nothing familial, I'm happy to say, but I seem to have mislaid my surgeon. You mind taking a look . . . ?"

"Surely."

Simon had Mosby lie on his filthy bedroll and lower his trousers and open his drawers.

"I ask only for my wife's sake," Mosby said, staring up at the smoke-darkened canvas of his lean-to. "I'd like to honestly write her that I'm on the mend. But I'll lie if I must."

"Looks like there was no impinging on the bone," Simon said, examining the wound.

"So I was told."

"Bullet from a Spencer carbine?"

"You know your trade, Colonel."

"Much pain when you walk?"

"Less so now than a week ago."

"Good." Simon noted the yellow ring around the bullet hole. Simple bruising rather than infection. "You may tell Mrs. Mosby in all honesty that you're on the mend."

"I'm in your debt, sir." Mosby fastened his trousers again, then sat up. He seemed relieved.

A Negro brought them each a cup of chickory coffee and a hardtack biscuit. Simon realized after a moment that this would be supper. He let his gaze pass over the rangers. All but one of them had gone back to their scattered fires to play euchre or just lie on their blankets and smoke. Yet, this gaunt man stood gaping at Simon, his beard dripping with tobacco juice. All four top incisors were missing, leaving the canines to jut slightly over his lower lip. A rougher sort than the others, who, despite their shabbiness, were still cavalier enough to have undone the middle buttons of their tunics in that devil-may-care affectation sported by Citadel cadets he'd seen as a boy.

"What d'you want!" Mosby suddenly hollered at the man.

He scratched an armpit, then moved off.

"There's what happens when cousins find a hayrick in the moonlight." Mosby chuckled under his breath, then slowly ran his hand through his hair before asking Simon, "You know what happened at Front Royal?"

"The executions?"

"Call them what you will, I had to make a promise to the boys. Next six prisoners who fall into our hands, we hang them. And now who the hell's first? A Southern-born sawbones. Sol Wolfe's son to boot. And Yankee preachers—least the ones I've suffered—say God doesn't have a sense of humor." He paused. "I suppose you're too high-Carolina to ask the boys for your own neck."

"Should I?"

"It might make things easier."

"For whom?"

Mosby smiled. "Sol'll get a kick out of that one."

"I'm a medical officer," Simon said, ignoring the further mention of his father. "Not even a prisoner of war."

"Says who?"

"Your own Congress."

"I wish that'd wash right now, Wolfe," Mosby said, sounding genuinely worried, "but Richmond's a world away."

Simon set his cup on the ground.

Hodgkins strode up to beg a word in private with Mosby.

Strangely, the colonel told him to say what he had to say in front of Simon.

"Sir," Hodgkins said, looking embarrassed, "I've overheard the men. They're *wondering.*"

Mosby thought this over for a moment, then barked across the hollow, "Damn you! Damn every last one of you to hell!" All faces snapped toward him. "I'll decide when *I* decide!"

When the men had turned back to their fires, Mosby said to Hodgkins, "That it?"

"Yes, sir—I should think."

The captain trooped away, red-faced, and Mosby chuckled again. "Poor Hodgkins. Fancies that at the end of this we'll all be English again."

"What will we be?" Simon asked.

"Different," Mosby said, his voice tinged with sadness, "just different."

One of the rangers swore against Custer's name.

Ignoring the outburst, Simon asked, "What's a Britisher doing here?"

Mosby shrugged.

"Has he ever explained?"

"Not really," Mosby said. "Oh, he fought with Garibaldi to free Italy, and maybe that's it. Still . . ." Then he broke into Greek. Excellent Greek.

Simon knew the citation. From Thucydides. " 'If one has a free choice and can live undisturbed, it is sheer folly to go to war.' "

Mosby grinned. "Very good, Colonel." But then his grin went and he stared at Simon, visibly puzzled. "Are you *really* for Africa?"

Simon dipped his biscuit in the coffee to soften it. "Yes, I am."

There was a silence filled only by the droning of mosquitoes. The first hard frost would kill them, Simon idly thought, waving them away, and then Mosby said, "You know, your father had me to dinner this spring."

Simon realized that it had probably been at the house his father had rented for Leah and himself in Richmond. His sister's last letter was nine months old, and he ached to hear how she was doing, but he let it go with: "Did you?"

"Yes. Some discourser, Sol. Another guest asked him how the Old Testament viewed slavery . . ."

That must have irked him. Solomon Wolfe hated having the mantle of Shem thrust upon him. That he'd been born a Jew and not a pure-bred Southron, he'd once joked to some close friends, could be laid to a divine sneeze at the instant of his conception.

"He said something that fascinated me," Mosby continued. "The authority for slavery's the covenant itself."

"Is it now?"

"You tell me. 'Thou shalt not covet thy neighbor's house, or his field, or his male slave, or his female slave.' "

"Ah." Simon saw that several of the rangers had gathered around the man Mosby had chased off. He was talking low and sullenly to them.

"You disagree?" Mosby asked.

"Pardon?"

"Is that the commandment in Hebrew?"

"Yes, but the word in question can also be translated as *servant* or *bondsman.*"

"Then Hebrew slavery didn't exist?"

"It did, within bounds. As my father well knows. What he's obviously forgotten is this—as Jews, we ourselves were slaves in Egypt. We know what it is to be a slave. To have no rights. No dignity. No hope. Job said of his *'ebed,* his servant or hireling or slave—take your pick— 'Did not He that made me in the womb make him? And did not One fashion us in the womb?' "

Mosby reflected a moment.

Simon could almost glimpse his father's leonine smile in the ranger's eyes, his love of argument.

Mosby then said, "But by your own admission just now, Job was a slaveholder."

"True."

"As were Abraham, Isaac and Jacob. Am I correct?"

"You are."

"Upright gents who eschewed evil, but owned slaves like any man of property in the South, right?"

"No comparison."

"Oh?"

"They were poor nomads, simple people, wandering the desert with their flocks, living no differently than those who served them," Simon said hotly. "Not exactly tidewater gentry, who have reduced the slave to an object for cruelty and lust—"

Simon stopped.

He realized that he'd raised his voice, while Mosby's face revealed nothing but polite interest.

"Is something wrong?" Mosby asked.

Simon had waded through this argument a hundred times before and never convinced a Gentile from below the Mason-Dixon Line that the entire spirit of the Torah was contrary to the Southern abominations of slave-breeding, slave-trading and slave-hunting. Time to change the subject. "This has nothing to do with the matter at hand."

"Which is?"

"My status as a surgeon."

"My boys at Front Royal were soldiers. That didn't stop Custer from murdering them."

Simon glanced away. No argument to that.

"What precisely's your job?" Mosby asked.

"Medical director for the Middle Department."

"For Sheridan's *whole* traveling circus?"

"Right."

"Good for you. Does that call for keeping tabs on enemy movements?"

Simon hesitated. Undoubtedly, Mosby had been a very good lawyer. In a shift that had almost slipped by unnoticed, he'd turned any explanation Simon might make into a plea for his life. He was now forced to tell the truth. "I wasn't spying on *your* forces."

"Who then?"

"One of our own cavalry divsions."

"Which?"

"The Third."

"Custer's," Mosby half-growled. He was obviously well posted on Union promotions. "The man himself?"

"Maybe."

Another smile came to Mosby's face, but this one might have been to mask his confusion while he sorted out his thoughts. "I find that hard to believe, Colonel."

"Will you agree that some things go beyond this war?" Simon asked.

"Most assuredly, sir," Mosby said, chuckling. "I'm from Virginia, not South Carolina." But then Mosby paused as if he could see where this was headed. "You're talking about criminal acts, aren't you?"

"Yes."

"What manner?"

"Just outside Winchester, I found a Dunker woman in a burning house. She'd been stabbed to death . . ." As Simon went on telling him about the first killing, Mosby plucked some moss off a stone and began rolling it between his fingers. He listened without expression for several minutes, then interrupted.

"D'you know which Confederates units were last to quit Winchester that evening?"

Simon admitted that he didn't. He hadn't even thought of it.

"Well," Mosby said, "most of them, I'm told, were Gordon's Georgians. Man of the law, John Gordon. I can't see—"

"I'm not saying your people did this."

"All right. Good." Mosby flicked away the moss. "Go on to the next ones."

That jarred Simon. "How'd you know there were others?"

"I was already aware of the Dunkards along the Front Royal pike. The German woman near Winchester is news to me."

Simon hesitated. How much more was Mosby secretly aware of? No way to tell. "Those Dunkers were the Hostedlers. I took them into Front Royal for autopsy, where the local practitioner—"

"Why, sure," Mosby suddenly exclaimed, "you're the one-armed Yankee surgeon!"

"Sir?"

"Who tried to save Henry Rhodes."

Was this another trap? But once again, Simon saw no way out but the truth. "Dr. Lazelle and I both tried, for all the good it did."

"Poor old Doc Lazelle," Mosby said.

Simon would've expected *poor Henry*. "D'you know him?"

"Knew him well."

"You mean he died?"

"Yes, a week ago. His son and I went to university together."

Something the practitioner had never revealed, and something Simon hoped Sheridan would never learn. Otherwise, his findings from the Hostedler postmortems would be discredited for the very reason Elias Deering had said they should be: Lazelle was a secessionist. Then it hit Simon in an echo of feeling. The kindly practitioner was gone. Another casualty of the Union advance Little Phil would never own up to.

"I know Custer was around Front Royal when the Hostedlers were killed," Mosby said. "Could he've passed by the woman's house south of Winchester?"

"Yes. But so'd half our army."

"Any wounds telling you that these Dunkards put up a struggle?"

"None," Simon said. "Which confounds me. I mean, there are limits to conviction. Instinct takes over at some point. These people went down to their deaths in almost total surprise."

Mosby tossed another stick of brushwood onto the fire. "I shot a man once. Before the war, I mean. But that was because he insulted me. This . . ." The fire popped, spewing an ember onto Mosby's bedding. He brushed it off, then licked his fingertips. ". . . this isn't that sort of thing at all, is it?"

"No," Simon said. He was getting weary. Going over the killings once again was doing it. And Mosby's expert questioning. If anything, it was convincing him of his own clumsiness with this sort of thing. Was Sheridan counting on just that?

"There's been another, hasn't there?" Mosby said.

"Yes."

"A woman?"

"Found on a farm near Harrisonburg day before last."

"And again Custer was in the area?"

Simon nodded. And Philip Sheridan.

He slipped his hand into his coat pocket. Deering's letter was still there, but that gave him no comfort. What if Mosby found it? The implications began to make his head swim. Truth or not, it could tip the balance in favor of McClellan and the peace Democrats, who were already saying the war was unwinnable, a moral outrage. Slavery would go on forever, protected by the sovereign borders of the Confederacy.

"Something wrong, Colonel?" Mosby asked.

"No, why?"

"You look powerfully vexed all of a sudden. Was the latest woman stabbed?"

"Yes."

"I see." Mosby warmed his palms over the fire. "And does Sheridan know about this?"

"All of it."

"What does he want done?"

"The murderer found out."

"Even if he's one of yours?"

"I believe so."

Then Mosby asked, "Some problem with that?"

"No." Simon decided to rise. "The only problem is my release. I demand to be let go at once."

"You can't do that, Colonel Mosby," a voice said from out in the ferns. The ranger with the missing teeth was standing there, holding a cocked revolver down at his side.

Mosby started to say, "What the devil—?"

"I seen this man before, sir," the ranger said, approaching. "Runnin' down off Little North Mountain, wavin' the colors as proud as you can with jist one arm. He ain't no surgeon, and it's time we answer Front Royal."

Mosby looked to Simon.

4:38 P.M.

HARRISONBURG

Custer was almost to the headquarters tents at the end of another day of widespread burning, when he came upon a scout from the 17th Pennsylvania. He immediately asked if Surgeon Colonel Wolfe had been found yet. The trooper said no. Although Custer had ridden forty miles since sunup, he left his column behind and galloped east with an escort of only two men.

At nightfall, they reached the barn in which Elias Deering had lain. Within minutes Custer did what Pettigrew had failed to do: find Simon's trail, a line of tracks heading southeast. But by then the darkness was full, and he knew that he shared it with Mosby.

"You want to push on, sir?" one of his troopers asked nervously.

It had struck Custer last night when Pettigrew came in without Simon Wolfe—how dear the surgeon had become to him. It was a kind of friendship he'd never experienced before. The freedom to admit most anything without fear of ridicule. Had there ever been a sweeter-natured Jew? And a wiser one? Other than Christ Himself, of course? But in the morning the retrograde movement Sheridan had ordered would begin, and the sea of gray—only temporarily parted by Little Phil's blue rod—would once again close behind the Army of the Shenandoah, swallowing any trace of poor Simon.

But poor Autie too.

There'd be no confidences with Simon. That more than anything infuriated him. He wanted to send for Libbie to share his winter quarters with him in Winchester, but there was so much more to talk over with Simon before he could do that with an easy mind. He wanted Libbie to find herself in the presence of the perfect husband, not the drunken boy who'd staggered past her window on his way home to the drunkard's stuffy nap. Only Simon Wolfe, with all his medical and moral knowledge, could help him become that husband. And how he'd looked forward to having her meet Simon. She'd adore him—he just knew it.

Pettigrew. If Custer were Sheridan, he'd whip the insolent bastard, then give him a running start ahead of a squadron with orders to shoot.

"There's nothing we can do tonight," Custer said at last to his troopers. "Let's go back."

At headquarters, he fetched an onion from the mess chest, then went outside again and flopped down in the grass. No stars. Just smoke. He bit into the onion and stared off, content not to think about anything. But his gaze had come to rest on Sheridan's tent. It was lit from within, and two silhouettes darkened the canvas. One had a bullet-shaped head. The chin of the other was spiked by a Vandyke.

Custer stopped chewing so he could hear the conversation. He couldn't quite make out the words passing between Sheridan and Pettigrew, yet the tone was unmistakable. Phil was dressing down Pettigrew. And royally too.

Bully for him.

Clenching the onion between his front teeth, Custer got up and brushed himself off. Then he crept up to the tent, sliding in behind Rienzi, who was standing at fodder, his black coat shining in the torchlight.

"Did you hear me?" Sheridan was demanding.

For once, the vinegar had been leached out of Pettigrew. "Yes, sir." His accent was gone too.

"Where's that goddamn *Herald* scribbler right now?"

"At mess with your staff, sir." And the correspondent was irked— Custer had heard—not to have found Mosby's corpse at Mount Jackson.

"This really blows it all to hell," Sheridan went on, quieter but no less disgusted. "Well, I can't have the body lying about, not with Wolfe out of the picture."

"Bury it?" Pettigrew suggested.

"What? And have it dug up by God knows who?" Lowering his head, Sheridan fell silent for a bit. "Burn it," he said at last.

"Sir?"

"Find an abandoned German farmhouse miles from here. Leave her inside—and put the torch to the place."

Pettigrew's silhouette could be seen saluting, then he came outside and around the end of the horse-line.

Custer had to beat a hasty retreat.

He went back to his own tent and sat at his table with his hands folded before him.

"My merciful God," he said after a while, "this isn't what I had in mind. Not this."

Simon had begun to suspect Little Phil. That's why the surgeon had seem so distracted last night. The enormity of it.

Maybe the time had come to switch horses again.

Phil was on the run, and Custer, for Libbie's sake at least, had to make sure that he didn't go down with Sheridan. If it came to that. And it seemed to be coming to that. No matter that Sheridan was advancing ever deeper into Virginia. McClellan had been doing the same in the fall of 1862 when Lincoln gave him the boot. Custer had avoided the bloodbath that hit the rest of Little Mac's staff, even though Washington had pegged him as McClellan's fair-haired boy. He'd taken leave to return to Michigan until the dust settled, the smartest thing he'd ever done, other than marrying Libbie Bacon.

"It's a blessing in disguise," he said out loud—Little Phil kicking him around like a stray dog these past days. It might prove to be the perfect time to be out of favor. "All right, all right then. I'm just where God wants me."

On this encouraging note, Custer got up and started for the mess chest and another onion.

6:43 P.M.

MOSBY'S BIVOUAC

Mosby was waiting for Simon to explain why he, a surgeon, had carried the Union colors down off Little North Mountain when a ranger officer rode out of the woods and into camp. The young lieutenant got down from his USA-branded brown charger—not the skinny bay Simon had seen him on before—and looped the rein around the picket rope. Then, almost shuffling from fatigue, he passed between the fires, nodding to the others in a cordial but aloof way. He stepped up to Mosby, saluted and said in a breathy voice, "Beg to report, sir."

"Anything urgent, Claude?" Mosby asked.

"No, sir," the ranger said, then glanced curiously at the ranger holding his Colt at the ready out in the ferns. "Just more of the same."

Mosby said, "Then it can wait."

The ranger finally looked at Simon full on, although the surgeon had the feeling that the man had already sized him up out of the corner of his eye. "Hello again," he said with the same dim smile he'd worn on the Manassas Gap line that morning in the fog. He had a slight Creole accent.

"You two know each other?" Mosby asked.

"I caught him napping," the lieutenant said. "I'm Claude Tebault."

"Simon Wolfe." Then he added pointedly for Mosby's sake: "I was the lieutenant's prisoner for a few minutes. Before he let me go."

"Between Front Royal and Strasburg?" Mosby asked Tebault.

"Yes, sir."

"Out alone?"

Tebault nodded.

Simon saw Mosby frown. Not the answer he'd apparently wanted. His mood had visibly worsened over the last several minutes. By twos and threes, the men were creeping toward his fire, and the rough-looking ranger, still drawn, was telling them about how Simon had borne the colors.

Mosby backed them off a few paces with a glare, then turned to Tebault again. "Did Colonel Wolfe carry weapons that morning?"

"No, sir."

"But he was alone."

"Yes."

Mosby frowned again, then eyed Simon. "That was Crook who came down on our left, wasn't it?"

"It was."

"Did you carry the colors for him, Colonel Wolfe?"

The words almost stuck in his throat. "I did."

The rangers gave out with a loud murmur, but Mosby silenced them with another look. "Why," he then said with deliberate slowness to Simon, "did you do that—if you are indeed a surgeon?"

"I *am* a surgeon, dammit."

"Then *why,* sir?" Mosby pressed.

"You won't like the reason."

"Try me."

"I picked up the colors from the dead bearer because my honor as a Union man was in doubt."

"You're not trusted, then."

"Not in all quarters."

"And you wish to be?" Mosby asked.

"Yes. I'm for Africa, as you say. I want no mistake about that, North or South."

"Then hang 'im for ol' Ethiopia and be done with it," somebody said from the ferns.

Mosby held Simon's eyes for what seemed an eternity, then motioned for Hodgkins to approach. He whispered something, and the Englishman strode off toward the horses, shouting for the Negro to come running.

"You look tired, Claude," Mosby said.

"Don't feel it." Still, Tebault seemed drowsy and remote as he blinked into the fire. Simon wasn't sure that he'd been listening to any of what had just been said. He was obviously unwell; the Army of the Potomac would've pensioned him out long ago. This, more than anything, convinced Simon that the Richmond government—his father's government—was on its last legs.

He was also convinced that the rangers were going to hang him. Mosby was caving in to them. This came over him not with a jolt of panic but rather with a sad, tired feeling. Running was out of the question. It wasn't fear of their guns that made it so. It was fear of a cowardly death, for he knew that his conduct during these last minutes would be widely reported—and he desperately wanted something of his works, his beliefs, to survive himself. It was probably foolish to believe that the whole of a lifetime can be validated by courage at the end. But he believed it, nonetheless, as much as Sheridan, Custer, Crook, Hayes and all the others did. He knew this now.

Simon saw the Negro hoisting his McClellan saddle over the sway-back of the worst-looking mount in the entire line. Hodgkins had already taken his medical kit and Pettigrew's field glasses. Apparently, they were going to string him up out of the saddle. Good, he thought. The fall might break his neck.

His mind was empty, and his body so heavy and slumberous-feeling he doubted he could have run even if Mosby had asked him to.

Then he realized that he had one thing to do while he still had some voice. "Colonel Mosby?"

"Sir?"

"I'll ask you to burn something for me . . ."

"Yes?"

Simon handed him Deering's letter about Sheridan. "I'm ashamed to say this—it compromises a lady's good name. But the fault's all mine. She's young and doesn't know who's worth her reputation yet. Certainly not me. Read it first, if you must."

"You think it necessary?"

Simon forced himself to say, "I'll leave that up to you."

Mosby hesitated, then dropped the letter into the flames unread. "Her name's safe. And I never meant to search you." Turning, he asked Tebault, "Can you deliver to the Valley tonight?"

"Right away, sir?"

"Please."

Tebault went to join Hodgkins at the horse-line.

Simon saw himself going down the mountain later, doubled over the back of a horse like a sack of wheat. He struggled against an urge to dig his chin into his breastbone—the rope was weighing on his mind more than he realized. He held his head high, although a little spasm of nerves rocked it once. Mosby didn't seem to notice. Steady now, he told himself. Steady . . . steady. It'll all be over in a few minutes.

"You have any debts to call in, Colonel?" Mosby asked in a quiet voice.

"None I know of," Simon said, not sure what the man meant but in no mood to belabor the conversation. He could feel the last grains of his courage trickling away, like sand in an hourglass. He wasn't going to beg, if that's what Mosby was asking.

Hodgkins came back, leading the plow horse by the bridle. "God speed, sir," he said.

"If I see him, may I give Secretary Wolfe your regards?" Mosby asked.

Simon began to say no, but then an unexpected feeling came over him—all at once, he vividly recalled riding in an open carriage with his father long ago, down their street in Charleston. Solomon suddenly kissed the crown of Simon's head and put the lines in his tiny hands to drive the team the last yards to their home, which was marked by a candle lantern held by their slave-butler. "Please do. And tell him, after everything, I often think of him. My sister . . ."

"Lovely woman."

"She is . . . give her . . ." But at that point Simon's voice gave out.

He was terrified of breaking down in the final seconds of this ordeal. Come death, quickly. He cleared his head with a deep breath. Then, all his fear, whatever its cause, snapped, and he felt regret, mostly, regret over things not said or written while there'd yet been time. Nothing was resolved. That seemed an awful waste.

And then, abruptly, Hodgkins tossed him the rein.

Simon stared at the Englishman, afraid to take hold of his wild optimism. "What—?"

"You do have a debt to call in with me, Colonel," Mosby said. "Tell Sheridan we don't hang men of honor, that you're going free for what you tried to do for that boy at Front Royal. Tell him Custer and the rest of the murderers won't be so lucky." Then he offered that high-toned smile of his. "I'd think about how hard you want to go after that criminal matter we discussed. Otherwise, you might find yourself unwelcome on either side of the Potomac. And that, I'm afraid, would leave you plumb out of countries."

Simon dropped his head for a moment, then nodded good-bye to John Mosby.

"Sorry for fobbing this plug off on you," the ranger went on. "We're not horse thieves, but our need of a healthy mount is greater than yours." Then he gestured at Tebault, who was riding toward them. "I think you'll find Claude interesting company down the mountain."

⊰ CHAPTER 17 ⊱

9:10 P.M.

TWO MILE RUN

Simon rode behind Claude Tebault.

The night itself was now his blindfold, more impenetrable than the handkerchief Hodgkins had made him wear on the way up the mountain. Between Tebault's horse and his own was a quick shivering of leaves—all Simon had to follow most of the time, for the lieutenant seemed to melt completely into the foliage at each turning. Still, as if the darkness wasn't deep enough, Tebault led him up a creekbed for several minutes of splashing higher into the Blue Ridge again. "I'm already more than lost, Lieutenant," Simon complained as they climbed away from the water.

Tebault said nothing, then plunged his horse off a ridge into a cedar brake. Simon held the rein between his teeth to keep his arm free for parrying boughs away from his eyes.

"Where'd you lose it?" Tebault suddenly asked.

"Antietam."

Simon thought that was the end of it until a while later the lieutenant said, "Where along the line?"

"In the Cornfield."

Tebault spurred his horse to jump a fallen log. "The two of us, then."

Simon went around. "Pardon?"

"I was hit out in the Cornfield too."

"Louisiana Tigers?" Simon asked, guessing from the accent.

"Yes."

Snow-white gaiters flashing along the ground. Sooty faces screaming toward Simon. And to both sides of him the profiles of his own Massachusetts men, also blackened by spent powder. Tonight, incredibly, he had stumbled onto the mirror image of that morning, something he'd never expected until years after the war, if ever. "Was that Stonewall at the Dunker church?" he had to ask.

"For a while." Tebault paused. "Except we never called him that."

"What then?"

"Old Blue Light, mostly."

Strange, Simon realized, for sometimes in his dream about that morning he saw Jackson's eyes as pale blue stars invoking death across the smoky field. "I take it you weren't captured after you fell."

"No," Tebault said, "I was carried off right away. Or so my orderly told me. Carried off by my cousin. He went back out into the corn after, and then he was killed." The ranger had found another faint path for them. "You weren't so lucky?"

"I lay out there all day, waiting for the stretchermen."

"You didn't go down in the East Woods?"

"No, out in the field. Under the sun."

"A shame," Tebault said. "A surgeon hit while tending to the wounded."

Simon decided to let it go at that.

Tebault came to an overlook and drew rein. He sat motionlessly against a broad glow, his long hair stirring around his shoulders. The jagged scar near his right ear showed deep in the orangish light glancing around his face. Simon crested the rocky spine a moment later and saw what was transfixing him: the Valley floor was sprinkled with hundreds of fires. It seemed as if all of western Virginia was going up in flames, that Sheridan was hurrying the poverty he believed would make the Rebels pray for peace even more than death itself. But Tebault appeared anything but prayerful; his eyes, reflecting the conflagration, were bitterly metallic.

"What stretch are we looking at?" Simon asked.

"Staunton to Harrisonburg."

They watched, hushed.

"Your army's starting north again," Tebault finally said. "We know how it moves by this pillar of fire at night, a pillar of smoke at day." He rode on. "What's it like in Winchester?"

"I'm sorry?" Simon asked, following.

"Lots of our wounded?"

"Yes. Several hundred."

"Are they treated well?"

"The same as our own."

"Good. What about the Germans?"

Simon was instantly on edge. "What of them?"

"I see so few anymore. Your army's taking them down the Valley, yes?"

Simon relaxed again. "True."

"Are they all in Winchester?"

"No, not for long at least. Provost details are escorting them over the Potomac."

Tebault rubbed his eyes. Simon noticed that the lieutenant's left palm was still bandaged. "Is your hand healing all right?"

"Fine."

"How'd it happen?"

"I'm not sure. You know how it is in a battle. Your blood is up. You're in a dream. You feel nothing till it's almost over." Tebault's glassy-eyed stare went to Simon's empty sleeve. "Did it come off cleanly?"

"No—amputated."

"Pity."

Simon nodded.

"Much pain?"

"Yes."

Tebault nodded thoughtfully, then gazed out over the fires again. "No pain for me. Just a swift blackness."

Simon almost didn't ask, but then went ahead. "Was it hard for you to come back?"

"Sir?"

"You know—to duty after your convalescence?"

Tebault fell silent. Then a moment later, he said with a soft laugh, "Sometimes I'm sure I didn't make it."

"What d'you mean?"

"I'm dead, Colonel. And you, you're just a fellow ghost. Everyone I meet is just a ghost. Some sympathetic, like you. Some like the demons of hell."

Simon had to put his heels to the horse to keep up. "Then your wound still troubles you?"

"Sometimes," Tebault said.

"Tell me how, if you don't mind."

"Now and again . . . it leaves me in a dead place."

"Dead place?"

"Yes, all shadowy. Like a stormy twilight."

"How long does this last?" Simon asked.

"Minutes, I believe. Maybe five or so. But it seems longer. Forever, sometimes."

"And how do you feel during this, Lieutenant?"

"Forsaken," he said. "Much as you probably did at Sharpsburg, waiting for the stretchermen."

The man was obviously suffering from some sort of seizure. He had no business being in the field. "What d'you do during this time?"

"Sir?"

"Are you alert? Can you walk?"

"No," Tebault said, sounding a bit mystified. "I think not. I can't remember much after, just the loneliness." Suddenly, his tone turned hopeful. "Are you familiar with this kind of thing, Colonel?"

"Somewhat . . . but I'm no specialist."

Tebault ripped off a creeper tendril that had tangled around his reins. "But there *are* specialists?"

"Oh, an entire hospital devoted to nothing but head wounds." Then Simon saw an opportunity to end this man's war, to get him where he belonged. "I believe I could arrange something for you. It might involve taking the oath—"

"No, Colonel," Tebault said sternly.

"I beg your pardon?"

"My head might need mending. But not my loyalty. I thank you, but no. We mustn't talk from now on."

An hour before dawn, the lieutenant halted and motioned for Simon to ride up beside him. They'd come down to a parquet of fields and woodlots, and a few hundred yards to the west a bonfire was visible through the trees.

"One of your picket posts," Tebault whispered. Then, once again, he offered that eerie smile. "I'm glad now I didn't kill you that morning along the tracks. I came close, because I knew you were scouting for your army and I had no time for prisoners. But God stayed my hand. For what purpose, I don't know. Good-bye and *bon chance.*" With that, he wheeled and started back toward the Blue Ridge.

6:57 A.M., OCTOBER 5

WINCHESTER

"Colonel—come quickly!"

Mother Haggerty's cry spun Cal Ames around on his stool. "What is it?"

"Mrs. Zelter."

"Oh pus," Ames muttered, before raising his voice again. "Be there in a minute!" He told the patient he'd been tending to hold the fresh linen pledget to his wound until he could return to tape it. Then he followed the matron down the corridor. Yesterday, Mrs. Zelter had been carried from Simon's room to a windowless chamber. Stout brick walls to muffle her screams. Also, her cot bindings had begun to abrade sores into her arms and legs, so Ames had thought it better to let her lie free on a straw-covered floor.

Her son's care had been given over to Pamunkey, but that couldn't go on forever. Another battle would come sooner or later, and all the orderlies would be needed as dressers. When the hell was Simon due back from Harrisonburg? There'd been no message from him, and Ames only hoped that he'd fared well with Sheridan. Little Phil was nobody to cross, not with that sulphurous Irish temper of his—and the life-and-death power that went along with commanding a Union army on campaign. He could shoot or hang whomever he damn well pleased, and even old Father Abe would say amen as long as Sheridan was whipping Jubal Early and burning the crops Lee needed to feed his troops at Petersburg.

Mother Haggerty had already turned the key and opened the door.

Ames went inside. The morning light flowed around him from the door, but his own silhouette cast the young woman in shadow. He stepped aside so he could see her. Then almost gasped.

"Good morning, Mrs. Zelter," he finally managed to say.

She was sitting quietly on the straw. A coy smile as if she'd been up to some small mischief these past days. Her eyes were lucid and bright, and she looked pretty instead of haunted once again—astonishingly pretty.

"Good morning," she said. "I'd like something to eat."

Ames said, "Certainly." Simon would be delighted. "Anything you want. Come, it's time to get out of this room."

12:00 P.M.

THE VALLEY PIKE NORTH OF HARRISONBURG

From far away she looked like a walking stick. But then, as Simon rode closer, she turned into a serpent, standing erect as all serpents had before the Fall, although she wriggled slightly through the shimmering of midday heat. Finally, she became what she truly was: an old Dunker woman with rheumy eyes, holding out a ladle of water to all who passed.

Simon accepted her gift and drank.

"Danke," he said hoarsely, twisting around in the saddle to see where she lived. Nothing but scorched fields for miles. Behind her, a gaggle of ravens were grubbing in the ashes for seed.

"Where do you sleep, *Oma?"* he went on in German.

In silence, she dipped into her leather bucket and offered him another drink.

"No thanks," he said.

Infantry marched past on its way down the Valley. She went out to the soldiers, who broke ranks to steal a gulp from her until the officers waved their swords and got them back in order.

Simon gently put his heels to the plow horse Mosby had given him. Again, but harder. The animal refused to budge. His tail swished once, then flagged.

Finished.

"Well, old fellow," Simon said, "I'm trusting this isn't just because I'm a Yankee." He dismounted and pulled him by the bridle across the pike into some shade.

A murk of old smoke lingered in the air, especially along the bottom lands, but it was no longer thick enough to ward off the sun. Hot again. The promise of autumn coolness had vanished and another summer, although less fiery than the first, was baking the Valley once more.

Indian summer, wasn't it called?

He sat with his back to a locust tree and closed his eyes. Mosby's face whirled in a red haze, watching, listening, weighing. Strange. Despite the noose Simon had expected at the end of that supper in the ferns, he'd felt at ease with John Mosby. More so than he had with any Union officer. He'd explained carrying the colors as a matter of honor, and the ranger, whom everybody in blue said was a brigand and a cutthroat, had understood at once. A man's honor wasn't truly his own. It was in the hands of others, and for that reason had to be constantly retrieved at a price. Usually death or injury. A Virginian saw this right off, a man who even as a boy had wrested his honor back from a fellow student who'd handled it roughly.

An hour later, the creaking of a wagon woke Simon up.

A family of Dunkers, fleeing north, slowed, then stopped beside the old woman. The mother and her two teenage daughters climbed down. Each in turn kissed the old woman thrice on the lips while clasping her right hand.

The father, darkly bearded, in a black tailcoat, came over to Simon. "Are you sick?" he asked in English.

"No," Simon said, rising.

The man nodded, then licked his sun-cracked lips and gazed anxiously back up the pike. Had he gotten ahead of his escort?

A pall of dust was rising above the trees, moving toward them. Probably cavalry, Simon surmised.

"I think maybe you are sicker than you know, English."

"How's that?"

"The arm."

"No," Simon said with a smile, "it came off a long time ago."

"Ah." The Dunker grinned. "I thought—"

"I know." Simon gestured toward the women. "They greet one another quite affectionately."

"Do they?" The man looked puzzled.

"The kissing."

His eyes widened a little. "Ah, yes. The holy kiss. In Romans, you see. The *Vorkampher . . .*"

"The apostle?"

"Yes, Apostle Paul tells us so. Salute brothers and sisters with a holy kiss. The kiss of charity."

"Where are you from?" Simon asked.

"Mount Crawford."

Not the family, then, Simon had seen Custer approach yesterday morning along Cross Keys Road. "Where're you headed?"

"Maryland." Then the Dunker added defensively, "We had some blue soldiers with us, but they said we are too slow and they left us."

"I don't care if you have an escort. Can you take the old woman with you?"

"We will try. But so many like her . . ." The Dunker frowned. "How do you call it? Their wits, yes?"

"Yes, their wits." Rebekka writhing against her restraints on his cot, salivating from the calomel. Wits. Mrs. Lazelle baking to keep her mind off things. Wits. Leah carrying on like a scullery maid over Israel's coffin. Simon shook his head to break the chain of thought. "Do you have enough food for the journey?"

The Dunker said nothing. Not much, then.

Simon dug in his pocket for a double eagle. "You can buy something from the sutlers along the way."

The man hesitated to take the coin.

"Is something wrong?" Simon asked.

"Gold and silver are signals to Satan."

"Then you can't have money?"

"Not too much. It makes a man greedy. But this will be all right, I think, English." He accepted the gold piece and quickly pocketed it as he started to return to his wagon.

"A moment," Simon said, delaying him. "I've heard that the Brethren won't swear oaths in court."

"That is true," the Dunker said. "It is in James, you see—'Swear not, neither by heaven, neither by the earth, but let your yea be yea, and your nay be nay.' "

"But a sister could still testify, though?"

"Perhaps. If she does not raise her hand or kiss the book."

"So, on those terms, she could be counted on to come forward with the truth," Simon said.

The Dunker stroked his beard, his eyes shrewd. "That would depend on many things, English."

"Such as her character?"

The man wouldn't say.

"What if that sister were Rebekka Zelter of Staunton?" Simon pressed.

For a second he thought the Dunker was going to walk away, but then he said, "I do not know this woman. But if faced with the truth and faced with a lie at the same time—a sister would spring to the plain truth. I believe this if she was brought up in the church, for it is harder than one thinks to turn away from the truth."

"If you don't know Sister Zelter, have you at least *heard* of her—?" A rumble of hooves out of the south turned Simon's head. The cavalry was nearing in a column of fours, and a lone horseman had dashed ahead of the formation, whipping his hat against the haunches of his mount. At his throat was a red cravat.

"My God, I thought it was you!" Custer hollered, reining up. "It *is* you, isn't it!"

"Yes, sir."

Custer jumped down, and Simon was surprised to get a quick embrace. "Where the devil've you been, man!" But before Simon could answer, Custer stepped away and began pacing, tapping a gloved finger to his lips. "All right, all right," he prattled on, "must get you to

Phil at once. He's been off his head with worry. You don't lose your medical director every day. Where's your horse?"

Simon pointed at the plug, now lying flat in the shade.

Custer made a face. "You're kidding." He turned to his color troop, which had just caught up, and ordered a sergeant to loan Simon his charger. "Hurry, man, you can double up with someone."

Simon saw that the Dunker family had hurriedly gotten underway again, having persuaded the old woman to join them. He climbed stiffly into the saddle.

"Going ahead to meet with Phil," Custer said to his adjutant. "I'll meet you on the Back Road." And then to Simon: "We're off!" Several hundred yards down the pike, just after they had galloped past the wagon of Dunkers, the boy-general doffed his hat and whooped at the top of his lungs, "You're alive and well, damn you!"

Simon smiled through his weariness.

"Here's to snug winter quarters, Simon. Evening chats before the fire. Ye gods, I was terrified Mosby got you!"

"He did."

Custer gawked for an instant. "You don't say!" Then he burst into laughter. "You trump, you! How'd you talk your way out of that one?"

"I'm not sure."

"But he let you go?"

"Yes, right after supper. Kept my horse and kit, though."

"Supper with Mosby!" Custer howled again, but then gradually sobered as he stared at Simon across the jolting space between them. "Could you find his lair again?"

"Never in a thousand years. Blindfolded. And it was just a bivouac."

"Well, no matter," Custer said, although he was clearly disappointed. "No matter." And then after a minute he asked, "What were you doing with those Germans?"

"I was taking a nap when they came upon me."

"A nap? Oh Simon, you're luckier than you know. Another mile, and we're swinging over to the Back Road."

"Sir?"

"We're the rear guard. Nothing but Old Jubilee's cavalry behind us." Custer shook his head, grinning. "You're immortal, Simon

Wolfe. Like me. We're two stars that won't ever burn out, aren't we, though?"

An hour later, they came upon Sheridan's flag flying from the porch of a farmhouse. The general himself was down at a large corral, smoking, studying a herd of perhaps two hundred horses that kept shifting nervously from place to place. Seeing Simon walk down from the house beside Custer, he plucked the cheroot from his mouth and stared as if he couldn't believe his eyes. He didn't look pleased, even though he finally forced a smile. "Well, strike the tent—it's my surgeon colonel. Looking tired as hell, but in one piece."

"And fresh from John Mosby's hideaway," Custer said.

Sheridan spat down into the ammoniac dust. "Really?"

"Yes, sir," Simon said.

"I've heard Mosby means to hang six of our boys."

"True."

"Your neck looks fine to me, Simon."

"Hanging was proposed, sir, but finally tabled."

A sergeant, one of the informal horse doctors to be found in each cavalry regiment, emerged from the herd and joined Little Phil by ducking through the fence rails.

"Well . . . ?" Sheridan asked.

"Worn out and starved, sir," the sergeant said, his arms akimbo. "Every last one. Pasturin' on broom-sedge these past weeks, I'd guess."

Sheridan pointed. "How about that pretty little sorrel there?"

"She's got the scratches." A foot disease. Virginia soil was infamous for giving it.

"Damn." Sheridan paused. "Well, they're not worth taking north, but I sure as hell can't leave them for Early." He gave a deliberate nod to his A.D.C., who then trotted over to a regiment of troopers lounging in the grass on the far side of a pond that was green with duckweed.

Simon was careful not to look toward Custer as he asked Sheridan, "Have there been any more incidents, sir?"

"Shame. They're good little mounts. Virginia horses." Then Little Phil turned toward Simon. "No . . . none we know of."

Simon breathed easier. Certainly by now anything at the Dunker farm on the Cross Keys Road would've been reported.

"When'd Mosby snatch you?"

"It was by his men. Mosby himself is recovering from a gunshot wound to the groin."

"How bad?"

"Painful, but he's apparently able to ride."

Sheridan took a long puff, then said, "Sergeant Pettigrew tells me you promised to catch up in a couple minutes."

"Yes, sir. I wanted another look around the farm." Simon could feel the old pulpiness spreading inside his chest.

"You didn't answer me, Simon."

"Sir?"

"When did Mosby get you? Nine o'clock? Ten? Midnight?"

Simon was kept from saying by the troopers, who came filing along two sides of the corral, gripping their carbines. "Heads or hearts, boys," Sheridan coached them, then rested his forearms on the top rail of the fence and gazed at Simon. "As soon as you rode after Pettigrew and the wagon?"

"Yes, sir. I'd just started back when the rangers overtook me."

"And Mosby just let you stroll out of his camp?"

Simon nodded. He felt that Custer was staring at him a bit too keenly.

"I see," Sheridan said. "Pettigrew says another ranger recently captured you. And let you go."

"Yes. The morning of the Front Royal attack one of Mosby's lieutenants found me on the Manassas Gap line." It was time to get off the subject. "What became of the body, sir?"

"Body?"

"The one in the corncrib. I wasn't finished with it."

"Sorry, I thought you were."

"Did you have her buried on the farm?"

"No," Sheridan said, "we gave her to some Dunkers heading north." Sheridan dropped his cheroot and stepped on it. "Why d'you think Mosby and his people were so kindly disposed toward you?"

"I don't know that they were, sir. I'm a surgeon, and they know how medical service should be treated." Simon decided not to give him Mosby's message. Not with Custer present.

"Of course." Sheridan smiled as if all his questions had been in jest. Then his smile vanished as he said to Custer, "You out of things to burn?"

At first, the boy-general thought he was being joshed, but then seemed to catch the faint rebuke. "I'm off again, sir," he said, stung, then walked up the slope.

Sheridan raised his hand, and the troopers loosed a volley. Horses screamed, and the herd scattered pell-mell, leaving behind several dead and dying. A gaunt roan tried to follow, dragging its crippled hindquarters through the dust.

Simon gave his back to the corral.

"Sad, isn't it?" Sheridan asked just over the crack of the Spencers.

Simon said nothing.

"Just got the word," Sheridan said. "The goddamn Sanitary Commission's coming to see our hospitals sometime in the next couple days. I'll let you know as soon as I find out myself. I'm taking over Belle Grove mansion down near Cedar Creek. When I get myself situated, I'll come to Winchester so we can get rid of the self-righteous prigs in short order."

Simon nodded.

"Worst sound on the battlefield," Sheridan said. "A horse dying. Must be his dumb ignorance that makes it so. I figure a human being has it coming, don't you, Simon?"

⊰ CHAPTER 18 ⊱

9:53 P.M., OCTOBER 6

WINCHESTER

Simon reached Amherst Street at tattoo so tired he wondered if he'd need help out of the saddle. Soft yellow lights crowded in on his confusion, danced watery circles in his eyes. The sound of the bugles from the cantonment of provost guards near the hospital faded back into the ringing of his ears. He felt as if he were sitting fifty feet in the air, and the slightest movement would send him toppling down to the cobblestones.

He really should've spent the night in Newtown, those last six miles up the darkened pike had nearly done him in.

A familiar silhouette was standing in the shadows on the corner, holding something pale in his arms, some sort of bundle.

"Pamunkey?" Simon quietly called.

The orderly stepped into a spillage of lamplight from a window. He had Hannes, and the child turned his face toward him as if expecting Pamunkey to speak. Simon could see at once that they'd grown attached. "How'd you know I was coming?"

Pamunkey tilted his head toward the walkway behind him, and Rebekka strolled out.

"An ambulance driver told us, Simon Wolfe," she said in a firm, clear voice. "He saw you helping some hurt soldiers along the pike."

Simon was speechless for the moment. She was restored—wonderfully so, her eyes bright and steady on his, her smile full of warmth. The slightest trace of the tormented woman he'd left strapped to a cot, screaming, was gone.

At last, he eased down off Rex's back and stood before her. "That's right," he said carefully, so moved he was afraid that she'd think something was wrong. "A runaway wagon crashed into some infantry . . ." He paused, looking more deeply into her eyes before saying, "You look well, Rebekka."

"I feel well."

Simon glanced questioningly to Pamunkey, who gave him a slow nod. She was indeed better, then.

"You're weary, Simon Wolfe," she said, brushing his cheeks with the back of a hand as if testing a child for fever.

He wished that her touch had lasted longer. Esther Monis had sometimes touched him like that. "That I am."

"How was Harrisonburg?" she asked. A hint of pique that he hadn't taken her with him?

Everything was being burned and plundered, but he made up his mind not to distress her. "The same."

She threaded her arm through his, and they started for the hospital. He stopped on an impulse, took Hannes from Pamunkey, and let the orderly lead Rex. Walking again, he asked, "How's Colonel Ames?"—only to see how she felt about her treatment.

"I don't know," she said, as if the man were of no concern to her. A good sign, maybe. Usually, when in the midst of her affliction, she only opened up about the things that upset her.

He kissed Hannes's cheek. The baby fretted a little, but it felt good to hold innocent life.

Then he gazed up Amherst.

A half-dozen men and women in plain clothes were coming down the street toward them. Simon saw at once that they were Dunkers, carrying bedrolls and linen sacks—probably all that was left of their worldly goods. They began to slow as they caught sight of the young woman in black homespun, and then the women, two of them in unadorned bonnets like Rebekka's, broke ahead of their men and began to outstretch their right hands in a graceful, almost beatific gesture. Simon expected them to close the last few yards to Rebekka and give her the kiss of charity.

But all at once the women stopped, then gathered their skirts in their hands and parted widely around Rebekka.

The men quickly followed, averting their faces from her.

Rebekka hurried on for the hospital.

Clutching Hannes, Simon ran to catch up. "What was that about?" he asked breathlessly. Too exhausted to be running.

"Nothing," she snapped.

"Who were they?"

"Not true Brethren."

"Please stop," he said. She did so, but her eyes stayed hostile. "Why aren't they true?"

"Punishment," she said with the sharp ping of a bullet.

"I don't understand."

"Punishment!"

"Rebekka—"

"They deny the punishment hereafter—that the wicked will receive according to the deeds of this body. They'd have the wicked go happily into paradise. Don't you see!"

"Rebekka—"

"Those who have wronged me would go happily!"

"Please—"

"I've been wronged too much to believe that!" Then she threw her arms around Simon, pressing Hannes between them. The child began to cry.

"The wicked will be punished," Simon said, disappointment washing over him as he held her—she was no better, after all. "I promise. But why did these people avoid you?"

"I *told* you—they're from a sect that's in error. They know nothing of the gospels."

"What's the name of this sect?"

"I . . . I don't know," she stammered. "I forget. What does it matter? They're in error. Are you listening to me, Simon Wolfe?"

Fleetingly, he thought to go after the Dunkers, make them explain to his satisfaction. But he had nothing left for that. He had scarcely enough energy to get him inside the hospital to his cot.

5:28 A.M., OCTOBER 7

ARMY OF THE VALLEY HEADQUARTERS, MOUNT SIDNEY

Jubal Early sat on his charger in the darkness, gazing northward from a low ridge. Sheridan had more than burned the Valley beyond recognition. He'd burned it beyond visibility. Nothing was out there except blackness, the stench of ashes. Early was half-convinced that the dawn he was awaiting would never come. Just eternal darkness.

But really, Phil Sheridan seemed too little a man to cause something this vast. *The locusts have no king, yet all of them march in ranks.*

A cough reminded him that Tom Rosser had ridden out to join him in the last few minutes. The young brigadier had showed up two days ago in advance of his six hundred veteran troopers, the Laurel Brigade. Many of them were natives of the Valley. How would they feel about Sheridan laying waste to their homeland, turning it into a valley of dry bones? Slaughterous, Early hoped. Ready to cut off the tail of Sheridan's army and beat him to death with it.

He'd finally convinced Lee that, if he were to do his job here in the Shenandoah, he needed some first-rate cavalry to shore up Lomax's belles, who saw their horses as a means of flight rather than attack. Marsa Robert had grudgingly spared Rosser from the defense of Petersburg. Early knew the big and swaggering cavalryman well; Rosser had served under him the winter before. There had been a few differences. The biggest was over Mrs. Rosser. Like Jackson and John Gordon, Tom didn't care for having his woman out of touch. Bad for soldiers to come home to the feminine graces after a day in the field; all those silks and flounces somehow made death seem too painful. A soldier had to get it inside his head that there wasn't that much to life. But

Mrs. Rosser wasn't along this time, and Tom, after the tedium of the Petersburg trenches, was ready to butt and blast the Yankees back into Maryland. That was all that really mattered.

Early realized that the dawn was finally coming. Rosser's straight-backed silhouette was taking shape against a thin grayness. West Pointer. Would've graduated with the class of 1861 had he not resigned two weeks before the ceremony to join Confederate forces. He was an acerbic young man, but only because he took everything so damned personally. You could just say howdy and wind up insulting him. Cavaliers.

"I'm giving you Wickham's division too," Early said at last.

"All right," Rosser said sleepily.

"Pursue the enemy, harass him—and ascertain his purposes."

Something winged overhead, a forlorn sound this time of the morning.

Then Rosser asked, "May I ask what our own purposes will be?"

Early paused. He could almost make out Rosser's bearded face now. "We're going to leap on Phil Sheridan's army one fine morning soon. Chew it up. Then I'm going to drag the sawed-off son of a bitch out of his tent and shoot him between his black little eyes with my own hand." He felt something like lust pass through him as he inwardly saw Sheridan squirming on the muddy ground, dying. "That's what the hell we're going to do before the snow flies, Tom." Early then sensed from the silence that followed that Rosser had his doubts.

But the young brigadier kept them to himself. "Who'll I be facing in their rear guard?"

"Custer, mostly."

Rosser chuckled contemptuously. *"Fanny?"*

"Pardon?"

"We called him Fanny at the academy."

"Why's that?"

"His complexion, sir. So pink and white like . . . well, you know what I mean."

Early sat quietly for a moment, watching the dawn brighten around him, not wanting to see the devastation that would soon take shape. But then he laughed too. Fanny.

10:00 A.M.

WINCHESTER

Simon stood on the hospital loading dock in a rank with his staff, listening to a band thump out what were said to be Little Phil's favorite marches. Buttons glittered on dress uniforms, and the midmorning sunlight beaded sweat on faces. The general had yet to show up from his headquarters at Belle Grove mansion south of town, and Simon had better things for the stewards and wardmasters to do than primp in hot wool and wait for the arrival of the U.S. Sanitary Commission. Even the colored attendants from the dead house, usually the most sublimely patient of men, were getting antsy.

A chaplain grinned as he huffed inside, carrying an armload of devotional tracts. "Mornin', Colonel Wolfe."

"Morning, Reverend." Simon started to check his watch, but then stopped himself.

As a sign of its growing confidence in the Medical Department, the Commission—a coven of sensation preachers and village doctors, according to most Regular Army surgeons—had dropped its formal inspection program earlier in the year. So why one now? Unless Sheridan, for some reason, had requested it. Once again Simon found himself wondering if Little Phil was building a case against him, this time for medical inefficiency. Cunning: on the one hand to have him head the Dunker inquiry, and then on the other to sack him for neglecting his regular duties. After hearing from Custer how Sheridan had deceived the correspondent from the *Herald,* Simon had no doubt that he was capable of it.

Cal Ames slipped in beside him, having just made a last-minute sweep of the wards.

"Well . . . ?" Simon asked.

"Fine, just fine," Ames said. "Relax."

No need for Simon to hide his anxiety from the man. Last evening, he and Ames had met in private to try to figure out why Sheridan had reversed himself and not forced Simon to go on furlough for the Jewish holidays. Cal was as baffled as Simon, but far less suspicious. His final answer was that Sheridan was at last sincere about getting to the bottom of the killings, and that Simon should rejoice—his views had prevailed.

But Simon couldn't.

He noticed that Ames had strapped on a sword. "Didn't know you owned one, Cal."

"Yes, yes—got it as a birthday present from Edna. But damned if I can find my green sash."

Simon had left his dangling off a limb in the East Woods. For all he knew it was still there.

Sheridan's standard fluttered around the corner, carried by his cavalry escort. Pettigrew and his butternut scouts weren't among them. These shorn and shaved troopers were as polished as silver service. On matched bays. Sheridan rode in an open carriage with the two commissioners, nabobs from Manhattan. Soft brandy smiles and huge bellies. Simon knew the younger of them to be a Unitarian minister, and the other an allopath, or physician of the old school, whose practice was making him a fortune now that most of the competition was in uniform. Little Phil looked like their teenage nephew they'd taken out for an airing.

The carriage pulled up to the dock.

Simon called his staff to attention. A chipper Dr. Twiss, despite his civilian duds, looked more military than any of them; the true surgeons were slouching with fatigue, their heads drooping. Since the start of the campaign in August, fully a quarter of Simon's doctors had been sent home due to exhaustion or illness.

Sheridan led the way up the steps, holding his saber against his leg to keep it from clanging against the iron rail. He returned Simon's salute with a tiny smile. "Surgeon Colonel. I trust all's ready for inspection?"

"Ready, sir."

Sheridan introduced the commissioners, who'd put on a grave air to let everybody know they weren't about to be hoodwinked, and Simon in turn introduced them to his staff. Twiss knew the allopath socially, or at least pretended to, so some long moments passed in which they chatted while Little Phil tapped the hilt of his saber with a finger. As soon as he could, Simon herded them all into the main ward, which finally—thanks to Mother Haggerty—was as orderly as any general hospital in Washington. The wounded were in clean nightclothes with ice and lemons at hand. Hard to believe that it'd been an abandoned factory only three weeks ago. The woman herself stood by, wringing her hands behind her black cape.

The minister cleared his throat and asked Simon if this was a division hospital.

"No, sir," he explained. "It's a transfer depot for the wounded of all three corps on campaign at this time."

"Kind of small for that purpose," the allopath said, examining a patient's record card. "Wouldn't you say, Colonel?"

"We're in the process of setting up a much larger facility under canvas, like the one at City Point serving Petersburg."

"And when can we see that?" the minister asked.

"Within the month, sir," Simon said.

"That long?"

"Only in the last week has it become clear that we'll be wintering in the Winchester area. A depot too far in the rear is useless." Simon glanced at Sheridan. Had he put the commissioners up to asking these questions? The general yawned behind a glove. Simon had never had difficulty with the Commission before; most of its members were gadflies, for sure, but the Army and Congress had needed prodding earlier in the war to clean up the medical mess. "Gentlemen, may I present the best medicine we can give to the Army of the Shenandoah—our matron-in-charge, Mother Haggerty."

She blushed, which shamed Simon a little. Did he praise her that rarely? Was he neglecting his people, what with all that had happened since that evening he'd come upon the burning farmhouse?

He made sure to smile approvingly at her. "Madam, would you please acquaint the gentlemen with your duties here?"

"Of course, sir . . ." She started haltingly, but soon found her usual salty confidence as she led the men in a snaking file through the rows of cots. All but the sickest patients sat up to watch the parade of uniforms.

Someone gently grabbed Simon's elbow from behind. It was Sheridan. "How're things going?" he asked in a subdued voice.

Simon knew at once what the general meant, but still asked, "Sir?"

"The Dunkers."

"Oh yes. I've been meaning to ask—did you get their names, sir?"

"What names?"

"The Dunkers to whom you turned over the woman's corpse."

"No." The general frowned. "Sergeant Pettigrew handled it for me, actually. And he's still up the Valley. When he reports in, I'll find out if he took names. But I rather doubt it."

"Thank you, sir. Sorry to trouble you with this. But it could prove important. Meanwhile, I've been making inquiries in town here."

At that moment Mother Haggerty shepherded the party into the next ward, but Sheridan kept Simon from following by taking his arm again. "Inquiries about what?" he asked, tightening his squeeze.

"The Brethren who took away the corpse. So far, none of the Dunkers I've questioned know anything about it."

Sheridan's grip was now almost painful. "I want a man in the stockade, and I want him there soon."

"Any man, sir?" Simon asked evenly.

Sheridan let go and stepped past Simon, flint-eyed.

But then the general interrupted Mother Haggerty to chitchat with one of the wounded about his regiment, the town in Vermont the boy came from. Everyone looked on with smiles.

Everyone except Rebekka Zelter.

She was standing across the ward, pressed against the wall with her arms outstretched. The bedside stool she'd been sitting on was overturned, and a tin cup lay in the straw at her shoes. The patient she'd been feeding was staring up at her in confusion, as if she'd shot to her feet in mid-sentence.

Simon went to her, but she fended him off with a hand.

"Rebekka, please," he whispered, "what is it . . . ?"

She continued to squirm against the wall.

At last, he tracked her hysterical gaze and saw that it was fixed on Philip Sheridan.

The general looked back at her with enormous sadness, kindness even. His eyes flared once, frighteningly, but then turned mild again.

Her entire body stiffened as if to take a blow. And then she began that awful screaming.

⊰ CHAPTER 19 ⊱

Custer trotted in front of his division. The noon hour was bathed in cool air, but he was uncomfortably warm. His face was positively hot. Tommy Rosser had been putting a twist on him for over twenty-four hours now; his old classmate had even carried off one of his battery forges and a wagon filled with contraband niggers. The rumor had quickly spread that Custer had lost his entire wagon train and a battery of guns to the Laurel Brigade, and last night in Strasburg Sheridan had hollered at Torbert to whip the invigorated Rebel cavalry or get whipped himself. The more he thought on it, the more Custer was sure that these blistering words had been aimed at him, not the cavalry chief. Phil had given him the cold shoulder for the last week, and now was putting him in a situation in which he'd either be killed or sacked for botching the charge. So be it.

Custer reined in.

Across a piddling creek called Tom's Brook lay a ridge of low, grassy hills. On one of them, near a laurel-trimmed flag, was Tommy, so bearlike Custer could pick him out even at this distance. Tom's Brook. Well, it was Tommy's for the moment.

Then, unexpectedly, affection rushed to his head like mulled wine. They'd been grand friends, Tommy and he, and a crossroads such as this—shelling each other's lines under a sharp October sun— would've seemed impossible to them on those dank Hudson nights they'd sneaked off together to Benny Havens for a drink. Was this the natural end of all friendships then? And for that reason alone was it folly to believe that Phil Sheridan would hold him, or anyone else, for that matter, in high regard forever? He prayed that it'd be never be so with Libbie. That he'd never pass out of season with Elizabeth Bacon.

He glassed the heights. Tommy had three brigades to his own two, plus the high ground and a battery of six guns up there to pour down cannister. But no matter. Sheridan had known this was how it'd be.

On a sudden impulse, Custer doffed his hat and bowed low in the saddle.

Faraway, Tommy turned to his staff, said something, then faced Custer and raised his own hat.

"That's it, Tommy." Custer laughed under his breath. "No malice." Strange that he'd felt such acrimony only minutes before; he loved Tommy Rosser, the scamp. Always had.

Then he wheeled and ordered sabers drawn. Metal rasped for a quarter of a mile. "Let's do it," he said to his adjutant.

The line started forward at a walk.

Custer looked around. Sun-glints on the sabers. Autumn paints swirled in the woods on the western face of Three Top Mountain. From the rear, his band was playing "The Girl I Left Behind Me," the sound fading fast. His eyes moistened, he was suddenly so happy. It was oddly sad to be so happy, for he knew that it'd never come again, at least not quite like this.

The line broke into a trot. And then into a gallop.

"Charge!" he bawled.

Through the stream he splashed and up onto the hillside beyond. Groundbursts here and there. A trooper to his right somersaulted out of the saddle. A guidon went down, and then a fragment struck a nearby horse on the nose, taking out a big chunk. The mount lowered its bloody head briefly, but kept up the charge. Valiant beast.

Tommy had the range. Damn him. Love him.

A sergeant had forgotten to remove the small bag of oats strapped to his saddle. It got punctured by shrapnel, and the man came out of the cloud of grain sneezing and rubbing his eyes with the back of his saber hand.

Custer grinned, then faced the torrent of shot and shell again.

7:33 P.M., OCTOBER 10

WINCHESTER

Simon waited a moment before knocking.

He glanced down the darkened lane he'd just walked up from the hospital. No one was in sight. Wood smoke rose from Winchester's chimneys, giving the impression that the town was quietly smoldering in cold, still air.

He finally rapped on the door.

A white-haired woman with a flattish face answered. "Good evening, Doctor," she said, her thin hands reaching out, "may I take your coat?"

"Please, Frau Bohn."

"Go right up, if you like."

"I shall, thank you." He tried to take the stairs without making noise, but they groaned at every step. On the landing he turned and smiled gratefully back down at the Mennonite widow, a woman so naturally kind he still couldn't believe his good luck in finding her. Cal Ames had arranged their first meeting, having remembered her from the height of the casualties when she'd come to the hospital to help nurse. She'd even made a favorable impression on Mother Haggerty, who invariably found fault with other women.

Simon crept to the door at the end of the hall, braced himself a moment, then went through it.

The lamplight was low. Pamunkey was sitting in a corner, rocking a sleeping Hannes. Rebekka lay in bed. He thought she too was asleep until her head lolled to the side and her eyes half-opened on him.

"Simon Wolfe?" she asked groggily.

He stepped over to the bed, but was careful not to touch her. "Yes . . . try to sleep." Ames and he, on the basis of her last episode, believed that they'd stumbled on something: if kept in a nearly light-less room with as little stimulation as possible, she tended to come around. At least to a point at which she stopped complaining of voices inside her head and fingers touching her neck. For this reason, he hadn't wanted Hannes distracting her. But after a night without him she'd begun shrieking for proof that the "Little Goliath" hadn't cut off her baby's head.

The rocking chair creaked. Pamunkey was resting Hannes atop a quilt Frau Bohn had put on the floor.

"Been to mess yet?" Simon whispered.

Pamunkey shook his head. His eyes lingered on the child. Had he once had his own children? Simon had no idea.

"Go now while I can spell you."

Pamunkey started for the door, but then stopped, bent over and took the small revolver from his boot. A Moore .32-caliber recently purchased from a teamster. He gave it to Simon, who dropped it into his right coat pocket before Rebekka saw. In his other pocket were a bottle of laudanum and a spoon.

"Simon Wolfe," she moaned again as the door clicked shut.

Simon slid a stool out from under the washstand and sat beside her. "I'm here. Try to sleep again."

"Take my hand."

He hesitated, but then held it. Maybe it was time to offer her comfort again. But everything he tried was a guess, a gamble with her well-being hanging in the balance.

She smiled wearily, a strand of hair caught in the corner of her mouth. "I can see you clearly today, Simon Wolfe . . ." She seemed to take pleasure from saying his name, although she was too far gone to be flirtatious.

"Can you?"

"Yes. And you look so very unhappy."

He gently pulled the strand of hair away from her lips. Talk to her. She wants to talk. "How can I be unhappy? It's a beautiful autumn night," he said. "Crisp. I used to take long walks on evenings like this. All the way out to Concord once."

"Stars?"

"Yes, wonderful stars tonight."

"I followed the North Star here."

"Did you?"

"Down the Valley. Looking . . ." Suddenly she shut her eyes and began to weep. "Do you know where he is now?" Sheridan, of course. Her little Goliath.

"No."

Her eyelids snapped open. Her face turned frantic, but maybe it was a good sign. Better than the utter lack of interest in her own safety, in life itself, she'd shown most of yesterday. "I mean," Simon quickly added, "he's not in town. He's most likely at his headquarters. Belle Grove mansion. Miles and miles from here." But then he asked in spite of himself, "Are you absolutely sure, Rebekka?"

She lifted her head off her sweaty pillow. "Do you doubt me?"

He squeezed her hand but said nothing.

"Do you doubt me, Simon?"

"Lie back down." Yes, he still doubted—even after seeing Sheridan rush out of the ward two days ago, his face stricken. Rebekka was not well. Simon kept this foremost in his reckoning, for all the other evidence had meaning only if she could be shown to be sound of mind.

Yet, there was doubt within his doubt about her condition and its effect on her story.

With sufferers like her, there always seemed to be a kernel of truth hidden somewhere in the delusions, something that made their frightening view of the world not at odds with reality, but more a variation of it. At Boston City Hospital, a hod carrier had been admitted screaming insanely that the Devil had taken up residence inside his skull. Months later, his autopsy revealed a brain tumor the size of an apricot. An adolescent girl from a respected minister's family had been brought to Simon's operating table after stabbing herself in the abdomen with a knitting needle. *Why, child?* She said that she'd been trying to escape forever a monster of decomposing flesh who kept creeping into her bedroom in the dead of night and doing unspeakable things to her. The police later learned from a family servant that the girl's father had forced unnatural relations on her.

So it might be with Rebekka Zelter. And the key to her rantings about hidden gold and the little Goliath on a black stallion might well be what Philip Sheridan had done before her eyes in the kitchen of that farmhouse.

Simon had waited all these weeks for her to react either to Deering or Custer. But then the explosion had come unexpectedly with Sheridan. She'd reacted instinctively—no denying that. And at the instant she started screaming, squirming against the hospital wall, he'd believed absolutely in her terror of the general. He still did. But, somehow, he couldn't quite close the last few inches to trusting her word. What if it were more interpretation than fact? More Devil than tumor?

And he admitted to himself that he was afraid of what this hitting the papers would mean to the election, to Lincoln and the Union itself. President McClellan would never press for slave liberation. Simon paused, wondering if his fear were simpler, more primal than that. Was he most afraid of what Sheridan, once crossed, would do to him? He knew that a part of himself was girding for that attack, for Sheridan to find Rebekka, destroy her and anyone trying to protect her.

A tap at the door, although soft, awakened Hannes, and he whimpered. Before answering, Simon picked him up to quiet him, hoping not to stir Rebekka.

"Sorry to disturb you, Doctor," Frau Bohn said, "but there's a general to see you. He's in the sitting room."

Simon tried to recall what he'd planned to do in this event. But he could scarcely think, Hannes was crying so loudly.

"Will you watch him for me?"

"Of course," Frau Bohn said, taking Hannes, cooing to him as she strolled toward the rocking chair.

Simon started down the stairs, his hand tucked in his coat pocket. If the general had brought along provost guards, there would be no choice. Rebekka could not be taken. This would be proof enough: Sheridan had come for her at last. Despite the danger, the quandary over what to do next, Simon almost looked forward to the certainty that it would bring. As he turned the corner at the bottom of the steps, his forefinger was wrapped around the trigger.

Yet, he had a shock as he looked across the sitting room. It was George Custer awaiting him, not Sheridan.

Custer said, grinning widely, "So this is where you've been keeping yourself." He smelled of a hard day—or several days—in the field, and his uniform looked faded from all the dust. "What's this about?"

"I have a patient here."

"Officer?"

"Civilian."

Custer flopped down onto a settee and crossed a boot over his knee. "Good for you. War won't last forever."

Simon tried to make it sound conversational. "How'd you catch up with me?"

Custer sat forward. Even more restless than usual. "Damndest day of my whole life, Simon."

He found a chair. "Today?"

"No, yesterday near Woodstock. Gave old Tommy Rosser a licking he won't soon forget. Oh, he came back at me once or twice, but—God help me, Simon—we were splendid. The boys and me. Smashed right through the Rebs, and from there it was off to the races. Races?" He suddenly fisted his hands in irresistible glee. "You know that's what I think I'll call it—the Woodstock Races!"

"Woodstock," Simon echoed. Earlier in the war Custer had been chided by the papers for the "Buckland Races," when Jeb Stuart had routed and chased him for miles. So much for originality.

"Well, I got all their wagons and guns, Simon. Even took Tommy's *saddle!*"

"General Sheridan must be pleased," Simon said.

Custer's grin fell as his eyes shifted toward the stairs. Frau Bohn was coming down with Hannes, and Custer shot up from the settee. "Well, who's this now?" He crossed the room in three bounding strides to meet them at the newel post. "Why, Madam, is this your grandchild?"

Frau Bohn glanced to Simon. "No . . ."

"My patient's son," he rescued her.

"Why, Simon, he's gorgeous!"

Simon felt a burst of pride that left him surprised with himself. "Yes, he is rather, isn't he?"

"An absolute love of a chap! Shamrock eyes and all! May I hold him?" Custer asked the widow, who gave up the child and offered to make coffee. "I'd adore some, Madam." He turned beaming to Simon. "My God, I want a son this pretty. What's his name?"

Simon thought for a moment. "Johnny." Not an untruth. At least not in translation.

"My grandfather's name." Custer bussed Hannes, who was picking at the gilt arabesques on the general's sleeve with a finger. "If Libbie were here, your patient would never get him back!" He sat again and gave the child a jiggling horse ride on his knee, but he seemed deaf to Hannes's charming giggles. "I hear that Phil has charged you with some sort of inquiry," he said.

"That's right."

"The Dunker business?"

Simon nodded.

"Any progress?"

"Some."

Hannes's forefinger explored Custer's teeth, and the general began sucking on it to a shriek of delight. "They're such great fun, aren't they, though?"

"I think fatherhood will suit you," Simon said. He thought Custer was mulling the prospect over until—

"I hope you won't take this the wrong way, Simon . . ." Custer's voice trailed off.

"Take what?"

"Well, it's just that I don't want you to hear it from the wrong person. Could be misconstrued." Custer turned his head toward approaching footsteps. "Ah, here we are—"

Frau Bohn came back in with a tinware coffee service. She poured two cups, then said, "Let me have him, General. He needs to be fed."

"Are you sure?" Custer asked with a look of disappointment.

"Yes, he was too fussy to eat earlier."

A final kiss, and Custer handed over Hannes before taking a sip. "God, he's a pretty. And how I love coffee, don't you?"

But Simon said, "As you were saying, sir?"

"Oh, yes." Custer set down his cup. "Since you've got this unpleasant business on your shoulders, I think you should know something. But only in the right context." He paused. "Yes, I think that's the right word. It's a matter of context."

"Know what?"

"Slow, my friend. Can't you tell? This isn't easy for me."

"I'm sorry."

"The early morning we moved against Front Royal," Custer began with obvious difficulty, "I understand Phil sent Elias with a message for Torbert."

"That's right," Simon said. "I heard him give the order to Deering myself."

Custer nodded thoughtfully. "Well, I have this from an impeccable source . . ." He paused again, making Simon take a deep breath. "Phil grew impatient for word from Torbert and rode out along the pike to Front Royal."

"Alone?"

"That's my understanding."

"How far?"

"No idea," Custer said.

"How long was he gone?"

"Two hours or so."

More than enough time to reach the Hostedlers' farm and get back to his field headquarters along Cedar Creek. "Would your source be willing to talk to me?"

Custer laughed as if astonished. "Of course not, Simon."

"Why not?"

"Well, I'm sure Phil's blameless—otherwise I wouldn't be telling you this. But still . . ." Custer stared down into his cup. ". . . he's our commander. And this sort of thing could so easily be misunderstood." He looked up again, smiling. "And he does have the power of life and death over each of us, doesn't he?"

Simon kept silent.

"Well," Custer sighed. "I just didn't want you to hear this from somebody unfriendly to Phil."

"I see. Thank you."

"But there's more."

"Another impeccable source?"

"I should say. *Me.* The poor woman found dead near our head-quarters at Dayton . . ." Custer laughed incredulously. "I heard Phil tell you that he gave her to some passing Germans."

"So?"

The brigadier sobered. "That wasn't the case at all. He had that heathen Pettigrew take her out to an empty farmhouse and then set fire to it."

Simon sat motionlessly, his eyes riveted on the man. "Are you sure . . . *absolutely* sure?"

Custer took something from his jacket pocket and tossed it to Simon—the scorched remnant of a Dunker prayer covering.

Simon could hear Hannes crying in the kitchen. He asked himself if this was the corroboration that could give sense to Rebekka's story, however confused she herself remained. Hayes. Rutherford had volunteered legal advice anytime Simon wanted it. Now was the time. Crook was reportedly billeted with Sheridan at Belle Grove. In all likelihood, that meant Hayes was there too. *Must see him in the morning, even if it meant risking a brush with Little Phil.* "This is quite hard to swallow," he finally said.

"Exactly. I'm sure Phil had a perfectly good justification for disposing of the body in the way he did."

"Yes. Of course."

"But what if we follow this through for a minute?"

"What do you mean?"

"A mental exercise, that's all," Custer said. "Did you examine the wounds on those poor people?"

"I did."

"Any idea what weapons were used?"

Carnal weapons. Rebekka's words came back to him. "A knife, bayonet or sword—something fairly broad-bladed. And a saber and a revolver. As far as I know, Sheridan carries only a saber."

"That's true," Custer said. "But as long as we're delving into the unthinkable—and we're both in accord that this is all absurd, aren't we?"

Simon nodded. He was slightly nauseous. He pocketed the scrap of muslin.

"Then," Custer went on, delighted to be of service, "we should probably remember that Phil has those around him who *do* carry revolvers and bayonets. Just like Rebel guerrillas."

Simon looked at Custer in silence, but inwardly he was seeing Pettigrew aim a Colt at him, a sheathed bayonet on the scout's belt. "Ridiculous to think that anybody in his right mind would carry out such orders."

"Yes, ridiculous. Exactly what I wanted to hear you say, Simon." Custer had come to his feet and was stretching his back. "Well, must be off. I owe Libbie a letter and—"

"You didn't answer me earlier, sir."

"Didn't I? To what?"

"How you found me here."

Custer took his hat and gloves off the trivet beside the door. "I want to be your friend, Simon Wolfe," he said without turning. "Your best friend, if that's in the cards. You saw me in my worst hour, and came back at me with nothing but kindness and understanding. I don't forget things like that. The truth is—you're not in a very enviable situation, right now. Please don't ask me how I know that. But I intend to look after you as well as I can. Oh . . . do you have a handgun at your disposal?"

Simon decided not to lie. "Yes."

"Good." Then Custer went out.

Simon fought the urge to go to the window and see if he had come alone. But what did it matter? Someone close to Sheridan now knew where Rebekka was, even if that person was playing both sides, as

Simon suspected Custer was. Then another urge swept over him, as if he'd left a child unattended too long: to make sure that she was well. He pounded up the stairs and found her sitting on the edge of the bed, putting on her bonnet. "What're you doing?"

"I must go," she said, a hot blush on her cheeks.

"Where?"

"To get my gold."

He came close to repeating what the Dunker man on the pike had told him—that gold and silver were signals to Satan. But he caught his tongue just in time. "Lie down, Rebekka. When you're rested, we can talk about this."

She knelt and looked under the bed. "Where are my shoes?"

"It's too cold outside for Hannes."

"He's used to it," she said, rising.

Simon put his hand on her shoulder and gently nudged her down again. Thankfully, she didn't resist. Her gaze left his face and bobbed around the room.

"Otis will be back soon," he said. "He'll keep watch while I'm gone."

She shook her head; weariness seemed to be overcoming her. "Hold me, Simon Wolfe," she whispered. "Soon I'll be dead."

He felt a chill—such resignation in her voice. "No, you won't."

"He'll find me again and kill me."

"I won't let him."

"You can't stop him. You're too kind to stop him."

Simon slipped the bottle and spoon from his pocket. He couldn't pour by himself. "I want you to take two spoonfuls, Rebekka."

She stared at him questionably, but then gave herself the laudanum.

"Very good," he said.

She toppled over against the mattress, landing on her side, burying half of her face in the pillow. One eye peered back at him, unblinking. The eyelid slowly closed. He waited several minutes, until her breathing grew deep and regular, then sat at the foot of the bed. He'd let Deering's letter be burned in John Mosby's camp. The only testament other than Rebekka's and his own that Sheridan must be stopped.

Pamunkey came back from mess, carrying a pot of coffee Frau Bohn had made for him.

"This won't go on for long, Otis," Simon promised. "I'm going to get her out of Winchester as soon as I can."

Pamunkey dumped almost all the sugar Simon had filched from the commissary for Frau Bohn into the coffee, then poured himself a cup and set the pot on the washstand before crossing the room to the rocking chair. Drinking heartily, he stared at the empty bedding on the floor.

"Do you have children, Otis?" Simon asked.

Pamunkey shook his head.

Another place. Another room. Another nut-brown face staring off in sadness. He tossed the memory out of his mind. In no mood to dwell on the past. He got up and gave the revolver back to Pamunkey. "Good night, Otis. And thank you."

The orderly snugged the handgun inside his boot.

In the kitchen, Simon stroked Hannes's head as Frau Bohn fed him some farina, then took his leave of the widow. He buttoned his coat and strolled out into the night. There seemed to be more stars than earlier. And he knew that he wasn't as bright and hard and cold as the least of them up there. Rebekka was right. He was too kind to stop Sheridan. A man who might well have already tried to kill him by sending him with Crook down Little North Mountain. And he'd obliged Sheridan by charging with the foremost rank, carrying a red, white and blue beacon that drew every shot within a mile.

Precautions. He must take every possible one from now on.

He shuddered to think what Rebekka's fate would be if he'd fallen at Fisher's Hill. Would she herself still be alive?

Reaching the hospital, Simon went directly to his room and latched the door. He took a small, plush-lined case from a desk pigeonhole. Inside was something new from Washington, a syringe to inject liquid morphine under the skin. He'd had no time to test it in the field, but now screwed on the brass needle with much effort, then worked the plunger with his thumb.

He regretted now telling Custer about his revolver. They would be expecting him to be armed with a handgun.

He began filling the syringe from a vial of chloroform, but then stopped, his eyes darting back and forth in thought.

"Pettigrew," he whispered.

Was Custer on to something? Was Sheridan using his scout to do this? It'd explain the wide range of the murders and the different weapons used. But for men to join together in such a mad thing required something horrendous of human nature, wouldn't it? "Good God," Simon said to himself with a bleak little laugh—the war itself was staggering proof of that!

But suddenly he wondered if he had begun to see the world through Rebekka Zelter's eyes. He prayed not. He tossed the syringe back into the case, half-filled, and prepared for bed.

Yet, as he lay in the darkness, he suddenly got up and put the case in his coat pocket.

⊰ CHAPTER 20 ⊱

10:35 P.M.

The door slammed against the inner wall. A figure stood framed by the lantern in the corridor, hunched as if he'd burned his hands or was about to pray. Simon rolled out of his cot and onto the floor. He waited on his back, breathless, legs doubled to drive the attacker back. But instead of lunging inside, the man staggered past the threshold a few steps and dropped to a knee.

"Pamunkey?" Simon asked.

A croak—forced, tongueless—broke from the man's loud wheezing.

Simon struck a match.

The flaring showed a face with a beard of spittle and dazed eyes. Pamunkey's pupils stayed dilated even when Simon drew the flame close. "Are you hurt?"

Pamunkey gave a drunken shake of his head.

"Is it Rebekka, then!"

A nod, then he flattened himself on the floor.

Simon lit the lamp and fumbled into his clothes, then groped inside Pamunkey's boot for the revolver. None of the cartridges had been fired. On his rush through the wards, draping his coat over his shoulders, he thought to find Cal Ames, but then decided that there was no time. No time even to draw a mount from the horse-line.

He ran through the streets.

Lamps still shone behind the windows. It wasn't late, then. He had finally dropped off around nine o'clock, satisfied that he'd come up with a workable plan for Rebekka's escape from the Valley. In the morning, he'd heavily sedate her, then seek out some Dunkers willing to take Hannes and her into Pennsylvania. Her narcosis would appear to be illness to anybody looking inside the wagon. Pamunkey, then, would follow these Germans and make sure that the provost guards didn't detain her, or—failing that—warn Simon that she'd been taken. Meanwhile, he himself would find Rutherford Hayes and, hopefully, ascertain a legal course that Sheridan couldn't derail.

But now, with Rebekka possibly seized, what could he do?

Frau Bohn was standing in her open door, Hannes screaming in her arms.

"Where is she?" Simon gasped.

"I don't know, Doctor." The old woman kept offering Hannes his thumb, trying to quiet him. "Your man woke me, running out. And then the baby started."

Simon bolted upstairs to Rebekka's room.

The only thing suggesting violence was the rocking chair. It lay overturned on the floor. But the bed had been neatly made. He pulled back the coverlet and felt the pillow. Still warm. He brought it to his nose. Still redolent of her.

She hadn't been taken, as first feared. She had simply gone to get her gold, as threatened. That she'd left Hannes no longer surprised him. It was part of her illness, this sudden and complete loss of sympathy toward those even closest to her. Nothing existed for her except the purpose of the moment, however twisted and confused, however opposed to how she would've seen the matter in her right mind.

Frau Bohn had come to the door. Hannes was dozing off; his head kept jerking as he struggled to keep it upright. "Are *you* all right, Doctor?"

"Well enough to ride after her," he said. "Go ahead and put him down. The bed'll do for now."

She laid Hannes on the coverlet, and at last he found his thumb. Simon was wondering when the moonrise would come and how low the temperature would fall tonight, when he felt the widow touch the back of his hand. "You care a great deal for Frau Zelter, don't you?" she asked.

"If you mean I want to see her at peace with herself—yes, I do."

The old woman smiled, but it didn't rise to her eyes. "I meant something else, Doctor."

"I know," he admitted. "There have been times when I've thought that myself. But it's not possible. Not with what ails her."

Frau Bohn seemed somewhat relieved. "And what do you think that is?"

Simon hesitated. Ames called it dementia, which was too general. Thomas Mayo at Oxford had written of *deficient sympathy* and *lack of affect,* terms that seemed closer to the mark in Rebekka's case, especially when describing her depression following a violent outburst. But so many questions remained. Simon had just written Oliver Wendell Holmes at Harvard, asking him for whatever he had on the subject; but it was still too soon for a reply. Finally, he said, "I believe she's a casualty of war. As much as any man you helped nurse in our hospital."

"It's more than that, Doctor. I think you should understand this about her. May an old midwife offer something?"

"Please, of course."

"I've seen this before. He was a bright and agreeable boy. But one morning he stood in the meetinghouse and shouted, 'My parents should obey the Lord. I am the Lord.' And then he tried to strike them with his fists." When Simon looked surprised, she added, "Oh yes, we plain people—Mennonites, Brethren, Amish—aren't free from these troubles of the spirit. We have our differences, how to baptize and such, but in this we're alike—and like you English. We have those who suffer demons in the mind. Especially now with the war. But the war is not the cause of all things. This boy had been reared without lovingkindness, Doctor. Even in praising him, his mother found a way to be cold. And I must say that long before that morning in worship I could tell it in his talk. The affliction. He was prideful, and blamed others too much. He had strange plans. Brilliant hopes laid before him by Satan."

"What became of him?"

"He had to be put in the asylum at Lexington. A bad thing, for we take care of our own people. But he'd turned dangerous."

Simon paused. "What do you know of Rebekka Zelter?"

"Only that these troubles you see aren't new. That is all I wish to say, for my own faults are many." Frau Bohn reached for the coffeepot Pamunkey had left on the washstand.

"Wait." Simon had just noticed the medicine bottle on the floor. There was far less laudanum in it than the two spoonfuls Rebekka had taken in his presence. He wished now that he'd given it to the widow for safekeeping before leaving for the night. So distracted. "What a fool."

"Doctor?"

He unlidded the coffeepot and sniffed. He could just smell the tincture of opium. He looked at Frau Bohn, then hesitated. "Madam, I know I've already asked too much of you—"

"No need. I'll take care of the little one while you're gone."

"Thank you."

He went back to the hospital and had Naomi saddled. Waiting beside the farrier's fire, he thought to enlist Cal Ames and the rest of his staff in the search, but then shook his head to himself. Others would frighten her off. He felt that he alone could coax her back.

"Has she been watered?" Simon asked the groom.

"Yes, sir—just 'fore you come."

Simon spurred the mare toward the pike, then turned south and put Naomi into a full gallop.

1:05 A.M., OCTOBER 11

NEAR NEWTOWN

Simon Wolfe had been wrong. They were not stars, those flaming specks that seemed brightest on the southern horizon. They were the gas lamps of New Orleans, fanning out into a golden dome behind the Massanutten.

The fingers touched the back of her neck, pushing her on.

But first she faced a blue sentry.

Ahead, his bayonet was sparkling in the sunshine, and she could hear the soles of his boots grinding over the pavement. He would ask her for her pass, and she had none. To get one from the blue soldiers required an oath, didn't it? A pious sister like herself could never take an oath. The morning she set out from Staunton and started down the

Valley, she'd been so foolish as to go up to a sentry—although that one had been gray, not blue—and ask him if he had seen her husband. He called for an officer, and that tired old man with a coat too large for him led her away to a house, where he asked her endless questions while Hannes cried and kicked his feet in the air.

Why was she heading north?

To find her husband, she said. She'd heard that he had been up along the Potomac.

Why did she need to go to him now?

She missed him terribly. Before going, he'd said that he didn't believe he would survive much more of the war. He was so sick. This had left her in such turmoil she couldn't sit still. Waiting was more than she could bear.

Did she think that her going down the Shenandoah would somehow hasten the end of the war?

Perhaps.

A peculiar notion, she realized, but it stuck in her mind. She'd begun her journey in a swelter of dread that if left alone a widow, unprotected, the demoniacs would steal her farm from her, the best and largest in the entire county. Yet, she might solve everything if only she could end the fighting, somehow.

The officer then said that now was no time to go into the lower Valley. A new Yankee general was camped with his vast horde at Halltown. Soon he would try to march south, and it wouldn't be safe for a woman of her "manifest charms" to be caught in the midst of so many enemy soldiers.

"Who is this new general?" she asked, fascinated, for he sounded dreadfully evil just from the way the officer said his name.

The officer reached back, took a newspaper off the table behind him and gave it to her. The drawing of a man's face leaped out at her. He had the cold and venomous eyes of a demon. She would never forget them. Nor his poisonous smile.

"Is he a giant?"

"Why do you say that?"

"He seems so large."

"No, not at all. He's a little Goliath, I understand, just a pint more than your fine young fellow." Then the officer tried to quiet Hannes by jiggling his foot. "Turn around and go home, woman. There's nothing for you down the river except misery."

But the officer had been wrong. Solution awaited her in the lower Shenandoah. So she'd made up her mind to have nothing more to do with the soldiers.

She now left the pike and took to the rolling grass. Crawly things rustled away from her approach. For the first night since last spring, there were no lightning bugs. Just an ocean of empty, black air. She walked and walked until there were different stars over the Massanutten, then at last fell wearily to the ground.

"Where are you?" she pleaded. "Why have you forsaken me?"

Silence.

She'd made a mistake by coming north. He wasn't here, and now she was convinced that he was back on the farm near Staunton, waiting for her, his thin cheeks streaked with tears as he roamed the empty farmhouse. He was so frightened and lonely most of the time. He was dead, he claimed, and loneliness dogged him without relief.

A noise made her start.

Voices were drifting from beyond the height on which she sprawled. Not the usual voices, the ones that accused her of having a wretched heart within her breast, a cage for what was hateful and unclean. Those were female.

She crept up the slope, afraid to go farther, but the fingers were hard on her nape. As she cleared the brow of the hill, the voices stopped with a shushing noise, and then a bladed flame shot out of the trees below, followed by a rumbly echo.

Something like a horsefly zipped over her head.

She crouched, wrapped herself tighter in her shawl and prayed.

Simon expected to quickly overtake her on the pike. But he reached the ruin of the farm where he'd first found her, then the bridge over upper Opequon Creek—and still there was no sign. None of the provost guards strung along the way had seen a young Dunker woman, or anyone for that matter. Then something she'd said came back to him: how she had made it all the way down the Valley from Staunton using the cover of darkness. Even though the sentries might wink at a wayfarer without a pass during the day, they'd hold any civilian traveling after dusk, pass or no pass, on suspicion of carrying Rebel messages through the lines.

Simon urged Naomi off the pike and let the mare pick her way across the darkened fields. She was badly lathered.

Some houses, lightless, came into view off to the left. The village of Newton, he believed. Ten miles out of Winchester, and not even a hint that he was on Rebekka's trail.

He hadn't moved against Philip Sheridan, and this was the consequence. He had to find some way to confront the general, to learn if he had indeed been inside that Dunker kitchen. But how? He would be going up against the most powerful man the Valley had ever seen, a virtual Caesar with thirty thousand Praetorians to command as he saw fit.

A musket shot reverberated out of the south, across the Middletown Meadows. Simon started to spur Naomi, but then held himself back. The mare was plodding over a field freshly plowed for winter wheat, and was already stumbling over the tops of the furrows.

Two more shots came in quick succession.

Somehow he knew that the gunfire was against Rebekka.

He dug in his heels, but Naomi balked.

"Please, Sissy."

At the sound of his voice, she broke into a halting walk, floundered, then finally trotted over ground that hadn't been cultivated.

More shots.

The pickets would open up on anything. They feared Mosby more than the devil himself, which seemed strange to Simon now, having met the man.

He charged over a rise just in time to see a muzzle flash from a patch of woods. His gaze went to the slope opposite the smoke, and he tried to listen for movement through the growth there, but Naomi's explosive breathing covered everything except the gunfire. No horsemen to be seen, telling him that Mosby's rangers weren't involved.

"Rebekka, run!" he shouted blindly. "Go behind the hill!"

Three more shots flamed against the darkness, and Simon galloped straight on for the riflemen. "Hold your fire!"

They didn't.

Instead, the flashes grew tighter as they focused on him. He'd expected this, but he cringed as the minié balls sprayed around him. He waited hunched over in the saddle for the second volley. It came in six or seven blazes that lit up the foliage along a front of thirty yards—a full picket post. Was he that close to Sheridan's headquarters?

Finally, he wheeled and dashed back up the slope, looking for Rebekka.

"Here, Simon Wolfe!" she cried, terrified. "I can't see you!"

He was riding toward the sound of her voice when she darted up out of the weeds, making Naomi whinny and rear. Simon slid down off the croup and held Rebekka under his arm. "Thank God." Her dress was soaked with perspiration, and she'd begun to shake, but she clung to him. "Quickly—we've got to move," he said. "They'll send the vedettes after us. We're too close to the headquarters at Belle Grove."

She went rigid in his arm. "Whose headquarters?"

Simon didn't want to remind her.

"Whose?" she insisted. "Sheridan's?"

"Yes. Come . . ." He helped her into the saddle, then climbed up after. He was reining Naomi off toward the north when Rebekka seized his hand. The mare pranced, confused.

"I can't go back, Simon Wolfe." Her grip tightened.

"There's no other way. I'm going to find some Brethren in the morning. Send you out of Virginia."

"To what place?"

"Gettysburg."

"No!" She tugged on the rein so that Naomi twisted around and started southward.

Simon didn't argue for the minute. He simply wanted to be away from the pickets—and the troopers of the 17th Pennsylvania who'd be out to investigate in short order. Maybe with Pettigrew in the lead. Ahead, no more than two miles away, a cluster of torches shivered against the last ridge before Cedar Creek.

"Is that it?" Rebekka demanded. "Is that where he is tonight?"

"Yes."

"Kill him, Simon Wolfe. Take your gun and shoot him."

He said nothing for a while, then: "I can't do that."

"You must."

"No."

"Don't you see? He'll take you next. When you're dead, what's to keep me from following? And then Hannes too? No one in the world will know what became of us."

It was true, of course. If Sheridan had had a hand in the killings, that is how he would silence the inquiry, the last remaining witness against him.

A big yellowish star hung low over Fisher's Hill. He kept riding toward it as they wound through some open pine woods—and away from the dirt road along Meadow Brook.

He was sweating coldly under his coat.

She craned her neck to catch his eye. "What're you thinking?"

"Quiet." He could hear hooves beating against the road.

Her lips moved, but she kept silent. Soon, the sounds of Sheridan's vedettes died away to the north.

"What will you do, Simon Wolfe?" Even more adamant.

"The thing you're asking for—it'd be the same as fighting."

"What's wrong with that?"

He almost reminded her that she was a Dunker. Carnal weapons—her husband, Jakob, lying in his grave for having refused to bear them. "I didn't leave Boston to fight."

She laughed. "Yes, you did. To help the blue soldiers kill Jefferson Davis's pet Jew."

"Don't say that."

"You yourself said it, Simon Wolfe. Said it of your own father."

"And I regret it." He took the revolver from his pocket, quietly snapped out the cylinder. "So don't imagine that all my feelings for him are bad." He put away the handgun, then rode on.

Belle Grove slowly appeared through the trees, an old dressed-stone mansion on the brow of a hill, the light from its tall windows flattening out over the tents on the front slope. "How pretty," she said with disarming sweetness, then grew quiet.

He turned in the saddle to check on her expression. A queer happiness had spread over her face. "You're going inside," she said at last.

"Yes. I'm not as saintly as the Brethren, Rebekka. I can take a life if I must. But only if I'm attacked first. Only if all doubt is removed."

A sentry challenged him, and he gave the countersign.

"You ridin' in from Winchester, sir?" the private asked, looking Rebekka over.

"Yes."

"You hear muskets earlier?"

"No." Simon started up the gravel drive.

"Do you have the gun, Simon Wolfe?" she whispered. "I saw you take a gun from Otis."

He flicked the rein over Naomi's ears to the groom, then lowered Rebekka to the ground before dismounting himself. She stared at him, motionless. He drew her over into the well of shadow beside the porch stairs.

"Stay here. If anybody asks, tell them you're one of the servants. Wrap this in your shawl." He took the revolver from his pocket and gave it to her.

Her eyes brightened with anger. "But—!"

He clamped his palm over her mouth. "Keep quiet and do exactly as I say."

He dropped his hand, and she said nothing.

"Use it only if Sheridan himself threatens your life," he continued. "Nothing less than that . . . do you understand?"

She nodded, her teeth bared. "I'll kill him."

"I know," he calmly said. Then he buried his fists in his coat pockets. Along the knuckles of one hand he could feel the cartridges he'd pried out of the revolver a few minutes back. He trusted that the astonishment of seeing the weapon in her grasp would be enough to give her time to flee into the darkness. If her word was good, she'd managed to slip away from Sheridan once before. He closed the fingers of his other hand around the small case holding the syringe. Surprising, the number of officers who'd been stricken by heart failure on campaign. The rigors and sudden excitement, Simon supposed. He took the syringe from his pocket and depressed the plunger. A squirt of chloroform arced out.

Rebekka watched with grim fascination. "What will you do with that?"

"Hopefully, nothing." He started up the steps.

Almost three o'clock. The evening had gone on long enough, and more than enough had been drunk for one soirée, but the boys were so enjoying themselves Sheridan once again put off turning out his guests. Most of them were Union sympathizers from Middletown and Strasburg. Since the victory at Fisher's Hill and then Jubal Early's skedaddle far up the Valley, more and more of them were coming out of supposed hiding. Of course, kick a gray behind and it's bound to turn blue. Several ladies were in attendance, nearly all of them in middle age. Still, the boys—except Crook, who'd retired to the library to sip brandy and view scenes of Antietam on a stereoscope—had found pleasure in the feminine company. A young Episcopal priest was still singing at the piano, which was being played rather poorly by one of

Al Torbert's aides. Only the genial Rutherford Hayes seemed to show any interest in their efforts. The rest of the boys were talking in that annoyingly loud way that comes when the bottles are almost empty.

"Phil—"

Sheridan turned as Crook laid a hand on his shoulder. "Why, here's the merry reveler."

"Like hell." Crook wasn't smiling. He'd seemed vaguely worried these past days. Said he sniffed a bushwhacking coming. "Anything back on that firing earlier to the north?"

"Bad nerves."

"Then I'm going to turn in."

Sheridan winked. "First heavy frost tonight—you wait and see."

Crook nodded, obviously catching Sheridan's drift.

The usual winter halt in campaigning was near. A well-deserved rest was in order for the Army of the Shenandoah, at least those of its elements which wouldn't be sent to rejoin Grant in the mud of Petersburg. But here, in a solid little brick town like Winchester, the boys would do just fine. And there'd be livelier soirées than tonight's when some of them sent for their wives. Sheridan especially looked forward to seeing Elizabeth Custer again. A warm-blooded girl, young Libbie. Of course, there was the usual fly in the ointment, reports that the Rebels were trickling down the Valley once more, even reoccupying their old positions on Fisher's Hill. But Sheridan was sure that whatever force Early might bring to bear against him—it would blow apart like a dandelion puff on the strong defensive position his three corps had taken behind Cedar Creek.

Crook, who'd been listening to the singer with a frown, suddenly yawned and said, "Don't see how a man can do that without getting red in the face. Night, Phil."

"Great day in the morning, George."

Crook went out.

Sheridan was ready to give his A.D.C. the deliberate nod that would empty the place when he heard Crook greeting someone in the foyer. The Carolina accent stuck out like a sore thumb.

"Good," Sheridan muttered. He wanted to talk to Simon Wolfe. But the surgeon immediately collared Hayes, took the colonel into a corner of the parlor and began speaking to him in low, earnest tones. He looked pallid tonight, haggard even, but was conversing forcefully enough. Hayes seemed a bit taken aback by what was being said to him.

Sheridan went over to the two men and interrupted. "What the devil you doing down here, Simon?" Wolfe's eyes, once they fastened on Sheridan's, seemed unable to tear away from them. "Everything all right?"

Wolfe still didn't answer, but he accepted a glass of claret from the orderly.

Then it hit Sheridan. Something new had been discovered. No use in shocking the guests. He pulled himself taller and said, "I just got a gift from Stanton. The stereoscopes of Gardner's Antietam pictures." Then he inclined his head toward the foyer. "Care to view them with me?"

Wolfe nodded after a second.

Sheridan closed the library door behind them. "Well, looks like you've gone and done it, Simon."

"Sir?"

"Worked yourself sick."

"No, sir—it's just late. I'm fine."

"We'll see," Sheridan said. "Sit down."

Wolfe sank into a chair across the table. He cleared his throat of phlegm, but said nothing, his eyes still hard on Sheridan's.

"Do we have another one on our hands?" Sheridan finally had to ask.

"No," Wolfe said.

"Then what can I do for you?"

"I'd like to ask about Taylor's *Medical Jurisprudence.* Haven't gotten my copy yet."

"Oh. Sorry. It slipped my mind. I'll go through the requisitions again first thing in the morning." Sheridan picked up the stereoscope, trained it on the table lamp and squinched into the eyeglasses. He was amazed by the depth of the image. But for the lack of stench it was almost like being on a battlefield. Confederate dead piled like rubbish in the Sunken Road. "I'll be damned. I can almost reach out and touch the corpses. Hot and bloated. Turned black as niggers by the sun." Sheridan paused. "What've you come to report, Colonel?"

Silence.

Sheridan glanced over the top of the stereoscope at him.

"Only that I'm getting close," Wolfe said.

"Christ, man, d'you have the son of a bitch?"

"Close."

Sheridan slapped the tabletop, and Wolfe started as if a pistol had just gone off. "Well, that's the best news I've had all day. Can you tell me when?"

"Soon." .

"Then you know who's doing it?"

"I'm almost sure."

"Well, *who*—dammit!"

"If you don't mind, sir, I'd like to keep that to myself up to the last possible moment. You see, I once very nearly accused an innocent man—"

"Deering?"

"Yes. And I don't want to repeat the mistake."

"Then you're sure Elias is off the slate?"

"I'm sure."

"Well, you're the scientist." Sheridan gave Wolfe the stereoscope. The surgeon took a quick look and handed it back. Sheridan had expected more of a reaction. He slid another twin-image into the scope: "The Dead of Massachusetts in the Cornfield." He offered it to Wolfe, who held his breath for the long moment in which he studied the scene. "Familiar, Simon?"

"Not really. I never saw it this way. I mostly remember the Louisianans coming on."

"Each man sees it differently, doesn't he?"

"Yes. Only God sees the entire picture."

Sheridan yawned. "I suppose."

Wolfe lowered the scope, seemingly in disgust. Odd mood tonight. "Did something you saw at Amherst Street hospital displease you, sir?"

"Such as?"

"The way I'm running it, maybe."

Sheridan smiled. "Of course not. What makes you think so?"

"You left so hastily."

That was it, then. A sensitive soul, Wolfe had inferred criticism from that unfortunate business. His wound had indeed deeply affected him, just as Crook had suspected. If he didn't improve over the next week or so, get his grit back, Sheridan saw no choice other than to replace him with somebody less damaged. No fault to Wolfe, though;

even stronger men had come away from the operating table with much of their manly spirit cut off. And campaigning always seemed to be hardest on the medical people—emotionally speaking. "The young woman who started the row . . ."

"Dunker, sir." Wolfe paused. "She witnessed the first killing. She was standing so close, there was blood on her prayer cap when I found her."

"Ah." Sheridan saw that Wolfe had put down the scope and buried his hand in a coat pocket. "I must tell you something, Simon . . . something personal . . ."

"Yes?"

"There's a touch of madness in my family. Nobody closer than a cousin, mind you. But I know that if someone or something sets them off, there's no peace till it's removed from their sight. At once. I know I'm not the handsomest fellow, but I seem to have set off the poor creature. It cut my comb a little, I'll tell you that much . . ."

"Yes, General—you certainly set her off."

"What would you say if we transported her north under special escort."

"*Sir?*"

"I'm sure Pettigrew and his detachment could see her safely across the Potomac." Sheridan was surprised to see that Wolfe had stood. "She is Dunker, after all. And you know the orders concerning them. Move them out. All of them." Wolfe stared so sharply at the middle of Sheridan's chest, the general wondered if his vest was awry. "Something wrong, Simon?"

"Respectfully, sir—Mrs. Zelter is my patient," Wolfe said, his voice raw, "and I will strike square in the teeth of any order that tries to take her from my care and protection . . ." He was leaning halfway over the table, his hand still in his pocket. ". . . for as long as she needs them."

After a long moment, Sheridan chuckled. "All right, as you say. Simmer down, dammit. I should've known better than to lock horns with an army sawbones over one of his . . ." He paused. ". . . his patients."

Wolfe took his hand from his pocket and stood straight.

"I'm thinking of a late supper, Simon. And then maybe a ride out to check the picket line. Care to join me?"

"Another time, sir," he said. And with that he started to leave. But he froze at the door, turned slowly, and came back to the table.

His face like stone, he took something from his coat pocket, a scrap of burnt white cloth, and tossed it on the table in front of Sheridan.

Then he left.

⩟ CHAPTER 21 ⩠

7:10 P.M., OCTOBER 12

WINCHESTER

Simon had ordered his field desk taken from his room and set up in the main ward of the transfer hospital. This arrangement made him more accessible to his staff, he told them. They'd been coming and going all day on errands to Shawnee Spring, where the huge tent depot was gradually taking shape. But that wasn't the real reason he'd moved from his room.

If and when the blow came, he felt that he'd have more warning out in the open.

He wasn't consumed by fear, exactly, but at noon—while catching a quick nap after a sleepless night waiting for Sheridan to send the provost guard after him—he'd dreamed that he heard a gunshot. Cal Ames, huffing like a steam engine in the dream, burst into his room, but Simon himself was mysteriously absent from his cot. Cal followed a trail of blood across the floor and out to the gray fringes of the dream, calling, "Simon . . . are you still with us, my boy?"

Whatever it was that had disturbed his sleep also turned his mind one more time to getting Rebekka and Hannes safely out of the Shenandoah. At the moment, he was trying to put together a letter to his sister in Richmond, begging her to care for them until the end of the war. Yet, his head kept spinning from the impossibility of it. Leah shared the house with their father, of course, and how would Solomon Wolfe feel about having Dunkers under his own roof?

Simon sat back and closed his eyes for a few moments.

Politically dangerous for the old man. Conscription was already despised in the South, and here would be Jeff Davis's Secretary of War harboring members of a German sect that would have none it. This evening was the beginning of Yom Kippur, and Simon had twice slipped in mention of the Day of Atonement, hoping to remind his father of the fact. But that was self-righteous, particularly since the letter was addressed to Leah.

He suddenly crumpled it.

An absurd idea in the first place. Grasping at straws. Richmond was more than a hundred miles away on roads that would soon turn to rivers of mud. Union cavalry was almost everywhere in between, scouring the woods for Mosby. Simon wasn't sure he could bring himself to ask Pamunkey to steal back into the Confederacy, and even under the best of circumstances he doubted that Rebekka could make the journey alone. Not without her mind giving out in some desolate place. And where would that leave Hannes?

He was beginning to see that the greater risk in his plan to let Sheridan have the first move was to Rebekka and Hannes. *God forgive me if she's telling the complete truth about what happened in that kitchen.*

She hadn't spoken a word in over twelve hours, since he'd come down the front steps of Belle Grove mansion and told her—no, he hadn't killed Philip Sheridan. "I'm not going to murder a man in cold blood." The look on her face. Recalling it still made his blood freeze. And then he'd had to wrench the empty revolver from her hands before she stormed inside herself. Arriving back in Winchester at first light, he'd lodged her once again at Frau Bohn's and watched over her until midmorning, when Pamunkey was recovered from his opium intoxication. He had to grab some sleep during the noon hour, or collapse. At two in the afternoon, the town provost marshal dropped by the hospital. All social on the top of it. But Simon had no doubt that Sheridan had sent the man to do a little reconnaissance work.

When would the blow come?

Soon, he believed. But then again he prayed that it would never fall, that his suspicion was wrong. But in the event it wasn't, two saddled horses were waiting at all times for him in the hospital stable, saddlebags loaded with provisions. He would take Rebekka and Hannes up into the Blue Ridge and find sanctuary with Mosby before he'd hand her over to Sheridan. He'd already left a sealed letter for the Surgeon General with Cal, defending his actions. Confronted by the guard here in the middle of the main ward, he would stand on the authority of his shoulder straps and go directly to his room to gather his coat and a few things, only to crawl out the window and run for the stable. As ungentlemanly as this means sounded, he was sure that it would get him to Frau Bohn's house, for only the officer heading up the provost detail would come mounted, and Simon had ordered his grooms to unsaddle and water that man's horse the moment he appeared at the hospital.

"There he is!" a bright voice called out. "Working as usual!"

Simon glanced up and instantly thought of the amputation knife he'd hidden in a desk pigeonhole.

Custer and Frau Bohn were coming toward him, the brigadier carrying a tray of food for her. A pair of hounds trailed them down the aisle, stopping now and again to sniff and lick the bandages of the wounded.

Mother Haggerty growled at Custer and shooed the dogs outside, but he only laughed as he set the tray on Simon's desk. "I think she's serious."

"She's serious." Simon said, rising, trying to mask his unease at seeing Custer with the Mennonite widow. It meant that he'd been to the house again. Thank God that the revolver had been left with Pamunkey.

"Frau Bohn . . ." Simon paused, working up a smile as he shook his head at her—she'd brought him the midday meal too. He told her that he should eat in the mess and spare her pantry, but she'd insisted, saying that it was a pleasure to cook for a man again. "My dear woman—you're too kind."

"No one's too kind, Doctor." But then she smiled at Custer. "Except perhaps the general here."

"Least I could do." Custer turned to Simon. "I came by to catch up with you, but I really wanted to see little Johnny. He rode me raw all over the kitchen. Next time I'm bringing along Tommy Rosser's saddle."

"She's better this evening," Frau Bohn said quietly, taking the cover off the plate.

Simon asked, "Is she?"

"Yes, even helped me with this and that."

"Good." Simon sat again. He'd intended to fast in observance of the day, but now took a big bite. "Wonderful." She'd included a pot of coffee, which she now set atop the desk so he might have more room on the tray. Coffee was a necessity. He had to stay awake until he came up with a solution. Last night, Rebekka and he had overtaken some more Dunkers on the pike, but she'd turned her face when he suggested that Hannes and she go with them. The best option still might be to sedate her, send her north with some Germans against her will.

"Well, I'll let you enjoy, Doctor," Frau Bohn said, taking her leave.

"Thank you again." Simon covered the plate as soon as she was out of sight. "What news, sir?"

Custer took the stool beside the desk. "Nothing but good, my friend."

"How's that?"

"Libbie will be here the first week in November."

"Wonderful."

Custer slowly ran his tongue over his lower lip, then asked, "What's wrong, Simon?"

"Wrong?"

"So glum tonight."

Inwardly, Simon was seeing Custer on his knees before Little Phil, hands joined, telling him that war was like having a woman. Had the two of them somehow taken it beyond simile? And now was Custer, having realized that Simon was on to their sport, ready to throw his commander to the wolves at a court-martial to save his own neck? "Sorry if I gave the impression," Simon finally said. "It's just that this new depot's weighing on me."

"Of course." A burst of nervous energy carried Custer to his feet. "It'll be a bully hospital, I'm sure." He took the lid off the coffeepot and inhaled.

"Would you care for some, sir?"

"Oh, don't bother," Custer said. "It smells good, but there's only one cup."

"I'll send for another."

"No, no." Custer leaned on his elbow against the top of the desk. "I'm going to find a nice big house for the three of us."

"Sir?"

"Libbie, you and me. I'm serious, Simon—you absolutely must stay with us over the winter."

"I'm afraid my place is out at the depot."

"What—with only canvas between you and the weather? I won't hear of it. Neither would Libbie. She'll want to know all about medicine. Harvard. Growing up in Charleston. She's so terribly curious about everything, you know. She's—" Custer's sunburnt forehead broke into wrinkles. "Simon, I really must ask you something . . ."

"Surely."

"The night you went with Pettigrew to recover Elias . . . ?"

"The night I was captured, you mean."

"Quite. Well, I heard you tell Phil that you were taken by Mosby's men as you were hurrying to catch up with Pettigrew and the wagon."

"That's right."

Custer smiled doubtfully. "That can't be."

"Why not?"

"First chance I got, I went out looking for you. Couldn't let Mosby have our medical director, could I?"

"Appreciate your concern."

"Least I could do." Custer paused again. "I came across your track. And it struck southeast. Toward Cross Keys Road."

"Did it?"

"Quite."

"Not the country for a city horseman then, is it?" Simon said. "I would've sworn I was heading northwest. Back toward headquarters."

"Poor Simon. No wonder Mosby got you. You must promise me something—no more skylarking beyond our vedettes. Not on your lonesome. Libbie will be crestfallen if you're in Rebel hands before she can meet you." His eyes sparkled. "Libbie doesn't want to see you in Libby Prison!" He grinned at his own joke, but then his upper lip slowly slid down over this teeth again. "About our chat the other evening . . ."

"Yes?"

"I was dead wrong about something."

Simon sensed what was coming. "In regards to Sheridan, you mean."

"Yes. I'm afraid I came out with a lot of chaff—when I shouldn't have. See, I had a long talk with Phil this morning, and you'll be happy to know that everything's straight."

"How d'you mean?"

"Well, something set me off cockeyed. A fuss between Phil and Pettigrew down at Harrisonburg. The truth of the matter—Phil was sore at him for losing you. I'd've hanged him, but Phil has a soft spot for those churls. Says he doesn't want to break their spirit. It'd ruin them for their nasty work."

Simon slowly said, "Did he explain why he had the woman's corpse burned?"

"Forgot to ask. But he did congratulate me for the Woodstock Races. God, how he laughed at that one." Custer lightly touched Simon's shoulder. "Well, I'm off. Must find my bed warmers, what if your matron hasn't chased them yapping halfway to Staunton." Then he bowed and walked out.

Simon sat back and exhaled. So Little Phil had managed to coax Custer back into the fold again. That probably meant the blow was closer than ever. He poured himself a cup of coffee. A slightly bitter taste, like chickory. It left his mouth tingling. Must remind himself to give Frau Bohn some more real coffee.

He looked for his letter to Leah, but then realized that he'd balled it up. *Finish it.* Custer's visit had just convinced him of the need. He would give the letter to Mosby, who might be persuaded to deliver it and the Zelters to the Wolfe residence in Richmond. If he left within the hour, he could have Rebekka and Hannes in the mountains by dawn. He was smoothing the paper on his desktop when a mild spasm rippled through his stomach. The tension of the past days. It was also giving him a smoldering headache.

But then, ten minutes later, a second spasm took his breath away. He glanced at his coffee cup. Empty. His tongue had grown numb.

He bolted to his feet, knocking the chair over behind him. He'd just started out into the ward to find help when another ferocious cramp stopped him short. The numbness was spreading from his tongue to his face. He fought the urge to double over and curl up on the straw-covered floor.

"Colonel!" Mother Haggerty cried. "What is it!" Then she turned and called for Ames, who came at a run from the mess.

"Simon!"

"Will you come with me to my—?" Simon bit off the words to keep from groaning.

Ames took him by the arm. "Can you stand?"

"For a minute," Simon hissed. "Give me an emetic. Powdered jalap. Then a stomach lavage."

"For what?"

"Monkshood."

"Good God, are you sure?"

Simon nodded. Countless times, he'd prescribed tiny doses of the herb as a sedative and anodyne. There was no antidote. Just the treatment he'd asked for, which failed more often than it succeeded. "Damn them!" he groaned. "Damn those bastards!" Ames helped him through the door of his room and onto his cot. He turned to go for the dispensary, but Simon seized him by the wrist. "If I'm still alive in an hour, get me out of here. Hide me, Cal. Hide me someplace. But if I go, get Rebekka and the baby away from this army. Promise me!"

1:00 P.M., OCTOBER 13

APPROACHING FISHER'S HILL

Jubal Early had started back down the Valley in force. His infantry and artillery were strung out behind him under a bright autumn sky. The going was slow because Sheridan, in pulling back the week before, had burned all the bridges. But this mischief had given Early every confidence that the Army of the Shenandoah meant to snuggle down into winter quarters—and not push south again into the desert of ashes it had left between Staunton and Strasburg. At least not until spring.

Surprisingly, there were still people in this desert. Dazed as hell, but they were waving at the troops. No cheering, though. Early ordered his mounted band to the front of the column. Not much of a band, just six musicians with tin horns, but they struck up "The Bonnie Blue Flag." That got the Valley folks cheering. With ginger. Women in coal-scuttle bonnets screeching to raise the dead, hands fisted. Old men hollering with spit on their lips. Early swiveled in the saddle to have a look back. It was in the faces of his men: they knew what these folks were asking. Not for Southern victory. It was probably too late for that. They were asking the Army of the Valley to spill blood, to put as many of Sheridan's robbers under the ground as they could before the bitter peace came.

A rawboned girl, barefoot and sooty, darted into the ranks and pressed something into the hand of an infantryman. Curious, Early wheeled and rode back for a look. "What d'you have there, soldier?"

He opened his hand. Not flowers or sweets. She'd given him some cartridges. Early hawed to himself as he galloped forward again. Yankee cartridges.

Fine ash was rising from a burnt field to the east.

The cavalry escort charged that way to see who was coming, but then soon relaxed and trotted back to surround Early on the pike. "Jim-dandy," the general muttered to himself, "just in time."

The approaching riders were some of Mosby's men, coming down off the Blue Ridge. Leading them was that crazy Englishman. But by no means was he the biggest loon in the group. The long-haired Louisianan was with them, looking as if he had just been startled out of a sound sleep by gunfire. Ever the loner, he trailed the others by a few yards. Partisans. Might as well arm a lunatic asylum. Still, despite their eccentricities, Mosby's boys were as hard as gristle. They'd slash or steal their way through the blue lines up ahead and come back with a map as good as the one Little Phil's topographical engineer had drawn for him.

Early laughed again. What an army.

Eyes closed, Simon could hear Leah padding around his room. He murmured her name, but there was no answer. Must be one of the household slaves then, come to open the curtains—for a sudden brightness had made him clench his eyelids tighter. He was going up to his father's property along the Catawba River today, and had meant to get an earlier start. He listened for some sound of his mother, but none came. She'd already taken a little paper of morphine then, and was lying out on the piazza, her eyes the same coppery tint as the sunlit river.

A breeze drifted over him. Odd, but it was light, like up-country air. No brackish smell of the tidewater in it. No rattle of palmetto fronds in the breeze.

The cane whistled toward collision with his arm.

"When's it ever been the fashion for a gentleman to be a saint!" Solomon Wolfe shouted.

And Simon heard himself coming back at the old man as cold as ice: "There was a time, I think, when a man didn't keep his wife, daughter, and whore all under the same roof—and still call himself a gentleman!"

"I *am* a gentleman!"

"You're a whoremaster!"

The cane whistled . . .

But no, Simon's confused mind was putting one thing ahead of the other.

He was staying up at the Catawba house, mostly to rest from the demands of his thriving practice in the North, but partly to see the dogwoods in bloom before his father's lumber mill got the last of them. He was at his morning toilet when a small, dark figure stepped into the mirror behind him. A boy of seven or eight with a coffee-colored face, clamping a Noah Webster spelling book under his arm. "Mars Simon, you call?"

Simon spun around, astounded. "Who are you?"

"Aaron, suh. Marie's boy." His mother's former woman, whom Simon had believed sold until this instant. And yet, he'd never really believed—for what true Southern gentleman would stoop to sell his slaves? And more than anything on earth, Solomon Wolfe—with the muted echo of Hesse almost gone from his pronunciation, desired to be a Southern gentleman.

"Come here . . ."

"Yes, Mars Simon."

It was more apparent—and shocking—with each step the boy took: Solomon Wolfe's eyes, his nose, the faintly amused curve of his lips.

"Do you know *who* you are?"

The boy lowered his gaze. "Yes, suh."

The cane whistled, and then Solomon Wolfe's face was twisted by remorse. Weeping, he reached out to touch Simon's offended arm, but it had already been cut off by the surgeon at Antietam and tossed on the pile.

Simon opened his eyes.

"Thank God," a man's voice said.

And then a woman's. German accent. "I'll get some broth." Footfalls clipped out of the room, down some stairs.

Simon turned his face toward the man, but the brightness was too much to make him out.

"D'you want some water, Simon?"

He nodded, at last realizing that it was Ames. His head was lifted slightly so he could take a sip. "How long?" he croaked; his throat felt as if it had been blistered.

"Going on twenty hours," Ames said. "More water?"

"In a while." It had burned going down his throat.

"Had me scared, dear boy," Ames went on. "First, almost total paralysis of respiration, and then last night I thought it was turning into pneumonia."

Simon's eyes finally adjusted to the light. He looked around the room, then sank back into his pillow and groaned.

"What's wrong?"

"Frau Bohn . . ."

"Downstairs, getting you some broth."

"Her house?"

"Yes," Ames said, "Pamunkey and I carried you here. No one will know, my boy."

Simon let out a congested breath. They would know. But he was too confused and exhausted to do anything about it. "Where's Pamunkey?"

"Sitting on the foot of the stairs—with a revolver." Ames paused. "Is that quite necessary, Simon?"

"Yes." At least it was good enough for now. He felt himself going under again. One other thing to sort out before he did. He asked Ames to bring Frau Bohn upstairs—alone. He must have then dozed off, for the widow's voice startled him.

"Yes, Doctor?"

He fumbled for her hand and squeezed. His voice was too weak to convey the urgency of this. *"Who* made the coffee . . . supper, last night . . . you?"

She hesitated. "No."

It sifted over him again, the feeling of arterial cold he remembered from the past two days.

"The general did," she continued. "He was just trying to be help-ful."

"Was Rebekka in the kitchen?"

"Yes."

"Coffee—did she touch?"

"Why, no."

"Positive?"

"She was never out of my sight, Doctor. I'm almost sure of it." Frau Bohn paused. "Dear Doctor, she nearly went out of her head again, terrified you might die. What are you saying?"

"Nothing." He sank back into the pillow.

He awoke several hours later. The daylight framed by the window was going, and a comfortable dimness filled the room, one he hoped wouldn't be broken by a lamp. He felt better than before. His dread— for he realized that's what he'd been living with ever since he found that poor woman dead in her kitchen—was gone, although he wasn't sure why. Everything was the same as it had been when he dropped off, yet his place in the world seemed preternaturally clear. The doubts that had held him in check these past weeks were now locked away like wasps in amber, powerless to sting him.

A rustle of cloth turned his head.

Rebekka was watching him from the bedside chair. Tears welled in her eyes. "Sometimes I forget how good you are," she whispered.

"I want you to ready yourself and Hannes. I'll be gone for a day or so, but then I'll come back for you." What he said next seemed like a small thing now. "We'll go together to Staunton."

At this, she began to cry. "You're so good to me, and I've done nothing but bring you misery."

"Please stop that, Rebekka." Strangely, her gush of emotion didn't move him. He found it tiresome.

"You can't cast all the demons out of me, Simon Wolfe. Not even you. As I have a soul to save, forgive me . . . please . . . as I forgive others."

Was he himself saved if he forgave Solomon Wolfe? Was that truly how it worked? Would he then be free of the demons that had taken possession of him that morning in the Catawba house? If so, it was done. He felt that he had forgiven his father in the moments he'd waited for Mosby's men to string him up. Yet, he now sensed that he was beyond all that. Not deliriously. But methodically, in much the same fashion that he'd put away his civilian clothes and closed his practice before leaving Boston with the 12th Massachusetts.

She eased down beside him on the bed and rested her face against his chest, snuffling. "Where will you go?"

"Back to Belle Grove."

She looked up at him. "What will you do there?"

"What I should've done in the first place."

"Are you *sure?*"

His mind was curiously easy. As if he were on the verge of acting out some premonition he'd had ever since he had set eyes on Philip Sheridan. It had been in Maryland, and Sheridan had shaken Simon's left hand as if he secretly wished to break it. "Wake me before first light," he said.

And then he slept again.

⊰ CHAPTER 22 ⊱

8:08 A.M., OCTOBER 14

CEDAR CREEK

A heavy frost lay on the Valley. The sun suddenly cleared Three Top Mountain, its blaze touching the sheen of crystals, jeweling the fields and woods. Naomi's breath exploded out of her nostrils and drifted back over Simon. He felt as if he were floating over the glistening pike, disembodied, but just when it seemed that he was beyond pain a spasm jerked him upright in the saddle. A more powerful one had awakened him hours before dawn. Rebekka was gone from the room, but Pamunkey was still at the foot of the stairs. He asked Otis for the revolver, then left before he alarmed the orderly with some sudden words of gratitude and affection. A parting smile had had to do.

Simon roused, tried to blink off his stupor.

Naomi's hooves were crunching over gravel. The drive from the pike to the front of Belle Grove. The stone walls of the house looked like those of a fortress in the flat morning rays.

He dismounted and gave Naomi over to the groom, who kept glancing back at him from the horse-line.

Several officers were coming and going from the mansion at a near-run. He hadn't expected such activity. He was almost to the steps when a familiar voice stopped him.

"Simon?"

He slowly turned. It took a moment for the face to register. Rutherford Hayes. "Morning."

"Did you hear it all the way in Winchester?"

"Hear what?"

Hayes waved off toward the south. Sporadic cannon fire was rumbling there. Simon had caught none of it until now. The monkshood had given him tinnitus, and there was still a faint seashell roar in his ears. "What's it all about?" he managed to ask.

"Bone of contention right now," Hayes said, waiting impatiently for the groom to bring his charger. "Some say it's just Rosser's horse artillery. Others say Old Jube's back with his whole gang. Well, off to find Phil."

It almost slipped past Simon in his mental fog. So light-headed he was swaying on his feet. "Where'd that be?"

"Down along the creek someplace."

"And Custer?"

"Not sure."

"With Sheridan?"

"No, on patrol on the far side of the Blue Ridge, I think." Hayes paused. "The other night, Simon . . ."

"Yes?"

"You started to ask me something about the law in regards to these Dunker incidents, and Phil interrupted. Do you want to set up another meeting?"

"No need now."

"Really?"

"Yes, it's all out of my hands."

"I see," Hayes said, smiling through his apparent unease. "Well, you must be quite relieved."

"I am. Thanks for your offer of help."

"Anytime." And then Hayes swung up into the saddle and was off.

Simon ordered the groom to water Naomi. That would give Hayes time to find Sheridan, report whatever he had to report, and then move on. Simon didn't want him to be a witness to this. He rather liked the man.

But whether he liked it or not, practicality had just come back into his life. Until now, he'd given no thought to how he would deal with Sheridan and Custer. He'd simply get it over with. There was poetry in doing it that way—and less chance of losing his nerve and backing down. But now Custer was out of reach, and Sheridan had taken off into what Simon supposed to be a growing fight. Still, he could have them both. His mind, abnormally clear for a moment, seized on how this was possible. He would shoot Sheridan in the middle of the skirmish. With stray bullets humming all around, this could be done with no one the wiser. And then he'd have Custer later, the same way.

Ten minutes later, Simon set off for Cedar Creek. He tested for a gait that wouldn't make him sick to his stomach. Only a slow walk seemed to do the trick.

He wondered if this turn of events was a blessing, after all. Had he shot Sheridan at the mansion, the general's staff would have no doubt wrestled him to the floor as soon as the smoke cleared. Court-martial and execution. And then Custer would've gone free.

Random shells were tumbling into the tents of the 19th Corps. Simon rode unflinchingly through the havoc, looking for Sheridan's flag. A major was taking cover behind an overturned limber; the team lay dead nearby, tangled in harness. "Where's Little Phil?"

"What's—" A ground blast, close. "What's that, Colonel?"

"Looking for Sheridan."

The major pointed through the trees at a farmhouse. "Saw him riding that way with Crook and Emory about ten minutes ago."

Simon put his heels to Naomi. He was heading toward a splutter of musket fire, but his only fear was that he wouldn't find Sheridan while the firing lasted. A field hospital had been set up around the farmhouse, but he didn't stop even though the surgeon-in-charge waved for him to do so. Instead, he rode down through a brushy pasture to Cedar Creek. Easy fordings all along the stream. Not much of a defensive barrier for the army to winter behind, he thought. His clarity of mind amazed him. Nothing seemed to escape his grasp.

About three hundred yards up the far slope, he saw Sheridan astride Rienzi on a rock ledge. Gathered around him were a half-dozen officers, including Crook and the commander of 19th Corps, Bill Emory. But Simon knew that, as the fight grew hotter, Sheridan would send these men off one by one with orders and messages.

He rode up.

Sheridan saw him first—and grinned, unexpectedly. "Can't keep away from the smell of smoke, can you, Simon?"

"No, sir." Simon realized that his voice was too soft. He raised it a notch to say good morning to the other officers. A moment later, Emory excused himself—wanted to make sure his boys were ready for whatever—and went back across the creek.

"This is what happens when you lay on your oars," Sheridan said. His eyes were so bright and unfocused Simon knew that he was chatting off his tension. "I think I still got my boot on their necks, but some of the boys have it otherwise. They think this is the start of a very warm October. Sent Joe Thoburn ahead to have a look. And Hayes to check the right flank."

"Joe must've found something," Crook said, then glanced at Simon. "You look sicker than a dog, Surgeon."

"Green apples."

Sheridan absently chuckled. "That'll do it surer than a pinch of dung. What the devil's keeping Thoburn?" He turned to Crook. "George, find out."

Crook went forward at a gallop. Two of the officers, a pair of lieutenants, trailed eagerly after him. That left only Sheridan's A.D.C. But the skirmish fire Simon hoped to use was still several hundred yards to the south, marked by bluish smoke that turned silver as it curled up into the sunlight.

Then he saw that Sheridan was staring at him.

"Something to report, Simon?"

"No, sir."

"Well, I've got no—" Sheridan interrupted himself and caught his A.D.C.'s eye. "Go back to our batteries. Tell them they better be ready with cannister. I don't want to make too much of this, but you tell those bastards to be ready. And aim at their legs—we're not hunting pigeons." The man rode off. "How about you, Simon?"

"Sir?"

"You got a feeling this could be it?"

Simon kept silent. Horrible urge to laugh. And he was getting nauseous once again, the knot of pain in his gut slowly unraveling.

Sheridan gazed south. "All right," he said in a voice with all the buoyancy gone out of it, "I bitched it up."

"Sir?"

"Burned that goddamned corpse."

"Why?"

"Because I had every reason in the world to believe that you were dead," Sheridan said, almost looking contrite. "Without you, how the hell could I ever get to the bottom of this thing? How could I explain to the papers? I'm a soldier, not a damn philosopher or a scientist. So sure, I let it get a twist on my judgment. I took the low road because it was fastest. And I'd do it again, Wolfe, because time's the one thing I don't have."

"Why didn't you just bury her on the farm?"

"And let somebody dig her up like you did Elias?" Sheridan stared off in quiet chagrin. "Who got you the Dunker cap? Some Judas on my staff?"

Simon wouldn't say—not to protect Custer, for he felt no need for that. He was just tired of talking. He wanted to get on with it and be done.

"You still don't understand, d'you?" Sheridan went on. "I'm trying to bring this war to an end. That's all. I don't have time for these moral trifles. If I did, if we were all lounging about garrison—I'd stand this *focking* army on its ear till I found out who the bastard was. I'd have 'em stand out in the snow in their drawers till somebody cracked. And you know I would, Simon."

The firing was inching this way, evidenced by the smoke and a clamor of ramrods, and then out of the ragged strands a handful of Union skirmishers appeared, shooting as they carefully backed out of a thicket. "Jesus Christ," Sheridan whispered, "they're being pushed."

Simon reached inside his coat pocket, then sucked in all the air he could and drew the revolver. He took a moment to steady his aim on the back of the bullet-shaped head and began slowly to squeeze the trigger.

"Christ!" Sheridan cried.

Simon flinched. For a split-second he thought that he'd fired. But it was a twelve-pounder going off somewhere behind him.

Sheridan was still in the saddle, gazing southward. "Ah—here they are. And none too soon!"

Two riders suddenly cleared the brow of the rise—Crook and Thoburn, coming back at a dead run, crouching over the necks of their mounts as if minié balls were zipping just above their heads.

Simon lowered the revolver. He was so agitated he twice hooked the muzzle on the flap of his pocket before he could put it away.

"What is it?" Sheridan hollered to them.

Crook answered, "Reconnaissance in force. Back to the farm, I say. We'll make a line there!"

Sheridan wheeled Rienzi, grinning at Simon through his obvious ill temper. "What'd I tell you?"

Simon watched the last of Thoburn's skirmishers coming over the rise. They were withdrawing in fairly good order, stopping to turn and squeeze off rounds as they went. Then he followed Sheridan back across the creek.

Near the farmhouse a courier dashed up to the general and reined fiercely at his bay's foamy mouth. "Sir—telegram!"

Sheridan scanned the yellow flimsy, then handed it to Simon with a loud sigh. "Read this."

It was from Washington. Secretary of War Stanton.

If you can come here, a consultation on several points is extremely desirable. I propose to visit General Grant, and would like to see you first.

Simon glanced up. He was fuzzy-headed. Too much was happening at once. Too much jarring noise. "Are you going?"

"Got to. They still want me to sweep through Charlottesville. Must get that fool notion out of their heads. Can you imagine what Mosby'd do to my communications? I'd have more goddamn troops behind me than with me!"

Thoburn's division was getting into line of battle in the pasture. "What about all this?" Simon asked over the drum roll, gesturing at the troops, but meaning the reappearance of Jubal Early in the lower Valley. "Can you leave in the middle of it?" He could feel Sheridan slipping away from him.

"It's nothing."

Simon knew that it would sound impertinent. "Are you sure?"

"Hell, yes!" But then Sheridan grinned. "Jubilee's just letting me know he's back in the county. He'll slip like a mole into his old works on Fisher's Hill. And that'll be it till the snow melts." He shook his head, still grinning. "You wait. In garrison we'll find that murdering son of a bitch. And then I'll let you and that little German girl yank the trapdoor on him."

Simon glanced around. Too many witnesses. And the wounded lying around the farmhouse were gazing at their general with the reverence he lit whenever he went forward. Couriers coming and going. Staff waiting at a courteous distance for orders.

But no, Simon told himself, as a shiver went down his back. He must do it regardless. Before Sheridan got away. The days until he returned from Washington would be a hell of second-guessing. There'd be no facing Rebekka if he went back to Winchester this way. Faltering now would be the same as sentencing her to death.

Then Sheridan made it easier.

"You know, Simon," he said, a conspiratorial gleam in his eye, "something just occurred to me. After Opequon and Fisher's Hill, I've got a few friendly ears in Washington. More than a few, actually. Rumor has it Lincoln's none too pleased with the present surgeon general. Maybe I could drop your name while in the capital. What d'you say to that?"

Simon immediately reached inside his coat pocket and gripped the revolver so hard his hand started to cramp. He was bringing it out again when—

"Surgeon," a voice drawled from behind.

Simon twisted around. Pettigrew was smirking there on a lathered horse. "Yes?"

"We need your services."

"Where?"

"To the rear a ways."

Simon hesitated. Had the sergeant seen him aim the revolver at Sheridan's head? He looked across the creek for the ledge, but it was hidden from view by a belt of laurel. Gray and light brown skirmishers, almost indistinguishable from the autumn brambles, were just spilling over the rise in a waving line, and then a brigade from the 19th was flowing around Simon, moving up to help Thoburn's division blunt the Rebel thrust.

Sheridan was nowhere in sight.

"Surgeon, you hear me?" Pettigrew asked.

"What is it?"

"You'll see." Pettigrew turned his horse with a jerk on the bit, then started off toward the northeast, his blue cape spreading behind him.

Simon watched him briefly, but then followed.

Whatever the sergeant had waiting for him, it might bring things to an end. Clear his head. Everything would be so much simpler if they fired the first shot. Reaction would be reduced to instinct.

He caught up with Pettigrew, who suddenly exclaimed happily, "Thunder, Surgeon! We finally got us a good twist on the sons of bitches!"

If he meant the growing fight around the farm, Simon was confused. It already seemed like another bloody draw.

They passed through the yet-largely befuddled 19th Corps and into the woods beyond. Shafts of strong morning light were pooling on the ground. The trees sloped down to a ravine that was shaggy with creeper. Pettigrew halted at its edge and shouted, "Find him yet!"

"Naw," a voice echoed up from below.

It took a moment for Simon to catch sight of the man. He was kneeling beside the small creek, drinking from his palm. One of Pettigrew's scouts. To his back was a grassy terrace, and on it were four more men. Two of them were from the 17th Pennsylvania: one sprawled dead with blood clotted in his beard from a facial wound, but the other was very much alive. He had his Colt trained on the two other men. They were rangers. Mosby's.

The Rebel still on his feet was bound at the elbows and wrists, and gagged. The other, in a red jacket, was flat on his back, his face almost colorless. Hodgkins.

Simon quickly realized what had happened. Pettigrew and his men had somehow ambushed the rangers. Still, Mosby's men had put up a fight, killing one of the scouts before being captured.

"This way, Surgeon." Pettigrew led him down a game trail through the creeper, across the creek and up onto the terrace.

Simon dismounted and went to Hodgkins. The captain had been shot in the left side of his chest and was breathing wildly. His lips were flecked with blood, his eyes glassy. The wheezing coming from the wound told Simon that more air was passing through it than through the man's glottis. Briefly, he rolled Hodgkins on his side: the ball hadn't exited. The captain seethed with pain, tried desperately not to breathe at all. "It's Simon Wolfe, sir . . ." There seemed to be a flicker of recognition in Hodgkin's eyes as they drifted over Simon's face. "I'm going to plug your wound, give you some morphine, then send back to the field hospital for an ambulance."

"The hell you say, Surgeon!" Pettigrew barked.

"What d'you mean?"

"I didn't fetch you to heal the son of a bitch. Just want you to bring him around a touch. You got salts? Enough so he feels the bite."

Simon asked, "The bite?"

And Pettigrew pointed at one of his scouts, who was flinging a noosed rope over the limb of an oak.

"Let's get on with it," the man said.

"When I say," Pettigrew snapped.

"Lord, he's already dead. Just look at him."

"When I say!"

Simon rose and went to Naomi for his kit.

"What you doin' there?" Pettigrew asked.

"I'm going to relieve the captain's distress."

"Will it make him dreamy?"

Simon didn't answer. He met the eyes of the other ranger, but quickly averted them. Too haunted. He knelt over Hodgkins again and cut the faded red cloth away from the wound. "You're not going to hang anybody, Sergeant," he said deliberately as he plugged the hole with lint. No time to seal it with collodion; that would have to wait for the hospital. "These men are soldiers. Duly enlisted just like you. And they're to be given over to the provost guard." The silence went on so long Simon had to look up.

Pettigrew was stroking his Vandyke with obvious amusement. "Ain't you a fine one, Surgeon."

Simon glared. "Surgeon *Colonel*."

A horseman thrashed up through the creepers from downstream, the hooves of his mount stirring a smell of rotten vegetation into the air. Another of Pettigrew's scouts. "Lost his trail," he said flying out of the saddle.

"Does it keep to the crick?" Pettigrew asked.

"Naw, I think he doubled back tryin' to skedaddle to his lines."

"How d'you know?"

"I bloodied him, I'm sure."

"Hell, boy, you was never close enough to hit him."

"I was close enough to see where'n somebody already walloped a bullet off the side of his head."

Simon glanced up. "A scar above the right ear?"

"Never you mind, Colonel," Pettigrew said. "You just bring fancy Dan around so he sees the pearly gates swingin' wide for him."

Simon stood. "No."

Pettigrew laughed in disbelief. "You say *no?*"

"Yes, I'm taking these prisoners with me. You're not going to hang them."

Unexpectedly, Pettigrew fell quiet, seemed to mull this over for a long moment. Then he nodded decisively, grinning. "You know, you're right, Surgeon. I'm not in the mood for a hangin' today." With that he drew his Colt and fired twice.

The standing ranger flopped down, squirmed for a second, then lay still. Hodgkins sighed as the air went out of him for the last time.

Simon staggered for a moment, but then brought out his revolver and peered over the sights at Pettigrew.

The sergeant continued to grin, although less brightly than before. "I know men, Surgeon," he said. "It's why I've lived so long in the middle of so much blood and destruction. Hell, I'm a goddamn Methuselah for an outfit like the Seventeenth. So I mean no offense now—but I look through your manly breast and see the heart of a woman. But don't despair. You'll do well when this war's over—and me, I'll just be a drunken nobody."

Then Pettigrew gave his back to Simon, got in the saddle, clucked his tongue, and led the others down one side of the ravine and up the other. They dissolved into the woods, the last man in line stringing the captured Rebel horses behind him.

Simon continued to blink over his sights for a while, then slowly the weapon sank to his side.

They had left behind their own dead, as well. Like a pack of dogs.

He covered Hodgkins's face by turning up the man's jacket, then picketed Naomi to a sapling and started down the creek on foot. Lieutenant Tebault was out here somewhere, hurt maybe. Then there was no doubt about it. He found a drop of fresh blood on a rhododendron leaf. And then another on a boulder midstream in the creek. A weir fed part of the flow down a wooden flume, and on one of the boards was a bloody handprint.

But Simon had to rest before going on. His guts were boiling. Over the clamor of the skirmish he could hear a rhythmic slapping of water. It was coming from down the shadowy ravine. He doused his face from the creek, then started walking again.

Bloody prints smeared the rocks wherever Tebault had scrambled over them. The trail was clear—Pettigrew's man had simply lost his nerve.

Through the leaves he could see a gristmill, one of the few in the Valley still standing. The flume he had been following was a millrace then, and the *slap-slap-slap* was coming from the waterwheel. The building was in disrepair, and as he watched, some pigeons flushed up through a hole in the roof and began circling.

"Lieutenant Tebault?" Simon called out—but not at full voice.

No sound followed. Except the whirring of wings overhead.

The last few yards of dirt up to the door were splashed with gouts of blood. A perforated artery had given out entirely.

Simon stepped inside.

Tebault was on the far side of the dusty, buckled floor from him. For an instant Simon thought that he was lying dead in the pile of cotton sacks. His pallor was like marble; his head lolling on a shoulder. But then, as he stepped closer, Simon noticed the slight tremors in the hands. One of them was compressing the wound to his left thigh. The other was still clutching a Colt.

"Lieutenant . . . it's Simon Wolfe. Surgeon Wolfe. You brought me down from the Blue Ridge. I'd like to have a look at your wound."

The eyes stayed shut.

Simon began to kneel, but his knees had just touched the flooring when Tebault bolted up from the waist and thrust his revolver in Simon's face.

Time slowed for Simon as he watched Tebault's thumb cock the hammer and his trigger-finger squeeze.

"Oh God!" he cried, hurling himself aside but knowing that it was too late.

Snick. The firing pin fell on an expended cap.

Then another.

Another.

Simon reached forward and seized the cylinder, kept it from rotating. The Colt was then easily pried from Tebault's weak grip. Simon tossed it across the room. "Do you remember me, Lieutenant?" he asked hoarsely.

The jade eyes were fixed on his, but then shifted away. He eased back down, his saber clanking in its scabbard, and began gnawing on his tongue. The exertion had brought on a clammy-looking sweat.

"Your femoral artery's been clipped by the bullet," Simon went on. "First I'll need to stop the bleeding . . ." He slipped the string from one of the empty meal sacks and tied it snugly around Tebault's thigh.

"Good . . . you can let go with your hand now. Do you have something you can bite?"

Tebault stared at him, questioningly.

"Something to clamp between your teeth? What comes next will hurt."

Tebault fumbled inside one of his coat pockets and came out with a piece of paper. He folded it up, champed it, then nodded grimly for Simon to go ahead.

The wound was large enough for Simon to use his forefinger as a probe. Tebault gave out with a muffled groan, then there was no sound from him except his labored breathing.

Simon couldn't locate the ball, but he could feel the femur. Contused. But not split or otherwise fractured.

Simon withdrew his finger, and Tebault spit out the paper.

"Good news. I think we can save the leg. If the surgeon can find both ends of the artery. And I'm sure he can. But first to the hospital."

"No," Tebault growled.

"The men from the Seventeenth Pennsylvania are gone. You're under my care now."

"No!" The lieutenant was sitting up again, his face alive with little paroxysms. Then he looked all around anxiously, sniffing. "Smoke!"

Simon thought maybe he meant gunsmoke, but he couldn't even catch that wafting in from the lines. "I smell nothing."

"They've set fire to the mill!"

"There's no fire," Simon said. "And the scouts are gone."

"Help me," Tebault cried, sounding utterly terrified, "before the dark comes!"

"All right." Simon saw it as a way to get him back to Naomi and then on to the hospital.

But he'd no sooner pulled Tebault to his feet than the man shoved him away.

"What is it?"

Tebault was staring up through the hole in the roof at the sky. His face had gone slightly blue, and he seemed unable to draw his eyes away from the patch of morning glare. He jammed his hand into his empty holster once. Again. Then, slowly, clumsily, he began spinning around. His arms flew up to the level of his shoulders as his grotesque pirouette gained speed. Drool crept out onto his cheek from the corner of his mouth. Around faster. Simon was too astonished to stop him. The old wound to the mastoid. Only something like that could bring on such a bizarre dance. Around as fast as his feet could shuffle. The bullet-damaged brain, sensing danger, was commanding the body to move in circles, keeping the heart and other vital organs inside a ring of flailing arms.

Suddenly, Tebault's torso overreached his hobbling legs, and he fell.

He lay still on his back, scarcely breathing. His eyes were half-shut, but they seemed to track Simon as he crept up.

"Lieutenant . . . ?"

Metal scraped metal, and Simon saw a flash of steel just before something tugged at his coat, yanking him off-balance. He scuttled backward. Cloth tore with a sharp rip.

Tebault looked loweringly up at him from the floor, the tip of his saber jutting from his left fist. He had instinctively tightened this hand so hard around the blade, blood flowed from the cracks between his fingers and dropped off his knuckles.

"My God," Simon said, faint-voiced. This was the way a man could use a saber to puncture instead of slash.

Tebault started toward him, his eyes murderously angry. Yet, he cried, "Don't hurt me!"

"I won't. You know I won't."

"Go away!"

"I want you to let go of your saber. It's cutting you."

"Go!" Tebault screamed.

Simon finally got his feet moving. But then, as he staggered for the door, he was overcome by a spasm. It faded into dizziness, but left his vision grayed out. An image burst inwardly across this blank field: the bandage Tebault had twice worn on his left palm, first after the Hostedlers, and then after the woman in the corncrib.

When he could see again, Tebault was only a few yards away and closing. He'd bitten his tongue, and his underlip was wet with blood.

"Stop, Claude!"

Tebault gave no sign that he'd heard.

It seemed to involve no decision. Simon had somehow slipped the revolver from his pocket.

"You have me at last!" Tebault roared, rearing back the blade to stab. "You have—!"

The report sounded surprisingly tinny. Nothing like the blast

Simon had expected. And then he saw—with shock—that he had hit Tebault three times. Not just once. Twice in the chest and a final bullet to the lower face.

Tebault was still on his feet. He'd been lunging forward, and the force of the bullets seemed to have stood him upright, freezing him. As Simon watched, spellbound, the look in the man's eyes changed from one of rage and terror to a confused squint, and finally a sad, dull expression.

Simon thought to try to catch him, to ease him to the floor. But he was still confronted with the point of the saber.

Then Tebault collapsed.

The smoke sifted up through the sunlight angling down from the hole in the roof. Simon sat on his heels. His legs had gone molten. A pair of pigeons fluttered in, roosted on a dung-encrusted rafter and murmured to him.

After a long while he stirred. His eyes suddenly widened. He remembered something from when Tebault had folded the paper. Gothic letters. He rose and went to the pile of sacks, on which it still lay, bearing the imprint of the dead man's teeth. He unraveled and smoothed it. The title page to a German Bible. Christopher Sauer, printer. Germantown, Pennsylvania. On the backside Simon found a rough sketch of the Valley from Winchester to Staunton. The locations of three farms were noted with the word "refuge" in English—and in a woman's hand. One was outside Luray, where Simon had never been. But the other two were familiar, as one was along the pike to Front Royal and the other near Dayton.

He looked up at the pigeons.

CHAPTER 23

The kitchen door was already open, and smoke was drifting out into the chill morning air. "Why, Doctor Wolfe," Frau Bohn said, kneeling before her cookstove, fanning a balky fire with a cookie mold. Rebekka was sitting at the table. She faced swiftly round at the sound of his boots on the floor, and gave him a searching look. He ignored it. Hannes was standing beside her, gripping her skirt for support. Pamunkey rose from a stool in the corner and nodded.

"Good morning," Simon said to all, then turned to Otis. "Take care of Naomi for me." The orderly went out, and Simon said quietly to Rebekka, "Please gather your things."

She asked, "Then what, Simon Wolfe?"

He came within a breath of saying—*And we'll see what you've done, woman.* But he let it go for the moment with: "Come to the hospital. I'll be waiting for you there."

"Go alone?"

"Yes, it's safe now."

She stared at him for a moment, then lifted Hannes into her arms and went upstairs.

Simon sank into a chair at the table.

Frau Bohn wiped her hands in her apron and sat across from him. "What is it, Doctor?"

He waited for the click of the bedroom door shutting, then said, "I know how hard it is for you to speak against others. Even when it's the truth. But there are things I need to know about Frau Zelter. Now."

Yet, the old woman looked hesitant once again.

Simon went on, "She told me her husband was murdered by a Rebel . . . is that true?"

"Yes," she said nervously. "True."

"What happened?"

"It's said he was martyred."

Simon asked, "Did she tell you this?"

"No, she's said nothing about Jakob Zelter. But I've heard it from others. How he wouldn't take up arms, and a gray soldier killed him for it."

"How—shot, stabbed?"

Frau Bohn shrugged. "I'm not—"

"Were there witnesses other than Frau Zelter?"

"Doctor, please, Staunton's so very far away. I don't know these things."

"*When* was Zelter killed?"

"I don't know. I only learned of it this summer from some Brethren coming through."

Simon fell silent. Martyrdom, then, was how the Dunkers of the upper Valley described the killing. Dunkers who hadn't been there. It might have been more sudden and meaningless than they wanted to believe. Simon now doubted that Jakob Zelter had refused service on that occasion, that he'd had the chance to talk over anything with his killer. "The Brethren have something they call the kiss of charity . . ."

"The holy kiss, yes. Not just the Brethren."

"What does it mean when it's withheld?"

Frau Bohn glanced away.

"Does it mean that person's being shunned?"

"Shunning is a word we Mennonites use," she said. "The Brethren call it 'disfellowshipping.' If you're asking me if Frau Zelter is still with her church . . . I don't believe so. I think she's become what is called a 'blemished one.'"

"The widow of a martyr is *blemished?*"

"That's the business of the Brethren. But if that's what happened, Doctor, I'm afraid her affliction is being mistaken for evil."

"So am I." He could see that there was no pump in the kitchen. The well was in the yard, then. "That evening General Custer helped you by making coffee . . ."

"Yes?"

"Who drew the water?"

"Why, Frau Zelter . . ." And then it visibly hit the old woman: how she'd let Rebekka out of her sight for a few minutes. "But you don't think—" Tears threatened her eyes. "How would she know poisons?"

"Weeks ago, we went on a walk out to Abraham's Creek. She knew the deadliest plant along the way on sight. And her husband was some sort of healer. Please say nothing about this to her." Simon rose. "I'm taking Hannes and her with me back to the hospital."

"Are you sure?"

"Yes, it's for the best that way. Good-bye. I can never thank you enough for your kindness."

But the old woman's voice suddenly stopped him at the door. "You must be careful, Doctor. Some things can never be whole again after they've been shattered. You must look after yourself."

Simon halted for an instant, but then walked steadily on without turning.

The sky was sulphurous, a misty yellow. He looked for some blue overhead, but there was none. It was as if the entire atmosphere of the Valley had been corrupted by the month-long burning spree.

Pamunkey was rubbing down Naomi outside the hospital. Simon stood watching him a moment before he said, "I've got something for you to do, Otis." The brush paused on the milk-white coat. "But again, it's up to you. In fact, I'd feel better if you said no . . ."

Pamunkey appeared to know what was coming even before Simon said it.

"I want you to go to Staunton." Deep into Rebel territory. Simon almost balked. Just hours ago, he'd promised himself never to ask such a thing of the man again. "You owe me nothing—"

But Pamunkey had dipped his head once. He would go.

Simon was tempted to clasp his hand and thank him, but then realized that he'd only embarrass the orderly. "Find the Pleasant Valley meetinghouse," he said instead. "The church won't have a steeple." Simon's saddle lay on the ground beside him. He reached down and took a small bundle from the valise. He unrolled it: a big linen bandage holding a lump of charcoal. On an edge of the cloth he'd written JAKOB ZELTER. "I want you to check all the grave markers for these letters. Then drape the bandage over the face of it and rub the charcoal against the words, like so—that way, they'll come through the linen. All right?"

Another nod.

Simon arranged for Pamunkey to draw the best mount from the line, then went inside the hospital. He would bet his life that not a drop of Jakob Zelter's blood flowed in Hannes's veins. But he had to make sure.

Cal Ames stood in the main ward with his fists on his hips. "Where the devil've you been?" he whispered angrily. "Mrs. Bohn said you got out of bed and rode off in the wee hours yesterday!"

Simon slipped the lock off a medicine chest and pocketed it. "In time, Cal. Everything. I promise." Then he strode on to his room, where he washed and changed shirts. But he felt no more refreshed when the knock came at his door.

He opened it on Rebekka and Hannes.

She didn't smile as she stepped inside. He saw her sickness again. It had shrunk for the moment into two black glints in her eyes, but it was powerfully there, waiting to burst out again in rage. Yet, he hid his unease and told himself that this state was better for his purposes than the blue depth of nothingness that came over her without warning. Morel, a French physician, had called it *dementia praecox,* an often brilliant child suddenly coming to the end of an intellectual life he or she could control. The onset was almost invariably at puberty. And so the seeds of Rebekka Zelter's madness were probably not in the war, as first thought, although Simon remained convinced that the bloodshed and hardship had taken their toll on her sanity. Those very conditions had unhinged stronger minds than hers.

"Sit down, please," he said, taking her few possessions which she'd bundled in her shawl and putting them in the corner.

She sat on his cot, letting Hannes loose to crawl across the blanket.

Briefly, Simon studied the child's eyes, the hard gaze of the trader looking for the sire in the colt, and then he knelt before Rebekka. He took her left hand in his. "Sheridan's been called back to Washington," he said cautiously. "We're quite safe for the time being."

Then he waited for her reaction. Waited to feel the tension flow into her hand at the mention of Sheridan. But it soon became apparent that the somber lassitude had come over her again. Was she even remotely in touch with herself this morning? Only one way to find out.

"I saw some awful things yesterday," he pressed. "Some of Mosby's men were ambushed. Killed. I'd met two of them before. A

Captain Hodgkins." He paused. "And a young lieutenant from Louisiana. Tebault, I believe his name was. Claude Tebault."

She looked up at him, but her expression stayed torpid.

Simon let go of her hand, then caressed her cheek as if to rouse her, to find her almost-smothered spirit.

She began breathing through parted lips.

He got up, opened the door and called for Mother Haggerty. Then he turned back toward her. The first winter of the war, he'd come upon a wounded boy, scarcely alive, with his hair frozen to the ground. Her eyes now reminded him of that boy's.

She realized.

The matron appeared. "Colonel?"

Simon picked up Hannes and gave him to her. "Please look after him for the time being."

"If you order, sir."

"I do."

Mother Haggerty withdrew with Hannes.

Simon took Rebekka's hand again and gently pulled her to her feet. She neither resisted nor helped him. He led her down the corridor to the windowless room. He let go of her hand, and she went at once to a far corner, where she slumped and wrapped her arms around her legs.

Simon shut the door on her, hooked the shackle of the lock through the hasp and closed it.

He returned to his room and finished reading Morel's paper, which had just arrived from Harvard. After inspecting the wards, he wrote to Deering's aged mother, telling her how Elias had met his end. She deserved the truth, he felt.

OCTOBER 17

FISHER'S HILL

Jubal Early had two choices. Either attack or slink back over the Blue Ridge. He couldn't winter his army in the Shenandoah. Not enough food left to stock a poorhouse. But he also refused to quit the Valley, to admit to Lee that he'd failed. That left one choice. He had to outflank and thrash Sheridan's horde once and for all.

The only question remaining was which flank to sweep around, so this morning he'd sent Jed Hotchkiss, his topographical engineer, and John Gordon, up Three Top Mountain. He would have gone himself but for his rheumatism, which as usual had grown worse with the first frost.

He spent the day along the west foot of the Massanutten, waiting for them, a stoop-shouldered figure perched on a flat rock. Autumn was in full gild, and the sun was warm on his back. But these did nothing to improve his mood: Mosby's men had failed to come back with themselves, let alone the map Early had counted on.

Gordon and Hotchkiss didn't get down off the mountain until after dark, and then had the audacity to eat supper before reporting to him.

But Early put his spleen aside long enough to learn how the Irish dwarf had arrayed his thirty thousand pawns along Cedar Creek. Gordon laid it out in detail, the bullet hole in his cheek especially pronounced in the glow of the fire. And Hotchkiss had sketched the prettiest map Early had ever seen.

"Then what d'you really think?" he asked Gordon when the Georgian had finished.

Gordon was staring into the flames. "Waning moon now . . ."

Early exhaled. Never liked being told the obvious.

"Probably perfect tomorrow night," Gordon went on. "Not too bright. Not too dim."

"Say it, John—you want a night march."

"Maybe, sir."

"Around which flank?"

"Their left. Second Corps could go around that way in darkness, then the rest could kick off against them right before dawn."

Early held Hotchkiss's map in his swollen, painful fingers. "Means the Second'll have to work down the north slope of the Massanutten, then cross North Fork at the bottom."

Gordon added nothing more, although his doleful eyes were firm on Early's.

"But what you tell me about their positions says one thing. Sheridan doesn't think we can do that. If he expects us anywhere, it's on his right."

Gordon nodded. "That's my impression."

"No mardi gras, night march on a mountain."

"Yes, sir," Gordon said quietly. "But Sheridan did it to us."

Early fell silent, thinking. Long odds, once again. But that was the only way to win against the numbers Sheridan had. Still, sending an entire corps down the steep north face of the Massanutten under a pale moon—and then spring a surprise on an entire Yankee army waiting below, dug in with well-rested pickets every few yards sipping coffee . . .

Gordon cleared his throat. "If it fails, I'll accept full responsibility."

Early glared at him a second, then laughed out loud—miffing Gordon. "I'll remember that, John, when they string me up in Richmond." He rose from his camp stool and tried to stretch the aching stiffness out of the small of his back.

"All right," he said at last. "Tomorrow night."

3:19 A.M., OCTOBER 19

WINCHESTER

Simon woke each time one of Rebekka's screams echoed down the corridor. A night of dozing and waking and dozing again. At last, he gave up on sleep and turned his mind to work, the depot that was almost finished out at Shawnee Spring. The tents were pitched, the stoves installed, and the sinks dug; all that remained was to start moving the patients from the churches and houses in which they lay.

But then, as he stared at the darkened ceiling, his thoughts strayed from the depot to Pamunkey.

The orderly had left for Staunton on noon Saturday. It was now late evening Tuesday or Wednesday morning—he couldn't be sure which. Not without getting up and lighting a match.

One hundred miles to Staunton. And that was by the most direct route—straight up the Valley. Pamunkey might have had to go through the Blue Ridge or the Alleghenies to avoid Rebel patrols.

Simon shut his eyes again, making up his mind not to worry until tomorrow night. Yet, he was worrying in that he couldn't sleep. Or was it more from Rebekka?

Over the past four days he had seen her drift from one mental state to another. All of Saturday she'd been lethargic, crouched in silence. Sunday's dawn had found her on tenterhooks again, sullen and resentful whenever she bothered to pluck a few words out of her dismay and hurl them at Simon. Yet, by evening she was much improved, and then seemingly herself by Monday noon. The animation and beauty came back into her face. Her sympathy came alive too; she even noticed that Simon was distracted about something. He told her that they could talk about it later, and then, during an instant of stunning clarity in her eyes, she said, "As I have a soul to save, I need you. And I thank you for all you've done, Simon Wolfe." He was so cheered by these changes he took her to mess with him. Yet, as they ate with the staff, she turned argumentative over nothing, first with Ames and then with Simon. Then she completely hushed the table by shouting that "the little Goliath" had ordered them all to murder her and Hannes. Two male nurses had to forcibly take her back to the windowless room. Ames suggested the usual dose of calomel, but Simon said no. He needed to see if there was a sequence to these stages—that if in one of them she regained her intellectual and moral faculties.

Moral faculties.

He himself had killed a man.

Quickly, he shifted on his cot and made himself think of something else.

He'd voted today with all the other men from Massachusetts. A moment of unexpected indecision as he touched his pen to the ballot. McClellan had no tone when it came to abolition, yet he'd grieved so over his casualties. Little Mac had genuinely hated the carnage. And he'd treated Southerners with what now seemed like courtly decency. But he'd also squandered his one and only chance to crush Lee at Antietam. My God . . . to think that the war could've been over in 1862. His brother-in-law Israel would not have been killed at Chancellorsville. And this would now be the second harvest of peace in the Valley of Virginia.

Then someone, almost noiselessly, opened the door and stepped inside the room.

Simon reached under the cot for the revolver.

He could smell stale perspiration, the soot that clung to anyone who'd come through the upper Valley. At last. He put down the gun, got out of bed and struck a match. Pamunkey was leaning against the doorjamb, his face grimed, flakes of dried leaves in his nappy hair. He'd lost his cap.

"You in one piece?"

A tired nod.

Simon lit the lamp, then couldn't help but to throw his arm around the man. "Damn, it's good to see you."

Pamunkey slipped the swatch of linen from the part in his coat. The material was smeared with charcoal. Simon took it and held it up to the lamplight. The white spaces left by the recessed letters and numbers jumped out at him:

JAKOB ZELTER

FEB. 1803

JAN. 1863

Simon made a quick calculation. Hannes was eleven months old . . . no, twelve now. Born a month early, Rebekka had said. Conceived, then, in late February of 1863.

Then, just when he seemed transfixed by the writing, he thrust the cloth back into Pamunkey's hands and said, "Burn it, please—at once."

He started down the corridor. He checked his watch. A quarter to four.

He unlocked her door, and the light from the corridor fell over her. She was lying on her bed of straw, awake. And watchful. He waited for an outburst, another scream, for her face was streaked with tears, but she lifted her head and watched him with a dull animal cunning.

He steeled himself. He remembered Little Mac's tenderheartedness. It had killed more than it'd ever saved.

Then, out of a disapproving silence, she suddenly smiled. It meant nothing, he told himself, but it still gave him pain.

"You're going to Staunton, aren't you?" she asked.

"Yes."

"And you'll take me, as you promised?"

"Yes."

"My gold's half yours."

"All right." Then he added, "I don't think Hannes should go. The weather can change."

"Of course," she said brightly. "We'll come back for him later." But her eyes told him that she never meant to come back. Her affliction was now so deep her son had ceased to exist for her. Only one human being alive meant anything to her, and Simon suspected that he was more fantasy than reality inside her mind, that madness left no room for genuine love. To her, love was but one more weapon in her arsenal to keep the demons at bay.

He offered his hand. "Let's go."

⇥ CHAPTER 24 ⇤

8:00 P.M., OCTOBER 18

EARLY'S HEADQUARTERS, FISHER'S HILL

John Gordon realized that Jubal Early was holding out his hand. "Good luck, John," he said over the clink of canteens being tossed in a pile, the rustle of knapsacks being stuffed with two-days rations. Nothing was said above a whisper among 2nd Corps, as if the men were already ghosts, silently working the darkness for absolution or whatever it was the dead wanted.

Gordon accepted Early's hand. "They're wildcats, sir. They'll do just fine."

A solemnity joined the two men for a moment. It might have passed for affection had it lasted a bit longer.

Then Gordon was off.

The water noise from Tumbling Run covered the slap of bare feet on the hard limestone of Fisher's Hill, the chafe of worn butternut at armpits and crotches. As the advance brigade came to the river, the first of two planned crossings, the moon rose. It was three days past full. Gordon thought he could smell yellow jasmine on the breeze, and his wife came to mind. It gave him a sore heart, remembering the sudden force of their good-bye this evening, the unthinkable passing between them like a shiver. But then, after fording the North Fork—icy cold that scalded the legs, for he'd gotten out of the saddle for fear of falling in if his charger slipped—his entire being was focused on getting the corps down the nose of the Massanutten in a bunch still fit to give battle at the bottom. They kept to a trail no better than a pig's path. It was full of twists, so he'd given the order that couriers, otherwise of no use tonight, be posted at each turning to make sure that entire companies weren't swallowed up by the tangles of laurel.

He paused. Beautiful—the line of butternut snaking along the path in the moonlight, skirting a cliff that dropped off giddily to the north. Twinkling beyond were the lights of Belle Grove mansion, Middletown and then, like a constellation at the farthest reach of the heavens, Winchester.

On this morning the war would be decided, surely.

But then Gordon had to smile to himself.

He'd thought the same thing in the dawn mists at Sharpsburg, and despite the valor and agony of the Army of Northern Virginia that day, his own agony along the Sunken Road, the war had gone on. It hadn't been decided. God, of course, would decide the issue in keeping with His own purposes, and John Gordon could only try to make his men and himself worthy of those purposes.

A screech owl sang mournfully from the density of woods ahead. It left Gordon with the feeling that all bonds with the past were broken. He'd felt this way before—usually before he got hurt.

But there was no use thinking this way.

Sometime after midnight, the leading regiment reached the bottom of the mountain. Gordon moved them in spread column down to the river, which they'd have to ford again, and ordered them to lie in the dewy grass and wait for the rest of the corps to close up.

Mist clung here and there to the black waters, just as it had to Antietam Creek.

He prayed that God's purposes for the coming light would not call for his men to die wholesale, like sheep with the rot. Other than that, he made no demands on the Divine plan.

5:05 A.M., OCTOBER 19

ALONG THE VALLEY PIKE

An opalescence grew behind the Blue Ridge, a spreading light like mother-of-pearl, and gradually Simon could make out the look on Rebekka's face. Eager and determined, as it had been leaving the hospital.

She rode Naomi, while he was on Rex.

At Mill Creek, about a mile and a half south of Winchester, they cantered through a checkpoint of the headquarters escort; all but a corporal's guard were still in their tents. Sheridan had come back from Washington yesterday, but had decided to spend the night in town rather than push on to Belle Grove.

Simon slowed Rex to a walk.

"What is it?" Rebekka asked, instantly suspicious.

He was searching for the ruin on the slope above them.

"What's wrong, Simon Wolfe?"

At last he saw the chimney standing against the purplish western sky. "I want you to see something . . ." He avoided meeting her eyes as he turned off the pike and rode through the gate in the stone fence. For a second he thought that she hadn't followed, that she was getting ready to flee, but then he heard the patient thud of Naomi's hooves behind him.

A husband nearly three times her age. These mountains had been her prison walls. But she'd thought no better of the hamlet near Gettysburg in which she'd been born and raised. What in her—evident even then—had made her marriageable only to an elderly Dunker from the faraway Shenandoah?

Simon knew that he'd soon find out.

He dismounted and wrenched a picket off the fence surrounding the kitchen garden. Smashed pumpkins lay rotting among the frost-withered vines, and a rat scampered under a washtub shot full of holes.

"What're you doing?" Her tone of voice was testy.

Simon waded into the ashes and embers, trying to figure where the kitchen had been. He began rooting around with the stave, squinting and holding his breath against the cloud of ashes he was raising. From the corner of his eye, he saw her slide down off Naomi.

"Staunton's a long ways," she reminded him.

"I know."

"Then why are we stopping so soon?"

Simon paused a moment. He thought he'd heard something out of the south. That murmurous rustle of far-off cannon. But he caught no more of it and went on sifting.

"What're you looking for?"

"The truth." He finally looked at her full on. "Nothing more, nothing less."

"We should go on," she insisted.

At last he found it. He closed his eyes for a moment, then opened them again, reached down and picked a blackened tibia out of the confusion of bones. He walked back to Rebekka, his boots crunching over the dunes of charcoal, and handed it to her.

"What is . . . ?" Then she fell silent.

He watched her face, which slowly filled with disgust.

"This begins with the death of your lawful husband, Jakob Zelter," he said calmly enough, although his chest felt tight. "Claude Tebault killed him. I won't say *murdered* because after what happened to his head, Claude wasn't in possession of his senses some of the time. Just like you."

"I don't know what you're talking about."

"I wish that were so, Rebekka."

In a way, Tebault was less guilty than she. He'd sprung at his victims out of terror—God only knew what phantasms he'd taken them for in the strange twilight that swept over him at the onset of his seizures. And his sudden lunging out of a dead faint accounted for the lack of defensive wounds on his victims. They'd crept forward to help a stricken man. Recoiling, Tebault had gone to his Colt first, but if he'd dropped it during his collapse he gripped his saber and used it as primitively as a bushman would a spear. It was as if he'd fallen back, in his jumbled fear, upon some ancestral portion of the brain.

Simon guessed that the man had expended all six rounds at Josef Hostedler, hitting him thrice, before taking his blade to Chlora. But he'd never know for sure.

Nor would he ever learn precisely how Elias Deering had met his end, although the fact that the provost marshal's fine horse had been left behind gave Simon some idea of Claude's confusion during these episodes.

Finally, Tebault had come around only to be horrified by what he'd done, or shut it up inside himself, unable to accept that he was capable of such violence—for he was, when in his right mind, a moral man. The bodies of the innocent Dunkers had been quickly hidden. Out of a desperate shame. As for Deering, there'd been no shame in killing an enemy, but Tebault had left him in dignity, his hands folded on his breast.

"Claude fathered Hannes," Simon now said to Rebekka.

The bone slipped from her fingers to the ground.

"And you stabbed to death the woman living in this house. That is what I don't entirely understand. Why her . . . why the others you turned Claude loose on?"

Would she run? He expected her to. But no, she stood her ground, glaring at him. Icy hate.

He grabbed her hand and pulled her off to the creek, the same screen of birches she'd hidden behind that evening after the Battle of the Opequon. The leaves were golden now.

Letting go of her, he hunted along the tiny creek for only a few moments before finding it. Just as he'd imagined. Still, taking hold of the thing, raising it out of the water, gave him a shudder of revulsion. It had the horrid magic of something that has taken a life.

She glanced at the butcher knife, then sank to her knees.

"You were washing the blood off your hands when I rode up on you that evening. Frau Kindig's blood." He realized that his tone had gone to acid. He took a second to control himself, then knelt before her. "Her name was Anna Kindig. Her sister was Chlora Hostedler. Claude killed her. And her husband. Josef had a cousin who lived near Harrisonburg. Her name was Christena Leibert. Claude took her life too. Oh, something else of note . . ." Simon paused again. "They were all related in one way or another to Jakob Zelter's first wife. Not to Jakob himself, as I first suspected." Two days before, he had finally found a Dunker who'd been willing to talk to him. An acquaintance of Frau Bohn's, whose daughter had suffered a shrapnel wound to the hand while the family tried to dash through the miles-long cavalry fight Custer started at Tom's Brook. Simon treated the girl in Frau Bohn's kitchen and won just enough of her father's grudging trust to learn of the web of relationships joining the victims. "I know now, Rebekka, that these women were behind the drive to have you disfellowshipped. And through Claude—his fits—I'm sure you saw a way to get back at them. But was that it, though—being thrown out of the church? I don't think being a Dunker ever mattered to you. I think it rather chafed. So why, Rebekka . . . why did you do this?"

Her answer was a breathless, vile laugh.

He looked at her amazed, and yet knew it was the sickness again, shamming unconcern, choking off her soul with a perversity she didn't feel.

"What brought you to this house—to Sister Kindig?"

Then, abruptly, Rebekka was crying, tears furrowing down through the ashes on her cheeks.

"That's it, woman. Tell me, even though it hurts."

"Anna Kindig saw me on the pike," she began tentatively. "She wouldn't give me the holy kiss, but she said it was her duty to feed Hannes. He was so hungry. Weak."

"You didn't come here with the idea to kill her?"

"No."

He put down the knife and pressed his palm to the side of her neck. Relief swept over him. She was feeling remorse. Thank God. But he still doubted that the encounter had been accidental. "Why'd you poison me?"

"You gave me no choice."

"How—?"

"Outside the big house, you said you could take his life only if Philip Sheridan attacked you first. Only if all doubt was removed. You told me he'd come back at you somehow, didn't you?"

"But you used Custer—why him?"

"In Frau Bohn's kitchen that night, he said Sheridan was very proud of him. That he was the Little Goliath's right hand. I asked him if you knew this, and he said yes. Everybody did."

Simon took a moment. "Did you want to kill me with that poison?"

"Never!" she said. "Just make you sick!" Then she sobbed. "I didn't know how much wild monkshood to use."

"Where'd you find it?"

"The field behind Frau Bohn's house."

"All right," he said, trying to settle her down by rubbing her neck.

Being this close to the truth, however haltingly she dished it out, made him anxious. He didn't want her to clam up again. "With time, I can forgive you this, Rebekka. But I've got to know *why* now."

"That's not true, Simon Wolfe."

He took his hand back.

"You can't forgive," she went on. "Ever. It isn't inside you."

"Why d'you say that?"

"Your father—how can you forgive me, if you won't forgive your own flesh and blood?"

The sun crested the Blue Ridge, and they were bathed in wan light. Simon looked eastward for a moment, toward Richmond, then lowered his head and said, "I've forgiven him, Rebekka."

"How?"

"What do you mean?" he asked.

"Forgiveness is a deed. Not just words inside the head. You must think of some deed to prove it to God."

"I will."

"Do you promise?"

"Yes."

She smiled with such tender triumph, Simon had to glance away. What a gift for seeing into others—if only it weren't soured and twisted by madness.

Finally, she said, "It was for Claude."

"My death?" he asked, puzzled.

"No, the Little Goliath's."

"You knew Sheridan's name, his face, before that morning in the hospital?"

"Yes," she admitted. "A gray soldier down in Staunton showed me a newspaper. There was a drawing of him from the shoulders up." She dried her cheeks with the hem of her skirt. "And I was angry when you wouldn't kill him. I wanted this for Claude and me. For all the soldiers."

"Explain," Simon said.

"Before he left me in August, Claude said that things were getting worse all the time for the rangers. Nearly every man he rode with had been wounded at least once, many twice. And there were more new faces than old. He asked me to prepare myself—he was sure he wouldn't last the war. I'd be alone. Alone with the demons." A look of nervous horror gave way to one of sly gratification. "He sees them too, you know."

"I know."

The tears started again. "It was terrible after he went away. All our dreams for after the war, to sell Zelter's farm and move to New Orleans—they were nothing if Claude died. I couldn't eat. I couldn't sit still. And how would I know if something happened to him? One morning, I just started walking north, hoping to find him. That's when the gray soldiers stopped me outside Staunton, and when their officer showed me the newspaper. Looking at the Little Goliath's evil eyes, I saw a way to end the war. To save Claude, save all the poor soldiers."

"By murdering Sheridan?"

She nodded.

"What made you think that would stop the fighting? The Union has lots of generals."

"I have faith, Simon Wolfe," she said adamantly. "The North is sick of battle and wants peace. That's what Claude tells me. So I have the faith of David, who slew Goliath by himself and sent all the Philistines running for the gates of Ekron. If Sheridan is dead, the hour will come when all the blue soldiers will lose heart and run back to the Potomac. I believe this."

And she, through Simon Wolfe, had come within a hairbreadth of felling the Little Goliath, he realized with a chill.

But he sensed that this had been only part of her plan. Sheridan had been but the last of several intended victims. "Did Claude kill Jakob in one of his fits?"

"Yes. I thought he was going to kill me too. Claude was standing behind me with his sword ready. But then he seemed to see me for who I am. He cried out as if his heart were breaking, then ran for his horse and galloped away into the snow. His long hair flying." She smiled wistfully. "He came back two nights later. So sweet. So soft-spoken. He wept. He said that some kind of demon was after him, and often it took up the bodies of harmless people—to trick him. So confused, my poor *cher*. He wasn't sure if he'd slain Jakob Zelter, but he asked for my forgiveness. I surprised him, Simon Wolfe. My gratitude overflowed, and I kissed his hands. I blessed him for freeing me of the old man. And from that night on, Claude and I were husband and wife."

"Rebekka . . . ?"

She slowly came out of her reverie, blinked at him. "Yes?"

"You meant to kill Anna Kindig and the others long before you ever saw Sheridan's face in the paper."

"What makes you say that?"

"You gave Claude something before he left last summer. A piece of paper."

"No," she said, "I didn't. I gave him some bread and a little testament to carry in his pocket."

Simon decided on another tack. "Why were all these women stabbed in the belly?"

"Because they did it to me. They followed me all the time, whispering insults. They said I was a wretched wife and a harlot for the gray soldiers. They crept into my house one night and gashed me—"

"Did Claude stab Zelter in the stomach?"

She hesitated a moment. "Why, yes. I think he was reading my thoughts. That is how I would've killed Jakob Zelter, and he must've known it because he loves me."

There seemed to be no walls between her idea of her own self and that of others. Is that what gave rise to such a frightening suggestibility? "Rebekka, that evening, did a blue soldier walk up to Anna Kindig's house?" Simon was thinking of Deering.

"An ugly little man with the mark of Satan upon his brow. But Sister Kindig was afraid to let him in. After a minute of pounding, he cursed and went away."

Something new occurred to him. "Could you see the pike from the kitchen window?"

"Yes."

He was only guessing, but it made sense to him. "Then you saw one of our troopers slash the old woman, didn't you?"

"Sister Kindig's neighbor. She was trying to get her cow away from the soldier, and he cut her."

"Was it the ugly man who'd come up to the house?"

"No, another."

"But within moments of seeing that, you stabbed Sister Kindig . . . yes?"

Nothing. No expression. Almost a lapse into stupefaction.

Whatever, the violent suggestion had put her long-standing plan into motion. Yet, how she'd guided Tebault's hand in this had been far from impulsive. Her powers of manipulation were formidable, and he saw now that he'd courted disaster by underestimating them, by supposing that she was too far gone in her sickness to have guile. Morel had stressed the link between high intelligence and the disease. Rebekka was unquestionably intelligent, but how in the world could she have predicted the brutal outcome she desired with each of these Dunkers?

"Could Claude feel a fit coming on?" he asked.

"Smells," she said. "Smells told him one was near. And a tingling in his left hand."

"Would he always have an episode after these signals?"

"Yes, even at the house in Staunton. He'd cry out and chop at the furniture with his sword. And usually he'd cut himself—"

"By the way he held the blade?"

"Yes. Dreadful bleeding. I'd hide in the woods with Hannes till he was better. He'd always get better. And then he'd weep in my arms and kiss our baby, saying that the demons had been at him again."

So she'd known full well that she was sending a rabid wolf among sheep. She knew the course and nature of his fits better than he did himself. Simon then asked, "You told him to go to certain barns in the Valley at those times, realizing that he'd harm the owners—didn't you?"

Again, she didn't answer.

"My God, he must've killed dozens over these past years."

"Oh no," she said. "There was a long while, almost a year, when he was perfectly well. It was a happy time for us, Simon Wolfe." A hint of joy in her eyes died. "But then this summer, he was thrown by his horse, and the fits started again. Worse than ever. One or two every week. Those awful Shenandoah women said . . ." She caught herself.

"What about them, Rebekka? What'd they say?"

"Demonic things. Untruths. Things they swore to, even, in the courts of the English."

Wait, Simon told himself—he'd overlooked a possibility here. Her mention of legal process raised it. "Was Jakob's first wife childless?"

"As barren as a stone."

"And what of Jakob's brother?"

"He had no brothers. No sisters, either," she said, forgetting her previous lie about the gold hidden on her brother-in-law's property. So she didn't always *spring to the plain truth*.

"Jakob's farm," Simon said.

"What of it?"

"If you could've been locked away for insanity, they would have had a claim to it. The first Mrs. Zelter's kin."

She looked at him spitefully for a few seconds, then spat out the word: "Yes!"

"If that happened, you couldn't sell it and go with Claude to New Orleans."

"Yes, yes! They came up to Staunton—all of them—last spring and gave the sheriff money so he'd take me away to the state house in Lexington. They feared for my baby, the sheriff told me. Thank God Claude rode in and put a stop to it!" And that had been the trigger that started the deaths. A property dispute, a simple probate matter. "What should we do, Claude and I? Go to Louisiana penniless? His mother and sisters are already starving. They have no home. I paid for that farm—paid for it in heartache each time Jakob Zelter coupled with me!"

"Rebekka—"

"I will end this war, Simon Wolfe, and then Claude and I will go away together. I swear on my love for him!"

"Your affection for Claude," Simon gently said. "It wasn't a healthy thing."

Her expression turned sulky and bitter. "Oh . . . ?"

"It was part of your affliction, Rebekka."

She began blinking rapidly.

"I've made up my mind to—" He stopped. A definite cannonade out of the south. No matter, though. Nothing mattered except making her see where she must go—and getting her there. "I know of a place in Boston, run by—"

"I won't go into an asylum, Simon Wolfe."

"It's more like a home than an asylum. Catholic sisters run the place. It's clean. Cheerful."

"Stop it," she snapped. "I can't do that."

"Why not?"

"I must find Claude. That's why I came down the Valley. I heard he was along the Potomac. But now you blue soldiers have driven him south again. So I must go back to Staunton. Wait for him there. He's probably already there. He worries so if I'm not there for him."

"Claude's dead, Rebekka. I told you that."

Her eyes were flashing. "You lied."

"Have you ever known me to lie?"

This gave her pause, but only briefly. "People always lie to me. So stop looking at me." She dipped her hands into the creek.

He knew then what he had to say. "I had to shoot Claude. He was having one of his fits. He was going to stab me, and I had to kill him." He was transfixed for a moment by the image of Tebault poised dead on his feet. When he went on, his voice was husky. "I threw the revolver in the mill race. Found some contraband Negroes to bury him and his comrades. If need be, I'll show you the spot—"

And then she flung creek mud into his face. He staggered back, wiping his eyes. When he could see again a few seconds later, she was holding the knife toward him.

He started to reach for her hand, but she flicked the blade at him. "Rebekka . . . put it down!"

The intention to strike was in her odd smile, yet she then said, "But for your kindness, Simon Wolfe." She got up and raced past him. "Claude waits."

"Rebekka, stop!"

She reached the horses twenty paces ahead of him.

Rex screamed, and then over the gelding's bucking croup Simon could see Rebekka gallop off on Namoi.

Rex went down on his forelegs, the knife buried in his abdomen.

5:35 A.M., OCTOBER 19

LOGAN HOUSE, WINCHESTER

Sheridan was awakened by his A.D.C. just as first light was filtering through the window curtains. The picket officer was waiting in the foyer. Heavy gunfire from the direction of Cedar Creek, he was reporting. "That'll be the reconnaissance Wright ordered for this morning," Sheridan mumbled, then rolled over and tried to go back to sleep.

But he couldn't.

Stirred, his mind kicked into thought. Mostly about his Washington meeting. Stanton and Halleck had finally caved in. There'd be no idiotic sweep over the Blue Ridge and through Charlottesville. The Army of the Shenandoah would be broken up—with Phil Sheridan's blessings. Unlike McClellan, he had no use for an idle army. Most of it would join Grant in the Petersburg area, while the remainder would dig in on the east side of Manassas Gap. Fine. His work in the Valley was done. He was satisfied, as was Grant, really. And Lincoln.

His aide had stepped inside the room again. Fifteen minutes, perhaps, had passed since the last interruption. "Sir, it continues," he said.

"All right," Sheridan said, throwing off the deliciously warm covers. "Get me something to eat first."

By eight-thirty, he was riding Rienzi down the pike through town. The women were shaking their skirts at him from the doorways. Traitorous harlots. But they were on to something. As soon as he cleared the houses he heard it with his own ears. A steady grumble. Massed batteries. He had to laugh in surprise. And admiration. "Old Jubilee—you're up to it one more time!"

At Mill Creek, his cavalry escort joined him, and less than a mile beyond they came upon a train of wagons jammed every which way on the pike in their haste to get north. Sifting among them were some of Crook's West Virginians, looking hangdog at having been caught skedaddling. The heroes of Little North Mountain.

"Turn around, you sons of bitches!" Sheridan shouted.

The men just gaped at him.

"Then ask those whores back in Winchester if you can borrow their petticoats!"

"Sir?" one of them was stupid enough to ask.

"Either that or tuck your lilies up the cracks in your backsides— because all the *men* in this army are headed back up the Valley with me!"

There was another wide-eyed lull, then the West Virginians cheered and turned around.

Sheridan laughed to himself again, then picked up the gait.

9:06 A.M.

Where the pike became the main street of Newtown the retreating army came to a standstill. Here, there were no open fields to turn out into and pass around the clog of wagons, caissons and limbered guns. Simon tied off the driving lines to the ambulance he'd commandeered, and stepped down. "Anybody see a German girl on a white mare?" he kept asking the infantry heading north.

Most made no reply. A few shook their heads. Some light injuries. The flaps of their cartridge boxes were wagging like black tongues, so at least they'd done some firing before turning tail.

Simon checked his watch. Ten minutes after nine.

Rebekka was most likely all the way to the oncoming Rebels by now. She'd delayed him twenty minutes by stabbing Rex. He had run down to the pike, stopped a courier and begged him for his horse. The man said no, he couldn't. Rex could still be heard shrieking. "Then at least go up there and shoot that poor beast!" No sooner had the shot echoed away than a two-wheeled ambulance raced down the pike toward him, its driver hell-bent for Maryland only because he'd heard from a local farmer that the army was completely routed, all its corps commanders dead or captured. Simon had relieved the man of the ambulance, turned it around and started south.

But now he was stalled.

Newtown continued to grow more cluttered. A riderless mount came trotting down between the wagons. Simon shouted for a mob of infantry to help him catch the charger, and surprisingly a few soldiers handed their muskets to their companions and cornered the horse long enough to let Simon grab the bridle.

He swung up into the saddle, then threaded his way south again.

He'd gotten the story in snatches from the men of a dozen brigades. How Old Jube had sprung an attack through the morning fog, overrun the camps along Cedar Creek and sent the entire army reeling back in panic. Yet now that early panic seemed to have played itself out. Many men had stopped alongside the road and made small fires to boil their morning coffee. They were joking among themselves, watching the traffic as if waiting for somebody to ride up and take charge. Not exactly the spirit of a beaten army.

But all Simon knew was that if Rebekka made the enemy lines, he'd never see her again. Why had no one noticed her? No other civilians on the pike. She should've caught every man's eye.

Then, on a sudden thought, he turned between two shuttered houses and dashed for the big sunstruck meadow beyond. No blue uniforms or glint of muskets showed on the grass. He felt sure that she'd ridden southwest of the pike to avoid the army. She had skirted the pike all her trek down the Valley.

Yet, he hadn't gone far when he saw some cavalry units in the distance, getting themselves in line to hold down the right flank. A crackle of carbine fire from the facing slope to the south told him that Rebel horsemen were testing them.

Simon caught up with the troopers in a grove of pines just before they went forward. "Anyone seen a girl on a white mare?"

No one spoke up. Bullets were nipping at the trees, sending down little showers of needles. Simon's mount kept pricking his ears at the sound.

He was thinking of turning back for the pike when Custer and his escort galloped in behind the line, guidon flying. The general's face was florid; his blood was up, and he glanced twice before he recognized Simon. "What the devil now!" he cried with a laugh, rising in the stirrups. "Lost again, Simon?"

"No." But what to say? "I'm looking for a patient."

"Well, pick a spot and break out your saws. You'll be up to your chin in them in no time at all!" Custer wiped the sweat from his face with a quick hand. "Tommy Rosser's been pestering me for this since dawn." He gave the word, and the line advanced at a walk. "Remember what I said about staying with Libbie and me," he said over his shoulder, then took his men into a trot.

Simon wheeled out of their dust.

He got back to the pike shortly after ten o'clock and started cantering toward Middletown. Fewer stragglers to be seen going north. The men squatting on the road cuts were from the veteran 6th Corps, and there was a determined air about them as if they meant to pull back no farther.

Where was she?

Suddenly, troopers on spanking bays were overtaking him. Sheridan's banner fluttered past, and Simon turned in the saddle.

Little Phil gave him a sere, questioning look, then grinned hugely and shouted, "That's it, Simon! Antietam!"

Simon said, "To hell with Antietam." But Sheridan was seemingly too exalted to have heard.

The general rode ahead, but soon reined up beside a handful of stragglers. Faces sooty with powder. "Hell, if you sons of bitches don't want to fight yourselves, why not come back and watch us fight!"

They smiled despite themselves, then about-faced and started south again.

The rout was over.

But where was Rebekka? Someone had to have seen her.

Unsure which way to go, he followed Sheridan. Some ragged lines had been formed ahead, and as the general approached them a young major whooped in relief. McKinley, wasn't it—Crook's newly promoted aide Simon had met the night before Fisher's Hill? He streaked behind the regiments, shouting at the top of his lungs again and again, "Little Phil is on the field . . . !"

A roar of approval went up.

Sheridan took it in with a wave of a hat, then halted on a knoll among some mounted officers. Crook, Emory—and Horatio Wright, whom Little Phil had left in command during his trip to Washington.

Simon kept at a distance. He could hear a heated exchange, but couldn't make out the words. Except once, when Sheridan boomed, "Hell no!"

After a while, Crook, trailed by an engineer, broke away from the conference. He passed close to Simon and said as if they were the best of confidants, "Phil says no more retreat. We stand here. Tonight in our old camps along Cedar Creek. So get your surgeons working wherever you damn well please. Just don't come to me if we get overrun."

"Sir—have you seen a young Dunker woman on my white mare?"

Crook seemed mystified by the question, but the engineer spoke up. "No woman, Colonel—but a saw a mare that color. Used up horrible bad."

"When?"

"Half hour ago."

"Where?"

The engineer pointed. "About a mile over here on the left flank. In a gulley below some wheat shocks."

Simon galloped east. He rode about two hundred yards behind the infantry, who were sheltering behind a long stone wall, and a hundred yards behind the batteries. The artillerymen, stripped to their trousers, were digging pits behind their guns. To the south, across a pasture strewn with boulders, he could see another wall. From it bristled the flags of the enemy. Catching their breath, bolting down their short rations, no doubt, after driving Wright several miles back from Cedar Creek since dawn.

He could see that fire had been traded here just minutes before. A yellowish haze was hovering overhead from the smoke, and the blood showing on the corpses had yet to brown. Apparently, 6th Corps had spun on its heels to fight, and the Rebels had hit them hard before falling back across the grass to the far wall. Maybe this skirmishing had slowed Rebekka. Kept her from getting across.

He found the grain shocks, and then a furrow that deepened into a gulch with crumbly banks. Midway down it sprawled something dusty white. Naomi. He galloped the rest of the way to her and dismounted. She was on her side, lathered, still panting. She raised her head slightly, put a glazed eye on him, but then lay flat again.

He patted her ribs, then got back in the saddle and started following Rebekka's tracks. They cut up the earthen bank and then struck south, as expected.

Beyond the infantry the pasture seemed silent and still—not even the rasp of a cicada. The men in the line seemed no more lifelike than those sprinkled in the grass. Most lay on their backs and let the sun beat down on their powder-darkened faces. Simon's gaze swept over them, then went back to an ammunition wagon parked in the shade of a solitary tree. Crouched behind it was Rebekka, obviously intent on figuring some way through the regiment to the Rebel side.

She shifted to the concealment of a brier when a teamster, laden with water buckets, started to come around the wagon.

She ducked down out of sight.

Simon was almost to where he'd last seen her when she apparently heard his mount's shoes ringing on the stony ground. She shot up and began running for the line, her cap flying off and her long hair unraveling.

"Please, Rebekka!" Then he hollered for the soldiers. "Stop her!"

But before any of them could shake off their exhaustion she'd run through them, bounded over the wall and was sprinting across the pasture. Simon started to give chase, but as he dodged among the soldiers several hands reached for the bridle.

His horse snorted and tried to back out of the throng.

"Colonel," one of them said, "you go out there and *we'll* draw fire!"

Simon leaped down and went over the wall on foot.

"We ain't comin' out to get you!" a voice warned to his back.

She had a hundred yards on him, and he knew that she was faster. "Rebekka!" he cried.

But then an all-too-familiar sound made him drop. He saw a tiny puff rise off the ridge to the south, and then red lightning seemed to split his head like an iron wedge. An airburst. His ears were still buzzing as he lifted his face out of the dirt and looked for her.

Nothing was moving out in the grass.

He scrambled to his feet and ran unsteadily for where he'd last seen her. "Rebekka!"

Then his heart stopped. He saw a skirt on the ground, bloodied and torn. But as he staggered ever closer it became a man's shirt, and the body proved to be that of a fair-haired Rebel who'd ripped open his tunic to have a look at his fatal wound.

A few yards beyond the corpse, Rebekka sat up, dazed, her hands over her ears.

He flopped down beside her, grabbed her arm. "We—!" Another burst. Closer. Sounds like pebbles passing through the grass. And the smell of rock dust from where the shrapnel had glanced off a boulder. He could feel her anxious breath on his cheek. "We've got to crawl back . . ." He gestured at the enemy. "They don't understand over there. They think we're skirmishers!"

She was smiling beautifully. The smoky breeze tossed a strand of hair across her eyes, and she took her hands from her ears to put it back in place. "Claude's over there. He'll tell them."

"*Claude is*—" Then he cut himself off. She was listening, but staring as if he were speaking a language she didn't know. He let go of her arm and reached inside his coat pocket. He brought out the title page to her Bible, unfurled it so she could see the map on its backside. The words in her own hand. "See, Rebekka!"

Her gaze went to the paper.

Simon waited, feeling as if the two of them were cut off from the rest of the world in the thunderous silence of the shells. He knew that he was right in doing this, yet felt cruel, jealous even. Was it too much for her mind to bear? Would she start screaming and not stop until a blood vessel burst in her throat? The earth heaved with a sickening lurch. Clods of dirt rained on them, but Rebekka was oblivious to the brown squall. She was spellbound by the page, which at last she took from his hand and inspected.

"There was no reasoning with him," Simon said above the din. "His injury made him another person. He never even—"

But then she was up and moving again, walking as if in a trance, still drawn to the south, holding the page down at her side. Through it all, he saw Leah drifting through the Richmond house, clasping the telegram about Israel's death.

Simon started to follow, but then stopped to throw off his coat. Maybe if the Rebel spotters saw no blue.

But then something massive took hold of him, slammed him to the ground. Darkness penetrated him. It was raining. He could hear the drops. He was on the piazza of the house in Charleston. With his mother. He saw her face clearly, felt a sharp joy, but then her body became as sheer as lace and through its dissolving figure he could see two horsemen just below the crest of the far ridge. Men in gray. They were artillery officers, he realized, for on the knob above them stood a signalman waving his white and red flag for the batteries to read.

Simon got up, reeling, wagging his arm. He then pointed at Rebekka.

One of the officers spurred his horse toward the knob. The other nodded deeply toward Simon. He understood.

"Thank God." Simon collapsed to his knees. The back of his hand had been nicked, and a little trickle of blood wound around his wrist. But he lifted his eyes to Rebekka. The smoke-dimmed sunshine was on her hair. She discarded the page and glided over the yellow grass as if in a dream, raising her arms. She seemed whole and healthy as she ran, delighted by the dragonflies flitting up from the weeds around her. Suddenly, she looked back at Simon and smiled. No rancor. No demons. No fear. It was as if the sentence of madness had been commuted, and she was running from the inexpressible joy of life itself.

The signalman was just beginning to spell out the new order to the batteries when a fountain of earth sprouted up where she ran.

The shower of dirt soon ended, but the smoke cleared more slowly. When it had curled off, the pasture seemed frozen in its own dust, as featureless as a desert.

⊰ Chapter 25 ⊱

A greatcoat Simon had been fitted for in July finally arrived with the mail. His Washington tailor hadn't pinned up the right sleeve, as asked, and Simon was trying to do the chore himself when Cal Ames dropped by his tent.

He saw Simon's difficulty at once, but warmed his hands at the stove for a moment before saying, "Let me have a go at that."

"Thanks."

"Headed somewhere tonight?"

"The Custers' party. Just to pay my respects."

"Good. Glad you're going." Ames finished pinning, then draped the coat over Simon's shoulders. He smiled, apparently not knowing what to say next, and then looked relieved when Mother Haggerty's voice asked for permission to come through the flaps.

"Enter please," Simon said.

"Dr. Twiss asks for your help, Colonel Ames." Then she turned to Simon and said in an obvious attempt to cheer him up, "You look quite handsome tonight, sir."

"Thank you."

"On my way," Ames said. "Well, enjoy yourself, Simon."

"I will." He had to force himself to add nothing more. Ames knew him too well.

Cal went out, and Simon gave the inside of his tent a final glance-over. No regret in leaving it, especially after the past month. He hurried out.

Several days of dismal rain had given way to an inch of snow that lay fluffily on the canvas and the ropes. Thankfully, the mud had hardened. Pamunkey came down the frozen street, on time. In his arms was

Hannes, so bundled against the chill only his eyes showed. Simon uncovered more of the child's face. A look of quiet expectation: however remotely, Hannes sensed that change was on the way again. A good change, Simon believed. "Well, let's get you two off."

He glanced up as Pamunkey and he walked. The storm had moved on, and a chain of stars linked the northern and southern skies. He would miss the winter night sky here in the Valley.

Beside the horse-line a covered ambulance was waiting for convalescents going home on leave. The steamy breaths of the mounts were sifting over it like smoke. Simon halted and took two envelopes from his inner pocket. One was addressed in German to "The Family of Frau Rebekka Zelter." The other simply bore Otis's name, which he could recognize. Simon handed him the first envelope. "This'll explain it to her people . . ." He had no doubt that they'd take Hannes with open arms, yet something had moved him to write that, in his judgment as a surgeon, the boy was as healthy in mind and body as any year-old he'd ever examined. Hannes was not *blemished.* "And this, my friend," Simon said, giving Otis the second envelope, "is for you. Should you chose to use it."

The eyes narrowed.

"It's a certificate of disability for discharge," Simon went on. "Authorized by me." He paused. Careful not to injure the feelings of this good man in any way. "You're as fit as anybody to serve, but I don't think this war will see another summer. Now that Early's beaten for good and Lee is penned up at Petersburg. What I'm saying, Otis—if you find a place for yourself up there in Pennsylvania, don't forego it for my sake. We're Southerners, you and I. We know something all the others here don't—when all's said and done, the South will still be the South." Simon gripped the man's hand for an instant, firmly, then kissed Hannes's cheek and closed up the covering again.

"Good-bye," he said.

The convalescents made room for them, and the ambulance was off, the usual clatter of the wheels muffled by the snow. It was twenty miles to the newly restored railhead at Martinsburg, but he trusted that Pamunkey would keep the child warm.

Naomi had been saddled and bridled, and Simon ran his hand over her forehead as the groom hung a pair of heavy medical saddlebags over her neck. They were filled with morphine and other medicines. "Well, Sissy. Ready for a bitch of a night?"

He mounted, then rode out of the depot toward the church spires of Winchester. He twisted around once for a look back. Nearly half the tents had already been struck, and soon the rest would come down. Most of the wounded from the Battle of Cedar Creek were now in Washington hospitals, and Ames was more than capable of seeing to the needs of those who remained.

Simon Wolfe's work in the Valley of Virginia was done.

He faced forward and rode on, unthinking. Brick facades gradually closed around him.

Upon his wife's arrival, Custer had appropriated a roomy mansion from a Confederate couple, who'd been allowed to stay in residence. Music now drifted from this house, and its windows spilled squares of light out onto the snow.

Simon left his greatcoat in the entrance hall and stepped into the main parlor. Candles everywhere making the skin of the ladies glow. And on the walls crossed sabers, regimental flags and garlands of evergreen. He drifted over to the buffet table, although he had no appetite. Turkey, cake, nuts, oranges and candy.

"Simon," a female voice said in mock reproach, "how long have you been here?"

"Just arrived." Simon gave Elizabeth Custer a peck on the hand. He realized at once that she was on edge, eager to make a good impression all around.

"Autie's with Phil," she said. "Phil needs a rest, I think . . . but he's a *glorious* dancer. Have you ever seen him on the floor, Simon?"

He smiled. "No." He hadn't expected to like this slender girl with dark eyes. She was no doubt willful and even pigheaded when the mood hit her, but she reminded him in many ways of Leah, who'd kept a tight grip on poor Israel. And chatting with Libbie had been his only solace of late. Through her, he realized once again that he preferred the company of women over men.

"What do you think of my new cutlery?" she prattled on, taking a knife from an assortment of several on the tablecloth. "It's German. Autie's been a darling and picking them up for me all over the Valley."

"Very good."

"So many bargains down here," she said happily, then put her arm through his and began strolling him around the room. He felt a bit like her beau. It was nice. "Those are the Glasses over there . . . lovely people, really." Stealthily, she pointed at the man and wife. "They do so appreciate our staying here . . ." The Glasses didn't look it. "They say it keeps them safe from the rougher element. D'you know what I mean?"

"Yes, I think so."

"There's that element everywhere, isn't there?"

"Everywhere."

"Never had colored servants before," she went on, nodding and smiling at her guests. "They really are marvelous, aren't they, though? Did you have them at your house in Charleston?"

"Yes."

She stopped. Her hand flew to her mouth and she blushed. "I'm sorry, Simon."

"About what?"

"That was indelicate."

"How?"

"It suggested that you yourself had slaves. And really, you're so . . . so *Northern.*" She paused, her eyes darting. "I've never hosted so many important people." She gave Simon's hand a quick squeeze. "You're Northern to the marrow. Autie says you found honor in our cause."

"And which cause is that?"

"Why abolition, of course."

The Custers, all those in this overheated room, were far from abolitionists, but Simon then differed with her for another reason.

"No?" she echoed, looking crestfallen.

"I'm afraid I'm Southern through and through, Elizabeth."

"But how can that be?"

"You stolid Northerners can find your honor in common causes. We hot-blooded Southerners are invariably failed by ours, so we have to resort to individual gestures."

"What kind of—?"

At that instant a side door flew open, and Sheridan and Custer stepped out, arm-in-arm, laughing. They both had bright faces, Little Phil's from drink, but Custer's no doubt from the affection he was being shown. And from the victory, of course. Cedar Creek had started as a Federal rout and ended as a Rebel one. Thanks to Sheridan's radiant courage on the battlefield. Rebekka had been on to something there. Had the Little Goliath been murdered days before that demoralizing hour in which John Gordon's division smashed through the Union line, the blue soldiers might well have lost heart and run back to the Potomac. They were already on their way when Little Phil turned them around, forestalling a stunning defeat in the Shenandoah just before most of the nation voted.

"Simon!" Custer exclaimed. "Bully you could make it! Has he gotten anything to eat, Libbie?"

"I'll eat," Simon said, "as soon as I beg a word with the general."

Sheridan sobered a little, but kept smiling. "My pleasure." Then he gave a toss of his head for Simon to go first through the door.

He shut it behind him, and they sat across the small dowdy parlor from each other. Sheridan poured a glass of port for Simon, who took more than a sip.

The general broke the silence first. "You off someplace tonight?" Sharp instincts, as usual.

"Yes, a sanitary inspection of the forward camps."

"Tonight?"

"Yes, they're useless unless they come out of the blue."

"You got a point there." Sheridan sat back. "Some pair," he said after a bit.

"Sir?"

"That Dunker girl and her ranger lover."

"Yes, some pair."

"Well," Sheridan said expansively, "you did what you set out to do. You got to the bottom of it. And I thank you. I've sent your report on to Washington."

"There's more than what I put in it."

"Oh?"

"The day you came to inspect the Amherst Street hospital . . ."

"Yes?"

"The way Mrs. Zelter reacted . . . and then the poisoning, all the rest . . . I was ready to believe that you'd done it."

"All the rest—you mean when I had that German woman's body burned?"

"That's part of it—"

"No, Simon," Sheridan said with a faint smile, "I want to know the *germ* that made you suspect me. The reason in your heart of hearts."

"I resented you."

"Is that it?"

"That's it, sir."

"I see." Sheridan's expression was momentarily hidden by his glass. But, when he put it down, he was no longer smiling. "Strange moment," he said, "that morning in the hospital. Truth is—I saw the other side of all this in that girl's eyes. The cruelty, I suppose. The waste. And I had to get out of there before my confidence went. Joe Hooker, for whatever the damned reason, lost faith in himself, and Lee whipped him royally at Chancellorsville. An army feeds on confidence, Simon."

"And resentment."

"I beg your pardon?"

"Till this thing in the Valley here, I kidded myself that I joined the Twelfth Massachusetts to end slavery. To save the Union. Marched off Beacon Hill that day so long ago with Daniel Webster's son to work wonders with the benighted South." Simon took a moment, then another moment. This was harder than he'd imagined, but it had to be said. "Rebekka Zelter used the war to further her own resentments. But, in her defense, she was mad. So was Lieutenant Tebault. What's our excuse? Nobody used this war more than I. My father. To get back at him. And then to get back at you."

"Why me?"

"Because you're a heartless son of a bitch who can kill thousands, maim three times that—and then wash down oysters with champagne." Then Simon quickly said it before he changed his mind. "I came close to killing you. Twice. Once at Belle Grove. And then again along Cedar Creek. Came within an inch of doing it."

Sheridan arched an eyebrow, but said nothing.

"God help us," Simon went on, "but it's the promise of righting wrongs against ourselves that seduces us into this living hell. That's what the Valley's taught me. And I thank you for it."

Sheridan just stared. A waltz drifted through the closed door. Then he burst out laughing—uproariously—before wiping his eyes on his gilt sleeve and hoisting his glass. "Welcome to the cavalry, Simon."

"Good evening, sir."

Yet, Sheridan stopped him at the door with: "But you know, it's the only thing that's going to stamp out slavery in this country . . . all that degrading personal resentment we're jamming down the Rebs's throats."

"I know that."

"Well, then, doesn't that put your lofty view between two fires?"

"Yes, it does."

Although there was no moon, a clear stillness drew him toward the Blue Ridge. At about three in the morning, he dismounted and walked Naomi around the last Union pickets.

Sheridan had hit the nail on the head, of course.

For Simon to leave the Army, to go back to Boston and take up his old comforts, yet still to believe in Union and abolition—well, there was moral confusion in that. And he was tired of confusion.

The Dunkers of Virginia had done better than himself. In their stand against slavery, they had not taken up arms against their neighbors. But neither had they forsaken their homeland for the safety of the North—at least, not until Sheridan had driven them out. And when this madness had exhausted itself, they would go home. They were Southerners. Their German had a Virginian accent.

Naomi shied. She'd caught scent of something in the woods.

"It's all right, girl," he whispered, getting back in the saddle.

The answer to his quandary had come only in the past week. Elizabeth Custer had been chattering away when something she said suddenly turned his head: "There's a place for each of us in this dreadful business, isn't there?" And then he'd seen what he would do. He would go on ministering—but not to an army on the offensive. He'd secretly arranged to make his way to Libby Prison in Richmond, a sort of voluntary prisoner-doctor, and then heal those soldiers who were simply fighting for their lives.

He would also ask his father to call on him at the first opportunity.

A voice echoed out of the darkness, commanded him to halt.

Simon dropped the rein and hoisted his hand as two men galloped upon him, one from the cedars in front, the other from the open side.

"Colonel Wolfe?" one of them asked, hushed.

"Yes."

"Colonel *Simon* Wolfe?"

"Yes."

Two revolvers were trained on him.

"Our boss quoted a Greek. You remember which one, sir?"

"What . . . ?" Oh yes. Simon smiled, then said, "Thucydides, as I recall." *If one has a free choice and can live undisturbed, it's sheer folly to go to war.*

"Very good, sir—you may lower your hand."

Simon finally realized that the rangers were dressed darkly—in Federal blue.

A third rider hurtled out of the woods behind them, reined up and said breathlessly that Yankee vedettes were all around.

"Kindly keep close, Colonel. And let's give them a song, boys."

Then, spurring their mounts, the three men raised their voices against the night. Mosby's rangers sang "John Brown's Body" as they led Simon at a trot toward the Blue Ridge. It got them through a pocket of vedettes without being challenged. Some of the Yankee horsemen joined in for as long as the rangers were in earshot, figuring maybe that the blue riders were their own cavalry heading out on patrol. The victory at Cedar Creek had seemingly convinced them that there were no Rebels left in the whole world. But there were always more Johnnies, and the war would drag on for months. Years, maybe. It was in God's hands. That was the only solace Simon could think of as he and the rangers climbed out of the Valley.

They reached Chester Gap at dawn and halted to make coffee. But for a mellow haze, Simon felt that he could've seen Richmond from that height.